DATE DUE

PRINTED IN U.S.A.

A Forgotten Murder

A Forgotten Murder

Jude Deveraux

THORNDIKE PRESS
A part of Gale, a Cengage Company

A Medlar Mystery.
Thorndike Press, a part of Gale, a Cengage Company.

Thorndike Press® Large Print Basic.
The text of this Large Print edition is unabridged.
Other aspects of the book may vary from the original edition.
Set in 16 pt. Plantin.

**LIBRARY OF CONGRESS CIP DATA ON FILE.
CATALOGUING IN PUBLICATION FOR THIS BOOK
IS AVAILABLE FROM THE LIBRARY OF CONGRESS**

ISBN-13: 978-1-4328-7648-7 (hardcover alk. paper)

Published in 2020 by arrangement with Harlequin Books S. A.

Printed in Mexico
Print Number: 01 Print Year: 2020

A Forgotten Murder

One

OXLEY MANOR, A COUNTRY HOUSE HOTEL ENGLAND

Two Years Ago

Puck didn't expect to find a body. She certainly hadn't been looking for the skeleton of a man no one seemed to remember. How she had mourned him when he disappeared. Her mother told her to stop sniveling, that at fourteen she had no idea what love was.

But she did know!

Now, so many years later, she was still at Oxley Manor, and this morning she was hiding from her mother — as usual. The absurdity that she was thirty-eight years old and still trying to escape Mummy wasn't lost on her. If her beloved cottage hadn't been gifted to her, she would leave Oxley. Maybe.

There were perks to living where she did. Today she'd been planning on going wildcrafting in the Preserve at the north end of the 130-acre estate. She'd made sure her phone's sound was off, put it in her shirt pocket and buttoned the flap. When her mother inevitably called and couldn't reach her, she'd say that yet again she'd forgotten the gadget. She let no one know that she used her phone to photograph all the plants she found on the estate so she could catalog them.

One of the farmers told her his grandmother used to pick yellow-leaved wild thyme there. She could use the herb in the wreaths she made and sold.

The Preserve was a dozen fenced-in acres that the owner, Mrs. Guilford, said were to be left untouched. No machines, not even people were to walk across it. Wildlife only. She had installed signs warning of danger, but everyone knew that Mrs. Guilford was trying for some conservation award so she could use it in the hotel's publicity.

At the edge of the thorn-filled woods, Puck stopped and listened. She was good at hearing what others didn't, adept at seeing what they couldn't. No one was nearby. She was thin and knew how to move without disturbing plants or animals. Not even the birds ran from her.

There was a lock on the gate and Puck knew the key was hanging on a rack in the kitchen, but she hadn't dared take it. It might be missed. Instead, she'd climbed over the fence. Inside, she walked slowly, leaving few crushed plants in her wake. She didn't want anyone to know she'd been there.

She walked in quite a way, across about four acres. Briars scratched her legs and something bit her on the neck. After a couple of hours, she hadn't seen any wild thyme so she thought she should turn back.

She decided to go out a different way so she'd be less likely to leave a path. She'd walked only a few yards when the ground suddenly gave way under her. She fell straight down for what had to be ten feet. Fortunately, she landed on moss and years of composted vegetation. It was a relatively soft landing but she was dazed.

Sitting up, she tested her body to see if anything was broken. Her ankle hurt and she was going to be bruised, but she was all right.

When she looked up, she could see the sky overhead. It was going to rain soon, and she was at the bottom of a wide, deep hole. Part of the sides were stone, some bare ground. Covering the top was a vine-covered roof made of very old iron bars. They had rusted to the point that, when she'd stepped on one side, the bars had given way.

The question now was how she was going to get out.

Standing, she checked her phone. It was working. The smartest thing to do would be to call for help. One of the farmers would show up with a rope and pull her out.

And then what? She was where she shouldn't be. People would delight in yelling at her. Treating her like a moron. Threatening her. Legally, she could be denied permission to roam the estate. She didn't want to think what her mother would say.

The consequences weren't worth asking for help.

As Puck looked for a way out, she wondered what the place had been made for. Ice storage? A root cellar? From the look of it, it was a few hundred years old. At some point, the top had been covered — and then left to rot. There were a few animal skeletons on the ground. Poor things had fallen in and couldn't get out.

She moved her foot around, testing the damage. Not bad. That was good, since she was going to have to climb up. The stones on one side were too smooth, too big for climbing, but she thought she could make footholds in the dirt part of the wall.

Looking up, she saw that a few feet down

from the top was a place that had been hollowed out to form a ledge. She could see loose rocks along the lip. They looked like they'd been stacked there. Above the ledge, the ground tapered back and there were hanging roots she could use to pull herself up. If she could just get to that shelf, she could get herself out.

The soles of her shoes were thick and not flexible enough for climbing. She'd be better off barefoot. She untied her shoes and took them off. What to do with them was a question. String them around her neck as she climbed? Too distracting.

She tossed a shoe up toward the ledge. The first one missed but she landed the next throw. It took five tries to get the second shoe up there. When some of the rocks rained down, she covered her head.

The climb was easier than she thought it would be. Years of tree climbing helped her place her feet.

She didn't realize how scared she was until she reached the ledge. In relief, she leaned back against the rocks. When they scattered, she didn't mind. It was good to be off the bottom — and to be safe. The rest of the way up would be easy.

Leaning back on her elbows, she gave herself a few minutes to calm her heart. Too bad she'd never be able to tell anyone about this adventure. Instead, she'd have to cover the top of the big hole and hope no one else fell in.

She drew her knees up to her chest and rubbed her ankle. The movement shifted the dirt enough that she saw something metal on the floor of the ledge. When she dug it out, she discovered it was a watch, dirty and corroded. She tried to see the dials but there was too little light. She wondered how it got there. Had someone dropped it over the side?

There were some sticks in the dirt and she used one to dig around a bit. What else was hidden in there? It was too dark to see much so she took her phone out of her pocket and turned on the flashlight. There was dirt, pebbles and sticks. Nothing interesting.

She was about to turn it off when she realized that what she was holding wasn't a stick. It was a *bone.*

With a gasp, she dropped it. Slowly, afraid of what she was going to see, she turned the light around. Behind her, deep in the shadows, stretched out, was a full, human skeleton. Strands of dark hair clung to its skull. Pieces of rotted clothing were beneath the bones.

As Puck turned off the light, she was shaking. Her trembling fingers touched the buttons to call her mother. *Come and get me! Rescue me!* she wanted to cry.

No! she thought, and disconnected.

She had visions of what would happen if she told of her find. The police and newspaper reporters would come with their flashing lights. The hotel would fill with tourists who loved the macabre. Oxley Manor would become an entry in books about *Places of Death.*

Puck took a few breaths and looked at the way up. She put the phone and the watch in her pocket and climbed out.

Once she got to the top, she threw up. Her stomach retched and heaved and emptied itself.

Still barefoot, she made her way to a tree and sat down. She needed time to think about what to do. When her heart had calmed enough, she looked at the watch.

Using her thumbs, she cleaned off the back, then held it up to the light. It was engraved on the back.

TO SEAN THORPE. FIRST PRIZE. 1991.

Puck leaned back against the tree and closed her eyes. Sean had been her friend, a *true* friend. That his body was here was proof that he had *not* run away as everyone said he had.

But then Puck had never believed what they'd said about him. The affair. The betrayal of everyone. They even blamed him for all that happened later. She'd heard them say, "If it hadn't been for Sean, Nicky would still be alive."

Puck told them that Sean wasn't like that. If nothing else, he wouldn't have left the horses without food or water. "Something happened to him," she'd cried. "I know it did."

But no one would listen to her. Certainly not the police.

She put the watch in her pocket, covered the broken opening with branches and left the Preserve.

For the next two years she didn't enter that area of the estate. And she never came close to telling anyone about what she'd seen.

Her only reaction to the horror of what she'd discovered was that she kept even more to herself. She'd always been a loner, but the effect of what she'd seen deepened her reputation of being "odd" and "different." But that was all right. Better that than being the one who had introduced murder to Oxley Manor.

Her silence wasn't altogether altruistic. She worried that the person who had put Sean in that place would find her shoes there. And that person would know what she'd seen.

Oxley Manor
Present Day

Puck was out of sight in the pantry when she first heard the name Sara Medlar.

"Never heard of her," Puck's mother said to Mrs. Isabella Guilford, the owner of Oxley Manor.

"She paid to restore this place, Mrs. Aiken," Isabella said. "I owe her —" She waved her hand. "I don't want to think of that, but let me say that I cannot turn her away. She and two others are flying in from Florida in three days."

"The house is closed." Puck's mother slammed a heavy copper pot down on the big oak table. Even though it had been years, she refused to accept that her beloved Oxley Manor was now a hotel.

"That's *why* she's coming. She's bringing her niece and her honorary grandson, Jack."

" 'Honorary grandson,' " Puck's mother muttered as she began chopping carrots. "I guess you expect me to cook for them."

Isabella gritted her teeth. Since the hotel was closed all of March and there were no guests, yes, Mrs. Aiken would need to do the cooking. Bella knew the cantankerous old woman would love being the boss of what she still considered "her" kitchen, but she also knew she'd have to coax her. Why oh why couldn't Sara come when the place was staffed?

"Just three of them?" Mrs. Aiken asked. "And all Americans? I don't know how to make pizza. Or those two-pound hamburgers."

Bella refrained from rolling her eyes. Instead, she straightened her shoulders. "This weekend will be a full house. There will be seven guests in total. All but Sara will leave on Monday. Her two are going to tour the Highlands."

"So what about *her*?" Mrs. Aiken asked. "What's *she* going to do?"

"I assume you mean Sara. 'She' as you call her, can do anything she bloody well wants. But she's staying here alone so she can write."

"About what?" Mrs. Aiken snapped.

Bella had her hand on the doorframe. "I don't know. She said she found some old story on the internet that everyone had forgotten about. Something about a couple of lovers who ran off together." She stepped into the hallway.

"Wait!" Mrs. Aiken called, and Bella looked back into the kitchen. "You mean that girl and the man in the stables?" Her voice was hoarse.

"I guess so. That was before my time."

"Who is coming?" Mrs. Aiken whispered.

This time Bella did roll her eyes. "I don't remember their names. Sara said they were part of a club and had a party the night the couple ran away together."

"Nadine, Byon, Clive and Willa," Mrs. Aiken said softly. "They're the only ones left." Her face had drained of color.

Bella hadn't thought of it, but Mrs. Aiken was probably there the night the couple ran off together. From Mrs. Aiken's expression, Bella knew she should be sympathetic. But why was that so traumatic to her? "Yes, I think those are the names. Sara wants to talk to them. I think she wants to use the runaways as a plot for a book." Bella sighed. "Since she retired from writing, that makes no sense. Maybe she's just bored. Whatever the reason, they'll need food. Can you do it? If not, I'll hire a caterer."

Mrs. Aiken seemed incapable of speaking, but her nod was good enough for Bella. In a few minutes, six girls were coming to clean and she needed to oversee their work. She quickly walked down the hall. "Deliver me from drama," she said, then hurried to answer the bell on the front door.

In the kitchen, Puck was still in the pantry, unseen by anyone. She watched her mother as she tried to put the sliced carrots into the pot. But her hands were shaking too badly. She dropped the carrots onto the floor, then went out the back door.

Puck slipped out of the pantry, went through the house, then outside. She hurried to her own house and grabbed her laptop. She wanted to find out who this Sara Medlar was. Thirty minutes later, she leaned back in her chair, her heart pounding in her throat. She'd read through all the hype: sixty million books in print, years on the *New York Times* Bestseller List, etc. That meant nothing to her.

What mattered was a small article in the *Miami Sun Sentinel.* A reporter said it was strongly rumored that Sara Medlar, along with her niece and her "almost grandson" had solved two old murders. "Murders that others dismissed," the reporter wrote.

When the Morris women were brutally murdered, people cared so little no one even noticed they were missing. They were Forgotten Murders. The police deny it, but the scuttlebutt is that the Medlar trio solved the case.

Puck stared at the screen. It was the same with Sean. Everyone had forgotten about him. And what about Diana? Was her body in that odious pit with Sean's and she'd missed it?

She made herself a mug of tea and sat back down. She hadn't kept up with the others who'd been in Nicky's group. After that horrible night, she'd never wanted to see any of them again. But now she was wondering what had become of them.

She spent the rest of the day researching and reading.

Two

"What do you think she's up to?" Jack asked.

They were on an overnight flight to London, first class courtesy of Sara. Kate and Jack were in the center, each with a seat that made into a bed, while Sara was across the aisle. Their TVs were turned off.

"Are you asking if I believe Aunt Sara just wants a vacation and that she's actually thinking of writing another romance?"

Jack gave a one-sided smile. "That's exactly what I'm asking." He waited for her answer.

"It's a mystery."

He chuckled at the double entendre: a mystery as to why and possibly a mystery to be solved.

Kate changed the subject. "Was Gil okay taking over your business?"

"He was glad to get rid of me. He said I was so emotionally involved with the remodel of the Morris house that I was a pest and . . ." Jack trailed off, not wanting to repeat his foreman's language. "He'll do fine."

"You need a vacation."

"What about you? Think Kirkwood Realty can live without you?"

Kate stretched her legs on the long seat. Just months ago she'd sold her boss's big house, and the commission was enough to allow her to take some time off. She'd been able to send money to her mother and had indulged her love of clothing with a few designer outfits from The Outnet. She did love a bargain! "I think they'll do very well without me. What do you know about this hotel?"

"Only that years ago Sara shelled out a lot to restore it."

"This must have been before she got together with you or she would have sent you with your tool belt to do the remodel." Sara had been a silent partner in Jack's construction company since he was eighteen years old.

"Okay, so what's the truth?"

"I think she's bored," Kate said. "For many years she wrote two books a year. That's a quarter of a million words. Then she retired. She had nothing but free time."

"So she traveled a lot. Saw the world."

"Yes, then she bought that big house and had you remodel it. That was exciting."

"Me or the house?"

"The house, of course." Kate was smiling.

"And we moved in with her."

"That was definitely exciting," Kate said.

"Especially since we solved a few murders."

"For which we got no credit."

"You *want* people knocking on your door asking you to help solve what happened to their great-uncle fifty years ago?"

"I thought this conversation was about Aunt Sara," Kate said. "If it's about me, I'm going to sleep."

"Beside me," Jack murmured.

"Behave or I'll switch seats with Aunt Sara."

Jack made a sign of hand over heart.

"Why is she sending us off to faraway Scotland while she stays at Oxley Manor?" Kate asked.

"To give us time to be alone? Just us in all that heather? Hey! Did you know that my ancestry allows me to wear the full Scottish regalia? How do you think I'd look in a kilt?"

For a moment, Kate blinked at that image. Jack was a *very* handsome man. She shook her head a bit to clear it. "Back to my aunt. In the last year —"

"Of peace," Jack said.

"Yes, in a year of peace and quiet, Aunt Sara has kept busy, but . . ."

"There's been nothing to keep her brain fully occupied."

"Right. I think maybe she's going toward something rather than away from it," Kate said.

"What makes you think that?"

"I, uh, did a little snooping about this hotel."

"No! You? Innocent Kate?"

She narrowed her eyes, but he just smiled. "In 1994, some friends were having a party at Oxley Manor. Two of them walked out the door and were never seen again."

"A male and a female?"

"Yes."

"Sounds normal to me. They just wanted to get away from everyone they knew. I've felt the same way many times." With a glance at Kate, he said, "Before I met you, of course. What else was there?"

"That's all I could find. It was a tiny piece in a local newspaper."

"Doesn't sound very mysterious. What made you think it has anything to do with this trip?"

"It was important enough that Aunt Sara

was using the clipping as a marker in the book she was reading. It was about true crimes. Don't look at me like that! I was curious about the book and the paper fell out."

"You think she's planning to stay at the hotel to research what happened while you and I go to bonny Scotland? I like that idea."

"You'd leave her alone to investigate all by herself?" She sounded shocked.

"She was researching her novels before I was born. Don't tell her I said that! She hasn't discovered that she's no longer about twenty-six."

Kate looked at him. "Aunt Sara might not know her age, but we do."

Jack groaned. "Please not a mystery to solve. I *want* a vacation in the Highlands. I grew up in Florida. I'm curious about cold weather. It gets to sixty-eight and I turn on the heat. Sara bought me a sweater for this trip. It's made of *wool.*"

"I grew up in Chicago and cold is overrated. And no one is keeping you from going anywhere."

"You're going to let me run around the Highlands in a kilt all by myself?"

"If that's what you want to do, yes."

Jack closed his eyes and said nothing.

"There's no law saying you can't wear a

kilt in England," she said softly.

Smiling, Jack opened his eyes. "I think we should wait until we get there and see what's going on."

"We have a plan!" Kate pressed the button to flatten her seat for sleeping.

"Why do I feel like I've just been manipulated?" he asked.

She smiled, but she didn't let him see her face. The truth was, in the last few months she'd also been a bit bored. Solving a mystery sounded good. Maybe not a murder but just finding out why someone did something. Obviously, the couple who'd run away together must have had serious obstacles in their paths. If they didn't, they would have announced their love and invited people to the wedding. So why did they feel the need to vanish? And why had no one heard from them since? Or maybe they had. The newspaper article was old.

But Kate knew that if the mystery of the disappearance had been solved, Aunt Sara wouldn't be arranging a visit to Oxley Manor.

Wonder what else she's done? she thought as she drifted off to sleep.

When they arrived in England, it was early morning. A black sedan picked them up at the airport. The driver had on a black suit, with a cap that you'd expect a chauffeur to wear.

Jack got in the back with Kate, while Sara sat in the front with the driver. They heard her ask the man about himself. He'd worked at Oxley Manor for years and picking them up was his last job before he left on holiday.

It took two hours of driving over express highways, then spiraling country roads before the car slowed down at a tall brick wall. A huge iron gate was in front of them. It was a rather plain gate, not flashy at all. To the left was a small brass plaque that read *Oxley Manor.*

At the security box, the driver tapped in a code, the gate opened and they drove slowly down a paved road. Around them was an expansive lawn, interspersed with huge old trees. Sheep dotted the lawn — walking lawn mowers.

After a few minutes they came to another gate, this one short and attached to low walls that disappeared on both sides through the trees. A small house stood by the little gate. It was two-story, all brick, with tall, stone-faced windows.

"Thinking of putting it on the market?" Jack asked Kate.

"I wouldn't mind knowing the number of

beds and baths."

"It's England. Twelve bedrooms, one bath."

"And you said you didn't watch *Downton Abbey.*"

Smiling, he looked out the car window.

The driver slowed down as they went around a corner and they saw the main house. It was long, spreading out over a hundred feet. It had Gothic overtones, with steeply pitched roofs and parts that jutted out to form giant bay windows that were two stories tall.

"Is that . . . ?" Kate asked, pointing to the front.

"It's a thirteenth-century chapel," the driver said. "Restored in 1928 by the sixth Lord Renlow."

"Then again by Bella," Sara added, pride in her voice.

Kate and Jack looked at each other. They knew who'd paid for it: Sara and the millions of books she'd sold.

The driver took his time going around the perimeter of the house, letting them see all of it. "The house is younger than the chapel," he said. "But parts of it are sixteenth century. The newest section was built in the 1700s. One family built it and their descendants still live here."

As a lover of houses, especially old ones, Kate could feel her heart doing little jumps.

Jack leaned toward her and whispered, "You ever look at me like that and I'll die happy."

"Looks like you'll have a long, sad life," she shot back at him.

When the car stopped, Sara nearly leaped out, said, "Bella," then took off running around the side of the house.

"Sorry about this," the driver said as he opened Kate's door, "but I have to drop you off at the back. Front's being worked on. The kitchen is through that door. I'll take your cases up."

Jack was standing next to Kate. Through the trees they could see other buildings. One was long and low. Stables, maybe? Corners of what appeared to be small houses were barely visible.

"How many people live here?" she asked the driver.

"Not many. Mrs. Guilford has a flat in the main house. Mrs. Aiken, the cook, and the head gardener have places. And there's Puck." He gave a little smile, sort of a smirk. "She has a house by the cemetery."

"Who is she?" Kate asked.

"Mrs. Aiken's daughter. She's . . ."

"She's what?" Kate asked.

"Different."

"What do you mean?" Jack asked.

"She is . . . fortyish, I guess. We have a saying around here that you can look at her but not see her. She's sort of invisible." He saw that neither Jack nor Kate liked what he was saying. "Sorry. Didn't mean to gossip. Anyway, the cottages are mostly for guests. They like their privacy."

"I would too." Kate turned full circle. "I'd like to stay in a cottage and walk over every inch of this place. And pet every animal."

"Moooo," Jack said.

That got a smile out of her. "I don't see any other people."

"That's because we close for the month of March. Old place like this needs constant repair. Guests don't like the sound of hammers. I'm afraid they're going to wake you up."

"They are music to Jack," Kate said. "Add a couple of power saws and he'll start singing."

The driver looked from one to the other for a moment, seeming to be curious about their relationship. Then he opened the black painted door to the house and they went inside.

The kitchen was divine. It had a huge oak table in the center and lots of open shelves full of copper pots, with dishes below. There was a giant Aga cooker against the middle of the back wall. It was a stove that was always warm, always fighting against the cold and damp.

"A lot of this is for the viewing pleasure of the guests," the driver said. "They want England to look like they imagine it." He moved a wooden slab to one side to expose a modern induction cooktop. "Microwave is behind those doors. Right now Mrs. Aiken has everything that doesn't look like a movie set covered up. She likes the old things."

He opened a big oak door to expose a built-in refrigerator. Inside, there wasn't a sliver of plastic. Little white pots had red-and-white-checked covers tied on with string. Cotton covered a big slab of cheese. There were several ceramic bowls.

"I like it," Kate said. "Where are our rooms?"

"Mrs. Guilford said you could choose any one you want. Except the Queen Anne. That goes to Mrs. Medlar."

They didn't correct him that Sara had never been married.

"That sounds lovely," Kate said. "We —" She broke off because the kitchen door was flung open so hard the glass rattled. A woman, grocery bags in hand, came inside with the force of a storm. "Look what you've done to my kitchen." She glared at the driver.

"I, uh, I'll take your bags up." The driver scurried out the door so fast he made the hanging pans shiver.

The woman was older, but looked to be strong and healthy. Short, iron gray hair, a cotton dress over a sturdy body. She was glaring at Jack and Kate.

Kate gave her a big smile. "I take it that you're Mrs. Aiken, the cook." She held out her hand to shake.

The woman ignored it. "I'm to cook for *them*!" Mrs. Aiken was scowling. "Worthless bunch, all of them. Parasites. Leeches every one."

Kate looked at Jack and gestured. *Does she mean* us?

"Poor little Nicky," Mrs. Aiken continued. "I don't know why he bothered. They were sucking him dry. They ate more than he could afford." She glared at them. "Do you mean to stand there? Go get the food!"

Jack and Kate nearly jammed in the doorway as they tried to get out.

Outside was a white van with the back doors open. Inside were boxes and bags of food.

As Kate took a bag, she glanced over her

shoulder. "Who are the parasites?"

"I have no idea," Jack said, "but I bet you a fifty that your dear aunt knows everything."

They loaded up with bags of groceries and headed back into the house.

In the kitchen, Mrs. Aiken was still glowering as she lifted a huge, heavy copper pot from a shelf and put it on the table.

"Could I help?" Kate asked.

The older woman looked Kate up and down and obviously found her wanting. "I've got a couple of village girls coming to help." It was a dismissal.

"That's good," Kate said. "Uh, mind if I ask what all this is for? If it's for the three of us, I can assure you that we can take care of ourselves. Jack is great at grilling and —"

"I already said it was for *them.* The ones coming. I swear I never heard of anything so cruel. They want a time just like the other one. How can that be done? Half of them are dead. And who wants to do over *that* time? That *night*? Broke my Nicky's heart, it did. And that playacting fellow. I knew he'd do something like that." She looked at Jack by the door. "You want something to eat?"

"No, ma'am, I do not." He and Kate hurried out of the kitchen.

"Ma'am," Mrs. Aiken muttered in disgust. "Sounds like I'm the queen."

THREE

Jack hadn't let it show but he was angered by what the driver had said about the woman called Puck. Nobody deserved to be thought of as "invisible." He'd known too many people who believed others were insignificant. Humans who were overlooked because they didn't fit the socially accepted norm of being friendly and gregarious.

It was the "invisibility" of a young woman he'd loved that had caused people to ignore her disappearance. Finding her and her mother had started them in mystery solving.

He'd never tell Kate, but he didn't like that Sara had arranged this trip under false pretenses. She'd said she wanted to do some historical research. But she didn't say that the history was barely twenty years old. Or that the people around here were still angry about whatever had happened.

He always wanted to know what was going on. To him, his job was to protect two women who were much too inquisitive and way too fearless for their own good. Right now, he wanted to know more about poor, persecuted Nicky and the "parasites" who allegedly stole from him.

Jack didn't think he was going to find out anything from Mrs. Aiken, but maybe her daughter knew something.

He turned back to Kate. She was looking at the exterior of the big house, and he wondered if she realized how much like her aunt she was.

"I'm gonna look around on my own," Jack said. "You go pick out a room for us and I'll see you later."

As he hurried away, Kate called out, "Rooms, Jack. Plural."

He didn't answer but he smiled. He walked around a tall hedge that hid the surrounding land, then walked down a gravel road, passing buildings that were well-kept. But he could see inside enough to know they were empty. Probably awaiting restoration.

Down one lane were four small houses, each beautifully kept. His guess was that they'd been built in the twenties when the old chapel had been restored. They were made to look Victorian Gothic but they weren't that old. His contractor's eye saw that they were in good repair.

Past the wall was a woodland. Trees were close, their tops overlapping to form a dense canopy. Ferns covered the ground.

When he saw sunlight along one side, he went to it. On the gravel lane was a little green utility truck. Jack owned three of them for his business. There were wooden-handled tools in the back that would be ruined if it rained.

Looking around, he saw no one. The entire huge estate was like it had been abandoned.

Beside the truck, along the lane, was a thick hedge of wild blackberry vines, heavy with unpicked fruit. When he put the tools inside the cab, he removed an empty stainless steel bucket and half filled it with blackberries.

There was a pretty pond with a trail around it and tall willows drooping down to the water. Clumps of reeds softened the shoreline. Jack knew from experience that if you sat very still, birds and wildlife showed up.

It didn't take him long to find her. When you grew up with a father like Jack's, you earned a PhD in hiding. He was so attuned to the shapes of nature that he saw the shadow of a human form sitting on a tree branch. As a child, he'd done that often. If he didn't move and drew his breath shallowly, people would walk past without seeing him.

Jack didn't show that he saw her. She was thin and her clothes were the color of the forest. It looked like she worked at keeping people from seeing her.

He sat down on the ground by the tree's roots. A little clump of mushrooms was to his left. He put the bucket of berries where she could see them.

Leaning back on his hands, he looked out at the water. After a few minutes, he had so quieted his body that he could hear her breathing. He ate a few berries. "These are good. Want some?"

There was no response, but he didn't expect any.

"I'm Jack, and it seems that I'm here to solve a mystery. Know anything about it?"

Continued silence. He ate more berries, then stretched out on the ground, hands behind his head. He was careful to keep his eyes on the water, not looking up into the tree.

After a few minutes he knew she was coming down, but he could hardly hear her. *She's good,* he thought. Lots of practice in being still and not being seen.

When she was sitting beside him, he slowly sat up and turned to look at her. The driver had said she was in her forties but she looked young. No worry lines, not even laughter creases. *Like those monks who spend their lives praying,* he thought. Smooth, clean faces.

She had straight dark hair twisted back on her neck, and she was very thin. Her green blouse and black trousers hung on her. She had on odd, flexible slippers. They wouldn't make a sound, or hinder her movements, whether in climbing a tree or scurrying through hallways.

Right away, he knew he liked her. Even felt a kinship with her.

When he smiled, after a moment, she gave a small smile back. He had an idea that she talked very little but listened a lot. "Hiding from your mom?"

Her smile broadened to show perfect white teeth.

"Me too," he said. "Your mother scares me."

They sat in silence for a while, listening to the water and the wildlife. "Where I live, there are alligators."

She lifted her eyebrows in interest.

"I watch blue herons dive for fish. And

soft-shelled turtles are in the water. Iguanas prowl around. They're huge, iridescent green and gold. If you sit very still, they don't run away."

He could see that she was imagining those things and she leaned back on her arms, her eyes on the water.

He leaned back beside her. "Do you know what this mystery is?"

She hesitated for a moment, then nodded.

"Who is Nicky?"

She sighed before she spoke. "He was to be the earl. He was going to inherit this place."

He liked her voice. Quiet, soothing. "Was? What happened?"

"He died in a car crash."

"And this was before or after the couple disappeared?"

"Two years after." Puck looked at Jack. "Will you help find out the truth? Sean was my friend and they hated him."

"Sean? He was one of the people who disappeared?"

Puck looked away as she whispered. "Yes. But he didn't disappear. He —" A voice came and she stood up quickly.

"It's just Kate," Jack said. "She —" But Puck had vanished into the trees.

"There you are," Kate said as she came

into view. She sat down beside him and ate a couple of berries. "Did you find what you were looking for?"

"And what do you think that was?"

"An orphan. A stray. Someone who needed to be rescued by Hero Jack."

He snorted. "Is that a compliment or a gibe?"

"You tell me." She waited for his answer.

"I didn't like what that guy said, so shoot me. And yes, I found her. There's something going on here and it's not good."

"She told you that?"

"Not in so many words. It's a feeling as much as anything. Nicky — who bad-tempered Mrs. Aiken seems to have loved — was the earl-to-be. Died in a car wreck two years after Sean disappeared."

"Sean Thorpe and Diana Beardsley."

"How do you know their names?"

"It was in the news clipping."

"The one you stole from Sara?"

She started to protest but then smiled. "The very one. I'm practicing to be a thief — like my father seems to have been. Do you know the combination to Aunt Sara's safe?"

It took some work not to show his shock at the casual mention of her father's predilections. "I know she doesn't have a safe.

Besides, the last I saw, half her jewelry was in *your* closet."

"Now who's snooping?"

He chuckled, ate some berries and leaned back on his arms. "So what's our room like? Just to be clear, I get the end of the tub without the faucets."

"You wish! But I did . . ."

"What?"

"I chose two rooms that have an internal door connecting them. Two baths though."

Jack didn't reply except to nod. If he found out that Sara had put them into a murder investigation like their first one, he wasn't going to let either woman out of his sight. Ever.

Four

Jack followed Kate back to the house. He wasn't surprised when she led him down corridors and up narrow stairs to reach their rooms. She was taking him through the servants' way: secret and hidden. He knew she could have gone to the front and used the main stairs, but she was trying to impress him with what she'd learned about the intricacies of the house — and she did.

She stopped on the third floor — or as the English said, the second floor — two floors above the ground floor.

"I saw all the guest rooms," she said. "It's all unlocked because they're cleaning every inch of the house."

"Who did you see?"

"No one. Isn't that great? It's like we own the place."

"Where is Sara?"

Kate shrugged. "I have no idea, but there's

a locked door in the western part of the house."

"Then that's where she is."

Kate had her hand on a doorknob. "I didn't know which room you'd like. They're all old-school English decorating. None of that Swedish minimal look for Oxley Manor."

Jack tried not to grimace at the vision he conjured: pink walls, pink bed draped in ruffles, little lampshades like from a doll-house. As Kate opened the door, he braced himself.

The room was large and tall, with floor-to-ceiling windows. The walls were painted a deep, dark red, the woodwork white. The carpet was gray with red medallions. The bed was — thank you! — not canopied. It had a plain white cotton bedspread. There was a desk, a chest of drawers, a chair upholstered in red paisley, a TV and a two-person dining table.

"Well?" Kate said. "You like it or not?"

Jack looked around. "I never thought of a red bedroom. Think I should paint my room at home?"

"I think the iguanas would love it." She was trying to hide that she was pleased that he liked what she'd chosen, but she couldn't.

"So where are you?"

She tilted her head to indicate the door on the other side of the room. "We should find Aunt Sara. I think it's time she told us what's going on." She headed to the door into the hall.

Ignoring her, Jack went to the connecting door. "What don't you want me to see?"

"Nothing." She made a leap to stop him from opening the door.

But he did. His eyes widened. "Holy merciful . . ." he whispered.

Kate frowned. "It's not *your* room so you don't have to look at it. Let's go."

Jack didn't move, just stared. It was like a child's fantasy of a princess room. The bed had a canopy shaped like the top quarter of an egg. It was decorated with carvings of fleur-de-lis with feathers on top, all covered in gold leaf. Yards of cream-colored silk flowed down and was tied back with bows at the four corners of the bed. And what a bed! Upholstered in silk and trimmed in gold.

The walls of the room were covered with dark yellow brocade. The carpet was off-white. Over the marble fireplace was an Edwardian painting of a pretty young woman in a soft, flowery dress.

Kate was still frowning, waiting for his

put-down.

Instead, he stretched out crosswise at the foot of the bed. He wouldn't dare let his shoes touch the cover. "This is what a woman's bedroom *should* look like."

With a smile, Kate lay down at the head, hugging an embroidered pillow to her. "You really think so? It's not too much?"

"It is way too much." He was smiling.

She turned onto her back and looked up at the underside of the canopy. It had been gathered like a fan, with a silk rose in the center. "I wouldn't want a bed like this at home. It's too much to take care of and I'd be scared of damaging it, but it's like a fairy tale. When I was a kid, I dreamed of a room like this. It's where the princess lives after she finds her prince. It's . . ." She stopped talking.

Jack kept looking up, but he reached out and took her hand. Kate's childhood had been far from that of royalty. She had a mother who was given to frequent bouts of deep depression, and uncles who were religious zealots, and . . . Jack squeezed her hand. "It's beautiful. Not as pretty as *you* but it shows you off well."

Smiling, Kate turned to look at him. "What did you and your invisible person talk about?"

He didn't let go of her hand. "She said —"

"There you two are," Sara said from the doorway, then gasped at the room. "Yeow! This is gorgeous. I'm in the Queen Anne room, one flight down. Beautiful but huge. Take the roof off and a helicopter could land in it."

She flopped down on the bed between them and they pulled their arms from under her. Sara took their hands in hers and looked from one to the other. "Nice place, huh?"

Jack sat up. "Cut the crap and spill all."

Sara and Kate were still lying down and holding hands. They were smiling at each other.

"Stop with the silent conspiracy," Jack said.

"He met Puck," Kate said. "He wants to save her."

"Bella and I saw her from a window. She makes wreaths and little potpourri bags. Sells them to the hotel and to shops in Bath and London. I was told they do quite well. Bella also said that her mother is awful. She —"

"We met her," Kate and Jack said in unison, their voices full of disgust.

"That bad, huh?"

Kate slipped off her shoes and sat up against the headboard. Sara did the same and sat beside her.

At the other end, Jack looked at both of them. He had never before realized that when Kate was Sara's age, she'd look just like her aunt. "Are you two ganging up on me?"

"We're preparing for the famous Wyatt temper." Sara looked at Kate, who nodded.

"You mean because I've been tricked and lied to? Manipulated, conned, played for a sucker?" he asked.

"I never lied," Sara said.

A tiny quirk of a smile appeared at the side of his mouth. "So tell the whole story."

"I saw an opportunity and I took it," Sara said. "Bella emailed me about the work they were doing during the March closing. I was on my laptop and I brought up Oxley Manor and found a little site that told of unsolved mysteries at great houses, then . . ." She shrugged.

"You read about the disappearance," Kate said.

"Exactly," Sara said. "Sent my curiosity through the roof."

"Mrs. Aiken told us of some guests who are coming," Kate said. "She's not happy about it."

"Is she really as nasty as Bella said?"

"Worse," Jack said. "Her poor daughter hides in trees."

Sara and Kate stared at him, waiting for more.

"I'm not telling anything." He was looking at Sara. "Who are the 'parasites' she has to cook for?"

"Parasites? Interesting choice of word," Sara said. "I think I'll go —"

She started to get off the bed, but Jack clasped her ankle. "No you don't."

Sara looked innocent. "You two are going to the Highlands, remember? I'm staying here to meet some people and ask questions. I want to find out what really happened to that couple. They just plain vanished. I dug through websites that do deep searching but there is no record of either of them."

"Maybe they changed their names," Kate said.

"Then that asks the question of *why* they had to do that," Sara said.

"The real question," Jack said, "is why you want to know."

"Maybe I'll write a mystery novel. What with the hotel being empty, I thought it might be fun to find out the truth."

"I'm still waiting to hear what you did,"

Jack said. "Something about a party."

Sara looked at Kate. "Bella's not too happy about it, but I invited the people who were there that night to come for a free weekend here at Oxley Manor. There are only four of them left."

"*Left?* As in still alive?" Jack asked.

Sara waved her hand in dismissal. "Will you stop being Mr. Grump? Yes, one of them died."

"Nicky, the earl-to-be, in a car crash," Jack said.

"I'm impressed. What else have you found out?"

"Puck the wood sprite tell you that?" Kate asked.

Sara and Jack looked at her. She sounded jealous.

"Sorry," Kate said. "Go on. Who are they?"

"All I know is that a group of friends had a party here way back in the ancient days of 1994." Her sarcasm was dripping. "Two of them walked out and were never seen again. Years later one was killed in a car wreck."

"And?" Jack asked.

"I told you. I did some digging — with Bella's help, that is. She put me in touch with a man who used to work here and I called him. What an accent! Very difficult to understand. He said that weekend wasn't just a onetime event but that the same young people were *always* here. The staff called them Nicky's Pack."

"That sounds more like dogs than people," Kate said.

"Or wolves," Jack added. "Go on."

"That's it," Sara said. "There were six of them. They attended Cambridge University together and came here every weekend and holiday. 'Pack of strays is what they were,' the man said."

"Doesn't sound like he liked them," Kate said.

"I don't think he did, although when he mentioned Diana, his voice got soft."

"Diana Beardsley." Jack smiled when Sara looked surprised.

"How did you know — ?"

"What about the others?" Kate asked. She didn't want Sara to know she'd accidently seen the newspaper cutting.

"Bella helped me find the names. She . . ." Sara sighed. "She didn't like doing it. But . . . you know."

"You paid for the place so she had to," Jack said.

"I don't like holding something over someone's head, but . . ."

"Couldn't be helped," Kate said dismissively. "What did you find out about them?"

"Sean —" She looked at Jack to supply the last name.

"Thorpe," he said.

"Yes. Sean was the stable manager. He wasn't actually in the group. He and Diana vanished, never to be seen again."

"It's been over twenty years," Jack said. "And no one has heard anything?"

"That's one of the first things I want to ask about when they get here."

"Who are the others and where are they now?" Kate asked.

"Nadine Howland," Sara said. "She and her father lived next door. Bella said he built a ghastly house."

"Got an invitation to see it yet?" Jack asked.

"It's on my list. She married a viscount so it's now Lady Nadine. There was a man named Clive who was the estate manager. He's a banker in London now. And a young woman named Willa. I had a really hard time finding her. She was the daughter of an aristocrat and I called the family."

"You did all this without telling us a word?" Jack sounded hurt.

"*What* am I supposed to do all day?" Sara shot back. "You think I'm old so I should sit around and watch TV? Look at photo albums and go over my memories? Or —"

"Don't use the age card on me!" Jack snapped back. "You could have told us what you were planning to do and —"

Kate, always the peacemaker, stepped in. "What happened to Willa?" She glared at Jack to shut up.

"I don't know. I found her sister in London and called her. She did *not* want to talk about Willa."

"Interesting," Kate said.

"I thought so too. I gave her my email address to give to Willa. I didn't think I'd hear back. But I did. Willa and I exchanged a few emails, and she said she'd love to come to a reunion, just give her a date."

"So you don't know what happened to her?" Jack was mostly over his anger.

"Not a clue."

"That makes five," Jack said. "Who's the last of the Pack?"

Sara took so long to answer that Kate and Jack looked at her in curiosity. Finally, she locked eyes with Jack and said, "Byon Lizmere."

Jack loudly sucked in his breath.

"Who's he?" Kate asked.

Jack and Sara were staring at each other.

"Okay, you two," Kate said. "Stop leaving me out. Who is this guy?"

"Before Last Night. Yesterday is Tomorrow." Jack's tone was reverent.

"We saw every one of his plays on Broadway," Sara said.

Jack hummed a bit of a song. "Is he coming?"

"Yes," Sara said. "I contacted him through his agent. I didn't speak directly to Mr. Lizmere, but he messaged me that he'd do anything to find out what really happened that night. He's driving up from London to be here." She looked at Jack. "You are going to sing with Byon Lizmere."

Jack snorted. "I'm not up to his league. Broadway? London theaters? Not even close."

Both women smiled. For all Jack's protesting, they heard the desire in his voice. Had his life been different, music would have been part of it. But he gave that up for his family.

Jack looked away. "Okay, maybe. Anything else you want, besides me making a fool of myself?"

"You made friends with the daughter, how about trying with the mother?" Sara said. "Find out what she knows."

"Mrs. Aiken? Are you crazy? I'd rather wrestle a gator."

"Jack, my dear, you can charm anyone."

She turned to Kate. "I couldn't persuade you to rummage in the attics, could I? We have Bella's full permission to snoop. You can see if there's anything in there about what happened."

Kate looked as though Sara had offered her the Key to Heaven. All she could do was nod.

As Sara got off the bed, Jack said, "And what ultrasecret thing are *you* planning to do? Or are we not supposed to know?"

"I'm taking my camera and a couple of lenses out for a walk. I figure that after all these people arrive, I won't get ten minutes alone. I'll see you for dinner with Bella. It's at seven." She left the room.

For a few minutes, Kate and Jack sat on the bed facing each other but eyes not meeting.

She knew what he was thinking about. "You'll do fine," she said softly.

Jack didn't want to think about, much less discuss singing for a professional of Byon Lizmere's caliber. It was his highest dream and scariest nightmare in one.

Sara wasn't the only one who could manipulate. He wanted to direct Kate's thoughts in another direction. "Wonder what the attic is like? I bet when Bella bought this place they cleaned it out. But isn't Bella a relative of the family who built this place? She might have kept a few mementos."

Kate tightened her lips. "Are you trying to get rid of me?"

"Did Sara say when these people are arriving?"

"If Mrs. Aiken is starting to cook for them, it's soon."

"So if I'm going to talk to her — and that seems to be my assignment — maybe I should go now."

"And you're sending me off to the attic." Kate was trying to sound put-upon, but there was so much excitement in her voice that Jack laughed.

"Go! Be Miss Indiana Jones and seek and find."

Kate leaped off the bed and was instantly at the door. "With Harrison Ford I'd be a Mrs.," she called to him as she ran down the corridor. She didn't seem to be aware that she was barefoot.

Smiling, Jack got off the bed, picked up Kate's shoes and put them outside the door where she could find them. She loved all things historical so much that he wondered if she'd miss them.

As he left, he didn't bother going back through the labyrinth Kate had led him through but went toward the main part of the house. It was silent, the lush carpets cushioning all sound. The walls were covered in pale gold silk brocade, and giant oil portraits were everywhere. The halls were wide enough that furniture was on both sides. Little half-round tables, small sofas, museum-quality chairs lined the way. As a builder, Jack knew the price of it all — and it had cost Sara a *lot* of money.

When he saw an abnormally narrow door, he opened it. As he'd guessed, it concealed a servants' staircase, where they'd probably hauled up buckets of hot water. He went down and wasn't surprised to enter the kitchen.

Mrs. Aiken was there with her pans and bowls. Jack took a breath, put on his most pleasant face and stepped forward. He smiled at the woman, but she glared back. "I was wondering where Puck is," he said.

"She's in that house Nicky gave her."

Jack blinked at the woman's tone. If her words were put in a text, there would be a skeleton emoji by "that house" and a smiley face with hearts by the word "Nicky."

Sara Medlar, you owe me, he thought, and cleared his throat. "Nicky liked Puck?"

"Young Master Nicky liked everyone. He was kind and generous to all. He would have made a wonderful earl. But someone killed him."

At that pronouncement, Jack wanted to run to get Sara and Kate and fly home. *Not another murder!* "I hadn't heard that," Jack said. "You think he was murdered?"

"Of course. That's what his father said at the funeral. 'Which one of you bastards killed my son?' "

"And the bastards were . . . ?"

"Them. The ones I'm supposed to cook for. They want to re-create that weekend when they killed dear Nicky. What I don't understand is *why*?"

"Sorry to be dense, but I thought he died years after that party."

"His body was smashed by a tree but his soul died that night. When *she* left him. She walked out with Nicky's heart."

Jack was confused. "Is this Diana? She and Nicky were a couple?"

Mrs. Aiken squinted at him in threat. "Are you here to interrogate me? Find out what I know to be true?"

Jack smiled in a way that he knew women liked. "If I say yes, will you tell me the story?"

She gave no smile in return. "You're like him."

"Nicky?"

"No, the other one. Thorpe. Worked in the stables." Her tone sounded as though the man was a criminal. "He used to come in here and steal food. I knew it was for someone he was meeting. Didn't know it was for the love of Nicky's life. Nicky could have had anyone, but he chose *her.* Then that man stole her." She looked at Jack as though it was his fault.

Jack would have liked to ask more questions but he didn't think he'd get anywhere. It was better that he change the subject. "Where is Puck's house?"

"Why do you want to know?"

She made Jack sound like a predator. "I —" He didn't say any more because a phone on the wall rang and she grabbed it. With a look at Jack like he was a spy trying to find out her secrets, she stepped into the pantry and loudly shut the door behind her.

Jack's first thought was *If there is a murder in all this, I hope she did it.* He'd like to see her in handcuffs. As he started to leave the big kitchen, the oven timer went off. He couldn't let whatever was in there burn. He opened the oven door and pulled out three sheets full of little potpies. They looked delicious. With a quick glance at the closed pantry door, he wrapped four of them in a white kitchen towel. There were half a dozen bottles of wine on the counter by the door and he took one.

He didn't run across the drive, but he certainly hurried.

Oxley Manor covered acres and there were buildings everywhere. Had there been people about, he would have asked directions but it was eerily deserted. There were fields with empty farm machinery. Houses with no signs of life.

Even if he found Puck's house, he didn't know if she'd be there.

When he came to a stone wall, a continuation of the one at the gate, he started to turn back. But then he saw a cemetery. The old headstones were covered in moss, the faces of angels blurred by time and weather.

At the end was a house. It was three stories tall, very narrow, with an octagon-shaped tower in the corner. At the bottom, almost hidden from view, was a pointed arch with an iron gate across it. It was not a place most people would want to enter, certainly not to live in. Jack had no doubt that it was Puck's house.

He made his way through the gravestones. The names were mostly Renlow, third, fourth, eighth, etc, earl of Oxley. He paused at one for a Nicholas, died 1996.

As he read the words about being a beloved son, a movement caught his eye. It was Puck standing in the doorway.

With a slight tilt of her head, she motioned for him to follow her inside.

When he got to the entrance, he saw that the gate could be locked. To get to the front door he had to go up a winding staircase. There was no way that someone could enter her house secretly.

He stopped at the top of the entry stairs and was in a tiny hallway with coat hooks and a bench. There was a heavy door — another security measure — standing ajar. He pushed it open and entered a large, light room with a kitchen at one end and a living area at the other. The rooms were separated by a huge oak table, which was covered with dried plants, spools of wire and string, and several pairs of pliers. On the walls were wreaths made of herbs. They were elaborate and beautiful works of art. No wonder they sold!

Puck was standing by the kitchen sink that was slate and big enough to bathe a calf. From the overhead rafters hung hundreds of tied bundles of herbs.

"This is beautiful," Jack said.

Her face pinkened at his heartfelt compliment.

He held up his packet of pies. "I stole

these from your mother. She'll probably kill me, so let's enjoy them before she ends my life."

Puck gave a laugh that was a bit like the sound of bells. It was quite pleasing — and he guessed that it was rarely heard by anyone.

Jack held up the wine bottle. "You have any glasses?"

She did. She also had cheese and mustard, pickles and olives. She filled a basket, then led him through a room that had a glass roof. She used it as a greenhouse. Her plantings were thick and lush.

At the end was a door that opened into a garden. For all that the English complained about the weather, Jack loved it. It was cool, a bit damp; the sun was bright but not broiling. The plants certainly did love the climate. The garden was a feast of greens that ranged from gold to almost black. Around the perimeter were fruit trees that had been trained to create a fence. The smell was heavenly.

Next to the house was a pergola covered in grapevines, a table and chairs beneath them.

"Wow," Jack said, as he put everything on the table. "This place is a knockout. And

I'm guessing that all these plants are edible."

"They are," Puck said, as they sat down at the table.

Jack opened the bottle of wine and poured two glasses.

"Will you tell me what happened?" Jack didn't think he needed to explain what he was referring to.

Puck hesitated. "What have you been told so far?"

"Very little. Your mother said — I think I understand this — that Nicky was madly in love with Diana, but the night of the party she ran off with the horse guy. And by the way, he was a thief and I look just like him."

He was watching Puck's profile and could see the muscle in her jaw working. Good! Anger often brought out secrets in a person.

"Later," he continued, "Nicky was so depressed at losing Diana that he smashed his car into a tree. Or maybe one of the other party guests murdered him. Or that's just your mother's theory. And Nicky's father's."

He was watching her but she was silent.

"Do you know what happened to the two runaways? Sara searched but could find out nothing. Kate thought maybe they changed their names, got new identities, but that seems drastic. I know that what happened to Nicky was awful, but the world is full of brokenhearted lovers."

Jack waited but Puck just sat in silence, her profile to him, her body rigid.

He tried to stamp down his annoyance but couldn't. He stood up. "I thank you for lunch but I need to help Kate. She —"

"It's not true," Puck said.

He sat back down and refilled their wineglasses. "What isn't?"

"All of it." She looked at him. "What people think isn't true."

Jack repressed a groan. He hated language that didn't say what was meant. "Was there foul play in Nicky's death or not?"

"I doubt it. He drank too much and drove too fast. That night he drank a lot, then stole his father's car because he'd smashed his own the week before. The police report said he was doing over eighty when he hit the tree."

"So your mother . . . ?"

"Romanticizes him," Puck said. "She practically raised him and thought he could do no wrong."

"But she —" Jack halted himself. Mrs. Aiken had actually raised Puck, her own daughter, but she hid in trees to escape the woman. "Your mother said Nicky's father thought one of the others murdered him."

"One of the Pack?"

Jack nodded. "Did everyone call them that?"

"Mostly. Bertie — Nicky's father — wanted to blame anyone he could."

"That's normal. He must have loved his son and —"

Puck made a scoffing sound. "Bertram Renlow loved no one, certainly not his son." She waved her hand. "None of this matters. It's Sean who is important."

"And Diana, since they ran away together."

"No," Puck said softly. "They didn't."

"You sound very sure of yourself."

She started to answer but didn't. "When the others get here, you're going to ask them questions, aren't you?"

"Yes."

"They will lie. One of them will certainly do what he or she can to not tell the truth."

He was staring at her. "You know something, don't you? Has Sean contacted you? Do you know where he is? If you do, please tell us so we can leave here. Kate wants to see Great Britain, but we won't leave Sara behind, and she won't leave until she has proof that there is no mystery. A couple of lovers ran off together. They're probably living on a sheep farm in New Zealand under new names because they didn't want people called Nicky's Pack to find them. I bet they have four grown kids now."

When Puck didn't smile at his jest, he knew she was hiding something. "Tell me what you know," he said.

"Not now." She stood up and began to clear the table, then stopped and looked hard at him. "Go and look at this place. At *all* of it. Keys for the little trucks are under the floor mats. Explore and *see*. Mrs. Guilford will be at dinner, but don't talk about *me*."

Jack knew he was being dismissed — and he knew when he was being given a message. There was something he was supposed to see on the estate.

He said goodbye and made his way out. He went back to the utility truck, found the key and drove around the estate.

Because Mrs. Aiken said that he reminded her of Sean, Jack was especially interested in the stables. He'd grown up working on cars, as his father and grandfather had done, but he wondered if, in a different time, his interest would have been horses.

The long, narrow stables were empty now, the stalls cleaned out, but they still had a feeling of the years they'd been used. He could imagine the place full of animals and people in riding suits.

The builder in him saw a way to convert the stalls into housing. He'd leave the stone walls, and especially leave the wooden floors that had been trampled and seasoned with decades of manure.

Smiling, he imagined some banker in a three-piece suit bragging about the patina of his floors.

Jack left the stables and went into the sunshine to further explore. He found a couple of foundations from demolished buildings. One looked as if it had burned down.

In the far corner of the estate was a closed-off area. A high fence had signs declaring danger and forbidding entry, saying it was a "wildlife preserve." Jack wondered what nesting critters lived in there. He'd have to ask.

By the time he got back to the big house, he had a layout of the acreage in his mind.

Had he been through enough that he'd found whatever Puck wanted him to see? Or had he imagined her message?

For all his hours exploring, there wasn't anything that stood out as unusual or mysterious. Maybe he should have climbed the fence of that place that was labeled "dangerous." Maybe he'd do that tomorrow. But everything depended on when the Pack was going to arrive.

As Jack headed up the stairs, he knew he didn't want to think of their arrival. Meeting Byon Lizmere was out of his realm of comfort. The man had written great music and even greater plays. The most magnificent singers in the world had performed his music at Carnegie Hall, Albert Hall, the MTV awards. Everywhere and everyone.

But I am supposed to sing for him, Jack thought as he headed for the shower.

FIVE

For dinner, Jack put on a clean white shirt and black dress trousers. He didn't know if he should wear a tie or not or even a jacket. From the look of the house, people liked to pretend they were Edwardian aristocracy, so he might be required to wear a tux to dinner — which he had, thanks to Sara. His only thought was to find Kate. Sara was probably outside, on her belly in the grass snapping photos of some ugly bug, and Kate was likely to be knee-deep in dusty old diaries.

It took a while, but he found a door that opened to a narrow stone staircase that led upward. From the worn-down centers, he knew he was in the oldest part of the house. At the top, he found unrenovated rooms. They had faded Victorian wallpaper and old metal beds. Servants' quarters.

"Bet Sara loves this," he muttered as he went down two long hallways, past doors with number plates, came to the ends, then had to retrace his steps before he finally saw an open door. Kate was sitting in a fat chair with faded upholstery, a big book across her lap.

She smiled when she saw him. "Have any trouble finding this place?"

"None whatever."

She laughed at his lie. "You look nice. Glad you cleaned up."

"Anything for my ladies." He stretched out on the bed and looked around. It was a very plain room with a small window and white cotton curtains. There was a stand with an old-fashioned bowl and water pitcher on it. The bed, the stand and the chair were the only furniture. "Bleak," he said. "You make any progress in finding out anything?"

"Not really. Tell me about your lunch date."

"How do you know about it?"

"From Mrs. Aiken. She was quite angry that you stole food. 'Just like Thorpe,' she said."

"I think maybe I look enough like him that his sins are piled onto me."

"Add your own sins and that's a heavy burden."

Jack snorted in laughter.

She lowered her voice. "Maybe it's the emptiness of this place but sometimes I feel like I'm being watched. Is your new girlfriend snooping around?"

"She has to stay away from her mother." Jack's jaw was clenched.

"She could move away from here, couldn't she? She's certainly old enough."

Jack frowned. "Puck owns a gorgeous house where she grows herbs for the wreaths she makes." He could feel himself getting angry. "It would be hard for her to move. She's quite intelligent and she —" He broke off as Kate was smiling at him. "You did that on purpose."

"Agitate the Wyatt temper and you learn all sorts of things. What did she tell you?"

"Nicky was drunk when he crashed his dad's car, and Daddy didn't love his son or anyone else for that matter. And Nicky was in love with Diana but she may or may not have run off with the stable guy. Puck thinks not. But then, I think maybe she had a crush on him."

"Wow, that's a lot," Kate said. "Sounds like you two befriended well."

Jack started to make a joke but instead told the truth. "She makes me want to defend her. I think she gets a raw deal around here." He looked at Kate. "What did you find out?"

She glanced at the book on her lap. He could see that it was an old-fashioned ledger full of numbers. "Just that this place was nearly bankrupt when Isabella bought it."

"You mean Sara bought it, don't you?"

"I doubt if her name is on any document, but Aunt Sara plowed a fortune into this house. She must have really trusted her friend to do that."

Jack raised an eyebrow. "Is she being paid back?" He knew Kate was good at finances.

"Yes, but slowly. When there's any money in the pot, it goes to renovation and expanding."

"Seems big enough to me."

"I agree. Did you see all of it?"

"I think so." He didn't say that Puck had wanted him to look around. "Have you met Isabella yet?"

"No. She's been in her rooms and Aunt Sara is —" She waved her hand.

"Alone with her camera," he finished. "Did you find anything about the missing people?"

"I got carried away looking at numbers. Protecting Aunt Sara, that sort of thing. I've been thinking about something. Maybe . . ."

"Maybe what?"

"Maybe you and I should leave all this

and go to the Highlands. We're booked for four days in a castle. We could go touring and see the sights."

"And I'd wear my kilt."

For a moment, they looked at each other. They'd never really been alone together. For all that they lived in the same house and for a while Jack had stayed in Kate's suite, there were always other people around.

"I'd like that," he said softly.

"You'd miss singing with this Byon guy."

"Yeah," he said. "I'd get out of that."

She laughed, then looked at her watch. "I better get dressed for dinner. And for meeting the illustrious Bella."

"Bottomless-money-well Isabella," Jack muttered. He got up and caught Kate's arm. "I'll be honest and say that I don't really care who ran off with whom. If it was up to me, I'd let Sara stay here and research to her little heart's content. We could pick her up on the way back. I'd like to see Scotland. I read that there's a place you can buy cashmere sweaters for practically nothing."

"Hawick," Kate said, smiling up at him. "It's on our itinerary."

He grinned. "Should have known." He let go of her arm. "I vote that we go. Let Sara deal with her mystery. You and I will go sightseeing."

"Let's do it!" Kate said. "We'll tell her in the morning. Think she'll be upset?"

"To be left alone in an old house with her camera and a mystery to solve? What do you think?"

"She'll be in heaven. I need to go. We're to meet in Bella's apartment at seven for drinks."

"That means dinner won't be until eight and I'm hungry now."

"Your American tummy will have to wait. I was told that they might be serving English beef." She was backing toward the door. "With horseradish sauce and buttered parsnips. But maybe that's just a rumor."

"Yeah?"

Kate laughed at his delight. "Don't be late."

"Where is Bella's apartment?" he asked, but Kate was already gone.

For a while he stayed in the barren little room, his mind full of the idea of a holiday with Kate. Sara had booked them separate rooms everywhere but he thought he could overcome that. Days of wine and heather, kilts and bagpipes. Time alone with Kate was something he'd longed for since the day he met her.

Now all he had to do was get through the

evening. Tomorrow they'd leave.

Smiling, he went downstairs to the drawing room. He'd look at some fishing magazines and get his mind away from the question of who Nicky loved, why Diana ran off with Sean and how Bertie didn't love anybody.

"I've got my own bad childhood," he muttered. "I don't need anyone else's."

Bella's suite of rooms were sumptuous. Draped in green and pink silk, Marie Antoinette would have envied the place. There were tall windows curtained in silk so heavy Jack wondered how the rods held them. He had to refrain from investigating the understructure.

As for Bella, she looked as regal as the room. She was tall, with iron gray hair and a solid figure. Not fat, not thin, but straight up and down. Her face was handsome, and her clothes . . . Even Jack recognized the straight-cut jacket as Chanel. He'd put money on it that her tasteful little brooch of colored stones was real.

Looked like the profits of the hotel weren't *all* being spent on renovations.

She was, of course, charming. Sara had told them that Bella grew up in the finest English boarding schools, had hobnobbed with the cousins of royalty. Smiling, Bella promised to take Kate shopping, admired Sara's latest photos and asked Jack about his construction work.

"Sara told me what you did for the Morris women," she said to Jack. "I thought you were a true hero."

"He was," Sara said proudly.

"We wouldn't have continued if it hadn't been for Jack," Kate said.

He could feel himself beginning to blush. "So what's for dinner?" he blurted, sounding like a workman who'd accidently been let into the palace — which he kind of was.

Bella wasn't perturbed. "English beef, what else would we serve?"

To save him, Sara began asking questions about the estate.

Mrs. Aiken did indeed serve a dinner of slabs of rare roast beef, with buttered parsnips and roast potatoes. The food was delicious, but her "serving" showed her displeasure. She loudly dropped bowls and a platter in the middle of the table while glaring nastily at Jack.

After she stormed out of the room, Bella looked at Jack with sympathy. "I'd apologize but that would imply that things will improve. It seems that you remind her of someone she greatly disliked."

"The groomsman," Jack said. "I saw his domain today. Nice building. Did anyone ever try to find him after he ran off?"

"I don't think anyone cared enough to search for either of them," Bella said. "I believe young Diana was planning to marry Nicky. Her leaving must have been a blow to him."

"And Mrs. Aiken adored Nicky," Kate said.

"I believe she did," Bella said.

"Surely, someone must have seen something between them before that night," Kate said.

"I have no idea," Bella said. "I never met any of them."

"What about the engaged couple?" Sara asked. "A happy woman doesn't leave without a good reason. When I left Cal, I —"

Both Kate and Jack leaned forward. They very much wanted to know why Sara had so abruptly run away from Jack's grandfather.

But Sara didn't complete her sentence. "I wonder if something else happened that night. Maybe Diana saw Nicky with someone. Or they had one of those arguments that puts an end to everything."

"Like when a man tells a woman that after they get married she has to quit her job and have dinner on the table exactly at six." They all turned to look at Jack. "I'd never say that."

He looked at Kate to back him up, but she just smiled, then she turned to the others. "Everyone assumes that the groomsman and Diana ran away *together* but what if they didn't? Maybe Diana saw something and said, 'I'm out of here,' then . . ." She looked to Sara to complete the story.

"Then Diana ran to the stables, said she was leaving, and the groomsman said, 'I'm fed up too. I'll go with you.' "

"Then they fell in love," Bella said with a sigh. "Oh, Sara, I do love your books!"

Kate smiled. "It seems that someone would have heard something by now."

"Maybe they have," Sara said. "From what I understand, none of the group has seen each other in years. We don't have any idea what they know."

"How sad," Kate said. "They went from being inseparable friends to not speaking to each other."

"All because of what happened in one night," Sara said. "Must have been dramatic. I look forward to talking to these people and finding out what really happened."

“Speaking of friendship,” Jack said, “I’d like to hear more about you two.” He was looking from Sara to Bella.

“It was cosmic,” Sara said. “Meant to be.”

“I’m afraid I intruded.” Bella looked at Sara. “You’re the professional storyteller — you tell it.”

“I only tell a story if I have a contract and a check arriving.”

Bella smiled. “I rudely shoved my way into Sara’s life.”

She shrugged. “The restaurant was so packed she was being turned away.”

“It was in New York, it was late and the rain was pouring.”

“Not a nice, soft, sweet English rain,” Sara said, “but a good ol’ New York blaster. It was turning umbrellas inside out.”

“The maître d’ told me I could wait until someone finished or . . .”

“Or leave,” Sara said. “Which is what I’m sure he wanted you to do. Couples give bigger tips than single women. But then . . .” She looked at Bella.

“Then I saw Sara sitting alone at a table. I said, ‘Oh heavens, there’s my friend. I’ll join her.’ So I went to Sara and she played along with it all.”

“It was the accent,” Sara said. “Of course I told the snobby man that she was my dearest friend in the whole world." She smiled at Bella. "And that was that."

"Yes." Bella smiled back. "The poor waiters! How annoyed they were that we wouldn't leave."

"We talked for hours," Sara said. "We had such a lot in common. Bella grew up going to top-drawer English boarding schools and living in a mansion, while I grew up in the slums of Lachlan, Florida. She was married and had a child and I had a life of writing and not much else. We were a perfect match."

The two women were smiling fondly at each other.

"I think it was our differences that were attractive," Bella said. "And Sara's fascination with history. I must say that my friend was very modest. She told me she'd written a few books. She didn't tell me she was a superstar in the publishing world. But maybe I should have guessed since I was staying downtown in a shabby little hotel while Sara was in a suite at the Helmsley Palace. I assumed it was a once-in-a-lifetime holiday."

"I was doing a new contract," Sara said, "and they wanted me there."

"I was in New York for an international hotel convention. I'd been in the business all my adult life and I was trying hard to interest someone in restoring Oxley Manor and making it into a five-star hotel."

"But *you* agreed to give her the money." There was no humor in Jack's voice.

"Not then," Sara said. "In fact, Bella didn't even tell me what she was trying to do until years later."

"I had too much pride to admit the truth to a stranger," Bella said. "Sara invited me to tea in the Gold Room the next day. That's when four women came up to us and asked for her autograph. Only then did I realize how successful she was. I, uh . . . I hid my own situation from her."

Sara smiled. "Four or five years later, after we'd exchanged a zillion emails, I came to England to do research and I saw this place. It was in bad shape."

"Sara is being kind," Bella said. "It was rotting. The roof was nearly gone. I'd given up trying to find a backer to repair it. The National Trust didn't want it as there was no money to go with it. And besides, in England, Oxley Manor is small, with no historical significance."

"What about the chapel?" Kate asked. "I haven't seen the inside, but surely it's important."

"If it were in the US," Sara said, "it would

be a tourist attraction, but here those places are a dime a dozen. Look at Savills website some time. Houses like this, in perfect condition, are always for sale."

"So you decided to take on the project," Jack said.

Sara narrowed her eyes at him. Sometimes his self-appointed role of being a protector was too much. "There have been *several* businesses that I have invested in."

Since Jack's construction company was one of them, he knew he'd been put in his place. When he drank from his wineglass, his eyes were glittering in amusement. Sara sure knew how to slash and burn.

"Should we go into the drawing room for coffee?" Bella asked, then looked at Sara. "Or the very strong tea that you like?"

"It's late so I think I'll say good-night."

"Me too," Jack and Kate both said.

Minutes later, they were heading up to their rooms. The main staircase was wide and impressive. They went up side by side. At the top, Sara turned to them and in a low voice said, "What is it that you two are dying to tell me? Other than insinuating about my friend, *in front of her,* that she's trying to rob me?"

"Uh . . ." Jack said.

Kate stepped forward. "He's just a worrywart is all. We want to ask if you'd mind if we went on the trip to Scotland right away."

"That's why I made the reservations."

"But we thought you wanted help with the mystery," Jack said.

She put her hand on his arm. "My darling boy, that was an excuse. I'd love two weeks in an empty hotel. Yes, there's a mystery to solve but I can do that. I think it will be an entertaining weekend with those people who are coming. You're sure you don't want a chance to sing with Byon Lizmere?"

Jack glanced at Kate. "I'm sure."

"Go then. You have my blessing. When you get back I'll have a story of great passion to tell you."

"Put it on paper and sell it," Jack said.

"I've taught you well." She kissed his cheek. "Now go to bed. Don't stay up late. Get some sleep. I'll see you two tomorrow." She kissed Kate's cheek.

They left her outside her bedroom, not even staying to see the big room, but hurrying upstairs.

Jack and Kate were a bit awkward outside their doors. Tomorrow they were going away. Together. Just the two of them.

Kate repressed a yawn. Jet lag was catching up with her.

"See you in the morning," Jack said. "If

you need anything, you know where I am."

"Right beside me. I mean —"

"I know." His hand was on the knob. "You can lock the connecting door if you want."

"I don't think I will," she said, then quickly went into her room and shut the door. The tall princess bed was gleaming in the light of a single lamp.

Suddenly, the long day hit her and she was exhausted. It took only minutes and she was in her pajamas and in the bed. Visions of men in kilts and the sound of bagpipes danced in her mind. She went to sleep smiling.

Six

Jack was in bed, sound asleep. "Get up," he heard Sara say. He glanced at the windows. The heavy curtains were drawn but he could see that it wasn't daylight. "Too early to leave," he mumbled, and turned over.

"We have to go." She sounded urgent.

Alarm ran through him. "Kate?"

"She's fine." Sara's camera was around her neck and a sling bag at her back. Wherever she was, she went out early to take pictures. "It's your buddy Puck. She wants us outside. Now, before daylight."

Quickly, he got out of bed and pulled on a pair of jeans. "Is she okay?"

"Yes, my rescuing knight, she's also fine. She's waiting for us. I'm going to get Kate. Make no noise."

"I'm intrigued."

"Me too." Sara's eyes were alight. She opened the connecting door and went into Kate's room.

Jack could hear them moving about. One of the things he liked about Kate was that she could dress in minutes and was always up for an adventure. Well, actually, maybe she was a bit too ready as well as too fearless and way too unafraid. Jack put his running shoes on. Whatever his women were up to at this hour, he planned to be there.

They met in the hall outside their rooms. Sara put her finger over her lips. No talking; no noise. Even with the hotel mostly empty, she meant to take no chances. Silently, they went down the carpeted hallway, then down the stairs. On the ground floor, Jack took the lead as he made sure no one was about. The exterior door was locked from the inside but he threw the double bolts aside.

Outside, it was quite cool, and their Florida-adapted bodies shivered.

"Wool," Kate said. "My new favorite word."

Sara was looking around. "She was here a minute ago."

Jack motioned for them to follow him as he led the way to a nearby clump of trees. With the sun not up yet, they could see very little. But Jack knew what he was looking for. He stopped at a big tree, reached up into the branches, and a hand magically appeared. Then a foot. Jack lifted his arms and swung Puck down with his hands on her waist.

Once on the ground, she looked up at him with adoring eyes.

"Really?" Kate's voice sounded like a hiss.

Sara was smiling. "Where to?"

Puck didn't speak but set out at a quick pace across dew-covered grass, always staying out of sight of the house. If someone looked out a window, they wouldn't be seen.

She led them to the back of an old stone building. There was a big wooden storage bin along the wall. When Jack lifted the bin lid, he couldn't see what was inside.

Kate turned her phone light onto the contents: tools, half-empty bags of fertilizer, ground stakes.

Puck reached inside, moved a few things and lifted a piece of chain.

Jack pulled it the rest of the way out. It was a chain ladder, what people in upper floor bedrooms used in case of fire.

Puck looked at Jack, letting him know that they'd need that. He slung it over his shoulder.

For a few minutes she disappeared into the building and returned with a new nylon rope, the kind used in rock climbing.

Jack glanced at Kate and Sara. Their eyes

were wide, but they said nothing.

They followed Puck across the estate, staying close to the trees. If the place hadn't been cleared of workers, they would have been seen, but it was eerily silent.

They reached the fenced-off area with its signs warning of danger and forbidden entry. Conservation Zone, a big placard read. If the place had been full of ravenous wolves it couldn't have been marked more clearly.

There was a locked gate, but Puck walked past it.

"Jack could open that for us," Kate said. "He has a criminal history and can break into any lock."

Jack started to defend himself, but Puck gave her funny little laugh.

Kate and Sara turned at the sound.

Sara was the first to break into a grin. She could always be counted on to say what was on her mind. "I think I like you."

Puck blinked at the bluntness, but then smiled. She led them a few feet away to a place with a fence post at an angle. She climbed over it easily. Jack went next, then lifted Sara down. He offered to help Kate, but she got over by herself. They followed Puck as she led them on a wavering path through ferns and grasses.

It was growing lighter, with the sun beginning to peep through the trees. As they went deep into the conservation area, they saw no signs of people. It was very quiet. Isolated.

Abruptly, Puck halted and they stopped behind her. She turned to them. "I have something to show you," she said. "It's . . . It's . . ."

"It's what?" Sara asked.

Puck hesitated.

"Whatever it is," Jack said, "we've seen worse."

"I don't think so," Puck said.

They looked at her, waiting.

"It's a body," Puck said softly.

The three of them didn't flinch.

"Does this have to do with what happened the night of the disappearance?" Sara asked.

"Yes," Puck said. "You're sure you want to see this?"

They nodded.

"Maybe Diana and the groomsman didn't run away together," Kate said.

"I know he didn't." Puck paused. "He couldn't."

"Ah," Sara said, and the others nodded. They had an idea whose body it was.

Puck waved for them to go stand by a tree. They did, but when she started to drag branches across the ground, Jack dropped the ladder and hurried to help her.

"No!" Puck cried, but not in time.

Jack had stepped where there was nothing. His left leg disappeared to his knee. To balance, he threw himself backward, and landed on the ground on his back.

Kate and Sara had seen him nearly fall, and they leaped to help.

Puck was across from them, startled at the sight. Jack sat up as Kate and Sara stood over him as though in protection.

"I'm okay," he said. "That's one serious hole. How deep is it?"

Sara got her camera, attached a flash, then stretched out on the ground on her stomach and took some shots. When she got up, they gathered around to look at the screen. They saw the hole, wide and deep, stone on one side, dirt on the other.

"It's medieval, for sure," Sara said. "Storage for something. My guess is it was for kegs of happy juice. Nothing like cold beer on a hot day." She looked at Puck. "So where is he?"

Puck nodded, liking the term "he" and not "it." She pointed on the screen to where the shelf she'd found could barely be seen. It appeared to be a pile of rocks.

Jack picked up the ladder and the rope.

"I'm going down."

"Me too," Kate said.

"Like hell you are," Jack snapped.

"I'm the cameraperson," Sara said, "and I'm the lightest. I'll go."

No one dared say that she was also the oldest. Pointing out that Sara was a grandmother's age would earn them her razor-sharp tongue.

Kate spoke. "Jack can use a camera, and he knows all about the apps."

"Aperture," he corrected, frowning. Kate was revealing something he'd confided in her.

"I've always known." Sara looked at Jack. "We're wasting time. Tie that ladder to a tree, then go down there and shoot what you see."

As he made the knots, Sara instructed him about photography. "You can probably do point and shoot, but check the screen. If the photo is dark, you're going to need to open it up as wide as it'll go. That's a one point eight lens so use it. And turn the ex comp. I'll adjust the ISO. Try the flash but it may wash the photo out. If it does —"

"Bounce the light off the wall," Jack said. "I got it." He was pulling on the rope to check its security.

"And do a few slow shutters so you get all

the details," she said. "Damn! I wish I had my mini tripod. Set the camera on the ground and —"

Jack kissed her forehead. "I'll be fine. Stop worrying." She handed him the tiny flashlight she always carried in her case.

When the ladder was in place, Jack put the camera around his neck, then started down. With just his head showing, he looked at the three women. "Edmund Hillary didn't have such a good send-off."

The women didn't smile as he disappeared below the ground level.

There was enough light from the top to see where he was. It was like an underground tower with a missing roof. He went down a few feet and there was the ledge that Puck had pointed out.

His builder's eye saw that the cutout wasn't natural. It hadn't been caused by fallen dirt but had purposefully been dug out. For what? If the place had been used to hold kegs of beer maybe workmen hid there while they drank. Whatever its original purpose, if someone looked down from the top, they'd see nothing, not even if people were there.

As Jack swung his leg over, he hung on to the ladder until he got his balance. He glanced up to see three worried faces staring down at him. From their position, they had to be stretched out on their stomachs.

When he was on the ledge, he didn't look to the back into the deep darkness, but kept his eyes on the front. The rocks looked to have been piled up recently. At least long after the place was built. Did someone try to hide what had been put on the shelf?

He took his time as he removed the camera from around his neck and set it down — but he didn't look back. He had an idea what he was going to see, and he wanted to be ready for it. No matter that he'd bragged that he'd seen it "all," bodies upset him. *No,* he thought, *murder infuriates me.*

To his left, he saw a pair of small shoes and guessed they were Puck's. He thought of how they got there. She hadn't said, but it was his guess that she'd fallen into the place, then thrown her shoes toward the top.

He turned on Sara's flashlight and looked at the bottom of the pit. Ferns, moss, rotten vines. Puck was light but if she had fallen, it was a wonder she didn't break her bones.

One by one, he picked up her shoes and tossed them up to the top.

"Thank you," she said down to him.

There was so much relief in her voice that he realized how afraid she must have been. And rightfully so. If someone had come to check on the body, they'd know Puck had been there.

With the shoes gone, Jack knew he must look at "him."

With the flashlight on high, he slowly turned to face the back of the ledge. He thought he was prepared, but he wasn't. A skeleton. A human being who'd been left there to rot. Uncared for. Unmourned.

"Are you okay?" Sara called down to him.

Jack sniffed and swallowed. Cleared his throat. How his father would laugh at him for his sentimentality! "Yeah, fine," he called up. "I just need to take photos."

"Of every inch," Sara reminded him.

"I will. I'll —" He broke off because he heard the ladder against the wall. "What the hell?" he muttered, then leaned out to look up. Kate was coming down. "You can't —" he began, but then reached out to get her, and pull her onto the ledge beside him. They were cramped close together. "You shouldn't be here. You —"

"Neither should you." She took the flashlight from him and turned toward the length of the skeleton. "He's —" Her voice broke.

Jack put his arms around her, and she hid her face in his shoulder.

"That poor man," she said.

"Right," Jack whispered. He wanted to

bawl her out for being there, but it felt so good to hold someone who was *alive* that he said nothing.

Kate pulled away. "Okay, that's it. Let's get to work before someone comes looking for us. Do you actually know how to take pictures with a real camera?"

Her sassiness almost made him smile. "Yeah. I know."

For the next twenty minutes they were quiet as they both took pictures, Kate with her cell phone and Jack with Sara's mirrorless camera. Between the two of them, they recorded every inch of the skeleton and the surroundings.

They tried to touch as little of the area as possible as the bones were loose and could be disturbed. All that held them together had rotted away.

"Wonder how Puck knows who it is?" Kate whispered.

Jack, camera to his face, shrugged. "No idea, but I plan to get every detail from her." He halted. "I mean . . ." He didn't need to finish his sentence. *If* they stayed.

Minutes later, he held Kate about the waist as she leaned out to shoot the interior of the cavernous structure.

"The sun's coming up," Sara called down to them. "We should go."

When Jack lowered the camera, Kate said, "Why is no one mentioning calling the police?"

"Is that what you think we should do?"

With a grimace, Kate said, "I don't know what to do." Her eyes were telling him that she didn't know about staying or leaving, or about a murder.

"Let's go to Puck's house and figure it out," he said.

Kate gave a last look at the place. "Do you think anyone's been down here lately?"

"No. I'll look more closely but I think the vines on top were untouched."

"Except where you nearly fell in." He steadied her as she leaned out to get on the ladder to climb up.

"Jack?"

"Yeah?"

"Do you think that whoever did this is still here?"

"If they aren't here now, they've spent a lot of time in this place. You'd have to be very familiar with this property to know about this old pit. I want to find out who fenced this area off."

"I have questions too." Kate started up the ladder, but paused. "How do we begin asking questions? Do we say we accidently found a body?"

"Yes, definitely," Jack said. "I'm sure that will make everyone feel at ease and tell us all they know."

With a grimace at his sarcasm, she climbed up the ladder.

Minutes later, they were in Puck's house. Puck and Sara were at the big oak table with a laptop and looking at the photos taken in the pit.

Jack and Kate were on the far side of the room, cups of strong, black tea in their hands. They'd seen all they wanted to and now needed time to calm down.

"What do we do?" Kate asked.

He knew what her real question was. Did they leave Sara there while they went on holiday? But everything was different now.

"The Pack is coming," Kate whispered as she glanced at Sara. "They're going to guess that we have a reason for calling them together. And what else could it be but that we found the body?"

"The irony is that we didn't have a reason, just Sara snooping. But now all they have to do is look around the area. Flattened grass will show that people have been there lately."

"Since the hotel is almost empty, they'll know it was us."

"And Puck," Jack said.

Kate nodded. "Her shoes were down there, but no one found them. Whoever hid the poor man probably hasn't been here in a while."

"But now they've been *invited* here." Jack ran his hand over his face. "All of this is *done.* If we called and canceled, they'd know something was up. Puck would be in danger."

"And us. Even if we go home, we might be in danger. We've seen a big secret. A *deadly* secret." She got up and refilled their mugs with hot water and new tea bags. She sat back down beside Jack. "I guess Scotland is out." There was a little sniff in her voice.

"There's no way Sara will leave, and I won't leave her." He looked at Kate. "And I have no hope that *you* will have sense enough to get the hell away from here." He sounded so forlorn that she put her hand over his.

"I really wanted to go," she said.

He squeezed her hand, then let go and sipped his tea. "Do we contact the police or not?"

"You think they'll take the time to dig into something that happened twenty years ago?"

"I'm sure they'd love to hear about Nicky who loved Diana and —"

"Bertie who didn't love his son."

"And maybe Diana dumped Nicky and ran off with the stable lad."

"Not a 'lad.' He looked like you, so he was one virile stud," Kate said.

Jack nearly spit tea at that. "Thanks. You made my day. What the hell do we do?"

"Lie," Kate said. "Act dumb. Pretend we're so in awe of Lady Nadine and Byon the Magnificent that we can hardly speak. We just listen and ask really stupid questions."

"So we act natural?"

She smiled. "Above all, we protect Aunt Sara."

"And you too since you're worse than she is. You cannot go anywhere by yourself. You understand me?"

"Are we talking about showers or bathtubs?"

He didn't smile. "I want a promise."

"I'll do my best."

"Not good enough."

"But it's the best you're going to get." She was glaring at him.

Jack was the first to look away. "I wish I could put us all on a plane for home," he said softly so only Kate would hear.

"Me too. When I asked if there was a mystery, I meant one where we'd research the history books. That man in there was *real.*"

"Poor guy. He was blamed for everything but did nothing wrong," Jack said.

"Except whatever he did that got him killed. If he was playing around with the emotions of women, maybe he deserved —" At Jack's look she took a drink of her tea. They had an unwritten rule not to blame the victim — until they found out that he or she deserved it. "Okay, it's too early for that. But there was something going on that he alone knew about."

"How do you figure that? No. Got it. Kill him and the secret dies. Think he was blackmailing someone?"

"Don't —" Kate began.

Jack cut her off. "Right. Don't blame the victim."

"I wonder who put his body in the pit?"

"Not a clue," Jack said. "I wonder exactly how he died?"

"We could call the police and get an autopsy done."

Jack didn't answer. He looked at Sara and Puck, their heads together. "If we dig deep enough, it's all going to be exposed. Not just here but to the world."

They were quiet for a moment as they thought about that. They'd had a lot of experience with the turmoil the press could create.

Kate spoke first. "I think it's time your girlfriend told us what she knows."

"She's not —" Jack began, then stopped. "She's the love of my life. We'll be married here. Will you be my best man?"

"Only if I get to wear a Tom Ford tux." Kate saw Sara signal them to come over and they went to sit at the table. Puck's supplies for her wreaths had been moved to the top of an antique chest.

"So what have you two decided?" Sara asked. She nodded at the pictures on the screen of the computer. "By the way, good job both of you. The photos are excellent."

"This is my finest hour," Jack said solemnly. "Praise for picture takin'. This is an historical moment." He was trying to lighten the mood but no one smiled. "Puck, you have any eggs I could scramble? I think this will take a while. We need sustenance while we make a plan."

The trio was used to working together and Puck fit in well with them. She pulled things from the fridge and the larder while Jack cooked. There was a skillet of thick English bacon, another of eggs scrambled in butter that had been churned at a local farm. Berries came from the Oxley Manor kitchen garden. Puck put a bowl of bread rolls on the table.

They sat down and dug in.

Sara was the first to open the dreaded conversation. She turned to Puck. "I assume you know that you're in danger from someone. Your shoes bother me. If the murderer didn't see them, you're fine. But if he —"

"Or she," Kate said.

"If someone did see them and did nothing, that means you're known to them. Knows you're the type to keep your mouth shut. Are you known for keeping secrets?"

"Yes," Puck said.

"But who saw the shoes?" Jack asked. "Or did they? I couldn't see that anyone had been in there."

"At least not this year," Sara said. "For all we know, those vines were cut back last year. All we can be sure of is that there was no trampling there in the last six months."

"We don't know when he was killed," Kate said. "Maybe he did run away, but came back years later. I don't know how long it takes for a body to, uh, become a skeleton. Maybe . . ." She trailed off. None of them believed that.

"1994," Sara said. "In May of that year Diana and the groomsman disappeared." She turned to Puck. "How do you know it's him in that hole?"

Puck went to a cabinet against the far wall, opened a drawer, removed the watch and handed it to Sara.

She read the inscription, then passed the watch to Jack.

"You found this by the body?" Sara asked.

Puck nodded. "It was on the ground under some leaves."

"You cleaned it?" Sara asked.

"With a toothbrush."

"So there's no hope that fingerprints were left on it."

"Oh!" Puck said. "I'm sorry."

"Probably wouldn't have been any anyway," Jack said. "I guess we're all aware that not reporting this to the police is a crime."

They nodded.

"Do we tell *anyone* that we found the body?" Kate asked.

"Bella should be told," Sara said.

"No!" Jack said. "Too many people already know."

"But the more people who do know, the less we'll be in danger," Kate said. "The killer can't do away with *all* of us."

Puck looked at them. "A fire. An explosion. Locked doors."

They stared at her in silent shock. But Puck was right. Locked doors at night. A fire started. Old Oxley Manor would light up in an instant.

Kate leaned forward. "Who do *you* think killed him?"

"Clive," Puck said.

"The banker?" Sara asked, and Puck nodded. "Go on. Plead your case."

"He's Nicky's cousin, but Nicky got all and Clive got nothing. Clive hated Nicky, and it was mutual. But they both knew that Nicky couldn't run the place without him. Clive said that when Bertram, Nicky's father, died, he'd get rid of me."

"Sounds like a nasty piece of work," Jack said.

Kate was more skeptical. She looked at Puck. "What did you do that caused him to say that?"

"Nothing specific. It's just that I knew things he didn't. It made him jealous."

Kate nodded in understanding. "Why do you believe Clive murdered the groomsman?"

"There was talk of making Sean the estate manager. Clive would have been out of a job."

"Clive wanted the job enough to murder to keep it?" Sara asked.

"He wanted what he thought might come from it," Puck said. "If Clive lasted until

Bertie died, he would have ruled the whole estate."

"Nicky was incompetent?" Jack asked.

"Yes," Puck said. "That's why he wanted to marry Diana. She could do *anything*." There seemed to be stars in her eyes at the mention of the woman.

"Seems like Clive would have killed Diana," Sara said, then they were all silent. Maybe someone did. She hadn't been heard from, but a body hadn't been found.

Kate changed the subject. "What about Sean and the women? I gather he was a gorgeous man and women liked him."

"Like you." Puck was looking at Jack.

"I can see that," Kate said. "Plays around with women's feelings, never serious about any of them."

Jack ignored the comment. "What was Diana like?"

"She cared about the horses," Puck said. "She was a very good rider and she fixed a broken leg on a swan."

"It still sounds like it was possible that Sean and Diana did run away together," Sara said. "Nicky and Clive were fighting to rule this place. Everyone seemed to be waiting for Bertram to die."

"I agree," Kate said. "Diana and Sean got fed up and left."

"And when Diana found out that Sean didn't love her, she murdered him." Sara looked at Puck. "Was she strong enough to put Sean's body down that hole?"

Puck didn't hesitate. "More than strong enough. Sean was slim and lithe while Diana was thick and sturdy."

"So," Sara said, "maybe there was a fight, an accident, and in a panic Diana hid Sean's body. After that, she disappeared."

"And she's still hiding," Jack said.

"She would have to be," Kate said. "Murder has no expiration date. This is all a mess, isn't it? Love and hate."

"Jealousy," Sara said.

"And death," Puck said.

"Murder," Sara said.

"Whether we like it or not," Jack said, "at some point we have to contact the police. They're going to be PO'd that we didn't tell them right away."

"Why don't the lot of you go — ?" Sara began.

Jack and Kate didn't let her finish her sentence. Their eyes said no.

"All right," Sara said. "We'll keep to our original plan."

Jack spoke first. "You were bored, with nothing to do. You heard of the mystery and you wanted to research it."

"I wasn't exactly bored," Sara said. "But I —"

"And since you paid for this place, Bella owes you," Jack said.

"And there's the singing for Jack," Kate said. "When you heard that Byon Lizmore was —"

"Mere," Jack and Sara said in unison.

"Whatever," Kate said. "When you found out *he* was here, you saw a bestseller in the making."

"If you tell him he has a place in my novel, he'll want part of the royalties," Sara said. "Any person who thinks they've given a writer so much as a single idea wants a cut. A woman at a party said I'd met her before and had used her name in a book so she wanted money. Her name was Beverly. She said I had *stolen* her name and I *had* to pay her. If someone begins a sentence with, 'Why don't you?' I walk away. If I write anything like what they suggest, they demand money. One time —" She cut herself off. "Right. Uh. I think we'd better say it's to be a highly fictionalized account of what happened. No real names used."

"Good idea," Jack said.

Puck was staring at Sara with wide eyes, but Jack and Kate were used to her impromptu tirades.

"Monday," Kate said. "This is Thursday. I vote that we give ourselves until Monday at . . . at teatime to solve this. We find out all we can by then and on Monday at 4:00 p.m. we go to the police and tell them where the body is hidden."

"And we pretend it's all for a book?" Puck asked.

"Yes," Sara said. "I used to spend months researching my historicals."

"Think these people will tell us anything?"

"For sure, one of them will want to know what we've found out," Sara said.

Kate drew in her breath. "We may have awakened a killer."

"It won't be the first time," Jack said.

Sara looked thoughtful. "Did someone kill Sean *and* hide the body? Or were there two people involved?"

They were silent until Jack spoke up. "I hope Byon wasn't the murderer. I really like his plays."

Sara said, "Although . . . prison is possibly a writer's paradise. I've often wondered about that."

"Because you thought about murdering someone and the possible consequences?" Jack asked.

"Oh yes. Many times." Sara looked at them. "We need to make some decisions here. This weekend the place is going to be filled with people, one or more of whom could possibly be a killer." She paused. "Or we could go home. We could just pack up and leave. As you said, we could call the police from the US. We could say we found the body when we were exploring. That would leave Puck out of it. She'd probably be safe."

"Probably," Kate whispered. "In this context, that's a frightening word."

"And we'd be leaving it to the police to find out who committed a long-ago murder," Sara said.

Jack raised his hand. "I vote with Kate. We search until Monday at 4:00 p.m."

"I agree," Sara said, then they looked at Puck. No one had to say that it was her neck on the line. "Maybe you'd like to visit Florida. I'll buy you a plane ticket to there or to anywhere in the world. You could —"

"No!" Puck said. "Sean was my friend. Besides, I've had a lifetime of watching. As the people here love to tell, I can be invisible. I could be useful to you."

Sara smiled. "I think you would be a valuable asset." She held her right hand straight out.

Jack put his hand over hers, then Kate, with Puck's hand on top.

It was a pact.

When they broke apart, Sara said, "I want to know as much as possible about these people before they arrive."

"Clive is tall," Puck said. "He is cold and always angry. He —"

"No, no," Sara said. "I want to *know* them. Like in a really good novel where they tell all about the characters. Show, don't tell."

Puck looked blank.

"Tell us something that happened," Kate said. "I think these people came here often, so tell us about one of their get-togethers. Take us through one of their weekends."

"I want to know about *you* with them," Sara said.

"During the week the house was quiet," Puck said. "Bertie lived here but he was gone most of the time. He liked to talk to people about his beautiful horses." There was fondness in her voice. "Too bad none of the animals he bought could run very fast. Sean said —" Puck waved her hand. "Anyway, Clive was here too but he stayed in his office." Her voice hardened. "Everyone kept away from him because he was so bad-tempered."

"And Sean was in the stables," Sara said.

"He had so much work to do," Puck said.

"He had to look after six horses by himself. Diana helped on weekends, but she was at university during the week. She —"

"Wait!" Kate said. "Wasn't Clive about the same age as the others? Why wasn't he in school?"

"He was for a while, but Bertie pulled him out after two years," Puck said. "Clive was an orphan. His grandmother was related to Bertie's. Clive's whole family had died by the time he was fifteen or so, and Bertie took him in."

"So Clive grew up in Oxley Manor?" Sara asked. "He was part of the family?"

"I guess," Puck said. "He probably had a room somewhere but I don't know where. At the top, maybe."

"And Bertie pulled him out of university after just two years and he had to run this place?" Sara asked.

"How he must have hated seeing the others return on the weekends," Kate said.

Puck shrugged. "I don't know." She looked up. "Back then I saw everything through the eyes of a child. All I knew was that Clive was a horrible man. I had to keep secrets from him, lie to him, trick him, sneak and spy, and —"

They were staring at her.

"I think you should tell us everything,"

Sara said. "And in context."

Puck took a moment to think. "What I remember is that the others would arrive on Friday and —" she smiled in memory "— things would begin to happen. But there was one weekend . . ." She stopped.

"Tell us about it," Sara said.

"It was when I saw Sean in the cemetery. And that was the day when I saw inside this house for the first time. Afterward, it became my own secret hideout. Or I thought it was."

"Nicky must have known you liked it because he willed the place to you," Jack said.

"He did. I thought no one knew where I hid from them all. But maybe it was only my mother who didn't know." Puck smiled. "But then, she knew very little about anything." She leaned back in her chair. "It was about . . . Yes, a year before they disappeared."

Seven

OXLEY MANOR

Autumn 1993

Puck sat in the big Oxley Manor kitchen with her mother. At fourteen, she was tall and thin and did her best not to call attention to herself.

"Really," Mrs. Aiken said in the tone of dissatisfaction she always used with her daughter. "Couldn't you at least sit up straight? You are so much like your father! I keep telling you that you need to make yourself useful around here. If you only knew what was actually going on! I worry that I may not have a job for long. And what about *you*? You have no real purpose here. You'll be the first one thrown out." She sighed at the futility of what she was saying. "*Do* something."

Puck had just finished chopping four huge onions and her eyes were red and burning. She felt no need to reply to something she'd heard many times.

"Go tell Nicky that lunch won't ready be until one thirty. I hope he's not upset by it being late." By the time she finished, Mrs. Aiken's voice was a purr. She *adored* Nicky. The son she'd never had.

Grateful to get out of the kitchen, Puck slid off the stool, went into the long hall, then up the old stairs toward the drawing room. When she heard music, she stopped and leaned against the wall to listen. Nicky was in there with his friend Byon, who was playing the piano. It was a tune she'd never heard before. Byon was a talented musician and a writer of very clever plays. He was oh so creative and everyone liked him. Well, maybe not everyone.

The music stopped.

"That was beautiful," Nicky said. "I especially like the chorus. What about the lyrics?"

"Haven't made them up yet," Byon said. "What do you think they should be?"

"About love, of course. What else is there?"

"A contract?"

Nicky didn't laugh. "You haven't heard from them about your play?"

"Nothing," Byon said. "I think I should write another one. Something lighter and easier."

"But I like the other one," Nicky said. "Lovers who never get together."

"People want a happy ending."

"That's so plebeian," Nicky said. "Not at all like real life."

"I agree," Byon said. "Love that is never achieved. Speaking of which, where is our darling Diana?"

Nicky scoffed. "With my darling father, of course."

At that absurdity, the two men laughed, and in the hall, Puck smiled. She knew they saw nothing "darling" about Nicky's father. She didn't think there was going to be any more music so she stepped into the drawing room. The two men were by the piano, their heads close together as they looked at the sheets of music.

Byon was the first to see her. "Ah, the elusive Puck. Illusion personified. And what can we do for you today my little waif?"

Puck could never tell if what he said was a compliment or if he was making fun of her. But then, most people felt that way about Byon's little quips. Whichever it was, they made Puck smile. "Lunch is late today. At one thirty."

"Let me guess," Byon said. "She is cooking something special for her beloved Nicky."

"Scallops with butter," Puck said.

"How prosaic," Byon said. "How simple. How divine. Tell me, is the butter browned? Clarified? Or is it dropped into a skillet in its raw state?"

Nicky spoke before Puck could. "I believe Mrs. Aiken measures butter rather than sauces it. The scallops will be immersed in cups of it. Am I right?" He winked at Puck.

She couldn't help but laugh — which was the objective of the men. Her funny little laugh delighted them.

"Oh," Byon said, "to find an actress who could duplicate that sound! I would write a play about it."

"And call it *The Sound of Angels,*" Nicky said.

"Perfect," Byon said.

Puck could feel her face turning red, but she was pleased by their attention.

Byon turned to Nicky. "Where did I see those pashminas? In a cupboard somewhere, I believe."

"Yellow sitting room." Nicky's eyes were alight. "We can use them for staging." He turned to Puck. "Get them and bring them down. They're in the bottom of the big walnut armoire."

She started for the door.

"Puck!" Nicky said. "If you see Nadine,

avoid her. Her father is here." He waved his hand. "They're . . . you know."

"Talking," Byon said with a laugh. They all knew that was a euphemism for arguing.

Puck hurried up the stairs to the yellow sitting room. It was small but it was very nice — thanks to Nadine. Or more correctly, to her father. Puck tried not to look at Oxley Manor too closely, but it was easy to see how shabby it was. Flaking ceilings, peeling wallpaper, furniture with the stuffing exposed. Clive, the estate manager, said that next year the roof had to be repaired, but no one knew where the money for that was going to come from.

Nadine's father was rich. Byon made fun of the man's accent and his bad table manners, but the cars he sold had paid for the old piano to be tuned. And he'd paid for the remodel of a bedroom and sitting room for his precious daughter to use when she stayed at Oxley Manor. He said that the ratty place reminded him too much of where he'd grown up. "I've come too far to put my daughter through that," he said.

The yellow sitting room was lovely and Puck enjoyed tiptoeing across the silk rug. The big armoire was on the far side. She opened it and there in the bottom were the pretty shawls that Byon and Nicky wanted.

As she reached for them, she heard voices.

Feeling panicky, Puck looked around for a way to escape unseen. There was no outlet. Without further thought, she stepped into the armoire, on top of the shawls. Unfortunately, they tilted and an edge kept the door from closing all the way. She tried to put herself into the far corner, out of sight.

"I'm doing the best I can," Nadine said as she entered the room.

"It's not enough," her father said in his rough voice, his heavy Suffolk accent making him almost unintelligible.

"I majored in art history — at your request. All in anticipation of becoming a lady."

"And what have you done with your fine education? You brought in that odious girly-boy, Byon."

"He's creative, fun. With a father like Nicky's, we need fun."

"And you introduced them to that boring little Willa. I think Bertram is trying to marry Nicky to her."

"Makes sense as she is aristocracy and her family has money. More importantly, she's our friend."

Mr. Howland held out a thick wad of cash. "Here. Take this."

"You're giving me money?" Nadine

sounded disgusted.

"I want you to pay that horseman to give you riding lessons."

"Absolutely not!" Nadine said. "I don't like horses and I despise that man. He laughs at us. He thinks we're all absurd."

"You are," Mr. Howland growled. "None of you know what work is. But ladies ride horses so you need to learn."

"So I can marry Nicky," Nadine said tiredly.

Mr. Howland's voice softened. "What's wrong with being a lady?"

"I —" Nadine broke off because she saw Puck inside the armoire. She turned her back to the cabinet. "All right! I'll ride the damned horses. Maybe I can find one with a 4 × 4 transmission."

"Now that's my girl. Go put on something expensive and work your charms on the earl and his lily-white son. I have to go." He looked around. "I can't stand this place. That guy downstairs is playing the piano again."

"It's his own composition. Someday Byon will be —"

"I've heard it before. He's going to be famous. When you run this place, you can have him over for fish and chips. I'll see you tomorrow." He hurried out of the room.

Puck held her breath. She didn't know how Nadine would react to having someone eavesdrop on her private conversation.

Nadine threw the armoire door open, then walked away.

Puck grabbed the pile of shawls and stepped out. "I —"

Nadine threw up her hand. "Don't explain why you were hiding in there. I'm sure it has to do with Nicky and Byon. You're their own little elf running their errands. But I'm glad to have a witness to what I have to put up with. Here." She thrust money at Puck. "Give this to the man in the stables. Tell him he's to teach me how to ride a horse — like a lady does. Maybe I should be glad my father isn't insisting that I ride sidesaddle."

Puck shoved the fifty-pound notes deep into her pocket. It was more money than she'd ever seen before. "Sean is a good teacher."

"What?" Nadine turned on her.

"Sean Thorpe. The groomsman. He's nice. He takes care of people."

Nadine was twenty-one years old and extraordinarily pretty. Her dark hair was always perfect and she wore clothes like in a magazine. She looked at Puck in speculation. "I've seen him enough to know that he thinks he's God's gift. He hasn't tried anything with you, has he?"

At first Puck had no idea what she meant. Then she thought, *Like the boys at school?* She couldn't help a tiny smile. "No, he hasn't."

Nadine caught Puck's meaning and she smiled back. "Go on, give him the money and set something up for tomorrow. Make it a gentle horse. I don't want to land on my backside in the dirt."

"I'm sure Sean will be gentle with you."

When Nadine laughed, Puck wasn't sure why. She ran down the stairs.

Nicky was sitting on the bottom step, waiting for her. The sound of Byon's playing filled the hallway.

"Take this," Nicky said softly and handed her a six-page legal document. "Find Diana and give it to her."

She took one end of the papers but he held on.

"Diana needs to go over this, but no one must see her do it." His voice dropped to a whisper. "I don't want my father to know that Diana reads about estate business. And Clive's not to know. *Especially* not him. Understand?"

"I do," Puck said, and Nicky released the papers. She stuck them in the waistband of her pants and pulled her shirt down. No one would see that she was carrying anything.

Nicky stood up. "Thanks, kid. You're the only person around here I can truly trust. I wish I could repay you. I'd wave a magic wand and give you three wishes."

"I don't need anything," Puck managed to say. Her face was crimson with pleasure and embarrassment.

"How about a place to hide from your mother?"

At that delightful thought, Puck's laugh rang out.

"I heard that!" Byon called from around the corner, then he tried — and failed — to replicate her laugh on the piano.

"Go!" Nicky said, and Puck began running.

She had a way to get to the stables so no one could see her from the house. She knew her mother kept watch. If Puck were seen, she'd be given more household chores to do. And if she said that she had to run an errand for Nicky, her mother would demand to see the papers Puck carried. Her mother would read them, then she'd talk to Nicky about them, then . . .

Puck didn't want to follow that train of thought. If someone else got hold of the papers, she'd never be trusted again — and she liked being trusted. Liked having a job to do besides chopping onions.

She heard Nicky's father before she saw him. She knew she was supposed to call him "my lord" but she'd never been able to make herself do it. When she was a toddler, she'd called him Bertie and he'd liked it. Her mother had forbidden her to continue using the name, but Puck hadn't stopped. Around other people, she referred to him as "Nicky's father." In the evenings, when the man was mellow from too much drink, she still called him Bertie.

Diana and he were together, as usual. Both of them were horse mad.

One night Byon had done a parody of the two of them talking. It consisted of snorts and lip flutters and pawing at the earth. It ended with the stallion trying to mount the mare, but she was too strong for him. She much preferred the young stallion, who was played by Nicky.

They all applauded and laughed hard at the little play. It was Nadine who asked if Nicky was playing himself as the winning stallion or was it the dark, handsome groomsman?

Nicky had *not* liked that! It took work on Byon's part to talk him back into a good mood.

Puck wasn't supposed to have seen any of that. The parody had been played well past her bedtime, but it had been put on in the central hallway and there was a balcony running around the top, a place where she could easily hide. Puck sometimes wondered if Byon put his plays on there because he knew he had a wider audience. She wasn't the only one who hid in the shadows to see his entertainments.

At the stables, she stood in the shadows and listened.

"He's beautiful," Diana said as she stroked the horse's nose. She had a deep, throaty voice. She was midheight, sturdy, all muscle as she liked to say. Her hair was short and blond, and she was pretty, but in a "best pal" way. Nothing about her was like Nadine, which was probably why they were good friends. No competition.

"He is gorgeous!" Bertie said. "I wish penny-pinching Clive could see that. Wish he could understand that a person has to spend money to make it. This boy is going to win! I can feel it."

"You're probably right," Diana said. "He certainly has the proportions of a winner. Those legs are magnificent."

Bertie gave a loud sigh. "Bringing you here is the best thing that son of mine has ever done."

"Nicky is a good man," Diana said. "He —"

"Spare me," Bertie said. "My son only cares about the next song that fancy boy writes. Do you know where he's from?"

"You mean Byon?" Diana asked. "In spite of his posh accent, I think he probably came from the same place I did. The slums of London."

"I believe you're right." Bertie chuckled smugly. "But at least you don't pretend to be someone else. He's a liar."

"Aren't we all?" Diana stroked the horse. "So when do we race him?"

"In six weeks."

"Then we have a lot of work to do to get him ready."

"You and Sean?" Bertie's voice was soft, sounding like love. He never spoke of his son in that tone. "Look at the time. I must go." Bertie left.

When it was quiet, Puck stepped into the light. She didn't like to think of her special spots as hiding places. To her, they were small areas of safety.

Acting as though she'd just entered, she went to Diana. Of course she was in a horse stall, pitchfork in hand. Byon said Diana put horse urine in tiny bottles and used it as perfume — and Nicky's father had been so enraptured that he was planning to deed her half his kingdom. His thinly veiled meaning was that Bertram was going to give her his son.

Diana didn't ask what Puck was holding out to her. She stabbed the fork upright and quickly read the papers. She took a pen out of her shirt pocket, made a couple of corrections, and handed the document back to Puck. "Get this to Clive ASAP. It should go out today. What are they up to?"

"Mr. Byon hasn't heard whether or not anyone is buying his new play," Puck said. "Master Nicky says he should write about love but still have a sad ending."

"Yeah," Diana said. "Nicky loves sadness. How is Nadine with her father?"

"She's to take riding lessons from Sean so she can become a lady."

Diana laughed. "That'll be fun to watch. Nadine has her father's love of cars and Sean only likes what can love him back."

Puck smiled at that. It was perfectly true. "Nadine's new Aston Martin seems to love her."

With a quick laugh, Diana looked up from forking the manure. "You're in good form today. Been listening to Byon's latest music?"

"Oh yes." Puck's eyes closed for a moment.

A noise at the door startled them. "Take that to Clive," Diana whispered. "And don't let him know —"

"Nicky told me." Puck slipped out the narrow door at the side of the stable. When she realized she'd forgotten to ask Diana where Sean was, she almost went back. But she didn't. She knew his favorite places so she'd find him.

As good as Puck was at not being seen, there was one person she never seemed able to hide from: Willa. Maybe that was because they were both so good at being invisible.

When Puck heard the "pssst" come from somewhere inside the overgrown, untrimmed hedge, she wanted to take off running and never stop.

Puck knew that the basic law of being a Secret Keeper was knowing who could be told what. She could tell Nadine and Diana what Nicky and Byon were up to and vice versa. Bertie was to be told nothing at all. Ever. She had to be selective about what she told Clive. Lying to him was acceptable but keep it simple. But the secret she couldn't tell *anyone* was that Willa was madly, passionately, insanely in love with Clive.

Willa was a younger child of the second son of a baron. Not high up in the aristocratic world, but her father had made money through some wise investments. Although, some people unkindly said he'd bought Apple stock thinking he was purchasing an American orchard. So maybe his money was from dumb luck, not wisdom.

Whatever the truth, he'd made a fortune and Willa had a trust fund. She should have been a good catch for marriage but she wasn't pretty and she was odd. Socially awkward. She tended to sit and stare at people.

Byon said she'd never had a creative thought or said anything interesting. "And that's what I love about her. If I can entertain *her,* all of Blighty will be mine."

It took them a while, but they got to know Willa. She was loyal, a good listener, and she adored the others. She was in awe of their talent and beauty. And Willa was protective of the people who'd befriended her. At university, a young man had dropped Nadine after a night when he got what he wanted from her. Three days later, he woke up in a bed full of stinging nettles and biting ants. He had to be hospitalized.

No one would have guessed that Willa had

done it if Byon hadn't seen the bites on her hands.

After that, Willa was a fully accepted member of their little group. "You're ours, darling." Byon kissed her cheek. "Even though we are quite terrified of you."

The others nodded in agreement. Willa had cried in gratitude — then bought them a case of some very fine champagne. In fact, she was the one who paid for all their food and drink. A local van arrived on Friday nights and it was full to the brim with the best of everything. They had only to mention a food or beverage and it arrived. All bills went to Willa.

Puck tried not to grimace at this interruption. She had places she needed to go. She stepped through a web of dead privet to where Willa was waiting for her. There were remnants of formerly grand garden rooms all over Oxley Manor. But they were being allowed to go to seed. Bertie had no interest in gardens.

Behind the hedge, the grass was a foot high. A few feet away was a crumbling old marble statue. A bird nest was at the top.

"You're going to him, aren't you?" Willa whispered. She was short and round, pudgy and shapeless, no curves anywhere. *Just like a good English sausage,* Byon said. Her face was plain. One time Nadine spent hours doing a makeover on Willa — but it hadn't worked. In a kind voice, Byon said, "You've made her into a drag queen. Do give her a bath." Nadine had mumbled that Willa was ". . . beautiful as you are . . ." and no one ever again tried to change her.

Willa held out an envelope. It was thick and cream-colored, with brown engraving. She probably bought her stationery wherever the Queen did. "Would you give it to him?"

Puck didn't know much about men but from what she'd seen, they wanted to do the pursuing.

"Don't look at me like that," Willa said. "I know I shouldn't be so forward, but how's he going to know what I feel unless I tell him? It's a poem and I spent days on it. I had to, uh, borrow some bits, but it's mostly mine. If nothing else, Clive will appreciate the literary merit of it. Maybe . . ." Her eyes widened. "Maybe I should show it to Byon."

Puck swallowed. She loved the man but he could be brutal. There was no doubt that Byon would rip apart whatever Willa had written. Puck thought fast. "Then it wouldn't be for Clive alone."

"You're right," Willa said. "It wouldn't mean as much if I shared it with the world."

Puck let out her breath. "I think I heard someone."

With a backward step, Willa looked about in fear. "You haven't told them about Clive and me, have you?"

Puck thought, *Told them you're making a fool of yourself over a man they don't like? Then watch Byon and Nicky feast on jokes so venomous they would put a cobra to shame?* "No, I wouldn't do that."

Willa smiled. "You're a good friend. Thank you." Turning, she disappeared through the decaying hedge.

Puck put the pretty envelope with the legal document inside the waistband of her trousers.

Clive's office wasn't far from the house. It was a long, low, brick building that had always been for the estate manager. It was quite pretty, but Clive complained that it was drafty and the windows were rotting — which was true.

She didn't bother to knock but opened the door and walked in. She knew from experience that if Clive knew it was her, he wouldn't let her in. One time when she knocked, she heard him turn the key to lock the door.

But then, she understood. If anyone sent Puck to him, it was *always* with bad news.

He was sitting behind his huge, gaudily ornate desk. For over a hundred years there'd been a plain wooden desk in there, but Clive had demanded that a Victorian monstrosity be removed from the house and put in his office. "After all," he said, "I *am* a relative." He liked to remind people that he was Nicky's cousin. "May as well be the chimney sweep," Byon said. "Too far away to inherit." It would have sounded sympathetic except that Byon couldn't stand Clive and often made him the punch line of his jokes.

Clive didn't look up when Puck entered. He was tall, thin, and starting to go bald. He had a large, sharp nose, and thin lips. "What is it now?"

Puck didn't speak, just pulled the papers out and put them on the desk in front of him.

He picked up the document, leaned back in his big leather chair, and scanned the pages.

To Puck's horror, she saw that Willa's letter had stuck to the back. Maybe he wouldn't see it.

But of course he did. "What is this?" He broke the old-fashioned wax seal, pulled out the single page, read it, then looked at Puck. "Where does she get this drivel? *My heart sings true?* Disgusting. And the worst of it is that I've been told by his lordship that I'm expected to marry her. All to keep this bloody job." He dropped the heavy vellum page in the waste bin, then looked back at the legal pages.

That Bertie wanted Clive to marry Willa was news to Puck. They all knew Nicky was to marry Diana. But it looked like Bertie couldn't bear to part with Willa's trust fund.

"Ah ha!" Clive stood up, document in hand. "I *knew* it! Diana did this. She tries to write like Nicky but she can't." He punched the pages with his finger. "I'll tell the earl about this. He'll be interested to hear what his son doesn't do."

Puck was trying not to look at Willa's heartfelt letter in the trash. How could she get it out without Clive seeing? "Bertie probably won't like hearing anything bad about Diana."

Clive's eyes shot fire at her. He was jealous that this scrawny girl was allowed to call the earl Bertie. And he was sickened that the earl genuinely loved Diana. But most of all, Clive didn't like being instructed in diplomacy by someone he considered a kitchen maid.

He quickly signed the document. "I will keep the knowledge to myself. For now."

He thrust the papers out to her. "Put this on the earl's desk. And this!" He held up a single piece of paper that had a lot of numbers on it.

Puck took the paper but didn't look at it.

"Go on. Read it. I know you will. You read it all, listen to it all. I *know* what you do."

Puck didn't have to look at the paper to know it was the monthly budget. He always printed the totals — always a deficit — at the bottom in red.

"He's buying another horse," Clive said.

Puck wanted to defend a man who had always been good to her. "Diana said it's —"

"Not the one that's already here." Clive's voice was getting louder. "It's another one. He thinks he's a brilliant judge of horseflesh. He thinks breeders admire and respect him. But they laugh at him. They tell each other to buy nothing that Bertram Renlow likes as the animal is sure to lose any race. They say —"

Abruptly, he dropped down into the chair. "Maybe I *should* marry that dumpy little woman. I'd get her idiot father to buy us a country house and I'd do nothing for the rest of my life. Could I stand her enough to do that?"

Puck had no reply to what he was saying,

but then she'd heard his self-pity many times before. While Clive was in his usual I-feel-sooo-sorry-for-myself collapse, she dropped the papers she was holding. When she knelt to pick them up, she slipped Willa's letter out of the bin. Without another word, she fled the office.

Outside, Willa was just a few feet away, her face begging for news.

"He quoted parts of your poem," Puck said. She knew how to pull truth from lies. "I think he was impressed."

"Really?" Willa's eyes were wide. Actually, they were kind of bugging out of her head. Not attractive.

"He spoke of you and marriage," Puck said. "And where you'll live on a country estate." She couldn't bear to break the woman's heart with the truth. "I have to go." She ran.

All Puck could think about was how much she wanted to see Sean. Whereas the others at Oxley Manor had rules about what she could and could not tell, there were no rules with Sean. He was apart from them. Separate. And he saw them all clearly. How they related to each other, how they needed one another.

She went to several places on the estate where he could usually be found, but he wasn't anywhere. His truck was parked by the stables so he hadn't gone into town.

Was he with someone? she thought. *Some fat, stupid village girl?*

Puck laughed at herself. She was getting as jealous as Clive. She was on her way back to the house when she saw him. He was on Lady Chance, one of the horses Bertie said would win races but never had. Sean was riding hard down the gravel road that went through the acreage. Puck didn't think she'd ever seen him ride so fast.

Her first thought was that someone was hurt. Nicky? Byon? Nadine?

Puck started running. Over the years she'd developed some speed, and combined with her knowledge of the grounds, she was able to follow him. He was headed toward the old cemetery. But why would he want to go there? No one ever did.

When she got there, she saw the horse tied to a falling-down fence post. Sean was among the gravestones, talking to two men, neither of whom she'd ever seen before.

Had it been anyone else, she would have figured out a way to hide so she could hear what was going on. But this was Sean. Her friend. She wouldn't intrude.

At the corner of the cemetery was the caretaker's old brick house. It was tall, narrow and boarded up. No one had lived in it for many years — and no one wanted to. The private Renlow cemetery had a reputation for being haunted. People were always saying they heard noises and saw lights there. Besides, the house was in such bad condition that it would cost a lot to renovate. Bertie wasn't going to waste money on it.

Cautiously, Puck went to the house. She didn't want the men to see her, but at the same time she was curious as to what they were doing.

When one of the men looked in her direction, Puck stepped backward — and fell inside. An old board had given way. When her weight hit it, she'd fallen back and the board had landed on top of her. The only sound was of her "oof."

She lay there for a moment, waiting for the dust to settle, and to see if anyone had heard and would come running. But there was silence. When she lifted the board off and set it aside, she saw the floor. It was inlaid tile in terracotta and white, with strips of blue. *Very pretty,* she thought.

For a moment she was torn between whether to go back outside and try to figure out what Sean was doing or to explore the house. The scary thought of Sean catching her spying made her choose the house.

It was three stories, with the ground floor little more than an entrance hall. Upstairs were half a dozen small rooms, with a couple of fireplaces. The top floor had two bedrooms and a bath.

The bathroom had a tub so big that it must have been installed before the walls were built. The room was dark, with the windows boarded up. She was about to leave when she saw something in the tub. Leaning over, she picked up a white mask. It was full face, with long holes for the eyes. The mouth was open and turned down. The bottom of the tub held yards of soft white cloth. Under it all was an old tape recorder. Before she thought, she pushed the play button. Out came eerie sounds of clanging and moaning. Quickly, Puck turned it off.

It looked like she'd found the source of the haunting. Masks, white drapery and recorded sounds.

Her question was *why?* And *who* was going through so much trouble to keep people away from the cemetery?

Puck peeked through the boards nailed over a window to look out at the old cemetery. It held over a hundred years of the Renlow family, plus valued friends and retainers. There was a Victorian marble mausoleum that looked like a military tent. Not that any Renlow had ever been a soldier, but one of them had kept the accounts for a British general who'd served in India. It was enough to lay claim to military service.

Sean wasn't far away from the structure. She saw him hand a small canvas bag to one of the men. In return, Sean took a paper bag.

Puck leaned back against the wall. Was the bag full of money? Was this about drugs? Was Sean buying them? Selling them?

This was a secret she did *not* want to have to keep. But she knew that this was one she was going to have to guard closely. If anyone found out . . .

When she looked out again, Sean was gone. She needed to find him but he mustn't know that she'd seen . . . Whatever he'd been doing.

She ran down the stairs. As soon as she was outside, she saw that her clothes were covered in dust. Sean would take one look at her and know where she'd been. With energy, she dusted herself off.

She caught up with him as he was walking Lady Chance back to the stables. Like always, she started walking beside him.

"What have you been up to this morning?" he asked.

"Listening to everyone."

"Oh?"

It was an invitation to tell all. And besides, Puck wanted to fill the air with words so she wouldn't have to think about what she'd seen. She told about the errands — including about Willa.

"Poor girl," Sean said. "If he marries her, he'll make her miserable." He looked at Puck. "And what's this about Nadine?"

There was a sneer in his voice, but it was understandable. Nadine arrived with fabulous cars from her father and they scared the horses.

"You're to give her riding lessons." Puck pulled the money out of her pocket and held it out to him. "She wants her first lesson tomorrow."

"No," he said. "Get somebody else."

"Nadine is a nice person." Puck sounded desperate, but then she was. If Sean didn't give Nadine lessons, her father would be angry, then Nadine wouldn't be allowed to come and she was good at keeping peace and — "Nadine is funny and interesting and she cares about people."

"You mean she cares about that group of misfits that hangs around here. Does she know it's her money they love the most?"

"I'm afraid she does." Puck was being honest. "But she has to do whatever her father tells her to do."

"And he wants her to marry the future earl." It wasn't a question.

"Sean, please. Nadine will get in trouble if you don't teach her."

With a grimace, he took the money. "All right. Tomorrow at 8:00 a.m."

"I don't think —" She'd been about to say that Nadine wasn't up that early but she didn't. "Fine. Eight in the morning."

"If she shows up wearing some riding costume from a BBC drama, I'll send her back."

"Jeans and T-shirt," Puck said.

Sean frowned but he nodded. "You're nervous about something. What is it?"

Puck could feel her heart pounding. "It's just Mum. Trying to escape her. And Clive's bad temper and . . ." She trailed off. Sean's face showed he wasn't believing any of it.

He stopped walking, then reached out and pulled something from her hair. It was a ball of dust. "You look like crap."

She started to make up an explanation, but she knew Sean would know she was lying. She was silent.

"So don't tell me."

He started walking but Puck didn't move.

Somehow, she was giving away too much about what she'd seen. "I'll see you later," she said. When he didn't answer, she headed toward the house. She'd gone only a few feet when she began running.

By the time she reached the house, she was out of breath. She went to Bertie's office. Sean joked that it was actually the drinking room as that's where the earl got drunk every night.

Puck put the document Clive had given her on the desk — which wasn't nearly as big or elaborate as Clive's. On the top was an open checkbook. She saw that Bertie had made out a check for fifty thousand pounds to Longbow Stables. The page of the monthly expenses Clive had given her showed that there wasn't that much in any account. The check would bounce.

Puck left the office and made a dash up to her room at the top of the house. She changed her shirt and ran a comb through her hair, then ran down the stairs to the kitchen.

"Where have you been?" her mother demanded angrily. "I've had this whole meal to do by myself, all while you've been outside daydreaming. You flit around like some butterfly, getting no exercise at all." She gritted her teeth. "It's time you started to grow up. If we're going to continue to live here, we all need to be *useful.* Indispensable, even."

Mrs. Aiken put half a pound of chopped up butter in a deep skillet. "What are they all doing?"

Puck ate a cherry. "Nicky and Byon are working on a play. Diana is mucking out the stables, and Nadine is going to take riding lessons from Sean. Clive is doing the accounts and Willa is writing letters."

Mrs. Aiken frowned at her daughter. "You're telling too much about these people. You're too young to know that there are secrets in this house. You need to learn how to keep what you hear and see to yourself." She glared at her daughter. "But you must tell *me* everything."

"I will try," Puck said. Her mind was on that house by the cemetery and what Nicky had said. A place to have some peace.

She watched her mother drop scallops into the puddle of butter. As Byon had said, the butter wasn't browned, or clarified, or sauced in any way. She tried not to laugh.

Eight

When Puck finished, Kate and Jack said nothing.

Sara broke the silence. "Interesting. They're different than I thought they would be."

"Frenemies," Kate said. "Nobody did what had been planned for them."

"Right," Sara agreed. "Nicky didn't marry Diana as Bertie wanted. Clive didn't marry poor, sad Willa."

"After that night they disappeared," Puck said, "everyone separated."

"Forever," Sara said. "I wonder . . ."

"What?" Jack asked.

"If they knew what had happened. I mean the truth. Did they know it was a murder?"

"Or murders," Jack said.

"Yes. They knew that two murders had been committed and that's why they separated so completely. A conspiracy of silence."

Sara looked at Puck. "We need to know what happened after Diana and Sean disappeared."

"Byon sold his play, *If Only,*" Puck said.

"His first big success," Sara said. "It was on stage in London for over a year and played in six countries. Schools perform it now."

They looked at her.

"I did a Wikipedia search."

"And Clive went to London and became a banker," Kate said. "I kind of feel sorry for him. He was trying to save the place but was hated for it."

Puck's face showed that she disagreed with that. "Nicky did ask Diana to marry him and she accepted. She said . . ." Puck hesitated.

"Said what?" Sara asked.

"That her ring was actually Oxley Manor."

"I understand that," Sara said. "At least Diana knew the truth of what she was taking on."

"And Willa?" Kate asked.

"Clive asked Willa to marry him." For a moment, Puck put her hands over her face. "We all knew that Bertie had bullied Clive into asking her. But Willa was ecstatic. She could hardly walk. She floated."

"What did Byon and Nicky say about that

engagement?" Sara asked.

"They were kind," Puck said. "Byon said it was all so awful that he couldn't think of worse than the truth."

"Bad for which one?" Jack asked.

"Willa. Byon said she was going to find out that Clive had nothing but contempt for her."

"How soon after the disappearance did he break their engagement?"

"Forty-eight hours," Puck said. "She came apart. We thought she was going to kill herself."

"Yeow," Kate said.

"Wonder what she did to him after they broke up?" Sara said.

"For something that big, I would think it was more than nettles and ants," Kate said.

They looked at Puck for an answer but she shrugged. She didn't know.

"Did you ever find out what Sean was doing in the cemetery with the men?" Sara asked.

"No." Puck's voice was a whisper. "The next day everything in the house was gone."

"You mean the mask and the recorder?" Kate asked, and Puck nodded.

"Did you see him with the men again?" Sara asked. "Maybe somewhere else?"

"No." When Puck stood up, she swayed

on her feet. "I . . ." The reliving of the past had exhausted her.

Sara stood. "We need to go. Bella will be wondering what happened to us."

Jack picked up Sara's camera. "We'll say we went exploring to take photos." He was reminding Sara that she wasn't to tell Bella anything about what they'd heard.

Sara opened her camera bag and took out two clean SD cards. She put the ones with the photos of the skeleton on them into her pocket. "Let's go take some pictures. I'd like to have something to show for our hours out." She looked at Puck. "Is it all right to say that you invited us to breakfast?"

"I doubt if anyone will believe that."

Sara frowned. As a writer, she knew all about isolation and being an introvert and how people criticized. *"You should get out more. You should meet people. You should —"* Fill in the blank. Everyone knew what she *should* do.

"Okay," Jack said over Sara's silence. "Let's give Puck time to recover."

Puck looked at Jack with smiling eyes.

They went downstairs to the ground floor, then outside, and stood for a moment in the cool air.

"Is it still morning?" Jack asked. "It feels like we left the house days ago."

"Discovering a murder does that to you," Kate said.

"Could have been an accident and a cover-up," Sara said. "We have no proof of murder."

Jack and Kate gave her skeptical looks.

"I agree," Sara said. She didn't take her camera when Jack held it out to her. "Why don't you photograph Puck's garden? Your love will show in the photos."

"Love? What does that mean? Love for the plants? The flowers are nice, but . . ."

Kate and Sara were looking at him. They knew that he had taken on Puck as his latest cause. In the past, they'd seen him risk himself for what he believed in.

"Yeah, okay, so I like her," he said. "That story of hers! She practically kept this place going. And they all *used* her."

"Except Sean," Sara said. "Anybody have any ideas about what he was doing in the cemetery? And no drugs. I am *sick* of drugs being given as the cause of everything bad. They're used in movies, TV, books. In *life*! Drugs were great as shock value back in the sixties, but now they're all anyone can think of. Parents dealing with drugs, masses of money being made, gangs. Drugs, drugs, drugs. We need to look for something else that could be the reason for Sean's secrecy.

Just *no drugs*!"

Jack and Kate were waiting patiently for her to get over her tirade.

"Sorry," Sara whispered, and looked off into the distance.

Kate spoke up. "I saw that the attics are full. Bet an Antiques Road Show person would love to go through them. Maybe Sean was selling something of value he found."

"You think the stable guy was allowed to wander through the house?" Jack asked.

"Didn't Puck say that Sean knew Bertram sat in his office every night and got drunk?" Kate said. "How'd he know that if he wasn't upstairs sometimes? *At night?*"

"Maybe he was having an affair with a pretty maid," Sara began.

"Or Diana," Kate said. "They both loved horses."

"Yet again, you two are plotting a romance novel," Jack said. "How about we take photos and figure out what we actually *know*?"

"With no romance?" Kate said with a sigh. "How boring."

"I'm here," Jack said. "Anytime you want romance, I can —"

"Boooo," Sara and Kate said in unison.

Jack tried to act offended but he was glad that some of the horror of what they'd seen that morning was being dispelled.

"I know where we need to go," Sara said. "And I've been dying to see it." She started down the road at a rapid pace, doing what she called her "New York walk."

"Where?" Kate asked Jack.

"I'm not sure but I believe 'dying' is the key word."

Since the cemetery was behind them, Kate knew where her aunt was going.

Jack led the way. He'd become familiar enough with the layout of the property that he could take them to the front of the big house in a roundabout way. There were few people inside the house, but all it took was one glance outside to see the three of them moving through the trees.

The private chapel in front of the house was a rectangle with a steep roof and a little covered porch jutting out on one side. One end had a tower with a tall cone of a roof.

They approached from the long side so they were hidden from the house. There was a narrow door with a lock on it. The women looked at Jack in expectation.

"We're going to get into trouble for this," he murmured, then pulled a knife out of his pocket. It had a tiny awl blade that he used to open the lock.

Sara was looking up at the chapel. "This

is a Victorian mishmash. Wonder where they got the pieces to put it together?"

As Jack pushed open the door, they heard the rusty hinges scraping. It had been a while since the door had been opened.

Inside, they gasped. The long, narrow and very tall interior was paneled in walnut in a design of squares inside squares. There was a header of carvings of sheep and their shepherds. The ceiling was beamed, with carved corbels. The end wall, from head height up, was an enormous arched window of stained glass. Each of the twelve panels showed a story from the Bible.

"So tell us all," Jack said as he looked at Sara. He knew that in researching her historical novels she'd learned a lot about period architecture.

"The original building is old, probably thirteenth century, but it's been changed. I think the tower was added later, mid-1400s would be my guess. That big window is relatively new, definitely Victorian." She turned full circle. "Somebody did some collecting and brought it all here and pieced this together like a puzzle. And whoever did it had taste and a whole lot of money."

"Not Bertram," Jack said.

Sara smiled. "I don't see a horse anywhere, so no, not him."

Jack went to the front, then grinned broadly. "Look what I found." He lifted the oak cover to a piano. "It's an upright grand," he said. "It's all iron inside." When he played a few chords, they echoed through the room. The acoustics were excellent. He looked around in awe. "You could play a harmonica in here and it would be as loud as kettle drums."

The center aisle was flanked by oak benches with pretty cushions. Sara sat down on one of them, and Jack put the camera bag next to her.

She reached into her bag and took out a notebook. As a writer, she surrounded herself with pens and paper. This notebook had a drawing of a camera with colored thread sewn on the outline. She didn't usually mix up her thoughts, and her camera book was for photo-related subjects *only.* But this was an emergency. "I want to go over what we've learned," she said.

Jack was running his hands over the woodwork. As a craftsman, he appreciated all that had gone into the carving. "You mean who had a reason to kill Sean?"

"Exactly," Sara said.

Kate was using her phone to photograph the big window. "Everybody had a reason."

"Bertie liked Sean," Jack said.

"As long as he worked here," Sara said. "What if he said he was going to quit? And I'm not discounting your Puck." She waited for a reaction from Jack.

"I thought of that," he said. "Killer clearing her conscience. But she was only fourteen and —"

Kate interrupted. "I still think it's possible that Sean left the night of the party, then came back years later and someone killed him. We don't have a date of death."

"Returned for what?" Jack asked.

"Maybe Sean killed Nicky," Kate said. "Returned, fixed the brakes on Nicky's car, then Sean was killed by Mrs. Aiken. She and Bertie hid the body."

"It seems everyone had the opportunity," Sara said. "And lots of little reasons but —"

"What does that mean?" Jack asked. " 'Little' reasons?"

"Jealously," Sara said. "*You love her more than me,* that sort of thing. But what about big reasons, like ownership of this place?"

"It was falling down. Who wanted it?" Jack knew about the expense and agony of renovating.

"Maybe Nadine," Sara said. "Or certainly her father. He was a success in business but was looked down on for his lowly origins."

"Diana was going to marry for it. Maybe

Sean threatened that," Kate said.

"Clive," Jack said. "He felt he deserved Oxley Manor. As for that, why didn't he inherit when Nicky died?"

"Byon said Clive wasn't in the line of succession," Kate said.

"The best ol' Clive could hope for was to marry rich, bland, kind of creepy Willa," Jack said.

"That poor woman," Sara said. "It was horrible that those two people disappeared but what really made Clive dump Willa? The disappearance didn't affect her money. What made him change his mind?" Sara picked up her pen. "Let's go over all this and see what we know."

"I don't think we *know* anything," Kate said. "We have only Puck's word and what she saw. She was a teenager and she had the serious hots for Sean. If she found out he liked someone else, maybe Puck hit him over the head with a brick."

"Then hid his body all by her skinny self?" Jack asked.

"She knew everyone's secrets so who wouldn't help her?" Kate's voice was rising. "They all wanted to avoid publicity and notoriety and —"

"They were certainly a pack of misfits," Sara said.

"Like we are." Jack's words broke the tension in the air.

Sara looked around the beautiful chapel. "I vote that we make this our meeting place."

"Suits me," Jack said, and Kate nodded in agreement.

They halted at a sound. "Is that a car?" Jack went to a little window that was high up on the side facing the house and looked out. "It's not a normal car. It's a Bentley. Beautiful thing."

The window was above the women's heads.

"Who's in it?" Sara asked.

Jack gave a low whistle. "A woman. Older, but she looks good. Very good. She —"

"I bet it's Nadine," Kate said. "Let's get out of here and arrive from the direction of Puck's house."

"Jack, can you relock the door?" Sara asked.

"Easier than unlocking it. But one look at those hinges and anyone would know they've been used."

"Can't be helped." Sara opened the side door. The old hinges made a lot of noise. They went through the trees so that when they walked across the drive, they didn't look as though they'd come from the chapel.

But before they reached the car, Jack abruptly left them. He mumbled that he had to do something, then disappeared around the corner.

"We're on our own," Kate said to her aunt.

The woman was standing by the car looking up at the house. She was simply dressed in a white silk blouse, black trousers, an Hermès belt. Her earrings, Cartier watch and a simple wedding band were gold. Her skin had that well-kept look that only a life of money and leisure could achieve. She was quite a bit taller than Sara and emphasized it by looking her up and down.

"Have my bags taken to the room to the left at the top of the stairs," she said to Sara. "I'm Lady Nadine and I'll be in the blue drawing room. Send Mrs. Guilford to meet me."

She was at the doorway before Sara caught up to her. "I don't work here. I'm Sara Medlar." She had on cotton trousers and a yellow polo shirt. They were dirty from lying on the ground around the pit.

Nadine halted, again looked Sara up and down. Obviously, the name meant nothing to her. "Oh?"

"I'm the one who invited you here."

"Did you? Yet you don't consider that working here? How extraordinary."

Behind them, Kate rolled her eyes. It looked like a Bitch War was about to begin — and she wanted no part of it. She picked up Nadine's two suitcases and paused behind the woman. "Aunt Sara writes novels and she restored this place." Kate's tone showed that she didn't like Nadine's attitude. "Nobody's here so . . ." She shrugged at the suitcases, then carried them between the women and up the stairs.

The first room on the left was large and beautiful.

Kate dumped the suitcases on the stand, then started to go down to be with her aunt. Instead, she turned away. Let Aunt Sara handle the woman. Kate headed toward the attic.

Downstairs, Sara did her best to smile. "Maybe we should go upstairs and I'll explain what's going on."

"If we must." Nadine went first. Inside the room, she looked around. "It's been changed. It's a bit gaudy now."

"It's for the tourists," Sara said. "They want everything to be more English than the Brits do."

Nadine's face had a hint of a frown.

Restylane or Botox? Sara wondered. Something was keeping her glower from wrinkling her face.

"You own Oxley Manor?" Nadine asked.

"No, but I did finance the restoration from the sale of my novels."

"And what is it that you write?"

"Women's fiction." Sara knew it was a cop-out but if she said "historical and contemporary romance" she always — *always*! — got smirks and dirty looks.

But Nadine wasn't fooled. She gave a half smile. "The ones with the lurid covers? Sold in every grocery and petrol station on the planet? *Those* books?"

Sara clamped her teeth together, gave a nod and wondered why she didn't leave her room.

"How quaint."

Sara didn't ask permission but sat down on a chair by the bed. "I'm writing a novel that will be based on the mysterious disappearance of the two people in 1994. I'm here to research."

Quickly, Nadine turned away, but not before Sara saw the color drain from her face.

Nadine opened her big suitcase. It was a Hartmann, the kind people used twenty years ago: no wheels, no carry strap, no telescoping handle.

Sara watched Nadine pull out a jacket that could only have been made by Chanel and hang it in the big walnut wardrobe. Since she had commandeered the room, Sara guessed it was the one her father had refurbished for her. While the rest of the house rotted. *Wonder if that's the wardrobe where Puck hid?* Sara thought.

"Mystery?" Nadine said, her back to Sara. "There was no mystery. Not even a disappearance, at least not in the true meaning of the word."

"Then what did happen?"

Nadine turned around and the color was back in her face. "I thought Byon was going to be here."

"He's coming. You're the first. They're *all* coming."

"What does that mean?"

"Clive, Willa, Byon and you. Mrs. Aiken and Puck are already here."

Nadine was looking at her in disbelief. "And this is for . . . for . . . ?"

"A reunion," Sara said. "But also to talk about what happened that night when the people disappeared."

"For your little books?" Nadine's lip curled.

Sara stood up. "I think this was a mistake. I'll talk to the others. Perhaps you'd like to leave. I can arrange —"

"No!" Nadine said. "I'll tell you whatever you want to know. It's just that it wasn't a mystery."

"Then what was it?"

"It was the end of . . ." She pulled a dress from the suitcase. "The end of something wonderful, and as we knew we must, we separated. We went our own ways. It's just that Diana didn't tell us where she was going."

"Wasn't she engaged to Nicky? And there was another engagement, wasn't there?"

Nadine shrugged. "Broken engagements are something that happen." She glanced at the bed and her mind filled with memory.

It was in this bed that Willa was screaming and threatening to kill herself.

Nadine looked back at Sara. "Isn't a broken engagement something called a 'plot device'? My guess is that a year later Willa married. She probably has three children by now."

"I don't know what's happened in her life," Sara said. "But she'll be here soon and we'll ask her."

"Yes, let's do."

Sara was trying to dampen her dislike of the woman, but it wasn't easy. Maybe she should go in a different direction. "All of you seemed to be good friends. Parting must have hurt."

"It did. Those were the best years of my life." Nadine sat down, a blouse on her lap. "This house was so shabby then. My father worried that the roof would cave in on us. But we didn't mind. Thanks to Willa, we had wonderful food. Byon entertained us endlessly and Nicky charmed us." She closed her eyes for a moment.

One of Byon's little "entertainments" was mocking them all. He portrayed Nicky as a useless fob; Willa was begging for anyone to love her; Clive was an inferno of hatred; Nadine was a low-class slut with money. Byon was madly talented, but too often he was despicably cruel.

"What about Diana?"

Nadine opened her eyes and smiled. "She was the sensible one. We were all dreamers. If we had food and drink, we were happy. Diana kept the roof patched. Before she came, we just put down buckets to catch the rainwater. I used to wash my hair in it."

She could hear Diana shouting at them for their laziness and self-centeredness.

"What about Clive?"

With a groan, Nadine got up and put the blouse in the wardrobe. "Clive wasn't really one of us. He wanted to be, but . . ."

"But what?"

"All Clive thought about was money. I wonder what he does now?"

"He's a banker."

"Of course he is. Locked away from clients, I hope. He could never get along with anyone."

Clive rarely spoke to them — which was worse than Diana's shouting and Bertram's cursing. Clive just sneered at them in contempt.

"Did you say Puck is here?"

"Yes."

"That poor thing. Her mother was a beast to her. We tried to protect her, but Mrs. Aiken was stronger than all of us. What does Puck do now?"

"She owns the house by the cemetery. She —"

"*That* house? It was derelict. But it had the most enormous bathtub in it. Is it still there?" Memories came to her.

Naked in that tub. A bucket of hot water being poured over her head. She could feel the slickness of the soap, feel the hands on her skin.

"I have no idea," Sara said.

"I'll have to go exploring. I guess Puck works for the estate."

"She makes herbal wreaths and sells them in London."

"How lovely." Nadine had finished unpacking.

"And what about Sean?" Sara asked.

Nadine looked confused. "Who?"

"Worked in the stables? You took riding lessons from him? He left the night of your party and was never seen again."

"Oh yes. Him. I didn't last long on those lessons. Horses terrify me — unless there are hundreds of them under the bonnet of a car. Do you have any more questions? If not, I'd like to change."

"Of course," Sara said.

Nadine had already opened the door and she closed it firmly behind Sara. The lock clicked loudly.

Sara hurried down the hall to the narrow stairs that led up. As she'd hoped, Kate was in the attic, seated on an old chair, her lap full of papers. Sara plopped down on an ancient sofa across from her.

"There's enough info here for a thousand books," Kate said. "Diaries from the Victorians, finances from the Georgians. I found some things from Queen Anne's time. Someone really should look at all this and value it." She looked at her aunt. "What did you find out from *Lady* Nadine?"

"Absolutely nothing. Everyone and everything was great and wonderful and good. No one had a bad thought — except about poor Clive. He was a monster."

"If there was so much love, why did they break apart and not speak to each other for twenty years?"

"According to her royal highness," Sara said with a sneer, "they left to . . . I want to get this right . . . 'go their own ways.' The end. Broken up and that's it."

"But there were two engagements."

"She said I should understand how insignificant they were. They are merely 'plot devices.' "

"Oh," Kate said. "Did you hit her?"

"I wanted to. She was rude, condescending and lying. After every person I mentioned, she'd get a little glazed look in her eyes. I think she was remembering the truth."

"Which she wasn't about to tell you."

"Jack votes for Mrs. Aiken being a killer. I think it was *Lady* Nadine. Who gets your vote?"

"Puck."

"Are you kidding?"

"Yes. But the others were taken. Puck was the only one left."

Sara grimaced. "I can hardly wait to meet the rest of this crew."

Kate laughed. "Should we draw straws? Loser gets the hated Clive."

"As long as Jack doesn't get Byon. We may never see him again. Speaking of whom, where did he run off to when Nadine drove up in her I-am-rich car?"

"No idea. Probably off to see Puck."

"And her giant bathtub," Sara said.

"With the ghost things in it?"

Sara's eyes widened. "Puck said that house was boarded up. But her ladyship knew about the bathtub in it."

"How interesting," Kate said. "And Sean used to skulk about in the cemetery."

"And the queen was . . . ?"

"In the bathtub?" Kate was smiling.

Sara grinned. "She thinks she told me nothing, but she may have told me something very *big*."

"And yet again, Sara Medlar dines on the living carcass of a suspect."

Sara's burst of laughter reverberated through the old room.

Nine

Jack was in the loft of the stables when the ladder crashed to the floor. He thought he heard footsteps but maybe it was just rats. In the back room, he'd found a bag of oats with a hole in the bottom. The loft was one big room with closed doors to the outside, where hay could be loaded. There were still some old harnesses lying about, but it was mostly empty, and the space covered the entire stable.

He was on his belly, looking over the edge and trying to figure out how to get down without breaking any bones when he saw the woman enter through a side door. From the overhead angle, he recognized her from her clothes more than her face. As Sara said, "Simple costs a *lot* of money." In that case, her black-and-white outfit cost as much as his new truck.

He opened his mouth to call out and ask if she'd mind putting the ladder back up, but she didn't stop and look around. Instead, she made a beeline toward the back of the building. She was walking so fast it was as though she was being chased.

He watched her until she was out of his view, then silently made his way to the next opening. It was covered by a flat, hinged door that was shut. She was directly below him and he wanted to see what she was doing.

Knowing that the hinges were probably as rusty as at the chapel, he lifted the door as slowly as possible. She was in what used to be the office and she was running her hands over the bricks of the wall. She seemed to be searching for something.

She moved farther down, out of his view. Jack leaned forward and lifted the door another inch.

The rusty creak seemed to echo through the empty stable. He drew in his breath, hoping she hadn't heard. But she had. She made a leap to the side and looked up. "What are you doing up there?" she demanded.

Jack lifted the door and looked down. "Sorry, I —"

He didn't finish because at the sight of him, the woman's eyes rolled back in her head. Her body went limp, and she sank to the floor. She'd fainted.

Jack didn't take time to think but threw the door back. As he grabbed the side of the opening, the door slammed down and the corner hit his forehead. He could feel the cut but he didn't hesitate as he swung down. The ceiling in the office was about eight feet high so he had less than two feet to go down. He let go, hit the concrete floor hard and jumped up instantly.

He tried to revive the woman but she was out completely. She was light enough that he had no problem picking her up. There was no furniture inside, so he carried her outside. To the left was a shade tree and nearby was a horse trough. A water spigot was beside it.

He put the woman down, leaned her against the tree and went to the faucet. There was nothing to hold water. He took off his shirt, wet a sleeve and went back to her. Using the wet fabric as a cold compress, he pressed it to her forehead, but she didn't respond. He cursed himself for not having his phone with him. Should he leave her to get the utility truck to drive her back to the house? Then call an ambulance?

When she turned her head to the side, he let out his breath in relief. "You're okay," he said softly. "You just fainted."

She didn't open her eyes. "Who are you?" she whispered.

"Jack Wyatt."

She kept her eyes closed. It was almost like she was afraid to look at him. "I'm Nadine."

Jack moved to sit beside her, placing his shirt across his lap. The sun felt good on his bare skin.

"So you're not a ghost?" she asked.

He understood. They'd all said he looked like Sean Thorpe. "Maybe I am. I steal food from Mrs. Aiken so she hates me. Sean and I share that. I'm not a horse person but my father and grandfather knew everything there was to know about the internal combustion engine. Maybe they balance out."

She was smiling. "Anything else?"

"I like Puck and don't like Mrs. Aiken." He looked at her. "And I've been to the cemetery." She didn't seem to understand that last statement.

"You don't sound like him."

"Cursed with an American accent, but give me a few English pints and I might change. Especially if the barmaid is busty."

She laughed. "You *are* like him." Finally, she opened her eyes and looked at him. "Oh my!" she gasped at his shirtlessness.

"Sorry. I needed a cloth. It was either your

shirt or mine."

"We all have lapses in judgment," she said.

When he caught her meaning, he laughed. He started to put his shirt back on but she took it from him.

"You're bleeding." She leaned across him and used the wet sleeve to dab at his forehead.

She was older than Jack, but damn, she was pretty. And her body seemed to be supple and firm. Since Kate had arrived in his life, there had been no other women. It had been a long, long time.

He put his hand over hers. "I'll do it." Her face was inches from his. Her eyes, her lips, her body were telling him that whatever he wanted was all right with her.

But Jack looked away and the moment was lost.

She leaned back against the tree. Their bodies were touching along one side. "You made me feel better."

"Don't see how," Jack said. He was wiping at his forehead. The cut was superficial, no stitches needed, but it did hurt. "I scared you half to death. You hit the floor pretty hard."

"I have a personal trainer who does worse to me. But it was a shock seeing him — you — again. He was always there. Nicky's father piled masses of work onto his employees. Sean . . ." She broke off and seemed to calm herself. "Are you here with the woman? The older one?"

"I'm with Sara, yes."

"And you want to know everything about us so she can put us in a book?"

Jack's hair prickled at this disparagement of Sara. "She's insatiably curious, true, but we'd like to know what happened." He hoped she'd confide in him.

"Why is this place empty?" she asked.

"Isabella closes it for a month every year for repairs and cleaning."

"I was hoping there'd be people here." She took a breath. "My husband died three months ago."

"I'm sorry," Jack said.

"Me too. He was a nice man. Not wildly exciting but he was . . . security. It's not easy to go from being a married woman to a single one. I catch myself saying 'My husband likes' and 'My husband wants.' But now I'm back on the market."

"So you're looking for a new one?"

"More or less. I've never had a job and I have no interest in being a 'career girl.' "

"Damn women's lib!" Jack said.

She laughed. "You're funny. Sean wasn't amusing. But maybe he would have been.

He hated all of us so much."

"But not Puck."

"No, not her. But then, she was a child who hid from her mother and ran errands for all of us."

"And kept secrets."

"Mmmm," Nadine said. "She believed she knew everything but she knew less than half of it."

"You knew the other half?"

She pushed away from the tree and looked at him. "As lovely as you are, you're not going to coax forbidden information out of me. I've already told you too much."

He leaned toward her and smoothed a strand of hair behind her ear. "Are you sure of that?"

She tilted her head as though she was about to kiss him. He didn't move away.

But Nadine did. "You are truly wicked." Smiling, she stood up. "I need to go see if Byon has arrived."

Jack got up to stand in front of her. "Hoping he'll introduce you to prospective husbands?"

"Brains *and* beauty. You are lethal." She stepped away from him. "For our own good, stay away from me and don't ask me any questions about anything."

Jack ran his hand down his bare chest.

"I'm afraid I can't give that promise."

Nadine made a little squealing sound, then took off at a fast pace toward the house.

Jack watched her walk away. That had felt *good.* It had been so long since he'd flirted with a woman that he'd doubted if he still knew how. Since he'd moved in with Sara, then Kate had arrived, he'd been Good Boy personified. No spending the night with a woman whose name he didn't remember in the morning. No raucous evenings with his friends, chugging beer and getting too drunk to drive home. It had been a long time since someone had pointed out that he was good-for-nothing Roy Wyatt's son.

"I have been good, good, good," Jack muttered as he put his shirt back on. "Disgustingly *good.*"

He started back to the house but when he heard a piano playing, he stopped to listen. It seemed to be coming from the chapel. Turning, he went to it. The door that he'd unlocked was half-open and he could hear the music. It was one of Byon Lizmere's songs and one of Jack's favorites. He pushed the door open and went inside. The man at the piano looked up at him and smiled — and as Jack walked toward him, he began to sing.

▪ ▪ ▪ ▪

After Sara left, Kate decided she'd had enough of being in a dingy attic. She went downstairs, put on walking shoes and left the house.

The gardens were so perfectly manicured that they didn't seem real. She would have explored them but workers were everywhere. Trucks loaded with trees were arriving. Women with buckets were going in and out of the house.

And Bella was in the middle of it all.

Kate stood in the shadows and watched her directing people. She was calm but no one doubted her authority.

Like Sara, Kate thought, and started down a narrow path that led away from the noise.

At the end was a long, low brick building. There were no cars around and it was peaceful. She looked in a window and saw a roomful of old oak filing cabinets. *Must be Clive's office.* She thought of Puck's story about him and wondered if his big desk was still there.

Since the door was unlocked, she went inside and opened a file drawer. It contained old, worn file folders full of receipts back to the 1970s. *Does anybody throw anything away?* she wondered.

When she stepped through a wide doorway, there was the biggest, gaudiest desk she'd ever seen. It had gilded carvings of cherubs with wings, and long shapes that swirled and curved. There had to be a dozen types of wood used in the thing.

"It's a monster, isn't it?" a man's deep voice said.

Kate jumped at the sound, her hand to her throat.

"I'm sorry. I didn't mean to startle you. Here, sit down." He quickly rolled the big leather chair from behind the desk. "I can assure you that it's quite comfortable."

Kate sat down and looked up at him. He was a handsome man, half-bald in an attractive way, late forties maybe. Tall, slim, well-dressed in a pale green shirt, dark trousers and perfectly polished loafers. "You're Clive."

He smiled, showing nice teeth. "I am. And you must be one of the inquisitive three."

Kate nodded. He wasn't like she'd imagined from Puck's story. He certainly wasn't the scowling, angry, full of hatred person she'd pictured.

"Are you here to find out who murdered Sean and Diana?"

His words so shocked Kate she couldn't speak.

"Too much too soon?" he asked.

"Murdered?" she managed to whisper. Did he know about the body? Had *he* put it there?

"Again, I apologize. I shouldn't have said that. It's just my theory. I've not said it out loud before."

Kate was staring at him in silence.

"Perhaps we should start over. I'm Clive Binswood and I work at Coutts Bank in London." He held out his hand to shake.

"I'm Kate Medlar." She shook his hand.

He glanced down at her shoes. "How about if you and I take a walk? I haven't seen the place in years and I'd like to see what Mrs. Guilford has done to it."

Kate was recovering. "Will you tell me your side of what happened?"

He smiled so warmly that she smiled back. "No one has ever asked to hear my side of anything about Oxley Manor. I assume you've been told that I was an angry young man. Disliked by all."

The kindness in Kate wanted to deny that, but she didn't. "Actually, yes. I expected you to have fangs and a forked tail."

He grinned. "No fangs. Haven't looked to see if a tail has grown."

She smiled as she stood up. "Yes, let's walk. Tell me how you first came to be at Oxley Manor."

"My guardian angel," he said as he held open the door for her. "At least that's what I thought at the time."

They walked side by side down a well-kept gravel path.

Clive was looking around. "It's hard to believe this is the same place. Bertram . . . He's —"

"Nicky's father. The drunken earl."

"You've been doing your research. Bertram didn't care about the place."

"Only about his slow horses."

Clive chuckled. "He said that when they made millions he'd repair everything. But he —"

Kate had heard enough about Bertram and his horses. "What about *you*? How was your angel involved in putting you here?"

"By the time I was fourteen, every person I'd ever lived with had died."

"I'm sorry," Kate said.

"I grew up in houses of grief and illness and tragedy. Only quiet sadness was allowed."

"Not good for a child," she said.

"Understatement. But I knew nothing different. I was the passed-around kid. After my parents died when I was eight, I went from uncle to aunt to cousin."

"Sure doesn't sound like fun," Kate said. "But I bet they were all so very glad to see you arrive."

"Their joy was overwhelming."

"Put you in the closet under the stairs, did they?"

He laughed at her reference to Harry Potter. "It was about that bad."

"Then came Oxley Manor."

"Yes. Then came this." He swept his arm out. They were by a pond that had tall cattails and ducks floating on the blue water.

"But I don't think you were welcomed," Kate said.

"Actually, I was. Nicky and I were the same age and he'd lived such a sheltered life that I was a novelty. I knew how to ride busses and how we could hide from his father. I knew —" He waved his hand. "Anyway, it was good for us both."

"What about you and Bertram?"

"Ever hear the saying that lazy people are brilliant at finding people to do their work for them?"

"No."

"Then I probably made it up. I worked hard to make myself useful so I wouldn't be sent away."

"Been there, done that," Kate said. He looked at her in interest. "Nope. This is *your* story. What changed?"

Clive lost his smile. "It was all wonderful — until Bertram pulled me out of uni after two years. He said Oxley was falling apart and I was needed here."

"Selfish in the extreme," Kate said. "I assume you were part of the group, but then . . ." She looked at him.

"In a single day, I went from being their friend to being their servant. And they bloody well let me know of my fallen status."

"No wonder you were angry. Why didn't you leave?"

They had reached an area with a long vista and there was a bench nearby. Clive motioned for her to sit and he took a place beside her.

"I was too afraid to leave. Oxley Manor was the only place I'd ever known any happiness. The world I'd seen outside was full of misery."

"And there was Willa."

Clive shook his head. "That poor woman. I was a beast to her. But then, they all were."

"I thought they liked her."

"Hell no! They put up with her because she paid for everything. And she applauded Byon's hateful little plays. All Nicky had to do was smile at her and she'd get out her checkbook."

"That is cold."

"Her family was worse!" Clive said. "She and I were alike in that we were terrified that it would all be taken away from us. I was scared that Bertram would run the place into bankruptcy, and she was afraid Nicky and Byon would do to her what they'd done to me. One day they'd decide she was out and she'd be told to leave."

"But if you and Willa married . . ."

"Yes, if she and I were together they might keep us both."

"You to run Oxley Manor and Willa to pay for it."

"You are exactly right."

She took a breath. "But it all ended on one night."

Clive took his time before speaking. "They didn't even notice," he said softly. "Nicky was engaged to Diana but she was gone for twenty-some hours before they realized it."

"And Sean?"

"They would have let the horses starve before they bothered to feed them. When the police came late in the day, they fed and watered the poor creatures."

"What do you think happened to those people?" She waited for him to say the *M* word again.

"I don't think they're alive."

"Who . . . ?"

Clive stood up, staring ahead at the garden. "I don't know what happened that night but I do know that everything changed. They were all different after that."

"It was a traumatic event."

"It was more than that. Deeper. It's like they all wanted to escape."

"Escape what?"

"Themselves, I guess. After that night, Nicky started drinking more than his father did. When Byon got his show in London, he ran off without so much as a goodbye. Nadine immediately married some man none of us had heard of, and Bertram's temper went from bad to vicious."

He turned to look at her. "I knew there was something else going on. Something much stronger, darker, than just a couple running away together. Whatever it was, it terrified me. Frankly, the atmosphere scared me. I told Willa I couldn't marry her, then I left. Whatever was going on at Oxley frightened me more than the outside world did. I took a train to London. I thought I'd spend my life washing dishes, but at least I'd be alive." He sat down beside her.

"And did you? Wash dishes, I mean?"

He smiled. "For years I'd dealt with a Mr. Davies at Coutts Bank. I was always covering for Bertram, always trying to manipulate what little cash there was. The day after I arrived, I went to him. He was . . . he was the father I'd always wanted. He hired me for a bookkeeping job, then made sure I went back to school. I became a chartered accountant."

"And now?"

His smile broadened. "Now I handle some of the biggest clients in the world. Last month someone specifically requested me. I spent four days with his family in their villa outside Paris. We did wine tastings, cooked, swam together. When I left, they told me to please stay with them anytime I'm in the country." He said it all with pride, with a hint of defiance.

"That's not how they thought you'd turn out."

"I know."

He sounded so proud that she laughed. "So maybe you came back to let them know that you aren't what they said you were."

Clive didn't answer with words, but his smile told her that was exactly why he was there.

It looked like the others weren't the only ones who didn't care a flying fig about what happened to Sean and Diana, she thought.

"Shall we walk?" he said and they headed down the path. "So who's here?" he asked.

"Nadine. I don't think she and Sara get along very well."

Clive laughed. "They wouldn't. Nadine much prefers men to women. I read that her husband died recently."

"Wasn't he a viscount?"

"Oh yes. Byon said we were to bow to her and call her 'my lady.' Is he here?"

"Not that I know of. I didn't see a Rolls."

Clive laughed again. "A Rolls and a very good-looking young driver. Male."

Kate nodded in understanding. "We've been told that Jack looks like Sean."

"If Byon is here, he'd better lock his bedroom door."

"Interesting." Kate wanted to get back to the subject. "If Sean and Diana were murdered, who do you think did it?"

"Could have been any of them. They —"

"Good heavens! What happened there?" Kate said.

Clive followed her gaze. They'd reached the far corner of the estate. Before them was the fenced conservation area that was clearly marked for no trespassing. But the gate was standing open and inside, the tall grasses were trampled.

"Looks like the sheep got in," he said. "Bertram bought them so he wouldn't have to pay gardeners to mow. Nicky and Byon used to dress them up in clothes they found in the attic. They thought it was hilarious."

Kate's mind was racing. So *this* is where Jack ran off to. He wanted to remove all traces of their footprints so he picked the lock on the gate and drove the sheep inside. She was willing to bet that he stayed with them, playing shepherd so they didn't fall down into the pit where Sean's body was.

"Are you all right?" Clive asked.

"Yes, I'm fine. I think we should close the gate."

"Good idea. I'll just ramble around inside a bit to check if any sheep are still inside, then I'll close it."

"No!" Kate caught herself. She didn't want him accidently stepping on vines and falling through — if he didn't already know where the pit was, that is. "I mean, sheep travel in flocks, don't they? So I'm sure they're all gone." She knew Jack would have counted them before he sent them out. So why didn't he close the gate all the way? Or did he?

She looked at Clive. She had no idea when he'd arrived. He could have gone to check if anyone had discovered the hiding place.

As they closed the gate, she tried to let her face give nothing away. "Good heavens! Sara and Jack will be wondering where I am."

"And I need to face them. Is Willa coming?"

"I don't know. Maybe." She was taking deep breaths to calm herself. Jack wouldn't have left the gate open. So who did?

"Maybe we can go together," Clive was saying. "When I face them, you can be my backbone. Byon and Nadine together won't be as bad as Byon and Nicky, but still . . ."

They heard a motor and emerging from the trees was a man in a dark green utility vehicle. He stopped in front of them.

"Mrs. Guilford sent me up here to look at the fence."

At least that's what Kate thought he said. His accent was so thick she could hardly understand him.

"It looks like sheep got inside," Clive said. "We closed the gate but there may be more in there."

"Then they'll have to stay," the man said. "I was told to lock it but that I was not to go inside. I might upset the nests." He seemed to think this was a great joke. He held up a new lock and Clive put it on the gate.

"Would you give us a ride back to the house?" Kate asked.

"Sure thing."

She got on the wide bench seat beside him, but Clive said he'd rather walk. "There are still a couple of places I want to see."

The driver took off, and as she waved to Clive, she wondered if he wanted privacy to check the pit. To see if it had been disturbed.

The driver was young and flirty and tried to impress Kate by driving as fast as possible across the bumpy land. But she was used to riding with Jack so speed didn't faze her.

Besides, she was heavy in thought about Clive. Who was he really? A grown-up version of the angry young man she'd heard about? Had he learned to cover his true nature? Even if he'd changed, twenty years ago he was a volcano of anger — and rightly so.

The question wasn't how he was now but what he was like then.

She was so engrossed in her thoughts that she didn't tell the driver to drop her at the back of the house. He had taken her to the front. She thanked him and got out, then waited while three women came out carrying plastic carts full of cleaning supplies.

She greeted them but they hurried past

her. Bella sure ran a tight ship!

Just as Kate was about to step inside, she heard music. A piano and a man singing. She'd know Jack's voice anywhere. Behind her was the chapel and she saw that windows had been opened. She had no doubt that Jack had done that. It was an invitation to . . .

"To us," Kate said as she ran into the house to get Sara. But she was coming in the back, her camera around her neck.

"You heard it?" Sara asked.

"Like a beacon from a lighthouse. Let's go!"

They went around the side to enter the chapel. Sara nodded at the hinges, and Kate knew what she meant. The marks they'd made earlier were now concealed.

As they had discovered earlier, the acoustics in the building were extraordinary. The piano and Jack's beautiful voice filled the pretty chapel. The sound hit the ceiling, spread out, then flowed down the walls. As Kate and Sara sat down, they were engulfed with the music.

Sitting at the piano was a short, chubby, man, plain faced. He was someone you could see one minute but forget in the next. But they knew this had to be Byon, and his talent made up for his lack of looks.

Jack had his back to them and he was singing a lively song about some girl he'd met. Kate had never heard it before. She'd always marveled at his ability to remember the words to songs.

When she'd told him that, he'd looked at her in disbelief. "The music *tells* you the words."

"But what if there's no music being played?"

"There's always music," he said. "It's inside my head."

Jack didn't see them, but Byon did. Abruptly, he stopped playing. "How about this instead?" He played a few notes of a melody.

"You'd kill me on that one. Too many high notes. Too many —"

As Byon began to play, the music drowned out Jack's protests. When he got to the part where Jack was to come in, he did.

It was a song about lost love, and even Kate could tell that it took great vocal ability. And emotion. According to the lyrics, the woman he loved had died and the song showed his grief.

Sara and Kate knew where the grief in Jack's voice came from. He'd had a hard time in his life and he put it into his voice. Only minutes into the song, Kate had tears running down her face. Sara was silently taking photos of Jack and Byon.

On the second verse, Nadine slipped in beside Sara. Minutes later, Clive sat down beside Kate.

When Jack's voice perfectly reached those high notes, the four of them in the audience were in awed silence. At the end, he still had his back to them. "I missed that one note and —" he began.

Behind him, the four rose to their feet and began applauding. The building multiplied the sound until it was a roar.

Startled, Jack turned around. His face was red but he was pleased.

When a fifth person added to the applause, they all turned to look. Mrs. Aiken was at the back of the chapel, a big basket at her feet.

Still clapping, Nadine said, "Byon wrote that when Nicky died. Mrs. Aiken —"

"I know," Sara said. "She loved Nicky."

"Worshipped him," Clive said, then he whistled and yelled, "Author! Author!"

Byon got up, took a bow, then held his arm out to Jack.

Jack's face reddened more but they could all see that he was happy. It was a lifelong dream to him.

Finally, they stopped clapping and Jack

came down to them. "I wasn't sure about some of the notes. I . . ." He shrugged.

Kate didn't say anything, just stood on tiptoe and whispered, "It was perfect."

Jack nodded in thanks.

"You were wonderful," Sara said and kissed his cheeks.

When Nadine also kissed him, the others looked on in surprise. Jack and Nadine obviously knew each other.

"Clive?" Nadine said, and held out her hand to shake his.

The three raised their eyebrows. It was certainly a cool greeting between old friends.

Byon was still onstage, apart and watching.

It was Mrs. Aiken who drew him in. She hurried down the aisle, pushed Nadine and Sara out of her way, then encapsulated Byon with her big arms. His face was smothered in her breasts. Her happiness, combined with the atmosphere of the church, made her look like she might float right up to heaven.

"So much for being a parasite," Sara muttered to Kate, then turned to Nadine. "Likes him, does she?" Sara said.

Nadine shook her head. "More than you can imagine. I do hope she brought food."

"Of course she did." Clive was craning his neck to look around the chapel.

"Willa's not here," Nadine said, "so you're safe."

Clive let out a sigh of relief.

"But I bet her family owns shotguns," Nadine said.

"As always, your humor evades me." Clive's tone let them see the angry young man they'd heard about.

Byon disentangled himself from Mrs. Aiken in time to hear the little jibes. "I see I nearly missed Round One." He looked at Mrs. Aiken. "Darling, do feed us. No, not in here. I fear the sanctity of this building will persuade me to confess my sins. The enormity of them would crash the ceiling."

In disbelief, the others watched Mrs. Aiken giggle like a teenager. "I'll take it outside."

"I have seen the light," Sara muttered.

Byon slipped an arm around Sara's small shoulders. "Aren't you one of those writers with masses of bestsellers and loads of cash in the bank?"

Kate stepped forward to defend her aunt, but Sara laughed. "Awards or money. Writers don't get both."

Byon gave an exaggerated sigh. "Alas, I have walls full of awards and shelves full of ugly statues. Perhaps we could share."

"I can see it now," Sara said. "I'll buy a label maker and put my name over yours."

They started walking out the door together. "Yes, darling, and I will add my name to your account as your spouse."

"Oh good! I've never had one of those," Sara said. "But I've consummated a few unions."

"Only a few? Darling, we must compare conquest stories."

The others were standing in the doorway, watching and listening, as the voices faded.

"Someone who can stand up to Byon." Nadine's voice was admiring.

"Usually, people flee him in tears," Clive said.

"Or threaten him." Nadine was looking Clive up and down. "Bring any knives with you?"

"Only one for you, dear Nadine."

They left the chapel.

Kate and Jack, standing inside, looked at each other.

"Think we have any suspects?" Kate asked.

"I think every person we've met here is capable of murder. Maybe they *all* did it."

They were watching the others through the doorway as they sat down to the picnic.

"What you did with the sheep was clever," Kate said.

"Stupid creatures. I nearly fell through that rusty old grating when I tried to keep them off of it. I just wanted them to run around, smash the grass and cover our tracks."

"I guess you closed the gate after you got them out."

"Of course I did. The sheep loved those virgin grasses, wanted to eat everything. It was tough getting them out. I latched the gate, but the lock was too rusty to put back on."

"Latched it, huh?"

"What are you dancing around saying?"

"When Clive and I got there, the gate was open about two feet."

"You and Clive? He's too old for you. He couldn't —"

Kate threw up her hands. "Would you stop it! Gate. Open. Get it?"

"Who — ? I see. Think lover boy did it?"

"Clive isn't my —" She glared at him. "I can see that Byon is already in love with you. And you sound like it's mutual. Be sure to hang your shirt over your bedroom doorknob to let everyone know you two are busy."

Jack laughed. "Nadine's the one who likes

me shirtless. Oh, Sara is motioning for us to join them."

"When were you shirtless around Nadine?"

He stopped in the doorway. "When she fainted at the sight of me and I carried her outside. I had to put a cold compress on her forehead so I used my shirt. She said I should have removed her blouse and used it. Too bad I didn't think of that." He went out the door to join the others.

"Bastard!" Kate muttered, and left the chapel.

They sat on the ground on a big blanket. Mrs. Aiken had ordered some of the cleaners to bring more food — and two pillows. Of course they were meant for her favorites, Nadine and Byon, but Nadine offered hers to Sara.

Jack and Kate hid their laughs. Sara hated anything that rang of "because you're old."

As they knew she would, Sara refused the pillow. "I'm fine." She sat cross-legged on the blanket.

The group divided itself with Sara, Jack and Kate on one side, Nadine and Byon on the other side. Clive was at the head. He was separate from the rest of them.

There were sandwiches and the little pies the English so loved, pâté, pickles, olives and three kinds of bread. For dessert there were tarts covered in berries and clotted cream. It was a feast!

"How lovely," Nadine said. "Just like it used to be. It's almost as though we're all here."

"Except for Nicky." There was longing in Byon's voice.

"And Bertram is gone," Nadine said. "Who is going to yell at us? Who — ?"

"I want to hear about Willa," Sara said.

The three English people barely lifted their eyes, but they exchanged looks. It was the most united they'd been since arriving.

Sara, with her keto diet, had a plate full of cheeses, sliced meats and olives. She looked at Byon. "What was she like?"

"Selfless." Byon looked at the other two and they nodded in agreement.

"I got the idea she was a dreadful person," Sara said. "A pest. Unwanted by anyone — except for her money."

Kate hid her face. She knew her aunt was baiting them.

Byon said, "Shall I tell you how we met her?"

"I'd love to hear."

He looked at Nadine. "You had only recently joined Nicky and me."

"I was there," Clive said pointedly.

"Yes, of course," Byon said. "But then you were a part of Nicky."

"Like his valet?" There was anger in Clive's voice.

"More like his second-best pair of shoes," Byon snapped. "Shall I continue or would you like more time to suffer?"

Clive gave Kate a look of *See what I have to put up with?*

"As I was saying," Byon continued, "we were together and at a grocery. We'd been up all night and we were tired and hungry and broke."

"I remember that we were trying to piece together five pounds," Nadine said. "My allowance wouldn't come in for another three days."

"Willa was ahead of us in the queue," Clive said. "But only Nicky noticed her."

"He was like that." Byon's tone was reverent. "He saw what others didn't."

"Describe her," Kate said.

"Plain," Clive said, and Nadine and Byon nodded. "In all the years I knew her I never saw anything to distinguish her. Not in looks or talent of any kind."

Byon looked at him in wonder. "I had no idea you were so perceptive."

Before Clive could retaliate, Sara said to Byon in annoyance, "Do try to subdue your venom. Clive appears to have been successful in spite of your belittlement of him. Get on with the story."

Clive looked like he was going to kiss Sara, and Nadine was wide-eyed.

Byon laughed. "Oh how Nicky would have loved you! Anyway, Willa secretly paid for the groceries of a woman with three children. Nicky saw what she'd done, but the woman didn't."

"She thanked some man," Clive said.

"And he told her she was welcome," Nadine added.

"What did Willa say?" Jack asked.

"Nothing," Byon answered. "She just stood there, unnoticed by anyone, and let the woman thank the wrong person."

"What did Nicky do?" Kate asked.

The three smiled and Byon leaned forward. "You *never* wanted to get on Nicky's bad side. That day, he tore them apart. Woman, man, cashier. All of them. Then he pulled Willa into our group."

"And that was it," Nadine said.

"And the lot of you got an adoring audience and an open checkbook." Sara got up and began taking photos of them.

"We did!" Byon said in delight.

Nadine didn't laugh. "We took care of her. Protected her. Her family was horrible."

"Or great," Clive said. "Depends on how you look at it. Her sister, Beatrice, certainly was beautiful."

"And talented," Nadine said.

"She could do anything," Clive said. "And she was tall and lithe. Utterly splendid."

"There was nothing about the sister that wasn't perfect." Byon smiled, but it was so malicious he looked like the devil.

Sara lowered her camera. "Tell me every word of it."

"Willa never said much about her childhood," Nadine began.

"She did tell me that she was the third of four kids," Clive said. "This was back when I was part of the group." He put up his hand to ward off Byon's comment. "I felt sorry for Willa."

Nadine continued the story. "One night, when we'd all had too much to drink, she told us that when she was a child, three different times, her family left her behind. Forgot about her. Once was when they were on holiday in France. She was nine years old and she found herself alone, but she managed to find a police station. She knew the name of the hotel where they were staying and the police called. Her family said they would pick her up when they finished dinner. She waited for hours."

"A forgotten person," Sara said. "No wonder she worshipped the lot of you. Did she invite her sister to meet you?"

"No," Byon said. "The sister invited herself. She told us that none of the siblings could believe that Willa actually had friends. They were curious about us, so the youngest sister was sent by the siblings to see what we were like."

"She took the bed and Willa slept on the little sofa in her own bedroom." Nadine's eyes glittered.

"And how did she fit in?" Jack asked.

The three of them smiled.

"She was charming," Clive said. "And so very helpful. Even then I was doing the Oxley accounts and she caught an error."

"She showed me some makeup tricks that I still use today," Nadine said.

"She gave Mrs. Aiken a recipe for piecrust that was easier and tasted better than any she'd made before," Byon said. "And she sang rather well."

"And she rode a horse like a wood sprite," Nadine added.

"She called someone about the roof, and it was repaired. For free," Clive said.

When they finished, they sat in silence, looking at Sara.

"I'm surprised you didn't murder her,"

Sara said. "I bet she was as welcome to you as a dinner with a Pulitzer Prize winning novelist would be to me."

"Less," Byon said.

"What did you do to her?" Kate asked.

"We released Nicky onto her," Nadine said. "On Sunday morning, Puck packed the sister's bags and set them outside. Mrs. Aiken called a cab. We stood by while Nicky told her that her jealousy made him sick. He said she couldn't bear for Willa to have anything so she'd come there to take away what little Willa did have."

Clive nodded. "Nicky said Willa was a better person than she could ever be."

"Did Willa hear this?" Kate asked.

"She was standing right there," Nadine said. "Her sister said, 'Are you going to let them treat me like this?' "

"And what was her reply?" Sara sat back on the cloth.

"Willa opened the cab door for her sister. Never spoke a word," Byon said.

"Then she walked back to the house." Nadine was smiling. "I'd never seen her stand up so straight."

They were looking at Sara as though waiting for praise for what they'd done.

Sara glanced at Jack and Kate, letting them know she'd speak her mind later. For now, she was keeping her true opinions to herself. "No wonder Willa loved all of you," Sara said. "So what happened after that night when the others . . . left?"

"Willa also disappeared," Clive said.

Nadine shot him a nasty look. "Only after you dropped her. What was it you told her? 'I'm not going to marry you.' No sentiment from you! Then you held out your hand for the return of the ring. Which, I might add, wasn't even a diamond."

Clive seemed unperturbed. "Ah, the cruelty and poverty of youth. I do hope she hasn't spent her fortune on . . . on cats. My bank and I could help her." He looked at Sara. "We don't know where she went or what happened to her. Wasn't she invited here?"

"Yes," Sara said. "She said she'd be here but she didn't say when."

Nadine was leaning back on her arms. "I wonder how she's made it through life. She had no defenses, no self-protection. And she was the most socially awkward person I'd ever met. What else could she do but go home? After the way Nicky treated the sister, I'm sure they butchered her. *We* were the only real family she had." She cut a look at Clive but he ignored her.

"Cried," Byon said. "My guess is that she

cried for years. She was truly heartbroken. She'd lost her friends and her engagement. It would have been a marriage in hell but —"

"Maybe not," Clive snapped. "We could have —"

Byon sneered at him. "You think if she'd bought you some country estate you would have been kind to her? Treated her like a human being? Or would you have blamed her for . . . ?" He waved his hand. "For all the misery you think other people have given you?"

"I was treated like dirt," Clive said loudly. "You threw me out of the Pack."

"Darling," Byon said, "you were never *in* the Pack."

Clive moved as though he was going to hit Byon. Jack looked like he was ready to get between them.

Nadine's laughter calmed them down. "Oh how I've missed this! What a dull life I've had. Cutting the ribbons at the village fête. So boring." She looked at Sara. "We weren't perfect but we did the best we knew how. And yes, Willa was our audience. She applauded Byon's plays, she professed love for a man none of us liked — sorry Clive — and championed lazy Nicky against his father."

"And don't forget that she looked at you like you were Venus come to earth," Byon said.

"There was that." Nadine was smiling in memory.

"What about Diana?" Kate asked.

"And Sean?" Jack asked.

No one responded.

"Anyone for a tart?" Byon's tone made it clear the conversation was over.

Ten

As soon as lunch was finished, the Americans escaped to Sara's room. It was the first time Jack and Kate had been in it and it was impressive. It was enormous, with a four-poster bed draped in cream-colored silk trimmed in blue. The walls were upholstered in blue silk. All the furniture was antique and exquisite.

There was a sitting area of a plump couch and chairs covered in blue-and-green chintz.

Sara took the couch, picked up her laptop, inserted the SD disk from her Sony a9 camera and began to look at her photos. "Well?" she asked.

Kate and Jack were in chairs across from each other.

"What did you think of how they met Willa?" Jack asked.

"I think you mean 'Poor Willa,' " Kate said. "Maybe it should be one word — Poorwilla."

Jack gave a one-sided smile. "It's a wonder they didn't nickname her PW."

"They used her," Sara said, "but it was better than she'd had. I know all about families that choose one child over another." She glanced at Kate. "Sorry." It was Kate's father, Sara's younger brother, who had been the favored child.

"That's okay," Kate said. "My dad probably deserved it."

Sara laughed. "Easy to get along with, charming but devious. Maybe you're right." She looked at them. "So who's on first?" She was playing on the old joke to ask who would tell first.

"I think Jack's had the most interesting morning," Kate said. "Singing with a superstar, stripping off half-naked for some woman. He should tell us all."

Sara raised her eyebrows. "Yes, do tell."

"It was nothing, really," Jack said with fake modesty. "Maybe I saved her life but . . ." He shrugged. "All in a normal day's work."

Sara and Kate groaned in unison.

"Okay, okay. I was climbing through the loft of the stables. That's where our victim worked so I thought maybe there could be something there. Then I saw this beautiful woman walk in and —"

"*Old* woman," Kate said, then looked at Sara.

"Age is relative," she said. "In this context, forty-six-year-old Nadine is *very* old."

Jack rolled his eyes. He knew when he was outnumbered. "Anyway, she was looking for something and —"

"Oh?" Kate and Sara said.

He smiled at having their attention. "I have no idea what she was looking for. Didn't find out." He went on to tell his story.

"How sad," Sara said when he'd finished. "I'm glad I can support myself. Nadine has to find a man to give her a home."

"Interesting that her husband didn't leave her taken care of," Kate said. "You'd assume that a viscount would have some inherited property."

"Nicky would have owned this place but he had no money." Jack looked at Kate. "So what about your banker boy? From what I've seen, I can't understand why he wanted to stay with people who put him down, belittled him, despised him."

"You adapt to your life," Kate said. They knew she was speaking of her mother's bouts of depression. She told them of all she and Clive had talked about. She waited for Jack's snide remarks but he was quiet.

"Another poor, unwanted person," Sara said. "This seems to have been misfit heaven. I read that if there's one male abuser in a stadium of eight thousand people and there's one woman who thinks she deserves it, they will damned well find each other."

"In this case, they all found one another," Jack said. "But one night two of them disappeared, then they all ran away separately."

"Four years of being afraid of the world disappeared," Kate said. "I think Clive was right when he said that the outside world was less scary than the little group at Oxley Manor."

"Every group has its hierarchy," Sara said. "And everyone has a place. They don't take turns being the leader."

"Sure as hell no one was going to take their turn at being a punching bag," Jack said.

" 'Today is my turn to be on the bottom,' " Kate mocked. " 'Rip *me* apart.' "

" 'No! No! Let me get kicked around,' " Jack parodied. "Said no one."

Sara was grimacing. "I bet if Poorwilla had tried to do something different, they would have stamped her down."

"For all that Clive said he hated his job," Jack said, "he was terrified of losing it."

"Until Sean's and Diana's disappearance forced him to leave," Kate said.

"I think they all know much, much more than they're letting on," Sara said. "Actually, I believe they're putting on a show for us."

"And getting truckloads of sympathy," Jack said. "Poor Clive with his tossed-around childhood."

"Nadine," Kate said, "so beautiful, so well-dressed, but oh so lonely. The martyred maiden who must sell herself to the highest bidder."

They looked at Sara.

"I agree. I think we're being played. One of them is a murderer."

"Or all of them," Jack said. "For all that they seem to clash, I think they're strongly bonded. I could see that Sean and Diana were about to interrupt their bond and they got rid of them."

"We don't know what happened to Diana," Sara said. "She could have killed Sean, then run away. Maybe the ones left behind hid Sean's body."

Kate nodded. "That's plausible. They wouldn't want the press and the police here. The publicity would ruin them."

"True," Sara said. "For the rest of their lives, they'd have a murder hanging over their heads. Byon's fledgling career would forever be tainted. Nadine might lose her viscount."

"Poorwilla would be ridiculed even more by her beautiful, talented family," Jack said. "She'd have to hear 'I told you so' for the rest of her life."

"Hide the body, then separate," Sara said. "Bookwise, this works. A plot always needs secrets. But are these the *right* secrets?"

"I think we need to ask more about Diana," Jack said. "Every time we mention her, everyone gets quiet. Let's —" He broke off as a loud crash came from outside.

"Somebody knocked over something," Sara said.

Jack was up before she finished. "I'll go look. From what I've seen of Bella, she'll have someone's hide." He left the room.

Kate turned to her aunt. "He's right. Bella really runs this place. There must be fifty people out there."

"She has help for the other eleven months, but she takes over for the yearly cleanup. She's a great believer in 'If you want it done right, do it yourself.' "

For a moment, Kate was quiet. "I didn't realize how good Jack's singing was. I've heard him with a bar band and at a funeral, but today was extraordinary."

"When he was eighteen I offered to pay for him to go to Juilliard, but he refused. He had to take care of his family."

Kate sighed. "Family." She knew all about the enormous pressure family put on a person. "His singing with someone of Byon Lizmere's caliber, meeting Lady Nadine — it's been quite a day for him."

Sara was watching her niece with the intensity of a hawk. "I think we both need to face the fact that someday Jack will discover how talented he is. The world will open up to him and he'll become famous. I have no doubt that, someday, he'll fall in love, marry and have kids. You and I will be left on our own."

Kate didn't like the visions that conjured. Jack on Broadway receiving a standing ovation. Holding roses and blowing kisses to his wife, Lady Fiona something. His beautiful little daughter would walk onto the stage and —

She looked at her aunt. Sara's eyes were sparkling. "Are you being a bitch?"

"Oh yes," Sara said. "I'm being so bitchy that I'm giving off red and orange flames. I'm sure I can be seen by satellite."

"Well, stop it. Save it for Byon."

Sara laughed. "He tires me out. I have to be on guard every second. It's almost as bad as being at a Romance Conference. Although, Byon is much sweeter."

"Jack's the one who has to be on guard. Byon looks at him like he's a two-hundred-dollar steak."

"Bet he looked at Sean just like that."

They looked at each other, eyes wide.

"If Sean didn't love him back . . ." Kate said.

"No wrath like a woman scorned," Sara whispered.

"Could he hide a body? He looks flabby."

"But twenty years ago? Sure he could."

Kate was thoughtful. "If Byon killed Sean, he had the rest of the night and all the next day to hide the body. The others were asleep and hung over. They wouldn't notice."

Sara nodded. "Even if they looked out the window and saw him, they'd probably yawn and say, 'Looks like Byon is hiding a dead body.' "

Kate laughed. "That would be Nadine. Clive would worry that the murder would affect his job."

Sara smiled. "Later, Bertram would yell at Nicky and ask if the murder was loud. He wouldn't want the horses to be frightened. They might lose the next race too quickly."

Kate was grinning. "Puck would be hiding in the shadows. She'd see it all and never tell anyone anything."

"And what about Poorwilla?" Sara asked.

"She'd say, 'Oh no! That's one less person to pretend to love me. Who do I pay to make it right?' "

Kate and Sara looked at each other, then dissolved into laughter.

When Jack opened the door, he saw both of them laughing hard. "What the hell have you two been talking about?"

"You!" they said in unison, then laughed harder.

It was later, after Kate and Sara had calmed down — they'd told Jack why they were laughing but not how it had started — that Sara found the note. It had been slipped into her camera bag. If at all possible, she didn't bother carrying it. She just put a medium telephoto lens on, stuck a battery or two in her pocket and went out shooting. That the bag had been in her room since they'd returned from Puck's meant anyone had access to it.

The note was on a heavy card and she held it out, facedown. She didn't turn it over until Kate was beside her and Jack was looking down over her head.

She flipped it over.

Nadine had a daughter. She was born November 1994.

Below that was a telephone number.

Kate was the math person. "That means Nadine was pregnant when Sean and Diana disappeared. She was far enough along that she knew she was."

Sara looked at Kate. "What was it Clive said about her husband?"

Kate quoted, " *'Nadine immediately married some man none of us had heard of.'* "

"She could have been fooling around with the guy she married," Jack said.

"And not tell her besties?" Kate said. "Not likely."

Sara held up the card. "If it was all on the up-and-up, why secretly slip us a note? I'm going to call that number."

"Shouldn't we wait until . . . ?" Kate began, but at the looks from Jack and Sara, she said, "Yes, do it now."

Sara got her cell and touched the numbers. It was picked up right away.

"Teddy here. What can I do for you?"

"Hi. My name is Sara Medlar and I'm at Oxley Manor with Lady Nadine. I believe she's your mother. I was wondering if —"

"My mother! You have a nerve calling me. Did she give you my number? I'll have my lawyer —"

"No, no," Sara said. "She didn't tell us about you. I don't want to cause any trouble but there are three of us here at Oxley trying to investigate the disappearance of two people in May of 1994. We —"

"You're calling *me* about *that*?" The young woman's voice with its upper-class accent was full of rage. "You can tell my mother that I'll never forgive her for a lifetime of lies. I never want to see her again. She —"

"We could tell her everything you want to say to her," Sara said quickly and loudly. "We're here. Come stay. Tell us all."

"I don't deal with liars!" She clicked off.

Sara looked at Jack and Kate. "Oh."

"Looks like we've uncovered a secret." Kate looked at Jack. "Nadine didn't mention that her daughter hates her?"

"Must have slipped her mind."

Sara was looking at the card. "I wonder who sent this? Who wants us to know about Nadine and her daughter?"

"A tattletale," Jack said. "He or she is saying, 'Don't look too closely at *me*. Focus on someone else.' "

"So how do we get her here?" Sara asked. "Or do we send Jack after her?"

"If the daughter is like the mother, she won't release him," Kate said.

"I'll go if I must," Jack said.

The women ignored him.

"Send her a photo of your room and say a weekend is free," Sara said.

"That doesn't seem like much," Jack said.

"Anger like hers needs an outlet," Sara said. "It's the cold I-don't-care kind of anger that doesn't respond." Sara used her cell to snap a photo of the beautiful room, tapped in an invitation, then used WhatsApp to send the text to the number on the card.

They stared at the phone in silence but nothing happened.

Sara and Kate sighed. "It was worth a try."

But then, Sara's phone dinged.

Eight p.m. The Josephine room.

They clapped raised hands in triumph. "I have to find the Josephine room," Sara said, "and make sure it doesn't smell like disinfectant."

"I'll cut flowers," Kate said.

They looked at Jack.

He was backing out of the room. "I'll go, uh . . . I think I'll . . ."

"You want to find Byon and sing some more," Kate said.

"Maybe." Jack disappeared out the door.

Kate and Sara laughed.

"Wonder what our Jack's future wife's wedding dress will look like?" Sara said.

"More like the other Kate than the Meghan one," Kate said.

"I agree completely."

They ran to do their tasks.

Just as Sara found the Josephine bedroom, her cell dinged with a text. She thought it was probably from Kate but when she saw the ID, she gasped.

"Everything all right?" the young woman who was cleaning the room asked.

"It's all perfect." Sara took off running to find Jack. It was no use texting him. He wouldn't check his phone even if he was carrying it. As she ran, she texted Kate to meet her at the back of the house.

She found Jack downstairs in the large drawing room. Byon was playing the piano and staring at Jack in adoration as he sang.

Standing in the shadow of the doorway, Sara got Jack's attention. She hated to take him away but she had to. She pointed to her watch, made a motion of driving, then zipped her mouth and jerked her head toward the back of the house.

He gave a nod of understanding and kept singing. He knew that quitting midsong would raise questions.

Sara went out the back. As she knew she would be, her dear, organized, up-for-any-adventure niece was waiting beside one of the hotel's cars, keys in hand.

"Is he going to drag himself away or do you and I go alone?"

"Don't know if he can tear himself away since he has an audience. Half the staff has spent the last hour dusting the balcony," Sara said.

"Puck's spy bridge? They're watching the Byon-Jack show?"

"Good name, and yes. But I think —"

Jack came out the door, took the keys out of Kate's hand and got into the right-hand-drive car. He put down the window. "Are you two going to stand there?"

Kate got into the front, Sara in the back.

"We waited for you for twenty minutes," Kate lied. "So who are you choosing? The magnificent Byon or the very old lady Nadine?"

"I'm waiting for her daughter." Jack looked at Sara in the mirror. "Where to?"

"The Red Bull Inn." Sara was tapping on her phone. "It's not in the nearest village to Oxley Manor. GPS says it's a whopping twelve miles away, and considering the corkscrew nature of English roads, it'll take about an hour. Turn left at the gate."

"I'll do it in thirty minutes," Jack said.

"Just don't forget that driving is on the left side of the road," Kate said.

Jack gave her a look to cut it out.

Sara read aloud about the inn from her phone. Built in the sixteenth century as a coaching inn. Fourteen rooms, a well-respected restaurant/bar serving three meals and drinks.

Twenty minutes later, Jack reached the village and parked in front of the inn. "Who are we meeting?"

"Guess," Sara said as she got out of the car.

Jack looked at Kate. "Poorwilla," they said in unison.

The inn had blackened beams and red carpet everywhere. There was a check-in area near the entrance, with a man standing there.

"We're here to see —" Sara began.

"I know," the man said. "But then, she's our only guest. I'll show you up."

The trio looked at each other as they followed him up the narrow stairs.

At the top, he stepped back. There were about ten doors standing open and half a dozen young women were going in and out of them, their hands full of papers and cell phones.

What was startling was that all the women were exceptionally pretty, and their clothes showed their well-toned bodies.

"I feel like I've walked into a 007 movie," Kate said.

"Me too." Jack's voice was in awe.

"I love coming up here," the manager said. "I use any excuse."

"So where is *she*?" Sara asked.

Jack spoke up. "I'll look in every room, question everyone until I find her. Wait here."

Sara clamped down on his arm.

"Buzzkiller," he murmured.

One of the young women came toward them. "You must be Sara Medlar." She offered her hand to shake. "Come with me and I'll take you to Meena."

Kate turned to Jack to mouth, *"Meena?"* but he was smiling at the women they passed — who were all smiling back at him.

They were led into what was probably the main bedroom of the inn. It was a large room with a bed at one end, sitting area at the other. The bed was heavy, dark wood and carved extensively. On the floor between the two areas was a woman on a yoga mat, her face turned away from them. She was twisted into an impossible posture.

The woman who'd escorted them in left, closing the door behind her.

"I'll be with you in a moment," the woman on the mat said.

The three backed up until they were sitting on a large chest at the foot of the bed. They couldn't take their eyes off the woman in front of them, who was twisting and turning into yoga positions.

"Jacobean," Sara said softly.

"What?" Kate whispered.

"The chest we're sitting on is Jacobean. Bed is Elizabethan."

"That was my number one question," Kate said.

Jack was watching the woman and said nothing.

She brought her body back to what a person would consider normal. Her back was to them as she sat cross-legged, hands behind her, clasped in reverse prayer mode.

Finally, she turned to face them. She was older, true, but her skin was flawless, her brows perfect, her lashes sooty black and thick. Combined with her body, she was an extremely attractive woman.

They stared at her in wonder. *This* couldn't be Poorwilla. Could it?

"I see that you've been told about me."

"*You* are Willa?" Kate asked.

"I was." She picked up a blue silk robe off the back of the couch and put it on. "Shall we sit and talk?"

They took their seats. "You used to be Willa?" Sara asked. "But now you're called Meena? Maybe as part of Wilhelmina?"

"Yes. Willa was too close to 'willing' whereas Meena is more 'I mean what I say.' "

"I'm intrigued," Sara said.

Kate leaned forward. "We want to know about your time with the Pack. Oh, sorry. I meant the —"

Meena smiled. "That's what we were called. It's an accurate label. And just like in a real pack, as long as we each did exactly what was expected of us, it was good."

"Clive was part of that?" Sara asked.

"Oh yes. The others needed both of us. For all that they sneered at him, he took care of them. But then, he was as afraid of being tossed out as I was. But I do think I was more desperate than he was."

"What happened if you didn't do what they wanted?" Jack asked.

There was a quick knock on the door and one of the pretty young women came in and handed Meena a clipboard full of papers. In large letters across the top was the name

Renewal. She glanced at the papers, signed, then the woman left the room.

"Where was I? Oh yes. When I didn't conform to their plan, they let me know of their displeasure. I found that out when I was attracted to a young lawyer here in the village. I saw him yesterday."

Sara's upper lip curled. "If you married outside the group, they'd lose their open bank account."

"And lose their talentless, adoring audience," Meena said. It was the first time there was a hint of anger in her voice. "They told me I was worth much more than a village lawyer."

"Elevating you and tearing you down at the same time," Sara said.

Kate spoke up. "Byon said you were devastated by Clive breaking up with you. He said you probably cried for years."

Again there was a knock on the door. Two women came in bearing trays loaded with tea, little sandwiches, scones and clotted cream. They set them down, then left.

The women only had tea, but Jack dug into the food.

"They all work for you?" Sara asked.

"Yes." Meena didn't elaborate. "Byon. How is he?"

"He's in love with Jack," Kate said. "He

plays piano and Jack sings."

Meena looked at him. "I can see that. You're just his type. Do you know you look like — ?"

"Yes," Jack said quickly. "Everyone has told me." He was on his fourth sandwich.

Meena took a breath. "It was over twenty years ago, but it's still hard to speak of. I know everyone thinks I left because Clive broke up with me, but that's not true. I think I wanted him to dump me. That way I'd be the innocent one."

Sara smiled. "You pursued him until he got rid of you."

"I think so," Meena said. "At the time, I didn't realize that's what I was doing, but I wasn't destroyed when the bastard so coldly told me to get out of his life. I think I figured that what would happen is that we'd end our engagement, I'd cry awhile, then we'd all go back to being our little family."

"And no one would ever again nag you to marry bad-tempered, unhappy Clive," Kate said.

"Exactly," Meena said. "They really are a very talented group of people. Has Byon put on a play for you? No? He will." She looked at Jack. "He'll write one just for you. With original songs."

Jack's face so drained of color that he

looked like he might pass out.

Meena laughed in delight. "He will definitely write for you."

"If it wasn't Clive, then what did cause you to leave?" Sara asked.

Meena's voice got lower. "It was Nicky." She paused to breathe deeply, as though to give herself strength. "After Sean and Diana disappeared, I went to him in private. I knew he liked both of them more than he let on. Nicky liked to be thought of as an Oscar Wilde clone, that he was above such petty emotions as a need for love."

"Or approval from his father," Sara said.

Meena shook her head. "How they despised each other!"

"What did Nicky say when you went to him?" Kate asked.

"He . . ." Meena took a moment to calm herself. "His words are emblazoned on my brain. I still remember them verbatim. Nicky said, *'We're all tired of feeling sorry for you. And right now we don't have time to give you sympathy, no matter how much you pay us to do so.'* Then he slammed the door in my face."

"That's horrible," Kate said. "He —"

Meena put up her hand. "It's all right. I needed that wake-up call. I knew he was telling the truth."

"As he saw it," Jack shot out.

"No, as it really was. I think I was some ravenous plant that fed off sympathy. Were you told about my family?"

They nodded.

"My siblings are selfishness personified."

"But then, you expected them to intuit what you needed and to give it to you," Sara said. "I bet they demanded whatever they wanted."

Meena laughed. "You have perfectly described the situation. But I didn't see it that way."

"I don't believe in blaming the victim." Kate's voice was rising. "I hate when people say 'If only you had done so and so, then he wouldn't have been angry.' In this case, you're being blamed for not being as selfish as they are. They should have known that you needed love and affection. Everyone does."

They were all staring at her.

"I like your attitude," Meena said. "You want to come work for me? I'll start you in a top management position."

"What *is* your business?" Sara asked.

"Do you tell the ending of your books at the front?" She didn't give Sara time to answer. "Don't look so surprised. I know about all of you. Estate agent, builder extraordinaire and a supposedly retired writer. You've solved two murder cases that no one else bothered with."

Jack looked up from a plate of scones. "We're public record, but you're a secret. How'd you go from Poorwilla to *this*?" The way he said it was flattering.

"After what Nicky said, I knew I had to leave. All through school I'd told myself that yes, I paid for things but they really did care about me. But it was like Nicky had taken a hammer and shattered the glass cage I lived in." She took a drink of tea. "To say I felt sorry for myself is too mild. I was absolutely and totally *alone.* I couldn't possibly go home. Beatrice was the most vicious of my siblings and she'd had time to make what happened at Oxley into a war. If I showed up there, they'd tear me apart."

"So what did you do?" Kate asked.

"As Byon said, I cried. I had so much wanted to *belong.* I especially wanted to be part of that set of beautiful people."

"And you were willing to do *anything* to achieve that," Sara said softly.

"Yes, I was. Money, marriage —"

"Revenge on people who hurt your club members," Jack said.

Meena smiled. "They told you about that, did they? Nasty little ants bit me mercilessly, but I felt it was a price I had to pay to get in." Her eyes lit up. "And it worked. For a while, I was part of them. It was glorious!"

"How long before you stopped crying?" Kate asked.

"I don't know. Six months? A year? I stayed in a little family-owned country hotel. They fed me, I watched old TV shows, I walked a bit but not much. I got even fatter than I was. I had crying bursts. I just didn't know what to *do.* I had been surrounded by so much talent that by comparison, I was a dead fish."

"So what happened?" Jack leaned back against the couch.

"My mother died and I *had* to go home. I had sent contact information to my family. Maybe I was hoping . . . I don't know, that one of them would turn up and say, 'We love you. Come home.' "

"Only happens in my books," Sara said.

Meena smiled. "You're right. No one contacted me until my father sent an overnight letter telling me about my mother. I was to return immediately. It was a command, not a request. I packed up, bought a small car and drove home."

She paused. "My family home. I hadn't seen it in a long time. It's bigger than Oxley Manor, and thanks to my father's money, it was in good repair. It was beautiful, but to me, it had always been a prison. A place of torture." She took a breath. "When I got there, I drove around the back, hoping no one would see me."

"I bet your little sister was watching for you," Sara said.

"Oh yes. She most certainly was."

ELEVEN

Summer 1995

Willa saw no one as she went up the back stairs to the bedroom she'd had as a child. It had been completely redone so she hardly recognized it. Her family had none of that useless sentimentality of keeping the room the way it had been when their daughter lived there. But then, Willa had no medals or trophies to display. She'd never hung posters of rock stars on her walls.

The only picture she'd hung up was one of Alice in Wonderland with a big pistol in her hand, her foot on a dead rabbit. Her mother had told her to take it down, saying it was "disgusting."

Willa had tried to defend herself. "They hang up pictures of naked singers. Why isn't that 'disgusting'?"

"Because *we* are normal," her brother Niall said. "You're not."

When Willa got back to her room, the

photo was gone. She never hung up anything else.

She put on a black knit top and matching trousers that Nadine had chosen for her. They had been loose but now fit tightly, showing all her lumps and rolls.

For a moment, Willa sat on the edge of the bed. It had been months since she'd seen Nicky and the others, and she wondered if they missed her. Did they ever think about her?

She looked at her watch. It was a few minutes until four. She'd timed her arrival for afternoon tea.

Standing, she smoothed her top, tried to suck in her belly, and went down the stairs. She heard voices from the Yellow Drawing Room, and she knew they were in there. She stopped just outside the room.

"Do you think she's going to come down or will she hide like she usually does?" Niall asked.

"She'll be here," Beatrice said. "But now she no longer has that vile little entourage around her. I fear that she was kicked out because she ran through the money. They —"

"Speaking of which," Nelson said, "does anyone know about Mother's will? Surely she left us something."

"She had nothing that was hers," Niall said. "It's all in Father's name."

"Here's to our very healthy father," Nelson said in sarcasm.

Willa leaned against the wall. For all that she'd spent on feeding her friends, she hadn't really dented her trust fund. She wasn't into fancy cars as her brothers were. Didn't own an apartment in London as each of them did. She didn't buy multi-thousand-pound gowns as Beatrice did.

"Do you think she has anything left?" Niall asked.

Willa drew in her breath. She knew he was talking about her.

"I doubt it," Beatrice said. "When I was there at that decaying Oxley Manor, her motto seemed to be 'If you pretend to love me, I'll give you money.' "

"Then she is surely broke," Niall said and they all laughed.

Willa didn't want to hear any more. She ran through the house toward the side door. She wanted to get as far from them as possible.

But she didn't make it. Coming inside was a little boy, about seven, and his pretty, young nanny. Willa had almost forgotten that Nelson had married and produced a son.

The boy ran to a big ceramic bowl set on a marble-topped table and started to pull it off.

"Martin!" the nanny said. "You can't play with that. It's eighteenth century."

"My mother says you are nothing and nobody. I don't have to obey you."

The look on the young woman's face was half rage, half depression.

For a second, her eyes locked with Willa's, and they shared identical emotions.

When the big bowl teetered on the table, the two women leaped to save it.

Angry, the boy stamped his foot and ran out of the room.

Willa and the nanny put the bowl back into place. "I better go get him," the nanny said.

"Maybe he'll go to the library," Willa said. "Some of the tall shelves aren't bolted to the wall. They could come crashing down."

The nanny's eyes widened in shock, then she smiled as she backed toward the door. "I'm Katrina."

"I'm Willa the Unwanted."

The nanny caught her breath for a moment, then laughed. "If *they* don't want you, then you must be doing something right."

There was a crash in the distance and the

nanny went running.

The encounter cheered Willa up somewhat. Her siblings usually surrounded themselves with sycophants who were afraid of them. Katrina was certainly different!

Willa slipped around the house so she wouldn't be seen. *Like Puck,* she thought, and tears gathered in her eyes. Would she ever see Puck again? See any of them again? When Sean and Diana returned, would anyone tell her?

But it had been months, and no one had contacted her about anything. It did cross her mind that since she'd not told them where she was, it would have hindered them. But they could have asked her family. They could have . . .

In the next second she remembered Nicky's words, and the tears gathered again.

She sat down under a big oak tree that she'd always liked, drew her knees up and put her head down. *It's time,* she told herself. Time to stop wallowing in misery and *do* something with her life. She was young; she had money. She . . .

When Willa heard a noise, she looked up. Katrina was coming toward her. Under her arms were two rolled-up rubber mats.

She didn't look at Willa, just unrolled the mats on a flat, grassy area. She stood on one, then looked at Willa as though to tell her to take the other one.

"I don't — I mean, I can't —" Willa began.

The woman wasn't a nanny for no reason. She gave Willa a look that almost made her say, "Yes, miss."

Willa took her place on the other mat.

Katrina put her legs in a wide stance and raised her arms. "We will salute the sun."

For the next hour, Willa tried her best to follow. It wasn't easy. She wasn't used to her newly acquired weight and she had trouble balancing. And the stretching just plain *hurt.*

But the good part was that for one whole hour she didn't think of her misery. Didn't think how she would soon have to face her siblings and father.

Katrina rang a little bell and they were done. She handed Willa a refillable bottle of water. Katrina took another one and for a minute they sat in silence on the mats.

"I despise your family," Katrina said.

"Me too."

"They say such terrible things about you that I thought you must be a good human being."

"I am," Willa said, and that made her feel better. "So why are you working for them?"

Katrina took a moment to consider before

she answered. “I was a yoga instructor. I had my own studio and held classes. I fell madly in love with one of my students and we married. I got pregnant instantly.”

She took a breath and Willa saw her blink back tears. “Six months later, his heart exploded. He was fine one minute and the next he was dead. The shock made me miscarry.”

“Oh,” was all Willa could say.

“I sold my studio. I couldn’t bear people’s pity. I wanted something new and I heard of this job and . . .” She shrugged. “Your brother thinks sex with me is part of what he’s paying for. I’m handing in my notice right after the funeral. Maybe you’ll give me a ride.”

“To where?”

“Italy? Greece? Wherever.”

Willa gave her first smile in a long time. “Me too. I plan to go down the rabbit hole.”

“Pistol in hand?”

Willa actually laughed. “How do you possibly know about that?”

“It’s a legendary Willa story. One of many that they have. They . . .” She stopped.

“It’s okay. I know what they say.”

“If you actually did, you might take a shotgun to them.” She stood up. “My break is over. Dear little Martin has probably broken a dozen valuable artifacts and I will be blamed for them all." She started rolling up her mat, then halted. "They're planning to do anything they can to get you to give them money. If they're nice to you, that's why. Nelson even bought you a gift." She finished rolling the mat. "Just so you know, the diamonds aren't real."

Willa rolled up her mat, put the straps around it and handed it to Katrina. "Thank you for this. It was good to get my mind off my own life for a while. And I'm sorry about your husband and . . ." She couldn't finish.

"Me too. I better go." Mats under her arms, she backed away. "Prepare to be wooed and courted."

"My checkbook and I will be eagerly awaiting them."

Laughing, Katrina ran toward the house.

Willa turned to go back to sitting under the tree, but she no longer felt like it. So her siblings were broke. And poor, pitiful, butt-of-all-their-jokes Willa was the only one who had anything left. How interesting.

She started back toward the house but instead turned away. When she was a child she'd played the solitary game of What if I Owned this Place? She used to keep sketch-books full of garden plans and she filled binders with decorating ideas. *Wonder if they're still here*? she thought.

When she had just enough time to get ready for dinner, she returned to the house. She had a black dress, but it was now too small. Instead, she wore black cotton trousers and a red sweatshirt with rhinestones across the top. Byon said it was the ugliest shirt he'd ever seen. "I love it! You should wear it to church and tell me what everyone says."

She didn't wear it to church or to anywhere else, but she did keep it. Byon had said he loved it and that was enough for her.

If what Katrina had said about the siblings was true, she'd know as soon as she saw them. When she walked into the dining room, saw their eyes widen in horror, but they said nothing, she knew Katrina was right. She smiled warmly at them. Their father didn't join them. He had dinner in his room.

"He's too distraught over Mother's death to talk to anyone," Niall said.

He'd better hire a food taster, Willa thought, but said, "I can understand that. They loved each other so very much."

Beatrice nearly choked on her drink. Their parents rarely spoke to each other.

At dinner, Willa was the center of attention. They asked about her life, her friends.

Thanks to Katrina's warning, Willa knew how to answer them. She said she was very happy and planning to buy a country estate. In Surrey maybe. Or Kent. "Maybe I should go to Devon."

Throughout the dinner, she smiled at their offers of financial advice, at the use of their London apartments.

After dinner, Nelson slipped her a bracelet. Niall gave her tasteful little earrings in a Tiffany box. She'd put money on it that they didn't come from that store.

She almost made it upstairs before Beatrice caught her. "I know we've had our differences in the past, but we're sisters and we love each other." She held out an old ring box. "Our dear mother gave this to me but I want you to have it."

Willa took the box but she didn't open it until she was in her room. The ring inside took her breath away. Memories flooded her. She and her mother were in the garden, Willa holding the basket while her mother deadheaded roses.

"Can't you hold it still?" her mother snapped, then jerked her hand back as a thorn pricked her. "See what you made me do? Now look, my ring is dirty." She took it off and handed it to her daughter.

Willa held it up to the light. Sapphires and diamonds. "It's so beautiful."

"I guess. It's owned by your father's family and goes to the oldest daughter. He has no sisters so I got it."

"Oldest?" Willa said. "That's me. Do I get it?"

"Are you hoping I will die so you can get a *ring*?"

"No, I meant —"

"Go away. Put it in my jewelry box, and I better never see you touch it."

Beatrice had been given *that* ring. The one that was supposed to go to the oldest daughter. But her mother had given it to the younger one.

Willa stretched out on the bed and stared up at the ceiling. She bloody well was *not* going to give her siblings any money. She'd lied about buying some money-eating estate somewhere. And then what? Live there alone?

What am I going to do? she wondered. Go to Italy with Katrina? Hey! Maybe she'd buy a yoga studio and she and Katrina would run it.

Smiling at that absurdity, she opened her computer. Actually, the idea of owning a business, a shop maybe, in some village appealed to her. It would be right on the high street. She'd meet people. Go to church on Sundays. Join the WI and learn to make jam. Maybe she'd sell the jam in her shop.

No, she thought. She needed to get a business that didn't make a person fat.

She wandered about the internet, then suddenly halted. There was a wellness center for sale in what looked like a really cute village. Actually, it was a nice-sized town. The center had yoga classes!

When the sun came up, Willa was still reading and making notes.

TWELVE

"And you did it?" Sara asked. "It worked out like you thought it would? No, wait. Tell it in order."

Meena looked up. "Have you ever seen traits in a blood relative that you hate but later find out that you have?"

"You mean like heart disease?" Sara asked. "Only without the heart."

Meena laughed. "Just like that. My siblings will do anything to get what they want. It turns out that I have some of the same traits. I did something awful."

"Please tell us," Sara said. "Please."

Meena laughed at her tone. "I started by lying to them. Hours after my mother's funeral, I saw that they were going to incessantly hound me for money. I had to stop it! I faked an email from my bank that said my account was overdrawn. I told them I had no money and asked if they'd help me."

"Bet they stopped being nice," Kate said.

"They certainly did! Beatrice asked for the ring back but I told her I'd sent it to the lawyer to settle some accounts. Invitations to stay in their London apartments were withdrawn."

"You learned lying quickly," Jack said.

"I'd had some good teachers. Family and friends. The next day, Katrina quit her job with my brother, and she and I drove away together." Meena's eyes twinkled. "My brothers said they'd always known I was a lesbian."

"And you started your business." Sara sounded proud of her.

"I did, but not as I'd imagined it," Meena said. "My fantasy was to be in a partnership, to be an equal with anyone who worked for me."

"Someone has to be the boss," Jack said.

"Yes, they do," Meena said. "I realized that in an instant. When I walked into the Wellness Center, I instantly hated it. I could see why it failed. It was for people wearing Prada, not clients who were overweight and ate pork pies by the dozen. There are moments in your life when everything changes, and that was one of them. I turned to Katrina to ask what she thought. But I closed my mouth. I realized that if I started consulting, it would never end. I'd have to ask her approval on everything."

"As you did with Nicky and Byon," Kate said.

"And Nadine and Clive. I didn't know I was fed up with it, but I was. I said, 'We're going to gut this place.' Katrina said, 'There's a lot we can use. Those sofas are —' I said, 'No. It all goes. I have a different idea for my studio.' Katrina hesitated, then said, 'You're the boss, Willa.' "

"And that set the tone forever," Sara said.

"Yes." Meena smiled. "And that's the moment I changed my name. No more Willing Willa or a willow that bends with every breeze."

Kate motioned to the room. "It looks like you succeeded. Your business is called Renewal?"

Meena smiled broadly. "If you were English, you'd know that there are Renewal studios all over the country. We offer every imaginable health service. All my trainers go through rigorous schooling. We — Sorry. You don't need to hear the sales pitch." She looked down at the tea table. "Our headquarters are in my family home. I bought it."

"You must tell us how that happened!" Sara said. "Did you put ants in their beds?"

"Did you see them again?" Kate asked.

"I didn't see or hear from them for eight whole years, not until I went back for my father's funeral."

"How many studios did you own by then?" Sara asked.

"About a dozen, I think."

"Were they impressed?" Kate asked.

"They didn't *know,*" Meena said. "With the name change, they didn't realize I was the owner. Oh! I wanted to arrive in a limo. I wanted to smash their faces in my success. But before that, I went to see a couple who'd worked there for years. I didn't want them to think I'd turned into a snob, so I stopped at their house to say hello. And truthfully, I was scared to see my siblings."

"Afraid they'd turn you back into the old Willa?" Sara asked.

"Yes, I was, but the couple couldn't get over how I'd changed. They said I wasn't the same person. They hadn't heard that I ran a business. I asked how their children were." She looked at Kate. "Their daughter had become an estate agent."

"Good choice," Kate said.

"In my case, very good. The man let it slip that he knew our family home was to go on the market the day after the funeral."

"Without your consent?" Kate asked. "Is that allowed under English law?"

"No, it isn't. It was assumed that I'd agree." Meena was smiling in a secret way. "In a flash, I came up with a plan. They called their daughter, she came over, and I made a low cash offer for the house and property. Then I told her what I had in mind. When it was all in place, I went shopping for clothes, and I bought some cheap hair dye."

"Back to Willa the Unwanted," Sara said.

"Yes. It was hard to slump in that position of *I Hate the World* but I managed it. I rented a cheap car and drove to the family home."

"And how were your siblings?" Sara asked.

"Eight years of hard living had taken a toll on them. They looked bad and they were frantic to sell the house. Beatrice started out by threatening me and I obligingly looked scared." Meena's smile was getting wider by the second.

"They were desperate to get me to agree because the agent had told them they already had a cash offer on the house. But they had only twenty-four hours to say yes or no. When they were told the company that wanted the house was Renewal, my siblings said that such a rich company could afford to pay more. They wanted to counter for a lot more money."

Meena picked up a chocolate brownie off the table and ate it. "I said they weren't being fair, that the house was falling down."

"I love this," Kate said. "My kind of espionage. Was the agent there?"

"Oh yes. She looked at me to nod yes or no at every question. Three times she stepped into the hall to fake a telephone call, but really she was looking at me. I made thumbs-up or -down behind the huge dress I was wearing."

"This is my fantasy deal," Kate said in envy.

"How much did you end at?" Sara asked.

"For my low offer," Meena said in pride.

Kate leaned back on the couch and sighed in satisfaction. "Less commission for the agent, but cash and a quick sale made it up to her."

"Everything was done quickly," Meena said. "I'd written a check and papers were signed."

"When did you tell them?" Sara asked.

"Late the next morning. I let them awake to champagne to celebrate. They needed it because the will had been read. Our father had left us each a pittance. He'd spent everything on the upkeep of the house."

"So you got a house that had been renovated." Kate was smiling in wonder. "And it was repaired with the money your siblings would have inherited."

Meena nodded. "I kept up the charade until the agent called to say that the sale had been finalized. At 2:00 p.m., Katrina arrived with three cars full of my officers." She looked at Jack. "They are a rather attractive lot."

"Understatement," Jack said.

"I got out of my disguise, put on something *very* expensive, then went downstairs to meet them. My sibs were there, smiling in triumph. They thought their money problems were over forever. My brothers were hitting on my officers." Meena was smiling in pleasure at the memory.

"I guess they were shocked when they found out the truth," Sara said.

"I'll never forget Beatrice saying, '*You* own Renewal? *You?*' "

They were silent for a moment as they imagined the scene.

"What's happened since then?" Sara asked.

"My siblings had spent everything, and one by one they came to me asking for jobs. But they believed they should be given all because their sister owned the company."

"Entitlement!" Sara sounded bitter. "One of the things I hate most in the world. 'You

have to give it to me because I'm *me*.' "
She grimaced. "Hope you rejected them."

"I did. However, remember obnoxious little Martin, my nephew? He came to me right after he graduated from uni and asked for a job. I gave him one but made him work his way up. He's an executive now, and I dearly love him."

"What about *you*?" Kate asked. "Your personal life?"

"Fifteen years ago, I married the son of the lawyer who handled all our deals. We have two children, a boy and a girl, and David handles all business for me."

"You are loved," Sara said softly.

"I am."

"And your brothers and sister?" Jack asked.

Meena shrugged. "They get by. Martin helps his father. The others . . . ? I don't really keep up with them."

"Still have the ring?" Sara asked.

"I do. I wear it often."

For a few moments, they sat in silence.

"What now?" Sara asked. "Will you go back to Oxley Manor with us? This time you *can* arrive in a limo."

Meena leaned back. "I've had a lot of time to think about those days when I practically lived with those people. I was so young and naive, so lonely, that I looked at them in awe. But the truth is that we were all misfits."

"We've seen that," Sara said. "Nadine . . ."

"Lower-class origins, upper-class education. Her accent was like the Queen's while her father's was barely intelligible. Nadine didn't fit in anywhere."

"And Byon," Kate said.

"Talented, probably from a poor background — we never knew for sure. We have no idea how he afforded school. Nicky was the saddest of us all. Disliked by his father, burdened with a rotting house that he'd been told he had to hold on to no matter what."

"Do you think he loved Diana?" Kate asked.

"Lord, no! They weren't even friends. But they both wanted Oxley Manor and were willing to do whatever was needed to obtain it. And Nicky would have done *anything* to get his father's approval."

"Murder?" Sara asked.

"Oh yes," Meena said. "But not Diana. He needed her."

"What about Sean?" Jack asked.

"He hated us all. I can't imagine why he stayed there. Even I knew he had job offers. Byon used to joke and say, 'He actually loves us.' But of course we knew he didn't."

"What do you think actually happened to them?" Sara asked.

"I have no idea," Meena said, "but I don't think Sean and Diana left *together,* not as a couple. They didn't match. Sean liked women who did their hair and makeup. Put together. Diana was pretty but in a natural way. Sean always treated her like she was his younger brother. We laughed about it."

"Did he — ?" Sara began, but a knock on the door stopped her.

A young woman came in carrying half a dozen heavily loaded shopping bags. She looked only at Meena. "I *hate* these things! I had to go to Oxfam for half of this. The shoes need to be disinfected. You're going to swelter with this padding on, and —"

"This is my stylist, Felicity," Meena said loudly.

"Sorry, I didn't see anyone else here. Can you talk her out of this?"

Sara was smiling. "If it's what I think it's for, I encourage her."

"I'm going back to being the Willa they remember."

It was time to leave. The three stood up and went to the door. Sara turned back. "So how do we treat you? Have we met you or not?"

"Not," Meena said firmly. "That way I can tell you my new story."

"The one they expect of you?" Kate asked. "Cheated out of your inheritance by your family, now living in a third floor walk-up, working at Sainsbury's, no friends." Sara was smiling.

"You should have written it for me," Meena said.

"Send me your text number and I will," Sara said.

Jack said, "You're assuming someone will ask. No one's asked me what I do for a living."

"Good point," Meena said. "I'll just be Poorwilla and that will be enough."

Jack opened the door.

"What about Clive?" Kate asked. "Puck said that at that time, you were quite, uh, taken with him. I know from experience that the past can sometimes swallow a person."

Meena pulled a huge ugly dress from a bag. "Along with Nicky's last words to me, I remember Clive's. *'Of all the things I want in life, you are at the bottom.'* " When she looked at them, her eyes were scary with anger and hatred.

Kate and Sara swallowed. They nodded goodbyes, left the room and started down the hall.

Jack spoke first. "I'm surprised *he* isn't dead."

"Think she's capable of murder?" Sara asked.

"Oh yes," Kate said.

"Hundred percent," Jack said. "In fact, I'm going to lock my bedroom door." He looked at Kate. "You better stay with me tonight."

"Hold your breath if you think —"

"What about me?" Sara said. "I'm all alone on a floor below. I need protection."

"I pity anyone who tries to tangle with you," Jack said. "Last week your right cross nearly tore my shoulder out of its socket." As he held the front door open for her, he looked at Kate over Sara's head. He didn't have to say anything. *Protect Sara* was between them.

Thirteen

Jack was driving them back from the inn.

"Wow," Kate said. "Just plain wow. I am *very* glad I never joined a club when I was in school. They seem to eat you alive."

From the back, Sara said, "You didn't join anything because your mother made you go home every weekend." Sara and Kate's mother were *not* friends. "There wasn't time for anything else."

"Then I guess she saved me," Kate said.

Jack looked at Sara in the rearview mirror. "Round One to young Medlar."

"But —" Sara began.

Jack raised his voice. "If a ladder falls in a stable and no one hears it, does it make a sound?"

"Explain," Sara said.

"I climbed up the ladder to the loft, but when I went to go down, the ladder was on the floor. I didn't hear it fall."

"So who did it?" Sara asked.

"Wasn't this when you met Nadine?" Kate asked. "Maybe she moved it."

"I can't see an elegant lady like her lifting a ladder. You need to balance it. Doubt if she has the experience."

"Ladies can do lots of things," Kate said. "She could have —"

"Who left the gate open?" Sara cut them off. "Kate, you said the gate was open."

She turned in the seat. "I didn't tell *you.*"

"I did," Jack said cheerfully. "Had lots of time while you were chasing after the banker."

Sara was looking at her phone. "There's no mention on the company website that the owner of Renewal has a husband and children."

"Could have left that out for privacy," Kate said. "English papers blur the faces of celebrity kids."

"Any David in charge of finances?" Jack asked.

"Yes, but there's nothing about him personally."

"Think she's telling a fib?" Kate asked. "Running a business takes a lot of time."

"With her anger-driven ambition, maybe she didn't have time for a family," Jack said.

"Maybe she's here for revenge," Sara said. "Or she needs to *see* the past. She can't release what happened to her until she fully remembers it."

Jack said, "Like you when you moved back to where you'd grown up? Girl from the wrong side of the tracks makes good? Rubs their noses in it?"

"Jack!" Kate said.

Sara was laughing. "Exactly like that. Whatever their reasons, they all seem to be full of anger."

"Except Byon." He caught eyes with Sara. "And no, I'm not giving in to your idea that prison is a haven for writers." He drove through the gate to Oxley Manor. "So what do we have so far? Ladder, gate —"

"Skeleton," Kate said.

"And enough hate to set off bombs," Sara said. "I don't believe your Puck is as innocent as she seems. She's spent her lifetime hiding from her hideous mother. That kind of rage builds up."

"Like a teakettle," Kate said.

"And soon it begins to whistle," Sara added.

Jack groaned. "You two! We could still turn this over to the police. I'd tell them I was trespassing in the forbidden zone, fell through the hole, then —"

"Got the rope ladder and investigated," Kate said.

"Then no one would ever know who killed Sean. I'm growing rather fond of him."

"You like him because he looks like pretty boy here," Kate said.

"Thank you." Jack smiled at her.

"I didn't mean it as a compliment. What you've done to poor Nadine is rotten. She thinks you —"

"Look!" Sara said loudly.

There was a very nice dark green car parked in front of the house. Standing by it was Nadine and a young woman who looked enough like her for them to know she was the daughter, Teddy. They were both frowning. Beside them was a large man, smiling fondly at them. The women had his jawline and they were set hard.

"Now we know why the English chose a bulldog to represent them," Sara muttered.

"Jag," Jack said. "If anyone wants to know. Eighty grand at least. I do admire that family's taste in cars."

"Looks like you're going to get to talk to the dad all about it." Sara waved, and the man smiled back. The two women didn't look away from each other.

"She won't win," Kate said under her breath. "Mothers *always* win."

"Not always," Sara snapped. "Sometimes —"

Jack's look cut her off. "One war at a time."

They got out of the car and started toward the group, but the young woman stormed inside, Nadine close behind her.

That left the man alone. He was staring up at the house.

Jack and Kate stayed in the background while Sara went to him. "Lovely, isn't it?"

"Not like I remember it. I was afraid it was going to fall down on my daughter's head." His colloquial English accent was very heavy.

"You must have some fond memories of your time here."

He chuckled. "Thelma Thompson and I broke the glass elephant right here in this house."

Behind them, Jack wiggled his eyebrows at Kate, and she elbowed him to behave.

"Don't believe I know her," Sara said. "Did she live here?"

"Who?"

"Miss Thompson."

The man stopped smiling. "Who are you?" he demanded.

"Sara Medlar. I'm staying at the hotel."

"Then you oughta go back to it." He stepped toward her in a menacing way. "This is private property."

Kate put her hand on Jack's arm to keep him from stepping between them.

"This place belongs to the Renlows. Nicky will —"

After a few blinks, Sara said, "I'm here to sell Bertie a horse. Fastest one I've ever seen."

The man's face changed to a smile. "He'll buy it then." He tilted his head toward her and winked. "And I'll lend him the money, like I always do. One day, I'm gonna collect, then Oxley Manor will be mine. I'll give it to my daughter as a wedding present."

"Who is she marrying?"

"Nicky, of course. She's gonna be a lady. I'm hungry." He walked into the house.

Jack and Kate went to Sara.

"Now we know who paid Bertie's bills," Jack said.

Kate said, "He seems to think his granddaughter is his daughter and that Nicky is still alive."

Sara gave a smile of satisfaction. "His mind is like having a living video of the past. Come on, let's go find him and ask a lot of questions."

"And encourage that poor man's mental problems?" Kate had slipped into what Jack called her "school marm mode."

"I prefer to think of it as letting him live in a world where he was happiest," Sara said. "He had wealth and power, and hope that the future for him and his beloved daughter was going to be nothing but happiness. It was a time before death and disappointment shattered everything he'd worked for and dreamed of. A place where —"

Kate put her hands over her ears. "Okay. You win."

"She always does," Jack muttered.

"So let's go." Sara ran into the house.

Kate looked at Jack. "You coming?"

"I'm going to take in the luggage."

"Don't you need a key to get into the car?"

"Puh-lease."

"Didn't mean to insult your criminal abilities. See you later." She ran after her aunt.

Jack didn't say that he'd noticed the young woman hadn't locked her car. He opened the trunk and pulled out the cases. The misery on the young woman's face bothered him. Nadine had a look of "please forgive me" but it was Teddy who appeared to be in pain. He thought it would be better if she weren't left alone. He hadn't said anything to Kate and Sara because he didn't want to be accused of playing "rescuing hero."

There was a woman cleaning the hallway

and Jack lifted the two suitcases in question. She smiled warmly at him and said, "Josephine."

He'd seen the sign on the door and knew it was at the top of the house. It was the only one of the former servants' quarters that had been renovated.

When he knocked, there was no answer. He set the cases down and was about to leave when he heard a sob. Then another. There was no way he could walk away from that. As Kate would say, "Leaving a sobbing woman would make you lose your hero badge."

The door opened easily. It was a small room, the walls painted with murals of a summer's day. The big, canopied bed took up most of the space. Sprawled across it was Nadine's daughter, her face buried in a pillow as she hid the tears that were making her body shake.

He sat down on the edge of the bed.

She felt the motion. "Whoever you are, go away!"

"I'm a good listener," Jack said softly.

She turned just enough to peek at him. "Who are you? You work here?"

"No. I'm a guest."

"I'm . . ." She put her face back into the pillow. "I don't know who I am. My father isn't really . . . I mean, my mother jilted my —" She cried harder.

"She seems to love you a lot." There wasn't any sympathy in Jack's voice.

"How could you understand? You're . . . You're an *American*!"

"True," he said mildly. "Any problems we have, we shoot it out. But then, we don't have disagreements with each other or our parents. And nobody jumps into bed with anybody else. You English have the market cornered on passion. No, wait! You are a bunch of coldhearted, unfeeling —"

She turned on her back. "You are reinforcing all we think of Americans."

"That we *care*?"

"That you have no sense of boundaries. You tell your life stories as soon as you meet."

"Better than crying into a pillow in secret," Jack said. "So what did your mother actually do?"

"I . . . She . . ."

Jack pulled half a dozen tissues out of the box on the side table and handed them to her.

She wiped her eyes and blew her nose. "I must look awful."

"A real troll."

She sort of smiled.

"My father — my beloved father who I adored . . ."

"Yes?"

"He . . ." She sniffed. "He isn't my father. I'm not related to him." Her voice was rising. "Granny isn't mine. None of his family belongs to me." Tears were beginning to flow again.

Jack couldn't bear it. She needed all the comfort he could give. He leaned back against the headboard and extended an arm in invitation.

"I don't know you and I shouldn't . . ." She went to him, put her head on his chest, and he held her with both arms. She cried some more, wetting his shirt, and his hold on her was snug.

"So who is your father?" he asked softly.

"A nobody. He cleaned the stables. He left my mother as soon as she told him she was expecting *me.* He didn't want me. He ran away with some dreadful woman. They —"

Jack had to work to keep calm. "Are you saying your father is Sean Thorpe?"

"Yes, that's the name."

"But he and your mother greatly disliked each other."

"Grow up!"

"Right." Jack glanced at the door. He

wanted to run to tell Kate and Sara. "Tell me everything."

Teddy moved away and blew her nose again. "I don't want to know all of it. Mother tried to tell me but I couldn't bear to listen."

"Are you upset because you don't think you still have the right to be called a 'lady'?"

"What a snob thing to say! I'm angry because I've been lied to for my entire life. She could have told my *real* father her situation. He would have saved her. He would have rescued us from a life of poverty. He was a man of honor and —"

"I don't think Nadine's father would have allowed you to live in poverty."

Teddy waved her hand. "That's beside the point. That man left her! Abandoned her. If she'd told me that long ago, I would have understood. Can you imagine what it's like to know your own father didn't *want* you?"

"Yes," Jack said. "Vividly. Did Nadine tell you when she and Sean first got together?"

"She tried." Teddy held out her hand and he gave her more tissues. "She said it was love at first sight. No! It was passion at first sight. But she said she couldn't tell anyone. I don't know why."

"They would have ripped her apart," Jack

said. "Like they did to Willa over her lawyer."

"What does that mean?"

"Nothing. Did she mention riding lessons?"

"I don't remember. Oh yes. She said it took months to make Gramps come up with the idea of giving her riding lessons."

Jack remembered Nadine saying about Puck, *She believed she knew everything but she knew less than half of it.* Looked like that was true! "Can your mother ride a horse?"

"Absolutely not! Horses terrify her."

"And you?"

"Won gymkhanas and trials. I was thinking of trying out for the Olympics, but —" She frowned at him. "Why are you asking me all these questions?"

"Just curious. Bet you can drive cars too."

"I've won a few rallies." She glared at him. "Who are you and why are you here?"

For a moment, Jack drew a blank. He couldn't think of a single thing that he could tell her. His mind was full of visions of the skeleton. He couldn't very well say *If your father did try to run away, it's quite possible that your mother murdered him.*

"Well?" she said. "I've just confided in

you, so tell me what you're trying hard not to say."

Perceptive little beauty, aren't you? he thought. He needed to change the subject. "What's wrong with your grandfather?"

"Early stages of dementia. He'll be fine for an hour, then suddenly start demanding that his secretary give him reports on the day's orders. He —" Her eyes widened. "We left him *alone.*" She scurried off the bed and grabbed the doorknob. "Come on, let's find him." She looked him up and down. "And don't hurt him if he gets nasty."

"Had to leave my six-shooter at home. Airport security greatly hinders us Americans."

With a look of disgust, she flung the door open and nearly tripped over her suitcases. "And put these inside!" she ordered. He heard her run down the hall, then the stairs.

Jack got off the bed. "Might have done you good to have a stableman as your father," he mumbled, then put the suitcases inside the room. He paused in the hallway. If Nadine's father knew the house, he might go upstairs. Especially if he used to "break the glass elephant" with someone who wasn't part of the family. A pretty maid, maybe?

He headed up to the top of the house.

■ ■ ■ ■

When Jack saw that the upstairs was empty, he went down and met Sara coming out of her room. She had on one of her simple dresses that probably cost what he paid his workmen for a week. "Have you seen Nadine's father?"

"He's with her. We're meeting downstairs for cocktails, and you need to change. I'm pretty sure Byon wants you to sing for him."

"Teddy's father is Sean."

Sara gasped. "Oh. Right. The man Nadine hated. Makes sense. She sure was good at keeping it a secret." Sara's head came up. "Think she told him the night of the party?"

"Then when he said, 'You're on your own, baby,' she bashed him over the head with a rock?"

"Something like that. Have you been with her daughter all this time?"

"Most of the time. She was a mess."

"And you healed her?"

Jack's lips tightened. "I *listened* to her. You two do the same with the old man?"

"We couldn't catch him. He wanted to see the changes in the house and gave us the slip."

"Where's Kate?"

"Getting dressed. You brought your tux, didn't you?"

"Of course," Jack said. "When do you think Meena will show up?"

"Remember that the name's back to Willa," Sara reminded him. "I imagine her hair will take some time. And makeup removal will take hours."

"She had on makeup today?"

"Aren't you funny," Sara said. "Go change into your tux." She smoothed his shirt collar. "Drive Byon crazy with the beauty of you."

Laughing, Jack kissed her cheek. "I'll be down as soon as I can."

"I forgot to ask what you thought of Nadine's daughter."

"Gorgeous. She rides horses like her father and drives cars like her mother."

"Oh." Sara's face fell. "She is quite pretty."

"And spoiled and demanding and doesn't appreciate what she has."

Sara cheered up. "Ah, too bad."

Jack shook his head, then started down the hall. "But exciting," he said over his shoulder. "She could give a man a good run. While it lasted. Short-term heaven."

Grimacing, Sara went down to the drawing room. Nadine and Byon were sitting together on the couch, their heads close, and talking privately. *Wonder if I could have the room bugged?* she thought. *I'd like to hear what they're saying.* They nodded to Sara but didn't stop their conversation.

Like Byon, Clive was wearing a tuxedo. He was at the drinks table and she went to him.

"Nothing has changed," Clive said. "The top echelon is together and I'm the butler. What would you like to have?"

"Gin and tonic," she said.

"How English. Sure you don't want an appletini?"

"Don't make me gag." She was looking at Nadine and Byon. "What do you think they're talking about?"

"Money, probably."

"Then they should include you, the banker," Sara said.

Clive smiled. "Thank you." He handed her a drink. "It feels odd after all these years of working *with* people to suddenly be excluded. And worse, it's making anger and resentment rise up inside me. I want to pour bourbon over Byon's head."

"And light it on fire?"

"Of course not," Clive said, but he was laughing.

"Have you met Nadine's daughter or seen her father?"

"No." They were at the far side of the room, their voices quiet. "Mr. Howland! He was sanity in the midst of chaos. The earl was spending madly, and Nicky was brooding over the futility of his life, then here came Mr. Howland, loud and giving orders."

"Did you know that he paid Bertie's bills?"

Clive nearly choked on his drink. "I knew money came from somewhere but . . ." He paused. "Mr. Howland wanted to buy Oxley for Nadine. He probably thought Nicky and his title came with it."

"Spot on!" Sara said.

"Didn't get it, did he? So what's he trying to rule now?"

"Nothing," she said. "He's as daffy as a drunken bullfrog."

"Odd phrase but descriptive. Probably wore his mind out with his schemes. Back then, there were whole minutes when I felt sorry for Nadine. What's her daughter like?"

"Jack spent time with her, says she rides as well as her father."

"Must have come from the viscount as Nadine *hated* horses. I still remember her complaints about Thorpe. She despised him! At the time, I thought her treatment of him was part of why he ran away. If he did. Maybe she . . ."

"Murdered him?" Sara finished for him. He didn't answer as his eyes went to the doorway. Young Teddy, her arm looped through her grandfather's, was there. She had on a slinky red dress with nothing on under it. You could see the indentation of her navel.

Clive gave a low whistle. "*How* old is she?"

"She was born six months after the party when her father disappeared." Quickly, Sara turned away. She wouldn't have dropped such news on Clive if there wasn't a mirror over the fireplace. If she'd been looking at him, he might have controlled his expression, but with her back to him, he didn't need to. Sara saw his look of shock — and it appeared to be genuine.

Cautiously, she greeted Mr. Howland, and he seemed to be back in the present.

"Lovely what they've done to the place, isn't it?" he said as they stepped to one side of the room.

Sara was facing him so she could see the others interact. Teddy seemed to be sulking, with her lower lip stuck out. She wasn't looking directly at her mother, but Sara felt that she wanted to speak to her. Whatever Jack had done, he seemed to have calmed the girl down somewhat.

Mr. Howland was waiting for an answer.

"Sorry. I missed that."

"I was saying what a splendid job this woman, Isabella, has done. Wish I could meet her. It's hard to believe that at one time I wanted to own this monstrosity."

"And Nicky," she said.

Mr. Howland looked startled, then laughed. "Poor Nicky. Nadine would have made mincemeat out of him."

"He was more suited to Diana?"

"She was the boss he needed. She ordered him about like the do-nothing he was." He looked around the room. "Diana would have done this — if she'd had the money."

"Where was she going to get financing?" Sara asked.

"She was planning to go into breeding horses."

"Not racing?"

"No. Too much expense. It was a secret, but one of the mares was pregnant by North Star. Ever hear of him?"

"No. 'Fraid not."

"It was kind of like crossing a Lamborghini with a Ferrari. I don't know how she managed it."

"What happened to the mare?"

Mr. Howland shrugged. "No idea. After Thorpe and Diana ran away together, everything stopped."

"What about Nadine?" she asked softly. "And the baby?"

Pain distorted Mr. Howland's face. It was like watching a play as Sara saw him change from rational to something feral. He turned toward the others. "Where's Bertie?" he bellowed. "I want one of his cigars. And I need to tell Nicky I have a car for him. He'll like it. It's fast." He stepped away from Sara.

"Damn!" she muttered. She'd missed the little window of opportunity to find out more of what he knew. Was he there the night Sean and Diana disappeared? What was his opinion of what had happened? Did he — ?

She was glad when Jack and Kate appeared in the doorway. They were laughing, probably at one of the many jokes they shared.

"There he is!" came a woman's voice.

Sara turned to see pretty Teddy looking at Jack. It didn't take a psychic to see that she was trying to annoy her mother. The sprayed-on dress, the blond hair caressing her face. She was what all mothers told their daughters not to be.

"He's the man who saved me." Teddy's voice filled the big room.

Everyone was mesmerized by her as she slunk across the room, the fabric of her dress clinging indecently.

"My darling hero." When she reached Jack, she slipped an arm around his neck and kissed him full on the mouth.

Jack didn't pull away, but Kate did.

Sara got in one step before all hell broke loose.

Like the bulldog he resembled, Mr. Howland went charging. "You bloody bastard," he yelled. "She's your daughter."

In one moment, he swept Teddy aside and went after Jack, head down, charging like an enraged bull.

Jack was fast and sidestepped the charge — which meant that Mr. Howland was going toward the wall. If he hit it, his head would be broken like a pumpkin.

Sara, Jack and Kate had spent a lot of time boxing, and they were used to punches and jabs that they had to duck.

Sara dropped her drink to the carpet and made three leaps to reach the man to grab him from behind. Kate was at his right side and she threw herself onto him, pinning his arm down. Jack put himself in front of the man.

They managed to stop him just as he was mere inches from ramming into Jack. But saving him didn't stop his rage. "I'll kill you," he yelled, and went after Jack.

Sara was behind him, her arms around his waist, her head on his back, but her light weight wasn't hindering him. Kate had his arm locked down, but he still went after Jack.

It was Nadine who stopped him. She got through the melee to stand in front of him. "He's not Sean," she yelled. "He's Jack. You don't know him. Not. Sean." She had to repeat it three times before it registered.

Yet again, he switched. The energy left him. He stood upright. In the present again.

Sara and Kate stepped away, but Jack stayed where he was, ready to take the man down if necessary.

Mr. Howland looked at Jack. "I'm sorry," he whispered. "I'm —" The man looked like he might die of embarrassment.

"How about if I take you to your room?" Jack's voice was kind and Mr. Howland nodded.

"I'm sorry," the older man said as they went up the stairs. His face was still red. "My mind comes and goes. I try to control it, but . . ."

"It's all right," Jack said. "We all have problems."

"A big, good-looking young man like you?"

"Me most of all," Jack said. "I look like a

man your daughter hated."

Mr. Howland gave a snort of laughter. "Far from it. She . . ." He took a breath. "I thought she was going to kill herself after he left. I would have lost her and my beautiful granddaughter both. Here. I'm in this room."

It was the Napoleon Room.

"They see me as a failed ruler," he said as he fumbled to find the key. "I lock it because I don't trust any of them. They're all liars and thieves."

Jack pulled a penknife out of his pocket. "Let me try."

"You *are* him. I liked him a lot. The son I never had. Before I found out what he did to my daughter, that is. Dropped her like garbage." He was looking down the hall. "This place is bringing back memories."

"About breaking elephants?" Jack was working the door lock.

"Oh yeah. I remember that night so clearly. They were arguing."

"Sounds like they were always arguing," Jack said.

"No. This was different. She was . . . desperate, that's what she was. And he . . . Well, he didn't care at all."

"You mean Nadine and Sean? She told him she was pregnant and he didn't *care*?"

Jack didn't like hearing that.

"No, not him. They were going to run away together. Nadine was packed and ready to go. But he didn't show up."

Jack got the door open. "So who did you hear arguing? Was it Diana and Nicky?"

"Maybe." Mr. Howland didn't move and he seemed to be thinking hard. "It was Nicky's voice but it wasn't. The woman talked like she'd learned how."

"You mean like she'd been in an accident and had rehabilitation?"

"No. Like me. How I'd sound if I studied how to speak like Prince William."

"We Americans would appreciate it if you did that. You okay to . . . ?" They both knew what he meant. Could he get ready for bed by himself?

"You think I could get something to eat?" Mr. Howland patted his big stomach.

"Sure. Mrs. Aiken —"

Mr. Howland let out a sound like a trapped pig.

Jack laughed. "I gotcha. I'll make up a tray and bring it up myself."

"Give me an hour," the man said. "Things take me longer now."

"Will do." Jack stepped aside to let him go into the big room. "One hour and I'll be back." He closed the door and was tempted to lock it. *In case he turns back into monster-mode,* Jack thought. Tomorrow he'd look at sealing Mr. Howland's windows.

As Jack headed back downstairs, he didn't see that there was a person hiding in the shadows. By the time he reached the others, everyone was there.

Fourteen

It was Kate who saw the van. She'd been watching the doorway, waiting for Jack to return from taking Mr. Howland upstairs, and she was worrying about him. When she saw a flash of light through the window, she thought, *Probably just a delivery.* Then she remembered hearing that Willa always showed up on Fridays with a van full of food. That wasn't necessary now though.

But then, Willa going back to who she was twenty-plus years ago wasn't necessary either.

Kate put her drink down and headed toward the doorway. Sara was deep into conversation with Byon, and Kate didn't want to hear it. Too much cat-fighting for her taste. Nadine was with Clive and looked quite bored.

She made it to the front door before Teddy caught up with her.

"Thank God!" Teddy said. "I wanted to

get out of there. It's like they've stepped into a time warp. If I hear them say, 'Do you remember?' one more time, I shall start screaming."

Kate wanted to get rid of the girl so she could see if it was Willa who'd arrived. "I think dinner is about to begin."

"Probably." She was looking hard at Kate. "So you're Jack's sister?"

"His friend. No relation at all."

"You two bed partners?"

Kate just looked at her, with no intention of answering.

"So you're not." Teddy was smiling. "Good to know. Who is that outside?"

"No one," Kate said. "I wonder if your grandfather is all right."

Teddy was staring at Kate. "Why do I feel that you want me to leave? Is this about Jack?"

Kate didn't answer.

"Something *is* going on, isn't it? I can feel it."

"Your mother —"

Teddy waved her hand. "Has no interest in me right now. She's trying to get Byon to introduce her to men. She needs a new husband — one with a fat bank account."

"Clive's available."

Teddy smiled. "What a nasty sense of

humor you have. He's so common he'd expect dinner on the table at six. My mother thinks the kitchen is a shortcut to the garage."

They heard a door slam.

For a moment the two young women looked at each other with the intensity of gunslingers about to draw their weapons.

Kate realized she was *not* going to be able to get rid of Teddy. Should she go back inside and wait until Willa appeared? There was no need to see her before the others did. She could —

Teddy decided the situation when she flung open the door and went outside. Kate was right behind her.

"Hello," Teddy said to the woman standing by the van. "I'm Nadine's daughter and you must be Willa. I've heard of you."

Kate stayed in the background as she looked at Willa in the outdoor lights. Gone was the sleek woman she'd met earlier. Her lashes and eyebrows had been dyed so pale they didn't seem to exist. Her clothes were faded and she looked like she'd gained fifty pounds. *Bland* was too strong a word to describe her.

"Hello," Willa said as Kate came forward.

Teddy went to the open side door of the van and looked in.

"You look horrible," Kate whispered.

"Thank you," Willa said. "My hair took hours."

"It was worth it. It's now frizzy and dirty."

"A touch of olive oil and some dark powder," Willa said proudly. "Anything new happen?"

"Mr. Howland attacked Jack because he thought he was Sean." Kate leaned forward. "Turns out Nadine and Sean were having an affair the whole time they were here." She jerked her head toward Teddy. "That's the result. Their daughter. She races cars *and* horses. And she cries all over Jack 'cause Mommy didn't tell her every private thing in her life."

Willa was blinking at Kate. "Is that jealousy or are you catty all the time?"

"I think it's always in there but it comes out in spurts."

"Sounds like a useful talent."

"It is. So what did you bring?"

"Food," Willa said. "I had Fortnum and Mason deliver everything."

"You two are chummy," Teddy said as she came around the corner of the van. "You talk like you've known each other forever."

"Kindred souls." Kate marveled at the way Willa quickly hung her head, as though she was someone who deserved to be ignored.

Teddy was staring at her. "I've seen you before."

Willa kept her head down and shook it no.

Teddy didn't give up. She moved closer to Willa and looked at her face.

"I think we should tell the others you're here," Kate said loudly.

Teddy didn't stop staring, then suddenly, a light came into her face. "Reverse Warrior," she whispered. She stepped away and went into the yoga pose. Legs apart, torso twisted, arms straight out. "Do I have it right?"

Willa gave up. She raised her head. "Right foot needs to be turned a bit. There. Now you have it."

Teddy dropped her arms and looked Willa up and down. "WTF?"

Before either of the other two women could speak, the door to the house opened and they heard Byon's voice. Behind him was everyone else.

"Keep your mouth *shut*!" Kate ordered Teddy.

"Please," Willa added.

Teddy was looking at Kate. "Only if you let me in on what's going on."

"Not on your life."

"I'll flirt so hard with Jack he won't be

able to resist. I have a bikini . . ." She held out her hand, cupped tightly, meaning the suit would fit into her palm. "And I'll sneak into his room at night. Naked."

"I hate you," Kate said.

With a smile, they turned to greet the oncoming Pack, while Willa stayed back, her head down. But in this case, she was concealing a smile.

Kate and Jack were with Sara in her bedroom. It was late but they knew they wouldn't be able to sleep. Sara was looking at photos on the screen of her camera. Kate was stretched out beside her, and Jack was in a chair.

"I'm exhausted," Kate said. "Too much food."

"Too many people," Jack said.

"Too much of everything." Sara turned her camera off and leaned back on a pillow. "I hated tonight."

"Me too," Kate said. "I wanted Willa to tell Byon to get it himself. Whatever he wanted, he expected adoring Willa to get it for him."

"And she did," Jack said.

"They handled the news of Nadine having Sean's child well," Sara said.

"You mean no one gave a flying crap,"

Jack said. "Clive snorted in a nasty way, as though it was all dirty."

"Sort of is," Kate said. "Nadine was lying to them all, sneaking around. She hated the horses but loved the rider."

"I think whatever Sean was doing in the cemetery had something to do with Nadine," Sara said. "Do we know when she told him about the child?"

"No." Jack told them what Mr. Howland had said about Sean and Nadine planning to run away together that night. "But Sean never showed up."

"What a horrible night that was!" Kate said. "They were supposed to be celebrating, but Clive dumped Willa and —"

"And Sean left pregnant Nadine alone." Sara looked at Jack. "How was Mr. Howland when you took his food up?"

"Great. Watching *The Terminator.* I wanted to stay with him. He must know a lot about cars."

Sara and Kate exchanged looks. Jack's father and grandfather and great-grandfather had been car people. Jack had spent much of his life covered in grease."

"And that night Nicky was in a *very* bad mood," Kate said. "He had to have been to tell Willa off like that."

"Willa has a temper," Sara said. "All the

toughness she has now has always been there. If Sean laughed at her and told her she was better off without them . . . She could have smashed him."

"Or shot him," Jack said. "We don't know how he was killed."

"There's more hate here than I originally thought," Sara said.

"But hate's what drives a murder, isn't it?" Kate sat up.

"No one seems to know that Sean is dead," Sara said.

"Think finding out that he didn't run away will help Nadine and Teddy?" Kate asked.

"I doubt it," Sara said. "Teddy misses her connection to people she loves. I heard her tell Nadine that she didn't know if her grandparents would continue to want her."

"They all probably know more than they think," Jack said. "Teddy was born six months after the marriage, but they had no more kids. Maybe the viscount was willing to marry a pregnant woman because he couldn't have kids."

"Good point," Sara said.

Kate yawned and scooted off the bed. "So what's on for tomorrow?"

"A sleep in," Jack said. "And I hope we meet no one."

"That means he wants to sing with Byon," Sara said.

"And watch that child, Teddy, run around in skimpy clothing."

"You do know," Jack said, "that she's just a year younger than you."

"In numbers perhaps but not in maturity."

"You wouldn't be upset to find out your father wasn't who you believed he was?" Jack asked.

In answer, Kate glared at him. In the last couple of years she'd found out that her saint of a father was far, far from sainthood.

Jack laughed at her expression. "Point made." He stood up. "Come on, let's go to bed. Tomorrow we can —"

He broke off at the sound of screaming. "That's Teddy." He threw open the door.

When the second scream came, Kate said, "Nadine."

Sara got off the bed. "Mr. Howland!"

In the hallway, Byon, in a blue silk dressing grown, was heading toward the stairs. Clive was already there and he was tapping his phone.

"What is it?" Jack asked.

"Mr. Howland killed himself," Clive said. "I'm calling the police." He gave his attention to his phone.

"No ambulance?" Sara asked. "No attempt at revival?"

Clive shook his head no.

At the end of the hall, was Mr. Howland's room. The door was open, light flooding the dark hallway.

Bella appeared in her nightgown and robe. "What happened?"

"I'm not sure." Sara hurried after Jack and Kate.

Byon had his arms around Nadine. As soon as Teddy saw Jack, she flung herself into his arms. She was crying hard.

Sara made her way through the people, Kate behind her, and into the bedroom.

On the bed lay Mr. Howland. His eyes were closed — and a plastic bag was over his head. On the table beside him was an open medicine bottle and an empty glass. There was a roll of duct tape on the bed. It had been used to seal the bag around his neck.

"We loved him no matter what," Nadine cried. "It didn't matter that he sometimes forgot things."

Clive was at the doorway. "The police will be here in a few minutes. They asked that we touch nothing and that we close the door."

"He needs us!" Teddy said, but Jack wouldn't let her get away.

"Come on," he said softly. "Let's go downstairs and wait." Jack led her down to the small sitting room and got her to sit on a couch. When Byon came in, leading Nadine, he put her beside her daughter.

Everyone watched the two women. Would their animosity hold through this?

When the two women clasped each other, they all let out a sigh of relief.

Mrs. Aiken came to the door. "All this ruckus! I guess I'm supposed to serve —"

Jack got to the door in two steps and pushed the woman out. "Get out of here," he ordered.

She stuck her nose into the air. "Well I *never*!"

"Too bad," Jack muttered. "Somebody should have."

Mrs. Aiken angrily went down the hall. Behind her was Puck. They hadn't seen her since the morning, since they'd seen the skeleton.

"Tea," Sara said to Jack and Kate, then headed to the kitchen. As she passed, Kate motioned for Puck to join them.

It was quiet in the kitchen, and Puck got out the big teapot while Kate filled the electric kettle.

For a while, they were silent.

"He didn't kill himself," Jack said. "He

was telling me how much he likes American action movies. We laughed about how he used to be busy all the time and now he could sit and watch a movie. We talked about cars. We . . ." He trailed off, looking down at his hands. "He didn't kill himself," he repeated.

Sara was pouring boiling water into the pot. "Who had the time to do it? Who left during dinner?"

"Everyone," Puck said.

They looked at her. "I was in the kitchen with Mother. She was angry about the tray Jack took upstairs."

"Why the hell — ?" he began, then clamped his teeth together.

"Puck is right," Sara said as she handed out mugs full of tea. "Everyone left the table at one time or another."

"Nadine was on the phone," Puck said. "She was angry about something. She was there when I took the potatoes in, but when I came out, she was gone."

They looked at Jack. He had sat between Nadine and Teddy. "Yes, they were gone for a while. Separately. Bathroom."

"I could believe Nadine is bulimic," Sara said. "You can't gain a pound when you're husband hunting."

"Byon left," Kate said. "He rubbed his

stomach and asked to be excused. He was gone for at least fifteen minutes.

"And Clive," Sara said. "His phone buzzed and he said it was work and he had to take the call. Said it was from Zurich."

"I liked Mr. Howland," Jack said. "Wish I could have met him when he was in the car business."

"Did he hurt you?" Puck asked. "Mother said he ran at you."

Jack waved his hand in dismissal. "He got mixed up for a moment, that's all. He thought I was Sean and said he knew Teddy was my daughter. Honest mistake."

"What did he say?" Puck asked.

Kate knew but didn't want to repeat it.

Jack didn't answer so it was left to Sara.

"Mr. Howland said *'I'll kill you. I did it before and I can do it again.'* "

"He didn't mean it," Jack said.

"It's possible," Sara said slowly, "that seeing Sean again . . . I mean you, Jack . . . awakened memories in him. He used to be a man of ambition and he wanted to overcome his origins. He wanted his daughter to marry an earl and live in an ancestral mansion."

"But she fell in love with the stableman," Kate said.

"She was going to have his baby," Puck said.

They looked at her. "We couldn't help overhearing."

"What else did you hear?" Sara asked. "Or see? Or intuit? What?"

They stared at her.

"Willa is different. When people are looking, she seems to like Clive, but one time, she . . . I don't think she'll write him any more love letters."

"Byon?" Kate asked.

"Something has hurt him." She looked at Jack. "But you are charging him."

"You mean like a dead battery?" Sara said, and Puck nodded. "I agree. Tonight he was quite animated in his storytelling."

"All his stories were *old,*" Kate said. "In every one, he said, 'Of course that was before cell phones.' What's he been doing for the last few years?"

Jack and Sara looked at each other. When Sara lived in New York, they often went to Broadway plays, but that was years ago. What *had* Byon written lately?

Sara looked back at Puck. "How is Nadine different?"

"I think she's afraid."

"Of what?" Kate asked, but no one answered. "If someone did kill Mr. Howland . . . Why? Who? Think Nadine knows something?"

All three women looked at Jack.

"I think you guys should leave. Go home." He looked at Puck. "You need to go with them."

Puck sat down on a stool. "Whoever killed Sean is *here.* In this house. If you leave, they'll know why."

"I think she's right," Sara said. "I don't believe in coincidence in book plots or in life. I don't know why Mr. Howland was killed, but I truly believe it has something to do with Sean's death."

"And Diana's," Kate said. "She could be, uh, hidden somewhere."

"I think —" Jack began, but stopped when they heard voices. "The police are here. Are we agreed on this? You're all going to leave?"

"No," Sara said. "We're a threesome, remember?"

"Maybe I should tell the police that I found the —" Puck began.

"NO!" they shouted at her.

"*You* know nothing," Jack said. "Understand me? I don't want to see you with a plastic bag over your head."

"Or shot and poisoned and strangled," Sara said.

Puck looked shocked.

"Agreed?" Sara said.

Puck nodded.

There was a single knock and Clive opened the door. "They want everyone downstairs." He gave a quick glance at Puck. "You too, I guess." He shut the door.

Jack shook his head. "What could *you* possibly know, right?"

The way he said it made Puck give her funny little laugh. At the sound, they went down the stairs feeling somewhat better.

It was late and they were all tired, but they sat in the small drawing room and waited patiently to be called by the police for questioning. Bella went in first. She was frowning when she entered the room and when she left ten minutes later, she was glowering. She refused to look at anyone, including Sara.

Nadine and Teddy, their disagreement seemingly put aside, went next.

Sara, who was a morning person, leaned against Jack and fell asleep. He put his arm around her and she slept against his chest. He offered his other side to Kate but she declined.

When Nadine and Teddy came out, they were crying harder. The others expected to be called, but the young police officer said the inspector only wanted to see Sara and everyone else could go to bed.

"I'd rather go in with her," Jack said.

"No, just her." It was said in the tone of an order.

With sighs of relief, Byon, Clive and Willa left. Puck sat down beside Kate. She wasn't leaving.

Jack woke Sara up and told her the officer wanted to speak to her.

"Me? Think he knows?" she whispered to Jack.

"Hope not. Bella already wants to kill us. I don't want to add to it. Yet."

Sara nodded in agreement and went into the room where the interrogations were being held. The officer was older, had a mustache, and was sitting behind a desk. He looked tired and bored, but his eyes perked up when he saw Sara.

"So you're the famous writer. That's interesting because I've always wanted to write."

Sara stifled a scream. *No! No! Not this. Not questions about writing. Or, more accurately, one question: How'd'ya-write-your-first-book-where-do-you-get-your-ideas?*

As she took a seat, she managed to smile without showing too many teeth.

"I'm about to retire." His tone was much too bright for the circumstances and the time. What was it? About 2:00 a.m.? It wouldn't be long before she'd have been up for twenty-four hours.

"I think I'd like to write a few murder mysteries. Seems like a good occupation. And lucrative. My wife would like that."

Sara thought about telling the truth, that most writers can't support themselves. She'd been lucky to have started in the glorious 80s. "What about Mr. Howland?"

"Suicide," he said. "Depressed. Couldn't even drive his own cars and he loved those! He was a good man. Back when those two ran away, Mr. Howland was a haven of sanity. He —"

Sara leaned forward. "You were *here*? On the night they disappeared?"

"It was my first case," he said proudly. "I was young then, and I remember it all."

Sleepiness left her. "I want to hear every word about that night."

He took his time before speaking. "I heard you were thinking of writing about our little mystery. Of course it wouldn't be ethical of me to tell the things I saw that night, now would it?"

I have been drawn into the bowels of hell, Sara thought. He was a true devil: a would-be writer. They all believed there was a "Great Secret" to writing. Learn it and the world was theirs.

She was too worn out to be nice. "What can I do to help you?" she said, which was code for "What's your price?" She crossed her fingers for luck. Please, please, please let him be a money wanna-be. Those were easy. Turn them over to an agent. The ones who made her crazy wanted to relentlessly question her until she finally divulged "The Secret."

"I think I'll need an agent," he said.

Sara genuinely smiled. "You got it. I'll connect you. Now tell me."

He smiled back. A bargain had been reached. "My boss hated the earl, Bertram. Don't know why."

"Probably lost money on one of his horses," Sara said.

"Good guess. His report said it was a couple of runaway lovers. No foul play, no mystery."

"But you were more astute." If it took flattery to get him to tell, she'd write a twenty-thousand-word treatise on the beauty of his 'stache.

"Don't mean to brag, but I was. Nicky . . . ?" He was testing her to see if she knew the characters involved.

"The heir apparent." She passed.

"Now, he was a real character. Wasn't

much liked in the village. He laughed at us, along with that music guy."

"Byon."

"Yeah, him." He paused. "Although I do like his music. Anyway, in the book I started, I thought I might —"

She broke in before he told her his entire plot. "You liked Mr. Howland. What about his daughter?"

The officer gave a one-sided grin. "She used to race cars with the boys of the village. That girl could downshift smooth as melted butter. We used to say Mr. Howland made her heart out of a carburetor with stainless steel valves."

"I bet Nadine was upset that night," Sara said.

"Catatonic. Staring into space. Never said a word. I think she thought something bad had happened because she ran out to the chapel to pray. If you plan to write about this, you ought to ask her questions."

"As one writer to another," Sara said, "I thank you for that tip."

The man smiled so widely she saw the fillings in his back teeth.

"What about Nicky?"

"He was a mess."

"Upset? Crying? Angry? What?"

"No. He was bruised. A black eye. A real

beaut. And his hands were red and raw."

Sara blinked. No one had so much as hinted at this. "Did anyone ask him why?"

"Back then, you didn't question an earl's son. If he'd said he hurt himself picking a daisy, he would have been believed."

"Everyone seems to forget that titles were given to the most violent, ruthless — Sorry. *Did* Nicky give a reason?"

"He said he'd fallen and that was it. I wasn't allowed to ask questions of him. It was considered disrespectful."

"What about the others?" she asked.

"They were all very quiet, like they were guilty of something. I asked a few questions but I was told to leave off, that they were sad at missing their friends."

"But you didn't believe that."

"No. I think every one of them was up to no good." He narrowed his eyes. "Did something happen that made you want to come here and investigate?"

"No," she said honestly. "I helped Bella restore this place and it's closed this month so I came to visit. And the mystery was just to keep the little gray cells going." She hoped he caught the reference to Hercule Poirot.

"You helped restore Oxley Manor? That means money."

Oh Lord, Sara thought. She'd put her foot in it. She took a breath. "Yes."

"So there *is* money to be made in writing books."

Back when there were bookstores and before people only read 140 letters at a time, she thought but didn't say. "If your book is good, yes, it can make money."

"So maybe you'll give me some writing tips. You know, as one author to another."

Sara knew the session was over. Would-be writers were obsessive creatures. They could think of nothing else. She stifled a yawn. "I'm not a young person," she said tiredly — and could almost hear Jack say, "Don't play the age card."

"I need to rest."

"Of course." When she stood up, he pulled a business card out of his pocket and handed it to her. "My private email is on the back."

She wasn't surprised to see it was "best-seller2846." Poor man. He had it bad. "So what about Mr. Howland?"

"Like I said, suicide. But we'll have to wait for an official verdict. No one is to leave before I release you."

Hope we don't have to wait until after my agent gets you a movie deal, Sara thought but just smiled. She left the room, closing the door behind her. Jack and Kate and Puck were waiting for her.

"Well?" Jack asked.

"Wants to write a book."

Jack and Kate groaned, but Puck looked askance. No one explained.

"Bed!" Sara said, and they all went upstairs.

Fifteen

The next morning, Sara was awakened by Bella bursting into her room.

"This!" Bella's voice was a controlled screech. She tossed a newspaper onto Sara, who could hardly be seen under the big down comforter.

Reluctantly, Sara rolled over and picked up the paper. It was one of the English tabloids that opened like a book. Usually, Sara loved them. They had the meanest, nastiest, most rotten gossip anyone had ever read. If it were printed in the US, there would be protestors with placards. But the British press was different.

She had to clear her eyes to be able to see — then wished she'd kept them closed. Murder at Oxley Manor? the headline read. Her mind couldn't quite comprehend what she was reading. *Wonder what size font that is. Sixty-eight? Or is it bigger?*

Bella was looming over her. Her face was

one giant sneer. "You have done this." She barely spoke above a whisper, but it was scary.

"I'm sorry," Sara said. "But it wasn't me who said we thought Mr. Howland was murdered." At Bella's expression, Sara thought, *Uh-oh. Wrong choice of words.*

Bella stepped backward and dropped down onto a little gold chair. "Do you know how hard I worked to get this place? My mother left me nothing. My father's wife made sure I was given nothing. I got out of school and I was alone. Penniless."

Sara was listening with wide eyes. In all their years of emails and visits, Bella had told her next to nothing about her life. But then, Sara hadn't shared the worst parts of her past either. Privacy was one of the things she liked best about their friendship. But as a lover of stories, she wanted to hear.

"I was in love," Bella said. "I was to be married, but when he found out that Oxley Manor wasn't to be mine, that I wouldn't get even a dower cottage, he left me."

Sara bit her tongue to keep from saying the cliché about how he wasn't worth having. But she didn't want to interrupt the story.

"Bertram," Bella said. "He . . ." She took a breath. "Do you know what it's like to suddenly have no one? No family? Nothing?"

"Yes," Sara said. "I do."

Bella ignored Sara's confession. Standing up, she pointed at the paper. "*You* caused this scandal. This must stop! I will *not* have everything I've worked for destroyed." She left the room, slamming the door behind her.

Sara read the article. It was worse than she'd imagined. And it was all about *her.* It said that:

> The "famous" author — who no one admits having heard of — Sara Medlar, is stirring up trouble. Is it just so she can revive her dead career?

It said that Sara had been discarded by the publishing world and now needed international publicity to put her books back on the market:

> Will she make the suicide of this poor, depressed man into a murder? You're not Miss Marple, Sara, so put away your magnifying glass.

Sara flopped back on the bed, engulfed by the covers. When she heard the door open, she didn't bother to see who it was. If it was a gunman, she'd welcome him.

Jack sat on one side of the bed, Kate on the other.

"Looks like you saw it," he said.

Sara put a pillow over her face. "Kill me now. Please."

"Killing is what got us into this problem," Jack said. "Who told them that we think it's a murder?"

"How would I know?" Sara removed the pillow. "I got bawled out by Bella."

"Wait until she finds out there's a skeleton in her conservation area," Kate said.

"She wanted everything in there protected from invasion and that's what she got," he said.

"Are you making jokes?" Kate asked.

"Trying to. Doesn't seem to be working. So what's our plan for today?"

"Go home," Sara said. "Home to Florida. I miss my iguanas and the Bird of Paradise flowers and —"

"Ha!" Jack stretched out on top of the comforter beside her. "We aren't allowed to leave, remember?"

Kate lay down on the other side. "Yes, let's do go home. We'll send Bella a note, using your most expensive stationery. 'Dear Bella, there's a skeleton in a hole in your backyard.

He was probably murdered by one of your guests, so for your own safety, send them away. Best always, Sara.' How does that sound?"

"Good," Jack said. "Everyone will like that. Especially whoever did away with Mr. Howland for whatever reason they did it. But they'll probably figure out that Puck found the bones. Too bad. Not our problem."

"If we warned Bella, she wouldn't tell," Sara said tentatively.

Jack snorted. "Like we thought nobody would tell some reporter — who we never saw — about you and murder and all the other lies in that paper? Isn't there a saying about only one person being able to keep a secret? Two people know and the world does."

"Probably," Sara mumbled. "Maybe I should go home and write a book with that theme. One person knows a lie, then she tells her bestie, then . . ." She shrugged.

Jack threw a leg off the bed. "Okay, I've had all the wallowing I can take. Besides, no one felt sorry for me on the Morris case when that reporter cut me to ribbons."

"You *slept* with her!" Kate and Sara said in unison.

"Yeah, well," Jack said. "She still —"

"This isn't about *you,*" Kate said. "We need to figure this out, but we don't know how. We—"

"Nicky had been beaten up," Sara said as she sat up.

Kate and Jack looked at her. "Who? Why? When?" they asked.

"The night of the party," Sara said. "Someone beat up Nicky."

"The cop tell you this?" Jack asked.

Sara nodded. "For a price. I'm to turn him over to my agent." She leaned back against the headboard, hugging a pillow to her. "Each person who was there knows something. Even if they don't realize that they know it."

Kate leaned back. "Something they don't want to tell."

Jack took the other side of the headboard. "Okay, Miss Plotter, what do we do to make them talk?"

"Ask for the *one* fact that no one else knows," Sara said. "Make them feel important. After breakfast, we'll—"

"It's ten thirty," Kate said. "Breakfast was hours ago."

Sara was surprised. She wasn't a person who slept much. "Who have you seen?"

"Everyone except Willa." Jack paused. "They make fun of her. Especially Clive.

He says she's just what he thought she'd become."

"He's probably glad he didn't get her to buy him a country estate." Kate sounded bitter.

"Watch out or he'll go after you," Jack said.

"Right," Sara said. "Considering that you're an heiress, that is a possibility."

Kate looked puzzled. "I'm not an —" She broke off when the meaning hit her. When Sara died, Kate would probably inherit. "I'm not going to think about that," she muttered.

"All right," Sara said. "We want to find out what really happened the night Diana and Sean ran away. Not lies but the truth. I want you two to go to each person and ask for *one* thing they know. Something no one else knows. Stroke their egos. Jack, you get Nadine, Byon and Teddy. Kate, take Clive and Puck."

"Teddy wasn't even born then, so what does she know?" Jack asked.

"Probably a lot," Sara said. "Coax it out of her. I have faith that you can do it."

"And what are you going to do?" Kate asked.

"Take a twenty-minute shower and get someone to give me a ride into the village. I want to know what Willa is up to. Jack, find out why Nadine went to the chapel that night. She said she was praying but I don't believe that. And I want you two to text me everything you find out. We'll meet at the King James pub at one."

Jack made some remarks about the "boss lady" being alive and well. He was grumpy at the idea of his task, while Kate was smiling. Like her aunt, she liked the mystery and intrigue. They left, closing the door behind them.

As for Sara, she needed time to be quiet. As a true introvert, people took energy away from her. Kate received energy from them, and Jack . . . Well, he just wanted the people he cared about to be near him.

Right now, Sara needed time away from them *all.* The newspaper article and Bella's wrath had been a blow. Sara had few true friends and she couldn't afford to lose any. She was feeling guilty. All she'd meant to do was come to England, see her friend and do a little research into what she'd thought was an old mystery. And she'd wanted an excuse to give Jack and Kate time alone. She'd meant to send them off to Scotland together. Maybe if they didn't always have a third person around, they'd . . .

She stopped. Forty-plus years of writing

romance novels was making her plan everyone's future. But the idea of the two people she loved most in the world getting together and . . . Heavens! How she'd like a baby to hold and spoil.

She made herself stop thinking in those terms. Thirty minutes later, she got a ride into the village in a truck with one of the workmen. He let her off by the pub. Across the road was a shop that sold English clothes: well-made and beautiful.

An hour later, she'd visited four shops and bought gifts for everyone at home. Jack's mother was going to love the teapot and cups. And his sister would like the crafts. Sara knew she should buy Kate's mother something but all the woman ever wanted was cash — something Kate knew nothing about.

The first text came from Jack.

Byon is frantic. His agent has someone who wants to hear his new music. He needs to leave asap.

Sara wrote back:

Police said he can't leave. If he resists, hint that he might be considered for Mr. H's murder.

Jack replied:

Devil is your bestie?

Sara started to answer, but a text came from Kate:

Clive says a billionaire is in London and wants to meet him. He's frantic to leave.

Sara stared at the phone. "Two frantics. How interesting." There was a packaging store nearby and she went to it, wrote out the addresses and turned the gifts — and a check to Kate's mother — over to them to send.

When Kate texted that Nadine had been invited to a party at Lord Hazeldean's so she really, really wanted to leave, Sara knew that something wasn't right. She needed to find out what was going on.

She sat down on a bench and began to send emails asking people she knew a lot of questions.

As soon as Sara saw Kate and Jack, she knew they had something to tell. They looked like they were ready to explode if they didn't release their information immediately.

They went inside the pub. It was awash in polished horse brasses, with a huge fireplace along one wall. The Floridians were sorry it wasn't alight. They took a table in the corner by a window that looked out to the street, then ordered great heaps of fish and chips.

"And tomato sauce," the waitress said. This was English for *ketchup.*

"No!" they said. "Malt vinegar."

The waitress gave a little smile and went away.

"So?" Sara said as soon as they were alone.

Jack motioned for Kate to go first.

"I want to say that asking for 'something no one else knew' worked. Clive was very pleased to be asked that." Kate paused. "Remember how Mr. Howland said Diana wanted to breed horses?" She didn't wait for an answer. "Clive thinks Sean was stealing semen from some big-time racehorses and selling it."

The visions that conjured made Sara say, "Ewww."

Jack laughed in a dirty kind of way. "Bet when he showed up, the horses came running."

"It was illegal," Kate said.

"That's what he was doing in the cemetery

with those men," Sara said. "Selling it to them."

"Probably," Jack agreed.

"I bet it was for Nadine," Kate said. "I wonder if he did know she was pregnant? He worked with animals so he probably knew the signs."

"Poor guy," Jack said. "In love, about to be a father and no way to support a woman who was used to great wealth. Her daddy had even remodeled a room for a place she just visited. How could he compete with that?"

"That gives Mr. Howland a motive for murder," Sara said. "He didn't want his daughter running off with some low-class nobody. He was an extremely ambitious man, and this handsome stable lad was destroying his life plan."

Kate was looking at her hands. "Maybe returning to Oxley made him remember what he'd done. Maybe he *did* take his own life."

Their platters of divine English fish and chips arrived. "Keto be damned," Sara mumbled as she shook the malt vinegar onto the fat "chips." In the US, they'd be called home fries.

The waitress left and they were alone again.

"What about you?" Sara asked Jack. "Find out anything interesting?"

Jack smiled. "Just a little."

"Out with it," Kate said, her mouth full. Their drinks were lukewarm.

"Byon said he didn't believe Diana actually liked men."

"Hated them or liked women better?" Sara asked.

"Sex," Jack said. "Liked women for sex."

"Proof that she and Sean weren't a couple," Sara said. "Damn! But I'd like to know what happened to her. What else?"

"Byon said that after that night, Nicky changed."

Sara closed her eyes for a moment. "I sometimes forget how good carbs taste. Anyway, how did he change? From what I gather, Nicky didn't have many friends, so after everyone left, he was alone with his father. He must have been depressed."

"Byon said that for the first year, he used to drive up from London every weekend, but Nicky was always angry and drunk. Byon stopped coming. Oh! And he said they missed Clive."

"But then, they were united in their hatred of him," Kate said. "It's a kind of bonding. Too bad. Clive seems like a nice guy."

"Asked you out yet?" Jack asked.

"Repeatedly."

"If he —"

Sara cut him off. "What about Nadine?"

"We had a nice heart-to-heart. She said this place is making her remember the truth," Jack said. "She told me about Sean and her."

Kate and Sara leaned forward, ready to listen.

"Tell us every word," Sarah said. "In detail."

SIXTEEN

"Sean was a great lover," Nadine said. "All those years of currying horses . . ." She raised her hands and moved them in a sensuous way. "He took his time. I've never . . ." She sighed. "No one since, if you know what I mean."

Jack nodded. "Losing him . . . I can't imagine how it hurt."

Nadine took her time before replying. "At the time I thought I'd die. To have it all taken away in an instant . . . I didn't know how to go on living. Willa had everyone's attention because Clive had dumped her, so I was alone. They didn't know about Sean and me."

"It's hard for me to see how you kept that a secret."

Nadine shook her head. "It wasn't easy. Damned Puck was everywhere. Sneaking here and there. But thanks to me, no one went to the cemetery house. Bertram was too cheap to hire a caretaker or to repair it. But that was good because it gave us a place to meet in secret. I came up with the idea of making people believe the house was haunted. Sean and I laughed as we set up the ghost equipment. We used the bathtub to —" She drifted away in memory of those days of the two of them together. Hands and soap and hot water.

Jack interrupted. "Puck found your hiding place."

Nadine came back to the present. "She did. She seemed to have fallen through a door. Knocked it over. Sean was very upset. We met in the woods after that."

"And in the chapel."

She looked startled. "How do you know about that?"

"Just a guess. And you were going to have a baby," he said softly.

She sighed. "I had been looking forward to telling Sean. Now that I'm older I see my stupidity, but back then, all I thought was 'Now Sean *can't* leave me.' "

"Did you believe he wanted to?"

"Yes and no. He'd said he couldn't see how it would work between us. We were pretty sure that when we told my father he'd disown me. He used to be . . ." She looked away as tears came to her eyes. "This afternoon I have to choose his coffin."

Jack put his hand over hers. "I'm sorry for all this. I liked the man."

"Even though he tried to kill you?"

"Especially because he tried to kill me."

For a moment, they smiled at each other in memory.

"It wouldn't have worked," Nadine said. "Sean and me. I can see that now. We wouldn't have lasted more than a few years — if that. Marriage is serious business. All he and I had was wonderful, fabulous sex. We looked at each other and clothes came off."

"Sounds good to me," Jack said.

Nadine didn't smile. "When I was with him, I couldn't see reality. He had a very quick temper. And he hated all of us."

"Except you."

"Have you ever loved someone and hated them too?"

"My father," Jack said.

"Then you understand. Sean and I didn't dare talk or the hate would have come out. My life was dealing with my father's ambition. He worked his way into upscale events — and he wanted me next to him."

"You were part of his showroom."

"I was. Some of my gowns cost more than Sean made in a year."

"And he stank of horses — which you hate."

"Exactly," Nadine said. "By the end, we were seeing our differences. No! We were seeing how alike we were. When I got angry, Sean got more angry. He had a truly vicious temper."

"When did you tell your father? And how did he take it?"

"It was weeks before I could admit to myself that Sean was actually gone. I kept thinking that he'd return. I soothed myself by planning my anger. I'd throw things at him, then he'd . . ." She held up her hand as though to stop that memory. "Finally, I had to tell my father about the baby — and I expected rage. I was sure he'd go crazy with anger. But he didn't. He suggested a solution."

"Your husband."

"Yes. A nice, quiet man to whom I'd never paid any attention. But then, with the fire of Sean around me, I couldn't see anyone else. So I married him. It surprised me that it was good. When I got angry, he held me and told me everything would be all right. I never would have married him if Sean had stayed. Sex causes us to do things that make no sense."

Jack said, "I'd like to hear your version of

what happened the night of the party."

"I don't know what actually happened. Sean and I were going to leave together. I know he'd packed a suitcase. I saw it. But I went to the stables and he wasn't there. His suitcase was gone and the place was empty."

"And Diana was missing, too," Jack said.

"Yes, she was." For a moment, Nadine's hands clenched into fists. "Everything changed after that night. I left Oxley Manor and I never went back. I didn't see Clive or Willa again until yesterday."

"What about the others?"

"I saw some of Byon's plays but not him. I never even told anyone that I knew him. I never heard anything about Willa or Clive."

"And Nicky?"

"I went to his funeral, but I didn't go to the house."

"Didn't Bertram say something there?"

"He said *we* killed Nicky, which I'm sure was true. When we left, Nicky had no one but his father. It was one of my father's cars that he crashed."

"Why did your father say that he'd killed Sean?"

Nadine's mouth tightened. "I . . . This is hard to say. I think maybe my father paid Sean to leave me."

"And he took the money?" Jack sounded

shocked.

When she looked at him, there was such hate in her eyes that Jack pulled back. "Looks like he did, doesn't it?" For all of her talk of having a better life without him, it didn't look like she'd forgiven him.

Seventeen

"Her phone rang and that was the end," Jack said.

"What if . . . ?" Kate said slowly.

"I know," Sara said, "what if Sean told her that he'd rather have her father's money than her?"

"She would have killed him," Jack said.

"And Daddy would have disposed of the body," Sara said.

"One thing is certain," Kate said. "They *all* had to show up here. No one could say, 'I don't need to go because I know who killed Sean. Me.' "

"Too true," Sara said, then looked at Jack. "You did a good job with Nadine. So what about Teddy?"

"No time to talk to her. I barely made it here on time."

"Too bad," Kate mumbled in a way that made Jack smile.

"So what's this about the frantics?" Sara asked.

They looked at her in question.

"Both of you used that word. Everyone is now frantic. They *must* return to wherever."

"To their lives," Jack said.

"Don't we all want that." Sara looked down at her empty plate. "Anyone up for some English custard?"

"Not me," Kate said.

"You'll regret this in the morning," Jack said. "Sugar *and* carbs?"

"I already regret it, but I need time to tell about the sleuthing I did on my own." Sara looked extraordinarily pleased with herself.

"The spotlight is on you," Jack said. "So spill."

"Well . . ." Sara drew it out. "It seemed an odd coincidence that every person here suddenly got an urgent message to leave." She smiled. "So I made some calls. In spite of what that hate-filled little tabloid said, some people have heard of me and *do* want —" She broke off at Jack's look of impatience. "Lord Hazeldean's office said there is no upcoming party. He's in Saint Lucia and won't be back for weeks."

"But Nadine said . . ."

"Right," Sara said. "Someone lied to her."

"What about Clive?" Jack asked.

"He works for Coutts." Jack and Kate looked blank. "It's where the Queen keeps her money and I happen to have a pound or two in that bank."

"You have a personal banker?" Jack asked.

"Oh yeah. He wears a tailcoat. Anyway, he made a few calls and found out some things. It seems that Clive isn't one of those rich money people who gets a percentage of his deals. He gets a salary. It's good but nothing to brag about. His boss told my banker that Clive is so hungry for acknowledgment, for praise, that if he asks for an increase in pay, they just let him have lunch with some big shot and Clive is happy for another two years."

"They did that to him." They knew Kate meant the Pack.

"Byon?" Jack asked. "What about him?"

Sara knew how much Jack admired the man, so she wanted to soften the blow. "His agent only talked to me because I said Byon wanted to put one of my books to music. It seems that Byon hasn't written anything in years. He's broke. He plays piano in a bar and lives —"

Jack threw up his hands. "Don't tell me any more."

"I wonder if Willa received an urgent call from her company?" Kate asked.

"From her husband?" Jack was frowning. "A man of Byon's talent should be living in luxury. He should —"

"You're only as good as your last book," Sara said. "And they remember the old stuff as perfect and wonderful. Anything new and they say you should retire, that your books have lost their magic. They say —" She cut off at their looks. "Sorry. I found out for sure that Willa has never been married and has no children."

"A great, whopping lie," Jack said.

"But I'm sure all the others are telling the truth," Sara said, and they almost laughed.

"Fake calls, made-up parties," Jack said.

"Don't forget the note left in Aunt Sara's camera bag," Kate said.

"Someone wants us out of here," Sara said.

"You think?" Jack said.

"We —" Sara began.

"Look!" Kate said.

They turned to the window. Across the road, a woman was standing outside a Victorian house that had been converted into offices. She was staring at the entry stairs as though trying to decide whether or not to enter.

"Isn't that . . . ?" Kate said.

"That is Meena," Sara said. "Owner of

Renewal. Successful to the extreme — aka Willa without her disguise."

"She shouldn't cover that body up," Jack added.

"I'm going to talk to her." Kate left before they could protest. She crossed the street quickly, but she still had time to work up anger. "You lied about having a husband and children."

"So what?" Willa said. "Did you want me to admit that I'm a failure as a woman? That's how they made me feel. And they still do."

"It was *your* choice to dress like a ragbag lady. You could have arrived in a limo and . . ." Even as she said it, Kate knew that a successful Willa would have taken the focus off Sean and Diana. Clive might even latch onto her. She sighed. "Okay, so what have you learned?"

"That's he's divorced and has two daughters."

"What? Who?"

Willa nodded toward the building, and Kate saw a sign for an attorney. "Is he the guy you liked?"

"Yeah. I saw Nadine go in there!"

"She's not after a village lawyer," Kate said. "She needs money. If she knew the truth about your business, she might propose to *you.*"

"Then I'd have to support that daughter of hers. No thanks." Willa kept glancing at the door.

"How old are his daughters?"

"Ten and eleven."

"They're young. It's been over twenty years, so he waited a long time before he married. Why don't you go buy his kids some gifts, something electronic, then show up as yourself? Tell the truth about your company. Invite him to tea."

"Nadine's still in there." Willa sounded defeated.

"Only *you* think she's so beautiful that men fall down in lust for her."

"You're the one who should worry. She's after Jack."

"That's because he looks like Sean. You left early this morning. Did you happen to have a work emergency?"

"How did you know that?" Willa sounded angry. "If you're tapping my phone —"

"We're not. What is the emergency?"

"Some woman in Manchester wrenched her back. She's in hospital and I better go see her. Maybe I can prevent a lawsuit. I'll be back before I'm missed."

"Not possible," Kate murmured, then said louder, "Tell me something about the night of the party that no one else knows."

"I . . ." She took a breath. "I think Clive saw everything."

"He told you that?"

"No. I, uh, I kind of followed him when he went outside. There was a fight. Loud voices. I was too drunk to know who it was. Clive was . . . I think maybe he was hiding from me."

"In the stables?"

"Not sure. I think —" The door to the office opened and Nadine came out. Immediately, Willa turned and hurried down the street, not wanting to be seen.

"Who was that?" Nadine asked.

"She was asking for directions. Did you see a lawyer?"

"Yes, he wrote my father's will. Everything was left to me and I'm to take care of Teddy." Nadine gave a look of disgust. "No debts but no money either."

"Your father used a lawyer from a small village?"

"Yes. Edward Terran. I always did like him."

"Willa mentioned him."

Nadine gave a little laugh. "I forgot about that. They used to walk around the estate together. He was a great history buff and loved to explore. He's the one who got

Bertram to fence off the conservation area."

"Before or after Sean and Diana disappeared?" Kate snapped.

"I don't remember. No, wait. I was about thirty months pregnant — at least it felt that way — and Dad came to visit my husband and me. He'd been to Oxley and had news. I remember he said Bertram caring about the birds was odd and it must have been for a tax break. I was too miserable with my body to listen much but I do remember that."

"What's the lawyer like?" Kate asked.

"Not bad. He's kept himself in shape. Let's just say that if I didn't need money, I'd go out with him."

"Did he ask you?"

"No. Not even close. Years ago, I tried, but for some reason, he liked Willa."

Who could imagine that? Kate thought. "Why did they break up?"

Nadine shrugged. "Nicky and Byon didn't want to lose her adoration — or the food she brought for us. Truffles cost a lot." She smiled at Kate's expression. "It was bad of us to break them up, but kids are a bitch, aren't they? I need to go. See you later."

Kate watched her leave. They broke up what might have led to marriage and children, but it was dismissed with "kids are a bitch."

"You weren't *kids,*" Kate said aloud.

Across the road she saw Sara and Jack watching her out the pub window.

If Kate's mind hadn't been on all that she'd heard from Willa and Nadine, she would have seen Clive sitting with Jack and Sara, and she probably wouldn't have entered the pub again. Ever since Kate had heard their remarks about her being an "heiress," she'd stayed away from him. The idea of someone wanting her for money was a new — and thoroughly despicable — idea. It made her have sympathy for Willa.

But Clive saw her before she could escape so she went to them. Sara had a big bowl of what looked like bread pudding and another one of thick yellow cream. When Sara saw the look in her niece's eyes, she ordered a second one.

Kate and Clive greeted each other, then he said, "Who was the woman you were talking to? I couldn't see her face but she looked good."

"She was asking me where she could buy gifts for her four kids."

Sara nearly choked, and Jack gave a cough to cover his laugh.

"Too bad," Clive said. "I'm between

girlfriends right now." He looked at Jack. "As I was saying, I'll just pop down to London for the meeting, and I'll be back in a jiff. You won't even know I've been gone."

Kate rolled her eyes. He was going to return to a place where he was being treated as second-class? Leave his job so he could fill drink orders for Nadine and Byon? Not likely.

"What's everyone doing at the house?" Jack asked.

Clive nodded toward the window. "You saw Nadine. She's taking care of . . . you know."

"The funeral arrangements." Sara was licking her spoon after every bite.

"How are she and Teddy getting along now?" Kate asked.

Clive gave a little smile. "Nadine wants to borrow the dress her daughter wore to dinner last night, but Teddy won't part with it."

"Couldn't she substitute paint for the dress?" Kate said.

Clive laughed. "Nadine is going to London with me. We'll leave early tomorrow morning. I'll be back in the afternoon, but Nadine won't be back until Sunday." Clive kept his head down as he said this.

"How's Byon?" Jack asked.

"He's looking for something. I think it's some music he wrote years ago. He said he left it with Nicky, which means it was probably used as a drinks coaster. But Byon is in the attic dumping boxes out." Clive leaned forward. "I don't know that woman, Isabella, but I think when she sees the mess he's making, she may disembowel him."

"And she will use me to do it," Sara murmured.

Jack spoke up. "Was Mr. Howland there the night of the party?"

"Party?" Clive said. "Oh, you mean the night . . . No, he wasn't. He didn't like any of us so he stayed away. I remember that Nicky was giving Nadine hell because she could have gone to Hawaii with her father. When Nadine said she wanted to be with us, Byon and Nicky booed her. They said she had some secret reason for wanting to miss a trip like that." His eyes widened. "If Thorpe is Teddy's father, I guess there was a *big* reason she canceled on her father."

"What did *you* see that night?" Kate said.

"Nothing much." Clive kept his eyes on his drink.

"Weren't you hiding from Willa?" Kate asked.

Jack and Sara were watching her, realizing that she had new information.

Clive looked serious. "I was *always* hiding from her. She was a true stalker, worse than Puck for sneaking around." He looked up. "She's different now. I don't know what it is, but there's something not the same about her."

"Such as?" Sara asked.

"I can't identify it. Or maybe I remember things differently. She used to have a look of 'Please don't hurt me.' That seems to be gone now."

"What do you remember about the lawyer Willa liked?" Kate asked.

"Eddie? Nice man. Very clever. He seemed a bit dull but he had a top-notch brain. One time I asked him why he spent so much time with someone like Willa."

"And what did he say?" Sara asked.

"He said 'passion.' That inside her was a lot of passion and he liked that. Personally, I never saw it." Clive looked at his watch. "I need to go. Tomorrow I have to make a sales pitch to some Asian billionaire about why he should put every penny he has with Coutts. Thanks for the drink. I'll see you later." He left quickly.

For a while they sat in silence. Kate and Sara finished their bowls of dessert while Jack drank another beer.

"Whoever believes that any of them will

return, raise her hand," Jack said.

Sara and Kate gave him looks of "get real."

"Let's go." Jack left money on the table. "I think we should talk about what we're going to do."

They drove back to Oxley Manor in silence.

Jack didn't drive around the house as usual. Instead, he parked out of sight on the far side of the chapel. When they got out, Jack held up a big key.

"Where did you get that?" Kate asked.

"Stole it off the rack in the kitchen," Sara said. "I noticed it was missing. If Mrs. Aiken discovers you took it, she'll poison your food."

"I can take her on," Jack said. "Maybe."

As they entered the chapel, they didn't need to say that it was the only place they felt truly private. There were too many people wandering around in the house. People who put notes in camera bags and spread lies.

Sara and Kate sat down while Jack stood.

"So what are we going to do for these ungrateful bastards?" he asked.

"If we continue, Bella may send Storm Troopers after us," Sara said.

"Doesn't matter," Kate said, "since they're all going to leave. For a few hours, anyway.

What a joke!"

"Maybe your Clive has room in his car for three more," Jack said. "We'll 'pop' down to London with him."

"And never return," Kate said.

"Those idiots!" Sara said. "They have no idea how easily their lives could be ruined. Puck is so angry about all this she might tell the police about the skeleton."

Kate groaned. "If a skeleton is revealed, the English tabloids would ruin them. Their names will be all over the papers."

"As possible murderers," Sara said.

"But they're keeping all the secrets to themselves," Kate said. "Just doling out tiny bits now and then."

Jack gave a malicious little smile. "The tabloids will ask who did it. Was it Clive, who was being forced to marry a woman he couldn't abide?"

Sara smiled a bit. "Or Willa, who was fat and dowdy and looked down on? That's not what the head of Renewal wants written about herself."

"Ha!" Kate said. "Willa is so ambitious she'd use it as an advertising campaign."

"Byon," Jack said. "He . . ."

Sara's eyes lit up. "He loved Nicky and was about to lose him to Diana —"

"Who loved Nadine," Kate said.

They couldn't help laughing.

"I would help them write it," Sara said. "How will the Queen's bank like a suspected murderer for an employee?"

"Nadine will never get a husband," Sara said. "And poor Teddy won't be a lady but the daughter of a murder victim."

"Willa's pristine yoga club tainted forever?" Kate said. "Her siblings will laugh at her."

"Which is the thing she most fears in the world," Sara said. "If the police get involved, public pressure will make them arrest someone. It's a coin toss as to who. All of them seem to have had motive and opportunity."

"If only they knew . . ." Kate said.

"If only we *didn't* know," Jack said. "We'd be in Scotland now." When he looked at Kate, his eyes told of his longing for a time with just the two of them.

When Kate felt the blood rush to her face, she looked away.

"That's it," Sara said softly. "We will *tell* them. No, we *show* them what's at stake."

"You mean the photos?" Kate asked.

"Yes."

They were silent as they thought about what she was saying.

Jack sat down on a pew, his arms across

the back. "They're a selfish lot. They'll turn on each other."

"Exactly," Sara said.

"How do we know who's telling the truth?" Kate asked. "I could see Nadine saying, 'I saw Clive shoot Sean. Now may I go see darling Lord Hazeldean?' "

"Proof," Jack said. "They have to show us proof of whatever they say."

"Like they have that," Kate said. "They all ran away that night and never looked back."

"Which proves that they have secrets," Sara said. "I bet Bella has a way to show photos on a big screen. Jack, you can set it up in here."

"Will your pictures show well blown up that size?"

Sara looked like her head might explode. "My new Sony has 61 megapixels. I can blow it up for a billboard. It —" She broke off as Kate and Jack were smiling at her. "Brats!" she muttered.

"What about Bella?" Jack asked. "Do we invite her or not?"

"Not!" Sara said. "She could close down the place. She could —" She took a breath. "Bella is going to hate me."

"It's not your fault. *You* didn't hide a body." Jack sounded dismissive. "So who's going to do what? Kate, it's your turn to deal with Mrs. Aiken. We'll need food or they won't show up."

"I think it's Aunt Sara's turn. That woman terrifies me."

"I need to choose photos and Jack is the IT guy. Looks like it's you," Sara said.

Kate groaned. "At least she has the food Willa brought." She looked at Sara. "If they're all making preparations to leave, how do we get them to meet us here?"

"Lie," Sara said. "Say whatever you have to. Appeal to their giant egos."

"Sounds good to me," Jack said. "Four o'clock this afternoon. Agreed?"

The women nodded.

It took the rest of the afternoon to arrange everything — and everyone was true to form.

Jack told Teddy he had some news about her father. That was enough for her. He flirted with Nadine and said he knew a few Florida millionaires. "Only M's?" It took him a moment to know what she meant. "It's Florida, not Nantucket. No billionaires available."

When Sara told Willa they'd found out something bad about Clive, she happily agreed to be there. "So much for revenge being dead," Sara muttered.

For Byon, she suggested they collaborate on something. Share the money. He protested that his schedule was full and he might not have the time. Sara shrugged, said, "Okay," then turned away.

"Four, is it?" Byon called after her.

Sara kept walking. "Whatever." She was smiling.

Puck just asked when and where. She didn't question them about what they were going to do.

Clive was the most difficult, but that was understandable. He really and truly wanted to get away from all of them. With every minute that passed, the others were reverting to the way it had been when Nicky was alive. Sara had even seen Willa staring at Clive in that fascinated way that stalkers do. Silent, watching, their eyes blank.

Jack set up the screen in the chapel, then taped cloth he'd found in a storage room over the windows. He didn't want to chance an outsider seeing what they were about to show.

"Everything ready?" Kate asked. "Do we tell them that the reasons they need to leave are lies?"

"No," Sara said. "We need as much urgency as we can get. Hurry up and do this so you can leave."

When Mrs. Aiken delivered the food, she looked at the screen and the blocked windows and said she was going to stay. Jack had to take her arm and lead her out.

The others arrived after the food did.

"What's this about?" Clive asked. "I really do need to leave. My bank called again. If I don't show up, they'll get someone else."

Sara smiled. "They are threatening you because they know you're the only one who can do the job. They need a numbers man who is charming. Who else is there?"

Clive softened under the praise and went into the chapel and sat down.

Nadine was next. "I do hope this doesn't take long. I need to condition my hair."

"I have a product I bought on St. Helena. You've been there, of course?"

"Certainly," Nadine said.

"Then you know what a center of beauty and luxury it is." Sara had been to the remote island a couple of times. Luxurious, it was not. "I'll give you a bottle."

Smiling, Nadine took a seat.

When they were all in place, Jack stood before them. It had been agreed that he would lead the presentation — mainly because he'd nearly begged for the right. "Let me have at them. Please."

The Pack wasn't much interested in what he was about to say. Their cups of tea and pretty plates full of sandwiches and cakes interested them more.

Nadine looked at Sara. "Did you take some nice photos?" Her voice was patronizing and full of the singsong baby talk that people often used on older people. It was a tone that always sent Sara into a rage.

Jack gave her a look to stay calm, then turned to the others. "Actually, these photos were taken by Kate and me. Sara wanted to go but since it meant rappelling down the sheer side of a hole in the ground, Kate and I said no." His words were meant to see who reacted, but none of them did. They just looked at him, not much interested. "Please put your teacups down."

"Yes, of course," Byon said. "We must give our attention to the show. Does it have music?"

"Hope so," Nadine said.

Jack nodded to Kate and the first photo came onto the screen. It was of the skeleton.

"A horror show," Byon said. "How divine."

There were three more photos, then a pause. A picture of the watch with its inscription came on the screen. To Sean Thorpe. First Prize. 1991.

A teacup crashed to the floor.

"That was Sean's," Nadine cried out.

The next photo showed a bony hand.

The room was silent.

Kate flipped through two more photos, then Puck turned on the light.

Sara, Jack and Kate were watching the faces of the audience. They were all in a state of shock — but they couldn't tell if it was from their discovering the death or from the death having been discovered.

Teddy was the first to speak. "Was that my father? If that watch was his, then was that . . . that him?"

"Yes," Jack said. "We believe he was murdered and his body was hidden."

"He didn't run away?" Nadine whispered.

Jack's face softened as he looked at her. "No. He didn't leave you."

Nadine put her hands over her face and began to cry.

Teddy was on the other side of the chapel. She went to her mother and put her arms around her.

"Are you *sure* he was murdered?" Clive asked. "Or was his body just hidden? Maybe he fell. Maybe a horse kicked him."

Willa, who'd been sitting in the back in disguise again, moved to the front. "If it wasn't murder, then why hide the body?"

She looked at Jack. "How did you Americans find it?"

They all seemed to know the answer to that. Everyone turned to look at Puck. She looked at the exit doors. How fast could she reach them?

"Stop it!" Sara said as she stood beside Jack. "You're not going to blame anyone but yourselves. We need to figure out who did this."

"Then you will write one of your bestselling novels about it?" Byon said. "Oh, darling, what a lucrative idea."

Kate stepped in front of her aunt. "If you want to be snide and sarcastic, so be it. I'll just call the police. We'll tell them how each of you had motive and opportunity. The press will love it! I can't wait to read the headlines. They'll love speculating on which one of you is a murderer." She had her phone in her hand. "Your emergency call number here is 999, isn't it?"

"Don't call," Clive said. "Byon, shut up!"

"Oh my goodness. The boy becomes a man." A glance from Clive made Byon quit talking.

"The police will try to find the murderer," Willa said.

"And it will be in the papers," Nadine whispered. "And on social media."

"Perhaps it would be better to leave this alone," Byon said. "After all, our dear friend Sean has been there awhile. Maybe we should leave things as they are."

"My father deserves justice," Teddy said.

"Maybe we could find him a place in the churchyard." Byon looked at Nadine. "Next to your father."

"What does that mean? You think *my father* killed Sean?"

"No, of course not," Byon said. "But he did offer him a million pounds to —" He shut his mouth.

"I see," Jack said. "The lot of you *do* know things."

Sara stepped forward. "What we need is a human sacrifice. Someone to burn at the altar."

She had their full attention.

"What my aunt means," Kate said, "is that when we do contact the police, we need to hand over the guilty person to them."

"And save them the expense of an investigation." Willa turned to Clive. "You disappeared that night. You went outside but you were nowhere to be seen."

"I was hiding from *you*." There was venom in his voice. "You were always throwing yourself at me. That night you had on a dress that exposed the upper half of you and you were always leaning over me."

"And you were tempted," Byon said. "Clive, my dear man, we all knew you wanted to jump on that. If Nicky hadn't laughed at you so hard, you would have grabbed onto her family fortune the way you're now going after young Kate and her bestselling millions."

"You fat, lazy bastard." Clive lunged for Byon but Jack grabbed him.

"Sit!" Jack ordered, then stepped back. "We all want to get out of here. We Americans most of all. We didn't want to get entangled in your nasty little Pack where you have predetermined winners and losers." He looked at Willa. "Which have now reversed themselves."

She smiled at him.

"All we want to know is — which one of you bastards killed Sean Thorpe?" Jack asked.

No one moved.

"As I thought," Jack said. "None of you are man enough to admit the truth, so we need to figure it out."

"Which one of you is the spy who sold the story to the tabloids?" Sara looked at Byon.

"It wasn't me," he said. "But how much do they pay?"

"You should find out," Clive said. "Your bank account is so low that —"

"Why you lying sneak. I'll report you to —" Byon began.

"Stop!" Jack ordered, then ran his hand over his face. "If I had a gun, I'd fire it."

"Americans," Byon muttered.

Jack gave him a look to shut up. "We need to figure this out. We have given ourselves the rest of the weekend. On Monday at 4:00 p.m., we turn it all over to the police. Whether we give them a person who is a murderer or just hand over the masses of information that we've gathered is up to you. Are you going to help us or are you going to continue to bicker?"

They looked like they were considering the matter. Only Willa spoke up. "I'll help. How about if I retrace my steps that night?" She gave Clive a little smile. "I'll show you where I was and where other people weren't."

"Looks like we have a lamb to burn." Byon was looking at Clive. "I'll get rosemary for seasoning."

"Can the rest of you show us what you did that night?" Kate asked.

"Of course." Nadine was holding her daughter's hand.

"It'll be useless," Byon said. "Without

Nicky, there's nothing."

"Who did he fight with?" Jack asked. "How did his face get smashed?"

They all looked straight ahead and said nothing.

Jack threw up his hands. "Your choice. We're not going to beg you to tell us."

Sara stepped forward. "We're not going to reenact an English murder mystery. We aren't going to plead with you to tell us what you know, then you say, 'How dare you?' It doesn't work that way. You tell us or not. But what we do get, we'll give to the police."

"If we don't have a murderer by Monday, the tabloids will speculate on each one of you," Jack said.

"I'm sure they'll be as kind to you as they were to me," Sara said. "That should be fun, right, Byon?" Her vision of headlines pointing out Byon's failed career seemed to project itself to him. His face turned a yellowish-green.

"None of us wants that," Willa said.

"Afraid your siblings will say, 'I told you so?' " Clive said snidely.

"They're too afraid I'll stop paying their bills to say anything bad to me." Willa gave a little smile.

Clive's face lost its smirk and looked at

her with interest.

"Love is in the air," Byon said.

"And the color is green." Nadine stood up. "I need time to digest all of this." She looked at her daughter. "We'll discuss this and decide what to do. Are we free to go or have we been imprisoned?"

Jack gestured toward the big doors in the back. "Go to London for all I care. I'm sure no one will even hint that you murdered a man who was bribed by your father."

Nadine gave Jack a look that nearly set his hair on fire. Then she put her nose in the air and left the chapel.

Quietly, the others followed. Even Byon seemed to have nothing to say.

When they were alone again, Jack, Kate and Sara looked at each other as they started putting away the video equipment.

"We did our best," Sara said.

"I loved your English murder mystery crack," Kate said. "I feel sorry for the detectives on TV having to deal with all the lies."

"Then figuring out the answer through superior intelligence," Jack said. "Wish I could do that."

Kate was looking at her aunt. "You have something in mind, don't you?"

"Willa said she'd walk us through that night. I know she still wants to know where

Clive was hiding, but I wonder about the others too. Maybe . . ."

"Maybe what?" Jack asked.

Sara closed her computer. "I have an idea about something. Would you two mind if I kept some secrets from you?"

"I would love it if you kept everything a secret," Jack said. "I mean like shoot Cupid's arrows into the sky love. I'd light candles of thanks. I'll name something after you. A kid maybe. I'll—"

Sara and Kate were looking at him with expressions of *too much*!

"Wouldn't mind it at all," he said. "What about you, Kate?"

"I'd be fine with it," she said politely.

"See you later then." Sara hurried out the door.

Jack turned to Kate. "I'll take care of this. Go. Have fun."

"Thanks." Kate hurried after her aunt.

Smiling, Jack finished clearing up.

Eighteen

It was early evening, and Sara was being bawled out by Bella. They were in her mini-Versailles of a bedroom — way too much gold for Sara's taste — and Bella was piling guilt onto her. "How could you do this to me?" Bella said for the third time. "You know how hard I've worked to make this into a world-class hotel. And I've succeeded. But this!" She held up the tabloid that had butchered Sara. "Murder at Oxley Manor. I've already had six calls asking to stay in the room where the man was murdered. Not suicide but *murder.*"

Sara kept her head down and looked as contrite as she could manage. But, she was thinking, *This is nothing. Wait until the world finds out there's a skeleton on your property.* "I'm sorry," she mumbled. Again. She wanted to defend herself, but she really was the one who'd started it all.

"They were going to leave." Bella was

standing over Sara like some great ogre ready to drop blows onto her head. "Then you met in the chapel and now they're all . . ." She turned on her heel. "I don't know what they're planning. Some of them are in the attic."

"Kate and Byon are looking for —"

"I don't care," Bella shouted. "I want them out of here."

"Bella," Sara said gently. "There are things going on that I can't tell you about."

Bella threw up her hands in exasperation. "Parasites, the lot of them. That Nadine is husband hunting. Disgusting. I think that daughter of hers was fathered by the boy who worked in the stables. How distasteful! The music man plays piano in a bar."

Sara was looking at her friend with wide eyes. "You seem to know a lot about them."

"They're not exactly quiet, are they?"

From what Sara had seen, they were a secretive lot. On the other hand, if Bella had done some research, Sara didn't blame her.

"What went on in my chapel?" Bella's eyes were intense.

"Showing off my photography," Sara said. "You know how vain I am about it. I have lots of pictures of the estate. You can use them on your website. Free."

"Next to the pictures of the Murder Room?"

Sara gave a weak smile. She was telling herself she should be like one of her book's heroines and demand, "How dare you say such a thing to me?" then she'd storm out in a dress with an eighteen-inch waist. But Sara just felt guilt. All the bad that was happening to Bella was caused by Sara's boredom and curiosity. "Everyone will leave on Monday." *If the police let us,* Sara thought. *By then, the skeleton will be exposed and hell will have been awakened.*

Sara stood up. "I need to . . ." She couldn't think of anything she needed to do except escape. She practically threw herself out the door. She didn't dare go to her room for fear Bella would find her. Instead, she ran up the stairs to the bleak servants' quarters, then up to the attics. Dear, calm Kate would be there.

Sara smiled at the sight of Kate and Byon together, surrounded by an untidy pile of boxes and suitcases and trunks.

"I can't find the box," Byon was saying. "Nicky probably threw it away. Probably threw them in the manure pile."

Sara rolled her eyes. The Enneagram divided people with nine personality types. Byon was a four. A true creative, but with extreme highs and lows. *Just like me,* Sara thought, and grimaced.

"We haven't even begun to make a dent in all of this stuff," Kate said. "It will take us days." When she saw Sara, her eyes were pleading for help.

"What's the box look like?" Sara asked. "And more importantly, what's in it?"

Byon sat down heavily on an old chair and dust floated up around him. He gave a sigh that told of all life's burdens. "Writing used to obsess me. It was like a disease that overtook my body and mind." He looked at Sara for understanding.

"Been there," Sara said. "And you kept every syllable you wrote, then put it all in a box?"

He nodded.

"The parodies!" Sara said. "You came here after that night. Did you write about *that night*?"

Again, Byon nodded.

"Hell and damnation," Sara said. "Get up and start looking. Tell us the size and color of the box. Kate! Call Jack. He can help search."

"He's with Nadine. She's up to something."

"Probably getting his clothes off," Byon said.

Sara and Kate turned angry faces to him.

"I'm in the midst of virgins. Stop the scowls. The box is about this big and it's blue. Maybe green."

"When did you last see it?"

"It . . ." His head came up. "I stayed in Nadine's room after that night."

"Of course you did," Sara said. "Finest in the house."

"Why not?" Byon said. "They all abandoned Nicky. I was the only true friend he had."

Sara's anger came to the surface. "Nadine left because she was pregnant with the child of a man who she believed abandoned her. Clive escaped years of bad treatment. Willa ran away because Nicky told her all of you were sick of giving her sympathy, no matter how much she paid for it. And Sean was gone because he was *dead.* Heaven only knows what happened to poor Diana."

Byon was unflustered. "Whatever their excuses, *I* was the only one here."

"You —" Sara took a step forward.

Kate placed herself between Byon and her aunt. "What happened to Nadine's things? Did she ask for them to be sent to her?"

"She turned her back on everything," Byon said. "Left her clothes and her friends. She —"

"Well, then, let's look for them," Kate said. "Find Nadine's clothes and we'll probably find your box of writing."

"Unless *you* wore them out," Sara said to Byon.

His lips twitched. "Only a few hats, darling. The rest didn't fit."

Sara laughed and the anger was gone.

It took them thirty minutes to find an old-fashioned trunk full of clothes fashionable about twenty years before.

"These are gorgeous." Kate pulled out a sky blue cashmere dress and a Chanel bag.

"Only the best for our Nadine."

Sara was leaning so far over the trunk she was half inside it. She was tossing clothes out to Byon and Kate. When she got to the bottom of the trunk, she had to brace herself at the side, but she came up with a red leather portfolio.

"That's it!" Byon clutched it to his chest.

"A 'box' of papers?" Sara said. "And blue or green? That is from Asprey's. So who gave it to you?"

"Willa for Christmas."

"I could have guessed," Sara said.

Byon sat down on the top of a trunk and opened the clasp of the beautiful portfolio and began flipping through the pages inside. "They're all here." He sighed. "That means

Nicky never read them. No one did." He looked like he might cry.

"Good!" Sara said. "Then no one can plagiarize them. We need to go over it all and see if there are any clues in there."

"They're all plays." He sounded as though that was a superior form of writing.

"The easy way out," Sara said. "No having to bother with scenery descriptions and literary glue." At their blank expressions, she said, "You know, getting people from one place to another. Standing or sitting? I used to use toy figures to keep up with who was where. Sex scenes were like directing traffic on an eight-lane highway, with everyone moving at a hundred miles per hour."

Byon's eyebrows were raised high. "Really? Maybe I should read one. Just for reference, that is. I could —"

"So what is in your plays?" Kate asked.

"I tried to write everyone's part in that night." He paused. "But back then, I thought it was all a joke. Diana and the groomsman had run off together. Quite amusing but not new. But after the little photo display . . ."

"Now it's different," Sara said. "What you wrote back then is very important."

Byon smiled at that.

"Willa said she'd walk us through what

she did that night," Kate said.

"Poor Clive," Byon muttered. "She followed him endlessly. Today it's called stalking."

"She was trying to please Nicky," Sara said. "Trying to please *all* of you. She was terrified of being thrown out of your nasty little group."

"We couldn't afford to toss her out," Byon said. "Literally. She fed us." His head came up from the case. "And she bought lovely things for us. If only we could look back at that time. We could —"

Sara was smiling. Glad he was finally understanding.

"A play," he said. "With actors!" He blinked a few times. "Jack looks like Sean."

"And the others are here."

They were looking at each other with wide eyes and heaving breasts.

"Is this writer sex?" Kate asked but they didn't answer.

"They will see only their own part." Sara was so out of breath her chest was like a runner's. "Do you know enough?"

"Not by a mile. Jack can get Nadine to tell all."

"Willa will love ratting on Clive."

"And it's all for a cause," Byon said.

"After your photos today, we have a purpose."

Kate was beginning to understand what they were thinking. "One of them is a murderer," she said. "One of the people here is going to lie to cover up and hide."

Byon and Sara didn't break eye contact.

"We'll not tell them. We'll do it one by one." Sara's voice was hoarse.

Byon nodded. "That dress." He pointed to a bit of silk sticking out from the pile of clothes. "Nadine wore that on that night." His eyes widened until they must have hurt. "You will film it."

Sara looked like she'd seen the Gates of Heaven. "I've always wanted to try video. It's the untouched red button on my camera. I'll need lights."

"London," Byon said.

"Yes. Clive. London," Sara agreed.

They turned in unison to Kate.

"Sorry, darling," Byon said, "but you must leave. We writers have work to do."

"And this lowly peasant has no place in that lordly kingdom," Kate said.

When they didn't smile, she left the attic, her eyes rolling back into her head. "The Writers' Pack," she muttered, and went to find Jack.

Nineteen

Two hours later, the whole house seemed to be abuzz with whispers. Byon and Sara had left the attic and were in a meeting with Nadine, Clive and Willa. They had their heads bent so close together their hair was touching. Since Kate wasn't invited to join them, she stood to the side and watched. At first, she thought it was her imagination, but Clive was sitting quite close to Willa.

Kate went upstairs to dress for dinner. *How Edwardian,* she thought. She put on nice trousers, a silk blouse, a soft jacket and pretty flats. *Screw the heels,* she thought, then went downstairs. They were all there and dressed up — except for Willa, who looked like a "before" photo — and they were all whispering among themselves. When they saw Kate, they quit talking and looked at her.

"I . . ." She took a step backward. They seemed to be discussing something that they didn't want Kate to hear.

Sara, sitting on the couch at the center of all of them, gave her a look to say GO! There was envy in her eyes.

Turning on her heel, Kate took off running down the hall. *Where is Jack?* she wondered. She hadn't heard him in the room next to hers so maybe he was outside.

She slipped out a side door into the dark night. She didn't think about where he was, she knew: the stables. There were path lights, but with all the day workers gone, she was alone. *Was this how it was with Nadine and Sean?* she wondered. There had been few workers then, so the grounds were empty.

As she hoped they would be, the lights in the stable were on and a door open. The sound of hammering made her smile. Jack and tools were like chocolate and raspberries, movies and popcorn, and in his case, men and iron.

Smiling, she went into the building toward the sound, then drew in her breath. Jack was sideways to her, nailing up a wooden panel — and he was shirtless.

Oh! but he was beautiful. Sometimes she forgot what other women saw instantly. To her, he was just Jack, the man who took care of her and Sara. Got them out of tough spots, kept them from getting too upset about things, and now and then saved their lives. And Jack *cared* about people.

He had stopped hammering, but he didn't turn around. "Keep looking at me like that and it won't end well."

For a moment, Kate considered that. But no. Not here, not now. She shook her head to get it back to reality. "What are you doing?"

He nodded toward the old desk behind him. On it was an envelope, yellow and curled from age. The words *TO MY LOVE* were on the outside. He went back to hammering.

She picked up the envelope and saw it was sealed. Had he been waiting to open it so they could do it together?

"There, done." He put down the hammer.

She looked from him to the panel he'd been working on, then back. "Let me guess. It was driving you crazy about what Nadine was looking for in here."

"You know me too well. You look nice." He leaned toward her, his shirtless body almost touching her, and put his lips by her ear. "Smell nice too," he whispered.

Kate's pulse started racing. "I'm not one of your —" She started to push him away. She put both her hands on his bare chest.

"Jack," she whispered as their eyes met.

There was a moment when they had a decision to make. Yes or no?

Kate leaned forward just a bit and so did Jack.

He was the one who stepped away and turned his back on her — and the moment was lost.

His shirt and jacket were hanging on the back of the old chair and he put the shirt on. He nodded toward the letter. "I remembered seeing that there had been new wooden panels put over the bricks. Probably put in to cover up decay. Lazy owners." He was talking fast. "I looked everywhere to find tools. Had to sneak them out from under Mrs. A's nose. Then I figured I'd get my shirt sweaty so I took it off. When I took the panel down, I found a loose brick, and there it was."

Kate was feeling more in control. His shirt was on, but not buttoned. She stepped forward and put her hand on his warm skin. She could feel the curve of his muscles underneath. "After this," she said softly, "let's still go to Scotland. Just us."

He nodded, seemingly unable to say anything. He touched her hair, just for a moment, but it was enough.

With a step back, he broke contact.

"What's it like inside?"

His words brought her back to the present. "Chaos. They're planning something. I've figured out some but not all of it. They get quiet when I enter the room."

"Do they?" He raised an eyebrow. "I have the keys to Nadine's Jag. How about if we go out to a pub about two villages away? I hear it has a live band."

She smiled. "Think they need a singer?"

"I think they have dancing."

"Then I'm ready."

He picked up the envelope. "And we'll read this."

"Should we? Maybe we should just hand it over to Nadine, unopened."

"Might be a clue." As he buttoned his shirt, his eyes were sparkling. He knew she wanted to read whatever was in that envelope.

"Yes," Kate said. "Yes to *all* of it."

"Oh how I wish that were true!"

With his funny-sad, longing-filled words, the tension between them was broken. They were back to a place where they could tease and laugh.

As they got into the car, Kate said, "Nadine won't mind if you borrow her car?"

"That woman would lend me her soul if she could."

"And the lacy knickers she covers it with?"

Laughing, Jack put the car in Reverse. Thanks to a father who didn't abide by anybody's rules, Jack had been driving since he was twelve. He whirled the car around full circle, then headed toward the gates. "This thing has been worked on. It handles well." He glanced at her. "You're staring at me again."

"Think you can drive while wearing a kilt?"

"Or without it. I doubt if I can live up to the heroes in Sara's books. They carry thirty-five-pound broadswords and ride heavy horses into battle."

"And wear chain mail." She sighed. "Never forget the chain mail."

"I'm not sure I'm strong enough to do that." He was teasing.

"I think you are. The way you climb ladders carrying two fifty-pound bags of whatever is strength personified. And you wear those heavy boots and that tool belt and —"

Jack pulled the car to the side of the road and looked at her. His voice was quiet, his eyes intense. "You know how I feel about you. I'm waiting for you and you know it. But there's only so much restraint I can manage."

Kate swallowed.

"If you want to leave this place tonight, we'll do it. A hotel? The backseat of this car? Whatever you want, I'll give it."

Kate's heart was pounding in her throat. "Scotland?" she whispered.

He looked away and seemed to be trying to make a decision. He put the car in gear. "Scotland, it is." He looked back at her. "Tonight is for *fun.*"

"Yes," she agreed. "We need some laughter."

Jack took the curves of the English country roads like a driver at Daytona. Beside him, Kate leaned back in the plush leather seat and smiled. Just a few more days and maybe . . . She glanced at him, saw the seriousness in his eyes.

The restaurant Jack had found for them was nice. White tablecloths, heavy silver. Next door was a pub that had a sign announcing the band.

"Eat first, dance later," he said as he held her chair out for her.

They ordered English beef.

"Now?" Kate asked.

Smiling, Jack handed the envelope to her. Carefully, she ran her finger under the tab and lifted it. There was a single sheet inside.

Tonight. Midnight. The beginning of forever.

She handed it to Jack, then blinked back tears. "Nadine went to him but he wasn't there. All these years, she's not known what happened to him."

"Maybe not. I still think she could have hit him over the head. Maybe he *did* accept her father's money."

"If Mr. Howland was in Hawaii that night, then he had to have offered the money before that. Sean would have left then. He wouldn't have been so cruel as to wait to tell her on the night they were to leave together."

"I like to think not. How's your dinner?"

"Great. Excellent. You?"

"Perfect. So what are the others plotting to do?"

Kate shook her head. "I can't figure it out. It's all very hush-hush. I think there's to be a play. We're all to act out what happened that night. I heard Nadine tell Teddy she was too fat to wear the dress she wore that night."

"Nothing like mother love, is there?"

"I understand. I'm a lot bigger than my mother."

"You are perfectly sized. Truly *perfect.*"

The way he said it made her blush.

"I guess we'll find out tomorrow." Jack sounded dismissive, as though he'd heard all he wanted to about the Pack at Oxley Manor.

It was as they were about to leave that they saw Meena — not her incarnation as the dumpy Willa — enter the restaurant with a man. The lawyer, no doubt.

Jack put his hand up to shade his face. "And it's another possible murderer and a body hider."

"You are horrible!" Kate said but she was laughing.

"Is there a back way out of here?" he asked the pretty waitress. He nodded toward Meena and Eddie. "They're her parents. We don't want to spend the night listening about the good ol' days."

"Sure," she said. "Through the kitchen."

"You're incorrigible." Kate took his hand as they ran through the kitchen and out the back.

"Horrible and incorrigible. I'm batting a thousand tonight."

They were in a dark alley with trash bins and empty boxes. There were lights on the buildings but one in the middle was out.

Jack caught her hand, and in a deft move, swirled her around until her back was against a wall. For a moment, he paused, as though asking if she was all right with him.

Jack kissed her. His body pressed against hers, his lips to hers. For all his desire for her, what was in the kiss was his longing for *her,* for this woman who had been his companion for years now. Talking, laughing, sharing. Good moods and bad. Danger and peace. Anger and calm. They were all there in the kiss.

When he broke away, he smiled at her sweetly. "The rest can wait."

He took her hand, and laughing, they went down the alley to the pub. It was already filling up and the band was on the stage. They went through the crush to the bar, got beers and made their way closer to the band. It began to play a mix of rock and roll and ballads.

Jack got them a tiny table near a wall. They put down their drinks and hit the floor. They had danced together very little, but they'd lived in the same house for years and they knew each other well.

He was a down and dirty dancer, while Kate had had classes in college. She could follow anything he did.

After an hour of nonstop dancing, Jack left Kate in a chair at their table and nodded toward the band. She understood. He was going to sing. She watched him talk to the five musicians and the female singer. They were smiling and nodding.

Kate wondered what he was going to sing. She recognized it within seconds. It was one of Byon's songs. She'd heard them practicing it, but Jack hadn't sung it all the away through.

Run away with me. Make my tomorrows your forever. Take my hand. Lead me away. I am yours.

As he sang, he kept his eyes on Kate. The audience saw where he was looking, and they stepped back, not blocking his view.

When the song was nearly finished, he handed the microphone to the female singer and she kept it going. Jack stepped down from the stage. He went to Kate, held out his hand, and she took it. Everyone cleared the floor as Jack led Kate in a slow dance, holding her body close to his. He dipped her back, then pulled her to him. Spun her out, drew her back into his arms.

When the singer finished, Jack held Kate tightly — and their audience burst into applause.

Smiling, Jack kissed Kate's forehead, then led her off the floor and out of the pub. Laughing, they ran down the sidewalk to the car.

"Okay?" he asked.

"I'm good. In fact, right now, this moment, my happiness meter is at a high ten."

He laughed. "Mine's about a hundred. Ready to go back?"

"No, but yes."

TWENTY

Jack woke to a soft, warm hand on his cheek. "Kate?" he whispered.

"Alas, it's only me," Sara said.

He turned over, rubbing his eyes. There was no light around the curtains so it was very early in the morning. "What's happened now? Found another body? Clive went berserk and killed everyone?"

"Puck wants us at her house. You usually sleep in a T-shirt but you don't have one on now. Anything on below it?"

"None of your business."

"Interesting," Sara said. "You were hoping Nadine would slide into bed with you?"

"I'm holding out for the daughter. Turn around. I have to get out of bed."

Smiling, Sara turned away as Jack slid on jeans and a shirt. "What's going on? Or is that part of your new secrecy?" he asked.

"You and Kate have a good time last night?"

"I always have a good time with Kate. If you don't answer my questions, I'm going back to bed."

"Kate's already up and ready to go."

"Ah. You're using enticement." He sat down on the edge of the bed to put on shoes. "Any climbing to do? Tunnels?"

Sara's face turned serious. "I don't know. Puck wouldn't tell me. That woman! If I didn't like her I'd be afraid of her. This house is locked at night, and my door was locked. But she still got into my bedroom."

"Wonder how she did it," Jack said.

"When we see her, you can ask, but that's not important. She said it was urgent that we get there asap."

Jack stood up. "How are you and Byon doing on the script?"

Sara laughed. "So you heard about that. You figure it out or did Kate?"

"She did. She's the brains — I'm the brawn."

"Have you been running around shirtless to make her *see* that?"

"Oh yeah. I've been about to freeze, but the look on her face was worth it."

They smiled at each other.

There was a quick knock on the door and Kate entered. She looked from one to the other. “What have you two been talking about?”

“Sex,” Sara said.

“Good,” Kate said. “You can teach Jack about it. You two ready to go?” She left the room.

Sara frowned at Jack. “You do know about boys and girls who love each other, don’t you?”

Shaking his head, Jack went through to Kate’s room. Behind him, Sara was smiling.

They tiptoed through the house, down the stairs and out through the empty kitchen. The big table was covered with bowls of chopped vegetables that Mrs. Aiken had prepared for the day’s meals.

“Dare you to mess them up,” Kate whispered to Jack.

“I value my life too much.”

Outside, the women followed Jack to find one of the little utility trucks parked under a tree.

Kate looked up. “Puck isn’t going to jump down, is she?”

“I wouldn’t be surprised by anything she did,” Sara said.

Jack drove them to Puck’s house and there were lights on inside. Outside was an old green Range Rover that looked like it had been used to ford rivers and climb rocks.

"Someone's here," Sara said.

"Oh good," Jack said. "Another murder suspect."

"Just so it isn't another body, I'm fine with it," Kate shot back.

Puck had to let them in through the downstairs gate. She didn't say anything, but her eyes showed that she was excited about something.

Upstairs, they saw a woman, fortyish, with skin that looked like it had spent a lifetime outdoors. She was sturdily built, not fat, not thin, and she looked strong.

Jack and Kate stepped forward to greet her, but Sara stayed back.

"You're Diana," Sara said.

She smiled. "I am. I saw the paper on the newsstand. Murder at Oxley Manor. What a headline! I was going to call, but then I thought it would be better if I showed up. I do like to answer questions about my death in person. Are they all here?"

"Yes." Sara sat down at Puck's big table, Jack and Kate beside her.

"Did you tell her?" Sara asked Puck and she nodded.

Diana took a seat. "I haven't seen the photos and I don't want to. Sean . . ." Tears came to her eyes. "It was all because of me. But he told me to go. I begged him to leave with me but he said he couldn't. He gave me his suitcase and I —"

"Wait!" Sara said. "Don't tell us now. Byon and I are going to write it all down."

"For the newspapers?" Diana sounded shocked.

"No," Sara said. "Tonight we're going to make a play about that night and act it out so we can find the answers. Unless you know everything and can tell us."

"No." Diana shook her head. "I know Sean had the gun and —" She broke off at Sara's look. "I don't know it all. If Sean was . . . murdered, I don't know who did it."

"What about hiding his body in the old well?" Kate asked.

"What well?"

"In the conservation area."

"You mean that old fenced-off acreage in the north? Bertie said there were fox holes there. He was afraid one of the horses would be hurt."

"Afraid one would fall down the hole and never be seen again. By the way, I'm Jack and this is Kate."

Diana smiled. "Puck hasn't stopped talking about you three." She looked at Sara. "Sorry about what my country's paper said about you. From what I read online, you've had enough success for a dozen lifetimes. Sure is better than trying to run a horse farm."

"Thank you," Sara said. "So that's where you've been all these years?"

"Yes. I guess I should have contacted them and told them where I was, but . . ." Her hands went into fists, her teeth clenched.

"But you never wanted to see them again," Sara said. "I can understand that."

"So how does this play thing work?"

"Today, one by one, everyone who was there that night is going to tell Byon and me what they did and what they saw. Then we're going to write individual plays for each person. No one will know what the others do."

"Just like that night," Diana said. "We didn't know where anyone was or what they were doing. Puck told me about Nadine and Sean. I guess she was why he wouldn't leave with me."

"How did you leave?" Jack asked.

Diana smiled. "On one of Bertie's pregnant mares."

"Impregnated by stolen semen," Jack said.

Diana nodded. "Right, but Sean and I figured that part was payback. Bertie was ripped off by every horseman in three counties. They owed him."

"Maybe I'm being presumptuous," Sara said, "but you don't seem like one of the Pack."

"That is a great compliment. Thank you," Diana said. "Nicky thought the world owed him, Byon gloried in his ability to use words and Nadine was obsessed with how good she looked."

"What about Clive and Willa?" Sara asked.

Diana gave a snort of laughter. "Talk about love-hate. Those two! Her family ancestry was all ol' Clive had ever dreamed about. He'd been tossed around by his own family, then here came Bertie. Offered him a ratty little room in the house in exchange for eternal servitude."

"And Willa?"

"Pathetic. She just wanted to belong. To anyone."

"If your own family doesn't want you," Sara said softly, "you hunger after being part of any semblance of a family that you can find."

Kate put her hand over her aunt's. "Tell us how you met them. I assume it's a happy story and we need some happy."

"I can tell it the way Byon told it to all of us. He expanded it, embellished it and made us laugh. He didn't like me much at first, but I eventually won him over."

The four of them leaned back in their chairs as they prepared to listen.

Twenty-One

Byon and Nicky were on their way back from university to spend the weekend at Oxley Manor. They were dreading it. Bertram would be there, ready to tell his son he was a wastrel. Clive was at school, but he was so eager to please he would arrive hours before the others did. To add to the horror, lately, Bertram had been asking Nicky when he was going to get a wife. "At least get *something* from your years at that school."

"We could go somewhere else," Byon said. "Maybe to . . ." He had no words to finish the sentence. Nicky's image at school was of a young earl-to-be who had responsibilities at his Great House. He couldn't just go drinking all weekend — or heaven forbid — *study.*

Besides, Nicky only liked a few people in the world — and the feeling was mutual.

When the old car slowed down, then stopped completely, they didn't know whether to be glad or terrified. They were on a country road with nothing around them but trees. They got out.

"What the hell do we do now?" Nicky asked.

Byon looked around. "Find someone to ask for help?"

"Are *you* going to walk?" When things weren't going his way, Nicky attacked whomever was nearest. Usually, that was Clive. "The income-sucker," Nicky called him. "Taking what isn't his."

They were leaning against the boot of the car, both smoking Spanish cigarettes, when out of the trees came a woman on a big horse.

When she saw the car in her direct path, she yelled, "Bloody hell!" then reined in. The horse, angry, confused and torn between obeying and fighting, reared up. The young woman gripped with strong thighs and iron fists.

It took minutes but she brought the animal under control and halted in front of the car. She dismounted, soothed the frightened animal, then tied the reins to a tree branch.

Nicky and Byon were in exactly the spot they'd been in. They prided themselves on being cool, on being "men of the world."

"What the hell are you doing?" she shouted at them. "You could have killed Raven."

"Is that your horse's name?" Byon asked blandly.

"Mare," she snapped.

"Forgot to look." Byon bent over, his head low as he looked toward the underside of the horse. "No dangly bits so you might be right." He straightened his shoulders and smiled at her.

She took a few seconds to decide on keeping her anger or not. She let it go. "I see you two at school." She glared at their cigarettes. "Do you ever stop smoking those filthy things?"

Byon took a long, deep puff, but Nicky dropped his cigarette to the road and crushed it with the toe of his custom-made Lobb shoe.

She looked at Nicky. "Oxley Manor, right?"

He nodded.

Byon was looking from one to the other, and he didn't like what he was seeing. Nicky was *his*.

"What's wrong with your car?" she asked.

"How would we possibly know that?" Byon snapped.

She gave him a look up and down that

was pure dismissal. He wasn't worth her time.

Nicky got out of his slouch and walked to the front of the car. "It quit running."

To Byon's astonishiment, Nicky's voice was deeper, more melodious than usual.

She looked at the old car, then deftly opened the hood. "Carburetor," she mumbled. She moved a few things around, then said, "Try it now."

Nicky got into the car and it started right away.

As she closed the bonnet, Byon got into the passenger's seat. He wanted to get away as soon as possible.

But Nicky got out and went to her. She was standing by her horse and he introduced himself with just his nickname. Usually, he gave his full name and title. "Best to start out by intimidating the enemy," he liked to say. Nicky considered all but about six people his enemies.

"Diana Beardsley," she said.

"How do you know how to repair cars?"

Byon's mouth dropped open. Nicky never asked anyone personal questions, mainly because he didn't *care.* He'd certainly never asked Byon about his origins. But then, Byon would have lied.

"My father is the chauffeur for Lord Haverley. We always helped keep the cars in repair but I loved the horses."

"How do you afford university?"

Diana laughed. "Saved the old man's life. He ran his best horse into a lake and the animal's legs were trapped. His lordship refused to get off, rightly thinking that the horse would panic. I dove in, went under, and cut the horse's legs loose." She shrugged. "Unfortunately, I got tangled and almost died, but I did save both of them."

"And he rewarded you," Nicky said.

"He did. He said he'd give me anything I wanted, even to half of his estate. I told him I already took care of the whole place so I didn't want it. I said I wanted to go to university. He laughed and agreed. So here I am."

With that, she mounted her mare and rode away.

Byon sat in the car and waited for Nicky to get in, but he didn't. He was staring at the road where the woman had disappeared. Byon went to stand next to Nicky.

"She would be able to take care of Oxley."

Byon bristled. "Your father would never fire Clive. And he can't afford *two* managers."

"I wouldn't ask him to, but if I *married* that woman he could throw Clive out. What was her name again?"

"Diana Beardsley." Byon's voice was full of horror.

"Write that down and find out where she lives. I'll send her a thank-you gift."

"Somehow, I don't think she's the flowers and candy type."

"What was that car part she mentioned?" Nicky asked.

"A carburetor?"

"Yes, that's right. I've met Lord Haverley. He drives Jags. I'll send her a carburetor from a Jaguar. Is there such a thing?"

"I would imagine so." Byon lit another cigarette.

"Then let's go somewhere we can buy one. Where do you think that is?"

"I have no idea." Byon's lips were tight in disapproval. "Ask Thorpe. He'll know."

"Good idea." Nicky got back into the car. When Byon got in beside him, Nicky took the cigarette out of Byon's mouth and threw it to the road. "No more of *that.* Diana doesn't like it."

Twenty-Two

"And that was it," Diana said. "On Monday, Thorpe FedExed me a carburetor from an old Jag. He included a note saying that he'd had it power washed so Nicky wouldn't get his hands dirty."

"That sounds like a put-down," Kate said.

"It was, but if you knew Thorpe . . . How do I explain? If Clive had said that, Nicky would have been furious, but Thorpe just made him laugh." She looked at Jack. "I guess you know that you —"

"Yeah, I know," Jack said.

"What happened next?" Kate asked.

"I was invited to Oxley." Diana paused. "I make fun of Willa, but when I look back on it, I wasn't much better off than she was. I was a chauffeur's daughter at a posh school. I didn't belong with them."

"But you did fit in with the Pack?" Sara asked.

"For a while, yes, I did. Bertie and I got

on well. He knew nothing about horses but he was trying. He so desperately wanted to make enough money to repair Oxley Manor before it collapsed."

"He didn't like his son." Jack sounded belligerent.

She gave him a sharp look. "Bertie spent his life trying to keep this place going, but he knew that Nicky would destroy it out of ineptitude and laziness."

"It sounds like you all needed each other," Kate said.

"Desperately." Diana looked down at her hands for a moment. They were strong hands that had seen a lot of work. She looked at Sara. "I have a twenty-five-year-old son. He'll be here soon."

Sara blinked for a moment as she took in this news, especially considering the boy's age. "He can play Nicky. We need —"

"No!" Diana shouted.

Sara was looking at her intensely. "How about if you and I go sit on the couch and you tell me everything that happened that night?" She aimed a pointed look at Jack and Kate.

He stood up. "Yeah, okay, we're leaving."

Sara took a piece of paper out of her pocket, made a few marks on it, then folded it. Jack took it and put it in his shirt pocket.

On the way out, Jack looked askance at Puck, and she nodded. He took two large bread rolls from a basket and some oranges, then he and Kate left the pretty little house and walked to the cemetery.

"So Sean was illegally selling horse semen to get money to support the woman he loved." Jack sat down on a concrete curb and used his pocketknife to start peeling the oranges.

"And Diana was helping him."

"That must have been a fun date."

Kate tried to look stern but she couldn't. "I feel sorry for Nadine. Diana said Sean gave her his suitcase, so when Nadine got there, everything was gone. She's lived with that for years."

"Maybe," Jack said.

Kate didn't reply but ate in silence. At last, she said, "So?"

"What do you mean?" He tried, but couldn't resist a smile.

"Give me that!" She made a lunge for his shirt pocket, but he leaned away.

Kate held out her hand. With a fake gesture of capitulation, Jack removed the paper Sara had given him, handed it to her, then leaned over her shoulder as she opened it.

It was a list of characters in the play and

who was to be whom.

"I'm to be Diana," Kate said. "Horsey girl. Like I know about horses. Let's see, the head has the eyes, right?"

"Who do you want to be?"

"Nadine, of course. Glamorous, rich, beautiful."

"And you have the most dramatic scene of finding that the love of your life is gone."

"Well . . . I did do a bit of drama in school."

He picked up a handful of pebbles, got up and went to the house to toss them at a window. Puck opened it.

"Tell Sara that Kate is going to play Nadine. Kate wants to be in love with *me*."

"That's not what I meant," Kate said. "I want the drama and the dress Nadine wore and —" Jack was smiling at her so smugly she stopped. "Maybe I'll get to bash you over the head with a big rock."

"For you, Kate, it would be worth it."

She groaned and looked up at Puck, who was still waiting. "Tell Aunt Sara I'll be Nadine. Teddy can be Diana. She knows how to ride a horse."

With a nod, Puck put the window down.

Kate turned to Jack. "So what do we do now?"

"Don't you need to get dressed for tonight?"

"Are you saying I'm so ugly that I need an entire *day* to put on makeup and a dress?"

"No. I didn't mean that. I thought you'd like —" He narrowed his eyes at her. "I'm not laughing." He tossed the orange peels onto Puck's compost pile, then started walking in the direction of the big house. "I bet there is some research you need to do. You'd help Bella if you straightened up the mess in the attic. Sara would appreciate that. Hey! You could help find clothes for the play and —"

"I'm going with you."

"I thought I'd take a swim. And hit the weights. If I'm to play Sean, I better get in shape."

"I'm going with you," Kate repeated.

Jack stopped walking. "I need some alone time."

"What are you up to?"

With a sigh, Jack admitted defeat. "It was Diana's mention of a gun. I'm going to go back and look for a cause of death."

"To the skeleton, you mean?"

He nodded.

Kate held out her arms. "I'm ready. Lead the way."

In the end, Jack felt like he half won as he persuaded Kate not to go down in the hole with him. To be fair, he hadn't had to say much. She didn't want to see the bones again.

"It's just that now I feel like I know him," Kate said. "He was in love and about to become a father."

"Am I hearing sympathy for his child, for Teddy?"

"After that dress she wore?" Kate sighed. "Okay, so maybe I am feeling bad for her."

"*You* grew up without a father, so —"

"So what?" she said loudly. "You're going to pity *me*?"

"Wouldn't dream of it." He took a step back. "You want to go down or not?"

"The more people who disturb the scene, the more . . ." She trailed off.

"Got it. You better stay here and make sure no murderer comes by and cuts the ropes and leaves me down there forever. You think my bones will look like Thorpe's?"

"You are so not funny. Are you going to rummage around in there a lot?"

"Not at all." He had Sara's camera bag and he withdrew four little black plastic cubes.

"What are they?"

"Lights. I'm going to use them and a stick

to see what I can find." He was standing at the head of the chain ladder they'd taken from the storage bin, and looking at the grass that had been eaten by the sheep. "Part of me wishes I hadn't done that. I'd like to see who's been here besides us."

"You think someone has?" Her eyes widened. "What if someone took him away?"

"My thoughts exactly. I wonder if everyone stayed in their rooms last night or if someone went out and down the hole."

"Jack, that's scary."

He grinned in a roguish way. "Guess I'll have to take my chances. Watch the knot on the tree." He climbed down the ladder.

Kate stretched out on her stomach. English grass was so soft and fragrant. Florida saw grass wasn't named that for no reason. It had to be strong enough to withstand the sun and a hurricane now and then. "Anything?" she called down to him.

"Not yet."

She saw a light come on.

"It's here. Just as we left it."

Kate let out her breath.

"I'm going to set up," he said. "It'll take a while."

Kate rolled over, did a sit-up, then let out a gasp of shock. There was a man sitting not three feet from her.

"Sorry," he said. "Didn't mean to frighten you. I'm Christopher Isles, Diana's son. So this is where it is?" He nodded toward the place where Jack had pushed the vines aside. The light from below was brighter now.

Kate was staring at him, not sure what to say. He was Jack's height, a little over six feet, with dark blond hair and blue eyes. He had on all khaki clothes, like he'd been on a safari. His accent was nice. "You're Australian?"

"Mom says I'm English. I was just born and raised Down Under. And please don't ask me to say anything about shrimp on a barbie."

"Wouldn't dream of it," Kate said. She tried to stop herself, but her eyelashes fluttered. He was quite good-looking!

"Mom told me about you and a famous writer and some guy who looks like Sean — whoever he is. She said his skeleton was found in a cave. Or in a hole. I'm not sure which."

"Sort of both. He's down there." She pointed.

"You're bringing him — it — up?"

"No. Jack's looking for —" She hesitated in telling too much.

He smiled in understanding, then stood

and offered his hand to help her up. "One thing for sure is that I'm not the murderer. I wasn't born at the time this guy disappeared."

"Me neither," Kate said, and smiled back. "I don't mean to be so personal, but, well . . . Who is your father?"

"I am the product of IVF and a donor from a catalog. My two moms call me 'untainted.' I have to work at not seeming to be 'too male.' "

"You're not doing a very good job," Kate said.

Chris laughed. "Don't tell my moms that. They'll feel they failed in their life's work of creating a man who cares about . . . well, about everything."

They smiled at each other.

"I was late getting here because I bought a horse. I'm taking him to Wales to my mother's cousin."

"Diana's?"

"No. My other mom. She's in Nelson on the station. All of us can't leave at once."

"So who have you met?"

Chris ran his hand through his hair. "Just a woman named Isabella. She seems to hate me."

"She owns Oxley Manor and she's angry that we've taken over the place." Kate leaned forward and her voice grew quieter. "Aunt Sara has been careful not to let her know there's a . . . you know on her property."

"Guess she won't be too happy when the police show up. You *are* going to tell them, aren't you?"

"Eventually. Did you hear about the play? You're going to be Nicky."

"Is he a good guy or a bad one?"

Kate held out her hand and flipped it back and forth. "No one seems to be sure. Byon adored him. Mrs. Aiken worshipped him. Not sure what Nadine feels about anything."

"What did Mom think of him? She —" He stopped. "Is someone calling you?"

"Oh! Yes. Sorry." Kate went down to her knees to lean over the well opening. "I'm here," she called down. "What do you need?"

"I found two of them," Jack said.

"Two of what?"

"Bullets."

"Crickey," Chris said. He was close beside her.

"Who the hell is that?" Jack yelled up.

"I'm Christopher Isles, Diana's son," he called down. "Need any help?"

"I damned well don't!" Jack shouted.

Kate sat back on her heels. "He's not going to be happy that you found us."

"I don't blame him. Who do you think did this?"

"Everyone is a suspect," Kate said. "Each of them had opportunity and motive."

"My mom, too?"

Kate didn't answer and she could feel her face turning red.

"What I was told is that after Mom left here that night, she and my other mother went directly to Australia."

"Oh," Kate said. "So she's English too? They met *before* the night Diana left?"

"Yeah. She was a trainer at a nearby farm. Met, fell in love instantly and . . ." He shrugged.

Kate smiled. "So Diana chose love over Oxley Manor."

"I really wish someone would tell me what's going on here. Does anyone actually think my mom shot a horseman, then ran off to Australia? I think she was saying she was engaged to him."

"Oh no," Kate said. "Diana was engaged to Nicky, who owned this place, and he couldn't care less about horses. Sean, who is down there, ran the stables."

"My mother was thinking of marrying somebody who *wasn't* horse mad?" He laughed. "She must have been temporarily insane."

"I think maybe they all were. She —"

"I don't mean to interrupt this little pow-wow," Jack said, "but why are you here?" He was on the chain ladder, with just his head above the ground.

"To offer help," Kate said. "He's come all the way from Nelson, Australia, and he wasn't born until after the night his mother disappeared. He's our one true innocent."

"And Teddy," Jack said as he climbed the rest of the way out.

"How could I have forgotten Teddy?" Kate mumbled. "Teddy is —" She broke off because her phone buzzed — as did Jack's and Chris's. "Please, please don't let anybody else be dead," Kate said.

"Do people often drop dead around here?" Chris took his phone out of his pocket.

"Here, there, everywhere we go," Jack said. "Put a shovel in the ground, hit a bone." He looked at his phone. It was a joint text to Kate and him from Sara.

> Find Christopher, Diana's son, and hide him. Don't let any of the Pack see him!! Mega important.

Chris's text was from his mother telling

him to go somewhere and stay out of sight. "And here my mother always told me I wasn't an ugly troll."

Kate laughed a bit too much at his joke; Jack didn't even smile.

"What are we supposed to do with him?" Jack asked.

"Toss me down the well?" Christopher asked in a way that was almost a challenge.

"Gatehouse!" Kate said. "I think it's empty now." She looked at Jack. "You can open the lock."

"Sure you don't want to get a kangaroo to break a window?" Jack asked.

Kate gave him a look that took the smirk off his face.

Jack sighed. "Okay, let's go, Crocodile Dundee. I'll take you there through the outskirts. Who's seen you since you got here?"

"Only Isabella," Chris and Kate said in unison, then smiled at each other.

Jack rolled his eyes.

"I have a horse here and —"

"Of course you do," Jack said.

"It's a big black stallion that only I can ride. Named Lucifer," Chris said.

Jack and Kate stared at him.

Chris grinned. To Kate's astonishment, Jack put his arm around the younger man's shoulders. "Chris, my boy, I'm starting to like you." They walked away from Kate. They were too far away for Kate to hear more of their conversation. At her feet was the chain ladder. Was *she* supposed to pull the huge iron thing up, hand over hand like an anchor? Then untie it from the tree and haul it back to the storage bin?

She looked about but the men were gone. She began pulling up the heavy ladder. "Give me back corsets and crinolines," she muttered.

When she got the ladder up — and she was sweating — Jack and Chris were standing there, both of them grinning down at her.

"I'm all for corsets," Jack said.

"What's a crinoline?" Chris asked.

Kate stood up, the end of the ladder in her hand. "I hate you both," she said, then let the ladder drop back down into the well. Let *them* pull it back up! She straightened her shoulders, put her chin up and walked toward the house. "Men are slime," she said over her shoulder. She didn't wait to see if they commented.

Twenty-Three

When Kate entered the house, the first thing she saw was Bella and her expression of rage. Her anger seemed to be so strong that she wasn't able to speak.

Kate tried to be cheerful when she said hello, but she sounded wimpy and apologetic. After all, Kate knew what was coming for her beautiful hotel.

Bella didn't say anything, just turned away and stomped up the stairs.

In the next moment, Kate heard Nadine. "Not there! Over here! These colors are all wrong. Who decorates like this anymore?"

Kate went to the door of the large drawing room. It looked like the entire staff of male workers was in the room — and they were moving furniture. Bella's neat, orderly room was being turned around, with couches put by windows, chairs in little groups. The room was being changed from a place that dealt with a large gathering into half a dozen private areas. It looked like Nadine was putting the room back to the way it was when the Pack had been hanging out there.

"No! No!" Nadine said. "That's Nicky's corner but that's Byon's chair. Put it by the piano."

Nadine looked up and saw Kate. "Isn't it wonderful about Diana? I was so afraid she was . . . You know."

"It is good," Kate said. "Everyone was happy to see her?"

"Ecstatic." She turned to a workman. "Table next to that chair." She looked back at Kate. "I hear you're going to play me."

"Yes. If you don't mind."

"I'm flattered. The green dress is upstairs. Teddy is going to be Diana." Nadine frowned. "That night Diana had on a mini-dress that was way too short. Maybe you can reason with Teddy about it."

Kate smiled at that. Getting Teddy to not do whatever she wanted was an impossible task and they both knew it. "Where is everyone?"

"Jack and Teddy are setting up for the stages. We've been told there are five acts and two of them are in the stables. Diana even brought a horse. How very like her! Clive should be back from London soon.

He bought the lights Sara asked for. Willa is in the attic. She's in charge of finding clothes for everyone."

"I guess Byon and Aunt Sara are holed up somewhere."

"Oh yes," Nadine said. "Byon was quite dramatic with the door. What have you been doing?"

Kate wasn't about to tell of finding two bullets and Diana's son. All that was of utmost secrecy. She faked a yawn. "Staying out too late and having fun. I need a shower."

She left before Nadine could ask more questions. The truth was that Kate did want some time to calm down, time to be alone. In her beautiful room, she took a long, hot shower, washed her hair, blow-dried it and put on clean clothes. So now what did she do? Or more precisely, which group did she join? Nadine? Willa? Jack and Teddy? Maybe she'd volunteer to type for Byon and Aunt Sara. Or maybe she'd go to the gatehouse and keep Chris company. She smiled at that idea.

In the end she went up the stairs to the attic. Willa seemed the safest bet. Kate's slippers made no noise so she caught Willa off guard. In a pile on the floor was Willa's old dress with its heavy padding, while Willa herself was sitting in a chair wearing her yoga gear. She was absorbed in what looked to be a photo album.

"You've been caught!" Kate said.

Willa gasped, then relaxed. "I thought I locked the door."

"Nope. Or at least not the one I used. Have you found all the clothes?"

Willa gave a one-shoulder shrug. "Enough of them. They were tossed into a trunk. It's a wonder they're still here."

"Aunt Sara said Isabella bought the house 'as is.' Intact. Even the trash bins were still full. I'm sure it has something to do with Bella being related to the earl. Keeping it all in the family, that sort of thing."

"I never saw that woman when we were here, and I'm glad I didn't. We had Bertram's bad temper to deal with. We didn't need hers added to it. I guess you saw Diana."

"Oh yes. Nadine said everyone was glad to see her." Kate's tone was asking Willa if that was true.

"Diana walked in at breakfast, acting like it was a regular day from years ago. She asked if there were any kippers." Willa was smiling. "It was very good to see her. Byon cried."

"And Nadine?"

"She was blinking back tears, but she got them under control. Diana made us remember the good times."

Kate looked at the clothes scattered about. "Do you know what everyone's wearing?"

"The men were easy. They're over there." She nodded toward an old coatrack that had three garment bags hanging on it. They had Post-it notes on them: Nicky, Clive, Byon. "I doubt if Byon's still fits," she said smugly.

"It's good you found them. I'll just look around for any of the, uh, other clothes."

Willa wasn't fooled by Kate's seeming indifference. "Yours is over there."

On a hanger on an old screen painted with butterflies was the dress Kate had only seen a bit of. It was a 1920s flapper dress of emerald green silk charmeuse. Around the neckline and the hips were wide bands of gold beads. Kate picked up the dress and held it at arm's length. "It's gorgeous."

"Everything Nadine wore was beautiful."

"She said Diana wore a minidress."

"I couldn't find it. I wonder if she still had it on when she left. If she rode a horse in it, she didn't leave anything to the imagination. Teddy will have to find something like it."

"A string bikini, maybe?" Kate said under her breath. "And what about you? What are you wearing?"

Willa groaned. "I did find my dress. Why did I think ruffles were attractive on me?"

Kate looked at her sitting there in her sleek, skintight yoga gear and couldn't imagine her in a dowdy, ruffle-covered dress. "So tell me about you and your lawyer last night."

"How did — ?" Willa laughed. "This is as bad as it was before. No one could do anything without the others finding out."

Kate didn't mention how the Pack had worked to break her and the lawyer up. Willa seemed to be remembering good things about the past. "How was your date?"

Willa closed her eyes for a moment. "Wonderful! He's like I remember. Smart and funny and caring."

"Did you tell him about Renewal?"

"Yes. And he said —" She took a breath. "He said he'd always known I had potential. I just needed to get away from the leeches."

"That being Nicky, Byon and Nadine."

"And Clive. Eddie thinks he strung me along, that he was after my fortune. Eddie doesn't like Clive much."

"No one seems to," Kate said.

"Eddie is coming tonight. Your aunt invited him."

Kate stared at her. *Does Aunt Sara think*

Eddie the lawyer is a suspect? "Have any other outsiders been invited?"

"The gossip is that the police inspector is coming."

"Really?" *The would-be writer?* Kate thought. "When did you hear all this?"

"At breakfast. It was a feast of food and information. Where were you and Jack and Sara?"

"At Puck's," Kate said quickly. *And searching inside Sean's remains.* "That's where we met Diana. If your new boyfriend is here, will you be Willa or Meena?"

Willa put the album down and stood up. "I think it's time to reveal my true self. What do you think?"

"Honestly? I think you should be Willa until after the play. Then when you take your bows, strip off to reveal Meena. It will be deliciously dramatic."

"Ohhhh. I love it! There are lots of ugly clothes in boxes around here. I'll just use one of them. I can —"

"Here you two are!" It was Nadine.

Willa jumped behind the screen and frantically motioned for Kate to toss her the padded dress.

Nadine plopped down in the chair Willa had been using. "You can come out. And you don't have to pad yourself."

When Willa said nothing, Nadine let out a sigh of exasperation. "Did you really think no one would see the difference in you? Well, I did anyway. I doubt if Byon or Clive noticed anything."

Willa took a moment to make her decision, then she walked — no, she strutted — from behind the screen to stand in front of Nadine.

The woman gave Willa a quick look up and down. "Same as always. Still sneaking, still hiding the truth. Nothing has changed." She picked up the photo album, seeming to dismiss her.

For a moment Willa looked like she was going to revert to who she used to be: the bottom member of the group, the one everyone looked down on.

Kate took a step forward, ready to intervene.

"Found a husband to support you yet?" Willa asked. "Sure you can get one at your age?"

Nadine looked up with eyes that sparkled. "The rabbit grows horns."

"Horns made of gold," Willa said. "What are you planning to wear tonight?"

"Since I have no part to play, it doesn't matter, does it?" Nadine went back to looking at the album.

Kate, standing to the side, let her breath out. It had been a short, terse conversation, but she could see that the dynamic between the two women had changed. They seemed to be equals now.

"It's going to be filmed," Willa said. "I'm sure you'll be introduced as the 'real' Nadine. Wear something conservative but sleek. And pearls. You still have those with the jade clasp?"

"Actually, I don't know." Nadine hesitated. "Were you grilled, interrogated and threatened by the writers?"

"Thoroughly." Willa looked at Kate. "I think your aunt might be worse than Byon."

"Did you answer all her questions?" Kate asked. "Or did you leave out key elements?"

"I told all." The two women looked at Nadine.

"I confessed everything, complete with tears for the past. That pearl necklace? It's part of my story." She looked at Kate. "Since you'll be playing me, you'll find out everything later." She looked back at the photos. "Here's Nicky and Byon. I remember that day. We all went swimming."

"Not me," Willa said. "If I'd shown up in swimwear, Byon would have slashed me to pieces."

"But darling, you couldn't have looked

worse than him. Even at that age, he was as flabby as a deflated balloon. Look at him."

Willa took the album. "So he is. But Nicky . . . I forgot how beautiful he was." She handed the book to Kate.

Kate looked at the photo — and the blood drained from her face. "This is Nicky?" she whispered.

"No one showed you any pictures of us?" Nadine asked.

"No." Kate slipped the photo out of the little black corner holders. "I have to go. I have to —" She couldn't explain. With the photo in her hand, she ran out of the attic and down the stairs to her aunt's bedroom.

As Nadine said, Byon had made the door dramatic. He'd taped on handwritten signs: keep out. do not enter. death to those who knock.

Kate pounded on the door with her fist.

"Go away," Byon yelled. "We're working."

"I have to see Aunt Sara," Kate shouted back. "It's important."

Sara flung open the door. "Jack?" Her voice held fear.

"He's fine," Kate said. "I guess." She showed the photo to her aunt.

Sara barely glanced at it. "I know. I have to get back to work."

"But Nicky is —"

"I know!" Sara said. "Now I know many things."

"So who killed Sean?" Kate demanded.

"That's the one thing we don't know," Byon called from across the room.

"Please," Sara said to Kate. "We're trying to get the scripts ready and we need every second. How's Chris? Has anyone fed him? Have you eaten?"

"I don't know. I don't remember. I guess he's fine."

Sara clasped Kate's wrist. "Go find Chris. Have a picnic. Clive is on his way back, so he and Jack will be creating the sets."

"He's with Teddy." Kate didn't like that she sounded like a petulant preteen.

"Diana is going to take her into town to buy a dress. It'll have to be shortened." Sara's eyes were pleading. She'd often complained that *time to write* was one of the biggest problems of her life.

Kate stepped back. "Okay. I'll steal food from Mrs. Aiken and find Chris."

Sara glanced over her shoulder at Byon, who was glowering for her to quit talking and get back to work. She leaned forward and whispered, "Take Nicky's tux to him. I think it'll fit." Sara gave Kate a knowing look, then shut the door.

Kate stood there for a moment, as the realization dawned on her.

Twenty minutes later, she had a basket full of food — Mrs. Aiken prepared it when Kate told her it was for the man who was going to play Nicky — and a tuxedo in a garment bag. She did her best to stay out of sight of everyone as she hurried to the gatehouse to find Chris. They sat outside and ate, and she told him everything she knew — and the two of them conjectured on what they didn't know.

Twenty-Four

Just after five, Jack arrived in one of the little work trucks in a flurry of gravel and dirt. He was carrying two sealed brown envelopes.

Chris and Kate were sitting outside, the lunch basket nearby.

Jack handed them the envelopes. "Read your parts and memorize your lines. Get to the house at six thirty." He looked at Chris. "Wear your tux."

"I need to get dressed," Kate said. "There isn't enough time for me to memorize anything."

Jack pulled a piece of paper out of his pocket. "Nadine isn't seen until Act Five. And by then, I'm dead."

"Who killed you?" she asked. "I mean, killed Sean?"

"You think I was told that?" He looked at Chris. "Your script is fat. I think you have a lot to do."

"I'll help you with your lines," Kate said. "We can —"

"No!" Jack said. "Orders from Queen Sara and Byon, the Court Musician. No one is to read anyone else's script." He looked at Kate. "Stay or go?"

She got in the truck beside him and looked at Chris. "You'll be okay?"

Jack snorted. "Do you mean can he dress himself, read and walk all the way to the house by himself?"

"Stop being a jerk," Kate said.

"I'm in character. Poor ol' Sean dies tonight." Jack turned the truck around, gave a thumbs-up to Chris and drove as fast as the vehicle would go back to the house.

Kate ran upstairs to her room, flopped down on the bed and began reading her pages as Nadine. In the first part she was in the bathroom. Pregnancy made her throw up. "A fun part to play," Kate said.

As she turned the pages, her eyes widened. What happened after Nadine discovered that Sean was gone fascinated her. It called for her to retrieve something that might or might not still be there.

She looked at her watch. Maybe she had enough time to do a little preplay searching. When she got off the bed, she saw the note that had been slipped under the door between hers and Jack's room.

Sara said you can't go and look. jack

Kate laughed. It was bad and good to be known so well.

She began to get ready for the evening in the beautiful green dress. It was going to be very interesting to watch the others when they saw Chris for the first time.

Try as she might, Kate didn't get downstairs until nearly everyone was there, including Jack. He was in his tux and drinking a beer. She went to him. "Shouldn't you be in the stables? And in jeans?"

"I'm part of the audience until Act Two." He was looking at Chris, who was standing close to Teddy. She did indeed have on a very short minidress. If she sneezed, she'd be eligible for a porno.

"How'd they react when they saw him?" Kate asked.

"So you knew who he looked like, but you didn't tell me?"

"I only found out a few hours ago. I saw a photo of Nicky, and Chris looks just like him." She was watching the others sneaking glances at Chris.

"I think we have a hint as to why she ran

away, but I hope I'm wrong. She must have —" He stopped when Willa came in, her arm entwined with that of a handsome man.

"Your parents have arrived," Jack said.

"I didn't tell her you said that." Kate put down her drink. "By the way, I think he's a possibility as the killer." She walked away.

"At least it wasn't *me,*" Jack said, but she didn't look back.

To Byon's dismay, only a cold buffet supper was served, but he did like that Sara allowed him to tell everyone their parts. He handed out a paper telling where each act would be staged and who the actors would be. "I will be reading the narrative bits. The actors not in the lights — and our thanks to Jack and Clive for their luminous job — are to stay to the side. You are not to get between the camera and the players. As in any theater, the audience is to remain quiet. However, at the end of each act, applause is appreciated."

Byon looked at Diana, his face sad. "Please forgive us for what we now know." He raised his glass. "Break your legs, my darlings."

Twenty-Five

Act One
Scene One

THE DRAWING ROOM AT OXLEY MANOR
WITH MOVE TO TERRACE

"Where is everyone?" Nicky asked. He was lazily slouched in the ratty old chair that no one else dared sit in.

"Willa is looking for Clive," Byon said.

"She is *always* looking for him. What is *new*?"

"Ah, the eternal search," Byon said. "Something new and different to entertain us. To make us sure that we actually exist."

Nicky didn't reply but went outside. He staggered a bit as they'd all had far too much to drink. "The last night," he said when Byon was standing beside him. But then, Byon was always nearby, always seeking more of Nicky than he wanted to give.

"It is a beautiful place," Byon said softly, looking out over what could be seen of Oxley Manor in the dark. But they knew what was out there. "It will be yours soon."

"The weight of it all will be mine," Nicky said. "And I am charged with looking after it and keeping it whole. Already, my ancestors look down on me." He raised his glass to the heavens. "They see a failure."

"You'll have Diana," Byon said.

"Oh yes, the wondrous Diana. Common as dirt, smart as a . . . a farmer."

He and Byon exchanged little laughs.

"We all do what we must," Byon said.

"Must?" Nicky's temper was rising. "You *must* write brilliant plays and become an international success. While I must plow the soil and —" In one swift move, he put his hand to the back of Byon's neck and kissed him hard on the lips. "You know what I want," Nicky said. "I have always wanted you. Not this place, not that woman. Not *any* woman. I —"

Nicky cut off when he heard a sound. Turning, he saw Diana standing in the moonlight. He still had his hand on Byon's neck. She had seen everything!

"I can't do this anymore," she said, then disappeared into the darkness.

"No," Nicky whispered. "She is my future.

She must —"

He started after her but Byon caught his arm. "Don't go. Stay with me. I'll write and make money and we'll run this place together. We'll —"

Nicky jerked away from him. "You? You'd drink it into the ground within a year. And you won't last. We are your inspiration. Without us, you are nothing." He ran after Diana.

ACT ONE
SCENE TWO

THE TERRACE AT OXLEY MANOR

For a few moments, Byon waited on the terrace. He'd been disturbed by what Nicky said, that Byon's ability to create was linked to *them.* Of course that was untrue.

Byon thought he heard a scream. It sounded like Diana the time the horse threw her. They'd all gone running, but Sean got there first. Nadine had made a joke about knowing who the hero among them was.

Byon took a step forward, but stopped. Nicky's words hurt too much, and running after Diana, who Nicky looked down on, wasn't going to help his cause.

There were more sounds, disturbing

noises that brought chills to his body. He went inside, closed the door behind him and poured himself a double whiskey. Whatever was happening outside wasn't his business.

ACT ONE
SCENE THREE

ON THE GROUNDS. VERY DARK

Diana didn't know where she was going — just that she had to face the truth. She stopped and waited for Nicky to catch up with her. She knew he was drunk but that was his normal state of being.

When he was close, she spoke. "I can't do it." Her voice was full of the regret she felt. This had been a difficult decision for her. Being mistress of Oxley Manor would give her the prestige she'd always yearned for. She'd had a lifetime of seeing her father ordered about, cursed out if the traffic was bad, having to pretend that he didn't see what went on: affairs, abuse, underage sex. Marriage to Nicky meant she'd be above that. *She* would be giving the orders.

But she couldn't do it. It was an old cliché: she'd met someone. It meant her future was now unknown. The only certainty was soul-crushing work. No luxuries, no prestige, no —

"Diana." Nicky was using that voice that meant he wanted something. "My dearest love, I'm sorry. I've had too much to drink. Byon means nothing to me. He —"

"I can't do it," she repeated. "I can't live like this."

"In luxury? As a lady?" He was stepping closer to her. She could smell his whiskey breath.

"It's not that. There's someone else."

Nicky smiled. "I don't mind. Have him."

"Her."

For a moment, he looked startled, then smiled broader. "That's even better. We'll give her a cottage."

She stepped back from him. "No. It would never work. We couldn't be a true couple. Your father would expect children. You couldn't —" She was trying to be as gentle as possible. "I'm leaving the country with her. We're going to have a horse farm and a —"

"And leave *me* with all of this to take care of?" His voice lost the coaxing tone. They all knew that Nicky could be vicious when he was drunk.

She looked around. It was very dark where they were and quite far from any building that contained people. "You have Clive. He can run it all if you'd let him. He's intelligent and he has ideas."

"Put myself under the rule of that prig?" Nicky was advancing on her. "I'd rather burn the place down. *You* are the solution. I chose you. I put up with you — a chauffeur's daughter! My ancestors are rolling in their graves — all for this pile of crap. All for this stone monster that is my burden in life. I let you *in.* I was going to — may God have mercy on me — defile my bloodline by *marrying* you. I was going to —"

Diana was sickened by his words and shocked that she'd never suspected the truth of how he felt about her. She drew back her arm to slap him. But she was so angry that her hand curled in a fist. When she hit his beautiful face, she heard his nose crunch.

He put his hand to his bloody nose. "You fucking bitch!" He sprang on her.

She fought him with all her might. She kicked and scratched and hit. But Nicky was a young man and he was strong.

The ridiculously short dress that Nadine had chosen for Diana rode up.

"You think I *can't*?" He was on top of her, holding her down. "You think I'm not man enough to fulfill my duties?"

There was a piece of stone nearby. It was the broken-off claw of a lion, fallen from what was left of a statue that one of Nicky's ancestors had thought would represent the family's glory. Nicky knew it was what he needed: a symbol of conquering his enemy.

He smacked Diana on the head with it. Her eyes rolled back, then her head fell to one side.

The sight of her lying there limp and helpless excited him. Diana, who told everyone what to do, who made people *like* her — something Nicky had never been able to do — was helpless beneath him.

His erection was as powerful as the stone lion's claw. It was easy to rip away the tiny briefs that Nadine had so thoughtfully persuaded Diana to wear. He entered her quickly and easily and was done in minutes.

Afterward, he stood up and looked down at her. She was still unconscious and that made him smile. He'd never before felt so powerful.

He fastened his pants, smoothed his shirt and jacket. His face ached. Bitch! She'd hurt him.

But as he looked down at her motionless body, he smiled. He had hurt her back.

Feeling the best he ever had in his life, he walked away, leaving her there. She had provoked him and she got what she deserved.

Chris stood up, leaving Teddy lying on the ground. He hadn't removed her underpants, but her dress was to her waist. The lights were on him and he knew the script called for him to walk away in triumph, but he couldn't. He went only a few steps, then threw up in the bushes.

Diana ran to her son and hugged him.

Byon was crying. "I never meant to cause that. I shouldn't have run away. I should have . . ."

Kate helped Teddy get up and put her arms around her. "I'm so sorry."

Sara stepped out of the darkness. "I must warn you that this horror doesn't let up. It's up to the lot of you if you want to go on or not."

Teddy pulled away from Kate, went to Chris and took his hand. "It's okay," she said. "I'm all right. You didn't hurt me."

"You're sure?"

"Yes."

Chris looked at his mother. "That . . . man . . . He was my father?"

Diana was too choked up to speak. She could only nod yes.

Chris put his arm around his mother's shoulders and looked at Sara. "I can go on.

I want to know the rest of it."

Sara looked at each person, the players and the audience. Standing to the side was the police inspector, and he gave a nod. Yes, he'd like to see what happened next.

"The show must go on." Byon's tone was one of disgust.

ACT TWO
SCENE ONE

GROUNDS OF OXLEY MANOR. NIGHT

When Diana came to, she was lying on the ground, her dress around her ribs, the bottom half of her naked. Her head hurt horribly. It took her a moment to realize what had happened. Nicky had raped her.

Always a woman of logic, she began to think about what she needed to do. Stagger back into the big house and confront him? Call the police? Then what? Court? The whole idea was absurd. She could envision the short dress she had on being shown in court. The jury would take one look and agree that she'd been "asking for it."

When she tried to move, she felt pain. There was blood on the side of her face. He must have hit her with something.

She held on to a tree to help her stand.

Her dress fell down to cover her but she still felt exposed, more naked than she'd ever been.

The things Nicky had said came back to her. She'd known that theirs was to be a marriage of . . . of what? The old-fashioned term "marriage of convenience" seemed to fit. They'd both wanted the same thing: Oxley Manor. Because she understood it, she believed she saw everything through clear glasses. Nothing rosy fogged her vision.

But now, with her body shaking, her mind traumatized, she realized she'd known nothing. She hadn't really understood Nicky — or herself. She'd always scoffed at books and movies about romance, so when love hit her, she'd been unprepared for it. She'd reacted as she never thought she would.

The night was quiet, but she could hear a wave of music coming from the house. Did she go back inside? Try to act as though nothing had happened?

A slight breeze came and she heard the soft whinny of a horse. Without another thought, she turned toward the stables, toward the familiarity of animals. And Sean would be there. Yes. She needed his comfort now. He would know what to do.

Her shoes were still on, not made for walking, but better than none. She was hurt and she felt dirty. Used. Discarded as though she was worth nothing. She staggered forward.

ACT TWO
SCENE TWO

THE STABLES

It was late, but Sean was outside the open double doors. A saddle was on a block and he was rubbing lanolin on the leather. He gave a quick glance to Diana when she stepped into the edge of the light. "Get tired of the noise of them?" he asked. "Too much booze? Too much cake?"

When she didn't say anything, he turned. She was in full light now and he could see her clearly. The torn dress, bruised body, hair wild. Blood covered the side of her face.

He didn't say anything, just dropped the brush and ran to her.

At the sight of him, her *friend,* Diana let go. She no longer had to try to be brave or strong.

Sean caught her before she hit the ground and carried her inside. There were bales of hay with a blanket over them and he stretched her out there.

He didn't have to be told what had happened to her. Her thighs were bruised, bloody and glistening. He spread a blanket over her, then got a wet cloth and wiped the blood off the side of her face.

"Nicky . . ."

"Ssssh," he said. "You don't have to explain."

"I told him I couldn't marry him. Helen . . ."

"Yeah, I know. I've seen the way you two look at each other. You almost set the barn on fire."

Diana gave a slight smile, but then the tears started. "I don't know what to *do.* Should I call the police?"

Sean's calloused hands were smoothing back her hair. "I wish we could. I wish I could say he'd be prosecuted, but it won't happen."

She closed her eyes but the tears kept coming.

"I want you to leave here. Now. Tonight," he said.

"I need to get —"

"No! Leave everything. Take Rona and go."

Her eyes widened. "But she's expecting —"

"I know. But *they* don't."

"Bertram will have the law after me. I

can't steal one of his horses."

Sean went to a tack cabinet, opened it and pulled out a suitcase. It wasn't very big, but it had locks and two leather straps encircling it. "I want you to take this and hold it for me. I'll meet you at the Rose and Crown tomorrow at 6:00 p.m. I'll see that Rona gets back here." He went to the stall and led the pregnant mare out.

"Are you leaving here?"

"Yes."

"Then let's go now. Together. This minute."

"I can't," he said.

"But what's to hold you here? Helen and I plan to go to Australia. Come with us."

There was a sound outside that made him stop and listen. "You have to get up and go now." He disappeared for a moment and returned with a pair of jeans. "Put these on and go to Helen. She'll take care of you. Tomorrow I'll meet you at the pub." He gave a bit of a smile. "I'll have a surprise for you."

He helped her stand, then turned away as she pulled on the jeans.

Sean got the mare saddled, with his suitcase strapped onto the back. He cupped his hands to help Diana mount.

But they weren't fast enough. Nicky was

standing in the doorway, and he was holding one of his father's guns, a heavy, old pistol. Everyone knew that Bertram kept them clean — and loaded. "Are you stealing a horse?"

"Borrowing it." Sean sounded cool, but his eyes were glittering in anger.

Diana saw that Sean was inching forward. A few more feet and he'd be close enough to leap on Nicky. But the gun could go off! She needed to get Nicky's attention onto her. "Yes! I'm leaving forever," she said, loudly. "You're a piece of filth and I never want to see you again."

"If you tell anyone what you made me do, I'll kill you," Nicky said, aiming the gun at her.

She tried not to look at Sean, but she knew he was getting closer. Her voice grew louder. "I'm going to the police. Right now. I'll tell them what you did. I may not win in court but your illustrious name won't be clean anymore. I'll say there are orgies here and —"

Sean leaped and the gun went off.

Diana held her breath as she waited to see what had happened.

Sean stepped away, seeming to be unscathed. He glared at Nicky for a moment, then turned to Diana. "Go."

She didn't have to be told a second time. She gave him a quick look up and down. The bullet must have missed him. She climbed onto the saddle and took off into the night.

Sean waited until Diana was out of sight, then he turned to Nicky, who was still standing there, gun in hand.

Nicky could see what Diana had not: Sean's side was bleeding.

Sean put his hands to his side. His voice was low. "You may get your kicks from raping girls and they may be too scared to take you to court but I'm not." He raised his bloody hand in a threatening way. "I will prosecute you. Attempted murder. Before I'm done, I'll see you in prison." He stepped back to the bales of hay.

Nicky, terror on his face, dropped the gun and ran toward the house.

PRESENT DAY

Kate was the first one to run to Jack. The fake blood on his side looked very real. Without thinking about what she was doing, she pulled his shirt out of his jeans and ran her hands over his ribs.

Jack had raised his arm and was watching her in amusement. "It wasn't real," he said softly. "I wasn't actually shot."

Kate looked up to see a few people staring at the two of them. Embarrassed, she sat back on her heels. "That will never come out of that shirt."

Under the cover of the bales of hay, he squeezed her hand — then turned to the bystanders. "Next act is in the kitchen. Better go get your places before they're all gone."

All but the police inspector left. "So young Nicky killed you?" the inspector asked.

"I'm not sure about that," Jack said. "I wasn't given a death scene."

"Interesting," the man said, and started toward the house.

Kate stayed where she was. "If it was only Nicky and Sean there, how do we *know* that Nicky shot him?"

"I think this is our Sara's storytelling. Remember I told you that there were two bullets with the skeleton? You were so busy drooling over evil Nicky's son that I didn't get a chance to tell you where they were located."

"I don't think you should throw stones at sons of bad daddies."

"Agreed. Anyway, one bullet was embedded in his lower ribs. The other one was in his skull."

"You told Aunt Sara that?"

"You think I withheld information from *her*? Not on my life! Don't forget that there are three more acts. I can't imagine what else has been put together."

"I hope the other acts aren't like these two. Too dramatic for my taste."

He held out his arm. "Help me up, will you? All this blood loss makes me weak."

She didn't call him on his joke, but put her arm around his waist, as his went around her shoulders. "What happened in the kitchen? I can't imagine Mrs. Aiken allowing anything to go on in her kingdom."

"I have no idea," Jack said, "but I believe Diana is playing Mrs. Aiken. Sara wanted Bella but she declined."

"Understandable." She looked up at him. "When this is done, I still want to go to Scotland."

Smiling, he kissed the top of her head. "It's my heart's dream."

They walked to the kitchen together.

ACT THREE

KITCHEN OF OXLEY MANOR

Puck was in the big walk-in pantry. Byon and Nicky had sent her there to get more of the tinned fish paste that Willa had brought. They'd all been smoking marijuana and were very hungry.

Actually, not everyone was smoking. Nadine had worn a beautiful dress but she'd spent the evening in the downstairs loo. Puck's mother had muttered "Women problems" in disapproval. It was like she knew some secret that no one else did.

Diana had been nervous all night, constantly looking out the windows. If a door opened, she jumped. She seemed to be expecting someone.

As for Clive and Willa, they were playing their usual hide-and-seek game. He hid, but if Willa took too long to find him, Clive changed places. As Byon said, "If Clive didn't have Willa to complain about, would we know he existed?" Byon would say most anything to make Nicky laugh.

Puck filled a basket with delicacies, all while knowing that tomorrow her mother would give her hell. No amount of saying, "It was for Nicky," would stop her mother's tirade.

When the kitchen door opened, Puck crossed her fingers. *Please,* she thought. *Don't let it be my mother.* Even though the others seemed to be in a bad mood tonight, they were still better than getting caught by her mother.

But it was, of course, her. Her mother started slamming pans about and muttering complaints. "I don't know why they expect me to do it all. They should go home and leave Nicky alone. He has too much to do. Too much to oversee. They are destroying him."

Puck had heard it all many times and knew her mother could go on for hours. Only Nicky was able to coax her out of a bad mood.

Puck was thinking about how she could get out without being seen when the door to the outside was flung open. She expected drunken laughter but what she heard was her mother's gasp of shock.

Puck peeked out. Nicky was standing in the doorway and he looked so terrible that she put her hands over her mouth to keep from crying out. His face was bruised and swollen. There was a long scratch down the side of his jaw.

Mrs. Aiken engulfed him in her big arms and led him to the chair at the head of the table. "Who did this?"

"Diana and I . . ." He caught his breath. "We . . . She made me do things. She *forced* me to do —"

"Shhhh." Mrs. Aiken glanced toward the

pantry as if she knew her daughter was in there.

Puck pressed herself back against the shelves and put her hands over her ears. *No! No!* she thought. *Don't let it be true that she knows about me.*

When Puck put her hands down, Nicky was crying. He had his face in his hands and he was shivering.

"I will fix it," Mrs. Aiken said. She pulled a little plastic case out of a drawer. "Nadine left this. Wash your face, then use this to cover those bruises. Don't let them see you like this."

"I don't think I can. I need —"

Mrs. Aiken leaned her face close to his. "You *need* to be who you are. This will go away. I'll make sure of it." With her big apron still on, her mother left through the kitchen door.

Puck stayed in the pantry and watched Nicky douse his face in the kitchen sink and use the liquid soap. He dried himself with a kitchen towel that he threw on the table. It looked to have blood on it. *Surely not!* she thought.

Then Nicky used the cosmetics in the little bag to cover what he could of the scratches and bruises.

It took him a long time to do all of it and

as he did, his body gradually stopped shaking. He'd entered the kitchen as a scared young man. Puck had never seen him so limp, so defeated. But now, the Nicky she knew was coming back. He was standing up straighter and his head was regaining that cocky tilt.

When he was finished, Puck held her breath. It was possible that he would come into the pantry, knowing she was there.

But he didn't. He stood, put his shoulders back and left the room. She heard him and Byon talking in the hall.

She stayed where she was for a while, but she was afraid her mother would return and catch her. Besides, Puck wanted to know what Diana had made Nicky do. Clean the stables? That would indeed traumatize him.

Puck went into the drawing room and everyone except Diana was there. She went to Byon and asked where Diana was.

"She was just here," he said. "Come and dance with me." He drew her to him. "Uh-oh. There goes Clive, slipping away. Bet you a fiver Willa will be right behind him."

"Are you sure Diana is all right? Nicky doesn't look too good." He was sitting in the darkest corner, his head down.

Byon leaned close to her. "I think Diana and Nicky had a moonlight premarriage tryst and he may have landed in the blackberry patch. He tried to cover it with makeup but he doesn't know how. I'll do it for him tomorrow."

Byon whirled her about.

"Everything is very strange tonight. Don't you feel it?" she asked.

"I feel as though something big is about to happen."

The music stopped and he stepped away. "Where's the food you went to get?"

"The dining room."

"Then let's go."

PRESENT DAY

The big lights on their tall stands were turned off, and Sara changed batteries and SD cards on her Sony. The audience was standing to the side in silence.

"I didn't know what happened to Diana," Puck whispered. "I should have —"

"You were fourteen!" Nadine snapped. "You weren't supposed to know, and none of it was *your* responsibility — especially when you'd been lied to."

They all looked at Byon. He was shaking so hard he sat down in a kitchen chair. "I thought I was telling a white lie. I didn't know what had actually happened. I didn't imagine . . ." He couldn't say any more.

"You weren't aware of the criminal activity of a man you worshipped?" Jack's voice was cold.

"Sometimes friends surprise us." Sara gave Jack a pointed look. Last year his best friend had shocked them all.

"Did you cover Nicky's bruises the next day?" Kate, ever the peacemaker, asked.

"I did," Byon said. "I did such a good job that the police didn't notice."

"We saw," the police inspector said. "We just didn't know it was covering anything — or that that much makeup was unusual on him."

"Right," Jack said. "No one has the right to question future earls about anything, and they can do as they damned well please."

Chris had been silent through this. He sat down by Byon. Tonight he'd learned his birth was the result of a rape and that his father shot a man.

Teddy put her hand on Chris's shoulder. "I think we need a break."

"For how long?" Sara asked.

"As long as it takes an Englishman to drink a cup of tea," Byon said.

"But that means another 350 years!" Sara said.

It took a moment before anyone responded, but it was a needed bit of levity.

"Puck to the pantry," Nadine said. "And let's not take so long with the tea. I want to see what's where." She looked at Kate.

"Me too!" They smiled at each other.

"Exposing more secrets," Clive said. He was looking at Willa as she and the lawyer leaned toward each other. They seemed to be talking about something serious. Now and then, one of them would glance up at Clive, then quickly look away. The next act was about Clive and Willa. He had his script for what he was to say to her but not what her part was. The truth was, he didn't remember saying the line as it was written for him — as Willa remembered the words. Since he doubted that he'd ever said such a thing, he felt he had a right to change the line to something kinder, something that presented him in a better light. The next time Willa looked up, he smiled at her. And she smiled back. *Everything is going to be fine,* he thought.

Act Four

A BENCH ON A HILL OVERLOOKING THE STABLES

It was dark in the garden, but Clive, playing

himself, knew his way around. The only light was from the stables down the hill. Both doors were open but there was no one there. Clive thought he should tell Bertram about that. Thorpe wasn't doing his job.

Willa was sitting on a bench and staring down at the light from the stables. He remembered that back then it seemed that he could never get away from her. He sighed but she didn't look up. "I should have known you'd be here waiting. I don't have time —"

"Be quiet!" she said.

"What?" Clive was shocked at her tone. He didn't remember her ever speaking to him this way.

"I'm listening. Something is happening here tonight, but I don't know what it is."

Clive groaned. "You and your drama. The group is breaking up, that's all. They don't know how they're going to cope with life if they don't have each other. Unlike me, who has to work all the time, they —"

"Diana rode away on a horse."

"Diana is *always* on a horse."

"Not at night. She'd be afraid the animal would be hurt. And I heard a sound."

Clive sighed again, this time louder. "And what was that?"

"An explosion. It . . ." She looked up at

him. "It sounded like a gunshot."

Clive thought he'd told Sara and Byon that he remembered explaining to Willa that Thorpe had been dealing with rats. He just didn't remember how the topic came up. He sat down on the far end of the bench and tried to keep to what had been said that night. "Thorpe didn't tell you that he's been chasing rats? He seems like the type to shoot at them."

She turned to him. "I guess *you* would poison them. Let them die slowly."

Clive looked shocked. This wasn't the way their conversation went in the past! She'd said she thought he was right. "No, I meant . . . What you heard was probably him." He needed to get this back on track. He'd remembered that she'd asked about their wedding. She was demanding that he set the date. "About when we get married, we —"

She stood up and glared down at him. "Married? Clive, of all the things I want in life, you are at the bottom." She turned and walked away.

Clive stood up and looked at the camera. "That's not what happened! I was the one to say that to *her*. She has no right to —"

"Cut!" Sara yelled.

"That wasn't the way it was supposed to

go," Clive said. "Back then *I* was the one who . . ." He trailed off.

"You were what?" Sara asked. "The person who had the power? *You* were the one who was wanted? Pursued? And now it's Willa who is the valuable one?"

"Valuable?" Clive said. "What's that supposed to mean?"

Everyone had their eyes on Willa, who was behind Clive. She was undressing. She unbuttoned her padded dress and let it fall to the ground. Under it, she had on a sleek, black, off-the-shoulder gown.

When Clive turned and saw her, his jaw dropped, his eyes widened.

Willa smiled at him very sweetly.

With a groan, Sara started to speak, but Kate put herself in front of her aunt.

"Meena!" Kate said sternly. "You didn't tell the information you were supposed to."

"Meena?" Nadine asked.

"Sorry," Willa said, but she didn't sound sorry. "For over twenty years I've carried that man's words with me. At last I released them."

All the women were nodding in understanding.

"What sound did you hear that night?" Jack blurted.

"I guess I heard the shot Nicky fired, and

I saw Diana ride away."

"Then what?" Kate asked.

Willa shrugged. "Nothing. Clive —" she give him a dark look "— showed up and said that . . . that horrible thing to me and that was it."

"I hoped you would remember something new," Sara said. "Clive isn't important. What happened in the stables is."

"I couldn't agree more," Willa said. "But after he said that to me, I left. I went back to the house."

"And cried," Nadine said. "And you took all the attention of everyone with your tears. Poor Willa. No one cared that *I* had just lost the father of my child."

"But you never *told* anyone of your problem," Willa said.

"I was to announce that the man I loved had run off with Diana? Really?"

"If you had confided in us, I would have told you that I saw Diana ride away *alone*. Ask Mrs. Aiken. She was there."

Everyone went silent.

Willa looked at them. "Oh. Sorry. I forgot that. When I was going back to the house in tears —" she gave another look of hate to Clive "— I heard someone. I hid and —"

"You were always so good at that," Clive said. "Hiding in bushes and —"

"Shut the hell up!" Sara snapped at him, then looked back at Willa. "You're sure?"

"Yes, I am. But you knew she was there. In the earlier scene she left Nicky in the kitchen to go 'fix it.' Right. I see." She looked at the silent police inspector. "I guess I'm a witness."

He nodded, then turned to Sara. "Isn't there more to your play?"

Sara looked at Kate. "You ready for the last act?"

Kate exchanged looks with Nadine. "Yes, I think I am."

ACT FIVE
SCENE ONE

THE STABLES AT OXLEY MANOR

Nadine was so nervous she could hardly walk. She couldn't believe no one had guessed her condition. She'd spent the evening being sick and hadn't drunk so much as a sip of the champagne Willa had shown up with. But everyone had their own problems. For all Byon's bravado, they knew he was terrified of moving to big, bad London and trying to make it on his own. Nicky was going to be left with his father — and Diana. Nadine wondered if she'd be able to return for that loveless marriage ceremony. Would they have a cake that was a replica of what they were actually marrying? Of Oxley Manor?

Laughter brought the nausea up and she halted to swallow it down. As she started walking again, she wished she knew where everyone was so she could stay out of sight. If any of them saw her and Sean together this late at night, they'd hurry to tell the others. They'd be gleeful at finding out that Nadine, who her rich father often called his princess, was in love with the low-class groomsman. All the snide, hateful things Byon had said about the man! Nadine had always pretended to laugh, but she did what was necessary to keep her father from finding out the truth.

When she'd told Sean she was pregnant, she'd braced herself for his anger. But he'd been ecstatic. He'd whirled her around as though they were a young married couple and everything was wonderful. When she'd told him her father would probably disown her, he'd hadn't blinked an eye. He'd assured her that they'd be fine — and she had believed him.

They'd made their plans to run away on the last night and it was all in place.

She clutched at her heavy handbag. It was

oversize and packed full. Even the wide straps were stuffed to the point of being lumpy.

She hadn't dared tell Sean, but for the last month she'd been collecting jewelry. She'd gathered all she had, all that had been her mother's and all she could coax her father into buying for her. He'd grumbled about the expense but he didn't really mind. What else was he going to spend his money on but his daughter?

She'd put everything into one big, black bag. She'd slit the leather straps and fed diamond bracelets into them. The lining, the pockets, were all full. On top, she'd put a few scarves — just in case anyone noticed.

With her breath held, she went through the drawing room. Byon and Puck were dancing together, Nicky was sulking in a chair, his back to them. Clive and Willa weren't there. *Chasing each other,* she thought. And Diana was missing. *Please don't let her be in the stables, snuggled up to some damned horse!*

Nadine made it out the side door with no one seeming to notice. When she got near the stables she saw the light — but she also heard voices. Up on the little hill she could see Clive and Willa. He seemed to be bawling her out. *Damn him!* she thought. He was angry that they were all about to leave on The Adventure That Is Life, while he had to stay and bear the brunt of Nicky's and Bertram's endless anger. He took it all out on poor Willa.

Finally, Clive seemed to have said something so nasty that even masochistic Willa couldn't take it. She ran down the path to the house, while Clive put his hands in his pockets and went the other way. He seemed to be feeling triumphant.

Too bad I won't be here tomorrow to take him down, Nadine thought.

When it was quiet again, she went to the open stable doors. There was a saddle on a stand outside. She thought it was odd that Sean had left it there. Even she knew that rain might hurt the leather.

She went into the stables and saw that it was empty of people. One of the horses was dancing about, its eyes rolling around, so she stayed away from it. The others also seemed agitated but for all she knew, they were always like that.

She went back to Sean's office but he wasn't there. Just last night he'd shown her his suitcase, all packed and ready, in the corner by his big tool chest. She'd expressed concern that someone would see it, guess the truth and tell her father.

He'd kissed away her worries, assuring her that no one, not even Diana, came to his office. And if they did, they would pay no attention to an old suitcase in the corner.

The suitcase was no longer there.

Maybe it was a sixth sense or just her being paranoid, but she *knew* something was wrong. Felt it in her bones.

She didn't know what to do. Wait for him to return? Go back to the house? Had he left her?

She went back into the center of the stables, facing the open doors, and sat down on a bale of hay. The horses seemed to be more agitated. *Shouldn't they be asleep?* she thought. *Did they miss Sean?* They made soft sounds when he was around and nuzzled against him. Sometimes, they almost made Nadine jealous.

"Be quiet," she hissed at them, but her words seemed to make them worse.

When she heard a sound outside, she ducked down beside the hay bales, but it was nothing. One of Bertram's dogs, maybe.

It was when she stood up that she saw the corner of white fabric. It looked like one of Sean's shirts, the heavy kind that he liked. Whatever was it doing back there?

She gave it a tug, and to her horror, out fell a pistol. It clattered on the wooden floor.

Nadine stood up, staring down at it in shock.

Sean had complained about rats in the stable, eating grain, opening bags, annoying his beloved horses. "I'd like to blast them off the earth," he'd said.

Surely he hadn't been shooting *at them,* Nadine thought. But if he did, then what? The gun fell down between the bales and he forgot about it?

She used the shirt to pick it up, not wanting to touch the thing, and rolling the cloth around it. She jammed it into the top of her heavy bag and covered it with a silk scarf. When she next saw him, she planned to give him a piece of her mind. His carelessness was dangerous!

There was another sound outside, only this time she knew it was one of the little trucks used on the estate. It had to be Sean!

She hurried to his office. Let him have a few moments of not knowing she was there. Let him think she hadn't shown up!

But it wasn't Sean who entered the stables. There was a little window, foggy from years of dirt that looked out toward the stalls.

Oh no! Nadine thought. It was Mrs. Aiken. She despised Sean and was always accusing him of stealing food. That it was Nadine who was taking it made her and Sean laugh.

Nadine knew that Nicky and Byon had sent Puck to the pantry to "rummage and appropriate" as they said. No doubt Mrs. Aiken had discovered the missing items and had come here in the middle of the night to accuse Sean. For those she hated, she never missed an opportunity to smother them in her anger.

Nadine did not want to be part of this!

There was a back door in the office and Sean kept the hinges well-oiled. She slipped out into the night, breathing in relief that she'd escaped.

But now what? she thought. When Sean got back and saw Mrs. Aiken there, he'd turn around and leave. But where would he go?

Instantly, she knew. The chapel. It was the only truly private place on all of Oxley. No one went there.

Except us, Nadine thought as she began making her way around the house. Sean was probably waiting for her there now. He'd hold her and laugh at all her silly premonitions.

"Nothing is wrong," she said aloud. "Everything is good." She hurried to the chapel.

Act Five
Scene Two

THE CHAPEL

Nadine used her key to open the door to the chapel. Sean had had copies made so they could leave the original key in the kitchen. In the past year they'd spent a lot of their time thinking of ways to keep their meetings secret. Evading Puck had been the most difficult.

"That child is everywhere," Sean said. "She sees everything. Hears it all." He believed Puck knew about them, but Nadine didn't agree.

As she opened the door, her breath was held in anticipation. This was *it.* The beginning of her new life. Marriage to the man she loved, a child on the way. She'd miss her father, but she had no doubt that as soon as he saw his grandchild, he'd forgive all. "I hope she's a girl," she whispered. Her father could spoil her, dote on her, shower her with gifts. He could —

The chapel was empty. Worse, it had that feeling that no one had been in there in a long time.

She sat down heavily on a wooden pew. Now what? Did she wait for him? She put her heavy bag down beside her. Maybe he'd had an emergency. One of the horses was sick. That she hadn't seen Diana in the house seemed to reinforce the idea. Yes, an animal was ill and they'd taken it to the vet.

She didn't want to think about the fact that they'd heard no noise of a trailer being loaded or that no one had commented on this happening. She also didn't want to think how much easier it would be for a vet to come to them.

Pregnancy was making her sleepy. Her head fell to her chest and her eyes were beginning to close when she jerked awake. The stone walls of the chapel were thick but she thought she heard a sound outside.

The window was high up and she could barely see out, but she saw one of the little trucks with its motor running. Nadine's heart seemed to skip a beat. Sean was here!

But no, Mrs. Aiken got out, went to the back and shoved what appeared to be a rolled-up rug farther back into the truck. It seemed to have been sliding out.

Nicky was in the truck, and he got out and helped her. The rug looked to be quite heavy. She watched as he tied a rope around the end of the rug and fastened it to the side of the truck. He jerked hard on it.

They got back into the vehicle and drove

away. Nadine had no idea what those two were doing in the middle of the night — and she didn't care either. She had her own problems to concern her.

She turned away, leaned against the wall and felt like her life was leaving her. Where was Sean?

She went back to the pew, meaning to sit down and wait for him, but she didn't. *Let him come to me,* she thought. He certainly knew how to get in and out of the house. Many times he'd come to her bedroom. They'd laughed as they'd tiptoed about during the night. Sean often went through Bertram's office. "I like to know what's going on around this place," he said. "Who's paying his bills?" he'd asked more than once. For all their sneaking, they were never caught.

She looked at her heavy bag. Did she take it back to the house? But what happened when Sean showed up later? That bag would be one more thing they'd have to hide.

Turning, she looked at the memorial plaque of a Renlow who'd died in 1856. It was embedded in the wall at floor level. One time Sean had kicked it. He'd been saying that all of Oxley was falling down. In emphasis, he'd struck out at the old piece of stone — and it had clattered to the floor.

It was a marvel it didn't break.

When it fell, they'd stood there in shocked silence. Inside they could see the end of a black coffin, its brass fittings tarnished and corroded.

"Not very big, was he?" Sean said.

Nadine couldn't help laughing. "Let's put it back before his ghost escapes and haunts us forever."

"A Renlow with me always?" Sean gave an exaggerated shiver. "Too horrible to imagine."

They put the plaque back in place and left.

It wasn't easy for Nadine to pull the stone out, put the bag inside, then get it back into place, but she did it.

When she'd finished, she left the chapel, locked the door and went back into the house to wait.

PRESENT DAY

Kate was standing in the chapel. It was well lit by the big lights. Sara was behind her camera and everyone was waiting.

Byon had finished reading the narrative, and Kate had done her job of looking out the window. In re-creating the past, Chris and Diana had been out there with the little truck and had lifted a rolled-up rug into the back.

When Byon got to the part where Nadine opened the grave, it made sense for Kate to do that. But she'd just stood there, the prop bag Nadine had lent her at her feet.

Everyone was silent as they stood there watching Kate.

It seemed that the possibility of finding a bag full of jewels overshadowed thinking about what Nicky and Mrs. Aiken had in the back of the little truck — and what they were tying in place.

Now all eyes, including the police inspector's, were on Kate.

Jack didn't ask why Kate was hesitating, he just went to her. "This one?" he asked softly.

She nodded.

Kneeling, he tugged on the stone but it didn't move.

"I glued it," Nadine said.

"Ah," the police inspector said. "That's why you returned to the chapel. We all thought you were praying."

"I was," she said. "In a way. But I was so angry I couldn't think clearly. I thought Sean had left me, that he was scared of . . . of our future. I wanted to seal him off forever." There were tears in her eyes. "I should have believed in him. I should have stood up and said that something was wrong. He wouldn't have left me and our baby. He wouldn't have —" Byon put his arms around her, and she cried into his big, soft shoulder.

Jack was looking at the stone. "It's a silicone based glue." He pulled a small knife from his pocket, opened it and ran the blade around the plaque.

He and Kate began wiggling the stone as they tried to get it out.

Everyone watched in silence. Sara was concentrating on Live View on her camera, recording it all.

Jack caught the stone before it hit the ground. What they saw inside made them gasp. There was a black leather bag, old and crusted with gray mold, untouched for years.

Kate took the handle to pull the bag out, then halted. She had to use both hands for the weight. After all, it was full of rocks — sparkly ones. Standing, she offered the bag to Nadine.

But Nadine shook her head no, and stepped back. She didn't want to touch it.

Jack started to take the bag but the inspector stepped in front of him.

"May I? There's something in there that I

want." He took the bag, set it on a bench seat, then started to unzip it. The old zipper stuck but it came loose quickly.

Inside was a pretty green-and-gold scarf. The inspector pulled it out and put it on the seat.

"My father gave that to me," Nadine said.

There was a white cloth inside.

"That's not a shirt," Sara said. "It's an apron."

The inspector lifted a flap of the cloth just enough to see the end of a gun. He closed the bag. "This is evidence."

"I guess there'll be fingerprints," Sara said.

"I'm sure there will be. And blood and hair and —"

Nadine gave a cry and Teddy put her arm around her mother.

"Sorry," the inspector said.

"What about Mrs. Aiken? She —" Sara began.

The door opened and a uniformed policeman entered. "All taken care of, sir. We got her just outside Cheswick."

Kate and Jack looked at Sara in question.

"I gave the inspector bits of the script as we wrote it. He knew what was going to happen." She smiled at him. "And he anticipated Mrs. Aiken's actions."

"It was the best writer's course anyone

ever had," the inspector said cheerfully. "To see the work in progress of two such talented, world-renowned authors was an honor. I never thought —"

Byon and Sara were smiling in such a pleased way that Jack stepped forward. Otherwise, the praise-hungry writers and the fanboy just might go on all night. "So you knew beforehand what Nicky and Mrs. Aiken did?"

"Yes," the inspector said. "And we predicted that she'd catch on to what we were doing and she'd flee. We were ready for her."

They all looked at Puck, who had an expression of horror on her face. Maybe her mother wasn't a murderer, but she was certainly an accessory.

"Mind if we borrow your lights?" the inspector asked. "We need to retrieve the remains." He looked at Sara, Jack and Kate in a way that said what he was thinking: He *should* arrest them for concealing evidence. *Should* bring charges against them. *Should* lock them up.

Kate gave him a big-eyed, pleading look. Jack turned as belligerent as his father often was. The infamous Wyatt temper was ready to show its ugly face. Sara did her best to smile as from one writer to another — then she handed him a business card. "It's from my agent," she said brightly. "He said to call him anytime. He'd love to hear your account of *this.*" She waved her hand about.

The inspector looked at the card and took a full minute to consider. Finally, he walked past them and left the chapel.

Sara's legs gave way in relief and she fell against Jack. He helped her to a bench. Kate sat beside her, Jack on the other side. They held hands.

"Do you think English prisons serve afternoon tea?" Jack asked.

"With scones and clotted cream?" Kate asked.

"I never, ever, *never* want to know," Sara whispered.

Byon placed himself in front of them, his hands on his plump hips. "You are *not* going to give that man the rights to this story! *I* am going to put this on the stage. No twopenny paperback novelist is going to overshadow *my* work. I —" He broke off because Sara, Jack and Kate were laughing.

"Extreme competition," Jack said.

Sara grinned. "I haven't even told my agent about the inspector."

"You may have to promise him a book just to get him to help keep us out of jail," Jack said. "Especially if he's like you and thinks prison gives writers time to work."

The others were leaving the chapel. They knew when they were being excluded, and those three were as solid as an oak tree trunk.

"Your agent can deal with the inspector," Kate said. "*Blood and Crumpets.* That's a nice title."

"Diamonds and Tea," Sara said.

"Puck Finds the Dead Man," Jack said.

They broke into more laughter, falling on each other. They were alone in the chapel.

Twenty-Six

Three Days Later

"I don't like it," Jack said. "It's all too pretty. What's that thing critics say and Sara complains about?"

They were alone in the small drawing room, and Kate had a glass of white wine. "That's a long list but in this case, I think you mean that the book's ending was tied up with a bow."

"Right," Jack said. "Critics of romances want . . . ?" He looked at her.

"Death of the hero or some such," Kate said. "They call it 'keeping it real.' Critics love misery."

He was swirling single malt scotch around in a Waterford crystal glass. "I still don't like it. There are holes in this story."

"The murderer was caught. She even confessed. I can't imagine what you don't like."

He sat down beside her, staring at her,

but she wouldn't meet his eyes. "You feel it too, don't you?"

"I feel bad about Mr. Howland, if that's what you mean. He didn't seem like he wanted to die."

"I agree. He and I had a good time that night and . . ." Jack took a drink of his whiskey.

"Mrs. Aiken said she didn't have anything to do with his death," Kate said softly.

"And we trust the word of a woman who cold-bloodedly killed a man?"

They sat side by side in silence. The last few days had been traumatic.

When the police got Mrs. Aiken to the station and began questioning her, she stayed true to her nature. She crossed her arms over her chest and said she'd done what she had to. There was *no other choice.*

"He was going to charge Master Nicky with attempted murder." She seemed to believe that anyone would have done the same thing.

"So you shot him," the inspector said.

She shrugged.

"Would you answer that question aloud?"

"Yes! Is that what you want to hear? I shot him and good riddance. He was a thief and he got above himself. *Somebody* was going to get rid of him *someday.*"

"Might as well be you. Is that it?"

Again, she shrugged. Then she leaned forward. "The *real* criminal is whoever killed dear young Nicky. *That's* who you should hang."

"Can't execute a bottle of rum, now can we?" the inspector said. "So let's start at the beginning. Where did you get the gun?"

After hours of interrogation, the inspector went to Oxley Manor and told Sara as much as he could. He couldn't give details but she knew them. Nicky raped Diana, then threatened her with one of his father's pistols. When Sean defended her, Nicky shot him. The wound hadn't been life-threatening, but Nicky was scared of the consequences. As he always did, he went running to the person who was the closest he'd ever had to a mother: Mrs. Aiken. And, as she always did, she took care of the problem.

When Mrs. Aiken got to the stables, Sean was wrapping gauze around his midsection. The bleeding had stopped, but he knew there was a bullet inside. If he hadn't been waiting for Nadine, he would have driven himself to the hospital. But he was determined to wait for her no matter what. Blood and a bullet weren't going to make him desert her.

Mrs. Aiken showed up in a rage. How dare he say anything bad about darling Nicky?

Sean, weak from blood loss, calmly told her he *was* going to file a police report. "Your precious Nicky won't get away with this."

Just as calmly, Mrs. Aiken picked up Bertram's gun and shot Sean in the head. She told the inspector she was very annoyed that she was left with a dead body to deal with.

She took off her apron, wrapped it around the gun and hid it between the bales of hay. "How was I to know that slut would find it?" she asked the inspector. "What was she doing sneaking around in the middle of the night? You should question *her.*"

Mrs. Aiken dragged the body into one of the horse stalls and the poor animal was crazed at the smell of blood. "I was hoping he'd trample that ungrateful wretch. It would have solved everything!"

But the horse didn't so much as touch Sean's lifeless body. When Mrs. Aiken came back with Nicky, Sean was where she'd put him — but the gun was gone. Mrs. Aiken didn't have time to do a thorough search and figured she'd look for it later.

She and Nicky rolled the body in an old rug and put it in the back of one of the utility trucks. They'd only gone a short distance when the body nearly fell out. "But Nicky tied it down," she said proudly.

"This would be when you were in front of the old chapel?" the inspector asked.

"I guess so. Somewhere near there."

"Then what?" he asked.

Her voice softened. "Nicky was a lonely little boy. I did my best, but I had too many responsibilities to take care of. And that daughter of mine was no help ever. Lives in a fairy world, she does."

"Where did you and Nicky take the body?"

"To an old well that only Nicky knew about. It was a dangerous place. I didn't like to think of him being inside that thing, but sometimes he had to hide from his father. He —"

"What about Sean?"

"Oh. Him. Nicky had a ladder that went down the side. He climbed down and I lowered the body. Wasn't easy. Nicky hurt his hands on the ropes."

"Poor guy," the inspector mumbled. "Had a hard life."

She cocked her head at him, seeing if he was serious or not.

"Then what?"

"He came up and we cut the ropes. The

next week, Nicky had some . . ." She lifted her hands. "Something put on it as a cover."

"An iron grid," the inspector said.

"Yes, that's right. Nicky knew how to take care of problems."

"A true saint." The inspector closed his notebook. "I'm charging you with the murder of Sean Thorpe."

"Don't matter," she said. "Nothin' matters since somebody killed Nicky. After that, I didn't care about —"

The inspector stood up. He couldn't stand to hear more about Saint Nicky.

"Tell my daughter to bring me some clothes. And I need somebody to talk to who will understand that I did what I had to. I had no choice."

"We'll be sure to find that person." The inspector left the room.

He went directly to Oxley Manor, and he and Sara isolated themselves and talked. Later, Sara told Jack and Kate everything.

"He said he'd never met a more cold-blooded person in his life," Sara said.

"Don't tell Nadine that part of the reason Mrs. Aiken felt justified in killing Sean was because he was a thief," Kate said.

"I agree," Sara said.

The two women were looking at Jack, who was oddly silent. "She keeps saying someone killed Nicky."

They knew he was thinking of his half brother, Evan. His death hadn't been an accident.

"Want to stay here and investigate?" Sara asked.

"No!" Kate and Jack said in unison.

"Still planning to go to Scotland?"

"Yes," Kate said.

"With all my heart and soul, I want to leave here," Jack said. "And I swear that if we see a dead body, I'll grab Kate and run away."

"Good idea," Sara said. "I'll ask the inspector when you can leave."

That had been days ago. They'd had to stay there while the police called each person in to give a statement about that night. Thanks to Sara and Byon's play, they had all remembered things that they hadn't thought were important.

Diana's testimony was invaluable. After she talked to the police, the others gathered. Diana cried when she told them that she didn't know Sean had been shot. "I wouldn't have left him if I'd known." After she rode away, she'd done as Sean had said — she'd gone to her girlfriend, who'd taken her in. As they'd planned, the next night, she took Sean's suitcase when she went to meet him at the pub. "But he didn't show up," Diana told them. "I knew something was wrong. I felt it. I should have gone back to Oxley but . . ." She looked at Kate.

"You couldn't bear to see your rapist," Kate said.

"I thought Nicky was my friend. I was going to *marry* him. How could I go to the police about him? Or even confront him in front of our friends?" She looked at her hands. "I took the coward's way out."

Sara spoke up. "If you'd gone back, I think one of them would have killed you too."

Jack and Kate nodded in agreement.

Chris took his mother's hand. "I'm glad you didn't return. Glad you left the country and had me."

She smiled at him. "I did —" She took a breath. "But . . . I did something unforgivable."

Sara leaned forward. "Does it have to do with Sean's suitcase?"

"Yes. It was full of money."

"I thought so," Sara said. "He'd been saving it for his life with Nadine."

"I knew what he'd been doing with the horses," Diana said. "It was through that that Helen and I met, so I couldn't be too angry at him."

"She supplied the horses and their . . . ?"

Kate asked.

"Most of them. I thought that if I took no money, I wasn't guilty. Besides, Sean seemed desperate for money. I thought maybe he was a gambling addict or something. I never thought it was all about love." She glanced at Nadine.

"When did you leave for Australia?" Sara asked.

"The next day. We'd booked a ship for a month later, for after I'd worked up the courage to tell Nicky I couldn't marry him. But after what happened that night, I wanted to leave immediately. I couldn't bear to wait."

"Did you see a newspaper during this time?" Jack asked.

"I did," Diana answered. "And there wasn't a word in it about Oxley Manor."

"Two lovers running away together wasn't newsworthy," Sara said.

"Especially since an earl was involved," Nadine said. "We keep our dirt quiet."

"And you had the suitcase full of cash," Byon said in awe.

"Yes, but I didn't know that for a couple of years. It was Sean's so I didn't open it. Besides, I just thought it held his clothes. Helen and I were busy trying to find jobs. It wasn't easy."

"And you had me to look after," Chris said.

Diana smiled. "We did." She looked at Sara. "A goat ate the corner of the old suitcase. It was in the loft of a barn and he gnawed a bit of it. When I realized what it contained, I again tried to contact Sean."

"You'd tried before?" Sara asked.

"I sent half a dozen letters to Oxley Manor," Diana said. "I never received a reply."

"Of course not," Sara said. "I'm sure Nicky or Bertram or Mrs. Aiken saw the letters and threw them in the fire."

"So they knew you were alive," Jack said.

"I would imagine so." Diana lowered her head. "We should have put the money in a bank account and waited for Sean to claim it. But we were desperate."

"Understandable," Sara said.

"What did you buy?" Byon asked. "Something wonderful or were you sane and sensible?"

"Both. We bought a farm. Good land, a few horses. We sold produce to a few stores. We . . ." She trailed off. "We have never been rich."

Sara looked at Chris — big beautiful, blond, gleaming with good health. "Looks to me like you're fabulously wealthy."

"I agree," Diana said, and Chris smiled.

"I agree, too," Teddy said loudly. "*Very* fabulous!"

The way she said it was so suggestive, so downright sexy, that everyone laughed. It was a good break from the horror of what was around them.

After the night of the play, Willa delighted in telling them her story of starting Renewal. She left out no details.

"It gets bigger every time she tells it," Jack said.

"It *is* big business," Sara said. "Bigger than one person can handle. And have a life, that is."

"You said what is on my mind," Kate said.

They smiled at each other.

"I know that look," Jack said. "What devious thing are you two planning?"

"Willa needs help," Kate said. "Someone who can organize."

"And be elegant while doing it."

Jack looked stern. "Willa's business is none of yours. She can handle her own life."

Kate patted him on the chest. "You're so cute when you act like you're in charge." She left the room.

Sara patted his arm. "I bet Bella has lots of tools you can play with." She followed

Kate into the hall.

Behind them, Jack was shaking his head. "DGI," he said loudly. "Don't Get Involved. It's a good motto. Use it."

The women were too far away to hear him — or they didn't want to.

Twenty-Seven

Jack was glad to stay out of whatever the women were planning. Instead, he gave his attention to Bella. They all felt sorry for her. Her beautiful hotel was again in the news, only this time was much worse. Skeleton Found, the headlines read. The Graveyard at Oxley. Another Murder at Oxley. Angry Spirits Invade Oxley.

They were able to keep the reporters off the grounds, but they were circling the estate, like carrion birds waiting to feast.

Several of Bella's employees refused to come to work, and she'd fired two who had talked to the press. The newspapers loved splashing Sara's name around for the second time. They spoke of "romance writers" as though they were filth, as the lowest of the low.

When Jack saw the women huddled together, he knew they were concocting some plan. Byon, annoyed at being excluded, said he was going upstairs to write.

"No you're not," Jack said. "We are going to help Bella. We're going to do some repairs, so you need to put on work clothes."

Byon made a face. "What happened to your being in awe of me? When we met, you were so nervous you could hardly speak. I liked that."

Jack gave a one-sided grin. "You know that saying about familiarity. Go change and meet us in the kitchen in ten minutes."

Clive also complained about Jack's bossiness. "I had years of servitude here. Damned if I'll do another thing for this place."

"Sara will take photos of you working on construction. Adds a dimension to your character. Makes you 'one of the people.' Don't you think your bosses in London will like that?"

Clive blinked a couple of times. "Give me five minutes." He took off running.

They spent the day repairing one of the outbuildings on Oxley. Chris knew how to do everything, and Jack invited him to Florida to work for him.

"I'm staying in Australia," he said. "My moms have made the decree."

"So you're ruled by the hens? Staying in with them?" Byon stopped. "That's a good title. 'In with the Hens.' " He hummed a bit.

Jack picked up the tune and hummed it too.

Chris surprised them by coming up with words. *"To pay for my sins with the hens."*

Clive was silent for a while, then he sang a bit in a baritone.

"I had no idea you had a voice," Byon said.

"No one ever asked me to join in. I could have —"

The booing from the other men stopped him.

"Time to give it up, old man," Chris said.

"Yes, your lordship," Clive answered.

Chris's eyes widened. "Never thought of that."

"If your parents had married," Byon said, "you'd have the title now."

"How about a DNA test?" Jack asked. "It would prove that he's Nicky's heir."

Clive and Byon groaned.

"You start checking for true fatherhood and the British aristocracy will collapse," Byon said. "It's all based on legal marriages, not who shagged whom."

Jack and Chris looked at each other and laughed.

By the end of the day they'd made progress on the building. "Tomorrow we work on the roof," Jack said.

"We'll do *Sound of Music,*" Byon said. "The roof will be our mountains."

They went in the house through the kitchen. It was a pleasant place without Mrs. Aiken there. A pot of beef stew was bubbling, homemade bread was on the table, a note from Kate beside it.

Beer in the fridge. Thank Puck for all of this. We women are busy.

The men sat down in their dirty clothes and ate it all.

"*This* is how I remember it," Byon said. "This camaraderie." He looked at Clive. "I didn't think about . . . about the others."

They looked at Clive, waiting for one of his poor-me statements. Instead, he said, "I have some really rich clients. I bet they'd love to meet you. Maybe they'll back your new play *Love and Death at Oxley.*"

It was seconds before the others could react.

Byon recovered first. "Jack will star in the show."

"Like hell I will," he said. "I have enough trouble trying to get Kate when I live with her. If I left her alone I'd never get her."

The other men burst into laughter.

"What?!" Jack demanded.

"Should we tell him?" Byon asked.

"If he's that dumb, I vote no," Chris said.

"I agree," Clive said.

"What does that mean?" No one answered Jack's question.

Byon looked at Chris. "You can play your father."

"No thanks. I'm going home, and I'll marry Teddy and have three kids."

Clive snorted. "Won't happen. She'll stay with her mother."

Chris leaned forward. "It's already started. The women are planning to open a Renewal studio in Sydney, and Teddy is going to run it. Nadine is going to become the manager here in the UK. The idea is to give Wilhelmina time off because she plans to marry the lawyer and have kids. Adopt or IVF. They haven't decided which."

The men were staring at him.

Chris shrugged. "If you grow up with two mothers, you learn the female language."

"I always suspected there was one," Jack said.

Clive spoke. "You're going to leave your farm and move to Sydney?"

"I was born into farming," Chris said. "I didn't choose it. But I do like the animals. I might look into zoo work."

"Job satisfaction over money," Jack said. "I like it."

"Teddy will earn more than you," Clive cautioned.

Chris smiled. "You old men and your egos. My generation doesn't believe in that sexist lunacy."

That night, Jack asked Kate what was going on.

"Just making plans."

"For Teddy to move to Australia and run a Renewal branch? And for Nadine to stop looking for a rich husband and support herself?"

The look of surprise on her face gave Jack great satisfaction.

"Who told you?"

"It was my clever deduction," Jack said.

"Yeah, right. We heard you guys singing. Will Byon give you credit in his new show?"

Jack, clean from a shower, stretched out on Kate's fancy princess bed. "So give me the facts, ma'am, on everyone."

"Seems like you already know it all."

He remained silent.

Kate climbed up to sit at the foot of the bed. "Nadine and Teddy are going through a three-month course to learn about Renewal. Diana's going back to Australia as soon as she's allowed to leave. She said Chris wants to stay here in England while Teddy is in training, then they'll leave together. Actually, Chris wants to spend more time at Oxley."

Jack nodded. "Wants to learn about his father, does he?"

"Yes, but I hope he doesn't think about what he could have had."

"He's got his feet on the ground. He won't do that. And what about Puck?"

Kate grinned. "That has been interesting. She visited her mother in prison and Mrs. Aiken was really nasty to her."

"As always."

"Right, exactly. When Puck got back, Teddy and I were hugging her in comfort, but Nadine got angry. Yelled at her. 'Have you never heard the word NO?' The next day Puck was only gone for an hour. Seems she walked out on her mother."

"Good for her."

"And then . . . drumroll please . . . Puck asked Willa if she needed anything to do with plants for Renewal, like maybe edible gardens."

"You think Puck would ever leave her house? Leave Oxley?"

"Maybe." Kate drew her knees to her chest and stared at the pretty bedspread.

"Okay," he said, "out with it. What else do you have to tell me?"

"Aunt Sara is going to stay here while you and I spend two weeks in Scotland." She waited for his reply.

"Sounds good." He looked at her from under lowered lashes.

His look was of such invitation that Kate got off the bed. "Aunt Sara says she wants some time alone but I think she's going to try to win back Isabella."

"How angry is she?"

"Very. It's a my-life-is-ruined level of anger and it's understandable. She grew up here. Restoring Oxley was her lifelong dream." Kate sighed. "She's been getting requests from people to hold séances here. They're saying Sean's spirit wants to be heard."

"They're probably right. Poor guy. I wonder if he had any family."

"Nadine says no, that Sean was orphaned young."

"He never got to see his daughter."

"And Chris never knew about his father," Kate said.

Jack rolled off the bed. "I like that the kid will be here with Sara, but I still wish she'd stay somewhere else. In London, maybe. She could go shopping."

"She feels guilty about what happened. She said we solved a murder but she lost a friend."

Jack frowned. "Sara *paid* for all this. I think that shows her concern for her friend."

"Money and friendship don't go together," Kate said.

Jack was still frowning. "I know you're right, but I wish she'd get out of this place. All the needless deaths that have happened here. Sara isn't thinking of joining a séance, is she?"

"Only if she could get a book out of it."

"I'll talk to her."

"Please do," Kate said.

He started for the door but paused. "Two weeks, huh? Just us?"

"No one else," Kate said.

Smiling, Jack went into his room and closed the door behind him.

Twenty-Eight

Sara was in front of the house saying goodbye to everyone. Diana said she and Chris had said their farewells the night before. "He's fascinated by what he's found out about the Renlow family and his . . . his, uh, father." She had trouble saying the word.

"At least he's not angry because you didn't tell him what really happened," Sara said. "There are some, well, unknowns about Kate's father. I dread when she finds out the truth."

"I wish you luck." Diana got into the hired car. She was going to the airport.

The rest of them — even Puck and Bella — were off to London. Nadine had talked Bella into taking a break from all the turmoil, and Sara had paid for a suite at the Connaught for three days. Reluctantly, Bella had agreed to leave. Puck was going to a meeting with Renewal executives.

Jack and Kate had rented a car, and it was

packed with their suitcases. Kate looked happy but at the same time nervous. They weren't used to it being just the two of them.

"You'll be fine," Sara told Kate. Jack was a few feet away, being repeatedly kissed by Nadine, Teddy and Byon.

"I'm sure I will be. Where's Chris?"

"Diana said he's reading about the Renlows."

Kate glanced up at the house. "Do you think you'll be able to patch things up with Bella?"

"I don't know. Maybe."

"Jack would warn you not to try to buy her friendship."

Sara smiled. "The dower house could use some work. That'll be expensive."

Kate kissed her aunt's cheek. "It's up to you. I can see that the prince is ready to go. It'll take an hour to get all the lipstick off of him."

Sara laughed.

"Keep in touch," Kate said. "Texts work here."

"You know me. I'm the empress of texting."

"True, but I also know that you get so absorbed in whatever you're doing that you ignore the outside world."

Jack came over, kissed Sara, then escorted

Kate to the car. He winked at Sara as they drove away.

For a few moments, Sara stood there looking at the empty parking area. To a true introvert like her, there was nothing so glorious as when everyone *went away.*

Smiling, she entered the house. She hadn't told anyone, but there was something still bothering her. Who told Clive that some billionaire client had asked for him? Told Nadine there was a party that didn't exist? Called Byon to go to London? Who put the note into Sara's camera bag?

Mr. Howland's funeral was in a few days. *Did* he kill himself? Sara trusted Jack's instincts more than she did what the police said, and Jack hadn't felt any of the despondency that foretold of suicide. It could have been spontaneous but . . .

Sara wrote a note.

Lunch at one. In the kitchen. Sara.

She slipped it under one of the doors into the attic. She knew she should find Chris, make chitchat, then invite him properly, but she had other things to do.

As soon as she was in her room, she called Eddie the lawyer. Sara truly hoped things would work out between him and Willa.

A secretary answered the phone. "Oh! Mrs. Medlar. I was told that if you called, I was to put you through right away."

"Thank you." When Eddie answered, she said, "I won't take much of your time, but —"

"Since I owe you my entire life, I am yours."

"How flattering. I was wondering if Mr. Howland ever told you a story about breaking an elephant."

Eddie laughed. "It was one of his favorites."

"Would you mind telling it to me?"

"He was kissing a pretty maid at Oxley Manor, and they knocked over a little glass elephant. I think it was valuable. The trunk broke off. The girl was so upset that she wouldn't see him again."

Sara waited for him to go on but he didn't. "That's it? That's not much of a story."

"Not by your standards, but Mr. Howland was heartbroken. He said that if it weren't for that damned elephant he might have married that young woman. But he said she was too scared after that."

"Scared of what? Or who?"

"Bertram, I guess. Or maybe Nicky."

Sara sighed. The story was a disappointment. "Thanks, and if you remember anything else, let me know."

"I will. How are you?" he asked.

Sara wanted to go, but she didn't want to be rude. And she also didn't want to give anything away. "Oh, just researching. I may write another romance set in an English manor house. Chris has been praying in the chapel. He wants to —"

As she knew he would, he cut her off. If there's one thing introverts learned early in life, it was that if you want to get rid of an extro, talk rapidly about some bookish subject and they'll go away.

"I'm sorry," he said, "but I have to take this call."

"Oh, okay. Stop by and I'll tell you my entire plot. I think you'll find it fascinating."

"Love to," he said, then clicked off.

Sara let out a sigh of defeat. That story of Mr. Howland was like buying a book with a bloody knife on the cover and finding a love story inside. The man's heart was broken. So what? Everybody's heart had scars. Sara's own heart had a Grand Canyon-sized slash that still hurt deeply.

She looked around the pretty room. What now? Part of her thought she should plan a way to make amends with Bella. Sorry we were shown a skeleton. Sorry your cook is a murderer. Sorry your relatives are a lying bunch of —

Sara saw a big box on a side table. How did that get to her room? She opened it and saw it was full of papers. On top was a note.

Thought you might like these. Byon.

She pulled out what had to be five hundred pages. They were tattered and stained, some in folders, some loose. As she flipped through them, she saw that they were written during Byon's college years. There were little character studies of his classmates. Sara smiled in memory. Cutting your teeth as a writer. Looking, analyzing, trying to make the mundane interesting.

Most of the stories seemed to be about Nicky. *Nicky's First Meal with Me. I Meet Nicky. Nicky's Best Replies.* "What? No bathroom stories?" Sara tossed those papers aside.

There were several short parody plays of the people around Oxley Manor. Sara read enough of them to see that Clive was often the butt of their "humor." Knowing what she did now, it was almost amusing to read about Poorwilla. That so-called pathetic person was now the one who was pulling them together. Yesterday, Willa said, "I always did take care of them. I just didn't know it."

"How true," Sara said as she picked up the last file. It was an old, white envelope. *Bertram's Drunken Stories.*

It was the first piece that she actually wanted to read. She snuggled down in an overstuffed chair and began reading. Of course the stories were slanted. The reader was to see Bertram as a joke, someone to laugh at. He was stupid, while the writer was superior in every way.

There was a story about Bertram's attempts to make money in horse racing. Byon had written Bertram as a buffoon, ridiculed by all the horse sellers — and by the young observers who did nothing but knew everything.

"He was trying to save Oxley," Sara said aloud. "And Mr. Howland was paying for it all. He wanted his daughter to have the best. It's just that he mistakenly thought Nicky and a falling-down old house were something to hope for."

The last story caught Sara's attention. *The Sister I Never Wanted.*

It was notes about something Bertram said when he was very drunk and very sad. He'd lost yet another race. "His words were slurred and hard to understand. He was giving up hope," Byon wrote in a way that was supposed to make people snicker. Bertram's lack of insight, his hope-without-a-reason, was meant to be humorous.

"She said she was my sister and I must let her run Oxley," Byon quoted Bertram as having said. "I didn't like her. She was too bossy."

"She wanted control. I told her to get the hell out. But still, she made me worry that I don't rightfully own the title."

That was it. Just notes. Sara put the page down, frowning. What was written sounded familiar but she wasn't sure why.

She glanced at her watch. It was ten to one. With the cook in jail, Sara had no idea what to do about food. She hoped the fridge was full, but she doubted if Bella had taken care of it before she left.

To Sara's delight, Chris was in the kitchen and it smelled divine. "Ah," she said. "Raised by two mothers."

"Yes." He was smiling. "I can cook and even iron."

"Is it too late for me to hope you'd marry me?"

He smiled. "Sara, I'd be honored."

She laughed and they sat down to eat.

For a while, they were both silent.

"Why do I feel that you're dying to tell me something?" Sara asked. "The air in this room is fairly vibrating."

"At home I take care of the finances. I should say that it's not because I'm male and therefore better at numbers. Women are just as good at math as boys."

Sara was smiling. "Those are stereotypes and not real."

"I've been in the attic all night."

Sara looked at him. Only youth allowed someone to stay up all night and look as dewy fresh as he did.

"Mom was against it, but I wanted to find out about my father."

"I have some stories Byon wrote and they're about him."

"Wonder how they were missed? It seems like someone went through all the documents in the attic. I found diaries from the 1800s and land contracts written in the 1500s. But most of the records from the late 1940s until the early 2000s are gone. Years of journals are missing, packets of letters have had those years removed. I saw nothing about my father or grandfather."

"Some of Byon's stories were in a case that was hidden by Nadine's old clothes."

"So whoever took the other documents may not have seen them," Chris said.

"You started this by mentioning finances. How does that relate?"

"I saw trunks full of dusty old ledgers, but I wasn't concerned with how much Lord Renlow spent on bacon in 1843."

"If I were writing a book set in that year, I'd be very interested in that. Money expenditure tells a lot about people."

"Too right." He pushed a spiral-bound notebook toward her.

Sara opened it. There were pages of notes about financial transactions, but Chris encouraged her to keep turning until she came to the heading *Mary Williams.* When Sara looked at him, he nodded, and she read aloud.

"Mary Williams, a widow, was hired as a maid at Oxley in 1948. In one year, she was promoted to head housekeeper and given three pay raises."

"Sounds like she was really good at her job," Sara said.

"So good that in 1950, there was a special allowance to pay for her new clothes. Twice."

"Unusual that the house paid for them."

"I thought so too," Chris said.

"There could have been an accident," Sara said. "One that the house was responsible for and they made amends."

"True," Chris said. He turned a page and ran his finger along a line. "December 24, 1950. A midwife was paid for delivering Mary's child."

"Ah. She was pregnant and the house paid for her maternity clothes." Sara leaned forward. "As a fellow researcher, let me guess what you did next. You went to the chapel to see if there were any records of the birth." Sara's eyes were sparkling. Historical mysteries were her favorite kind. "What did you find out?"

He picked up his phone and showed her a photo of an entry in the Parish register. *Bertram Nicholas Renlow born 24 December 1950.* The parents were listed as Hume and Sybilla Renlow.

"Bertram . . ." Sara whispered.

He showed her another photo. It was of a couple standing by a Christmas tree at Oxley Manor. The man was fastening what looked to be a spectacular diamond necklace around the neck of the woman. She had on a 1950s dress with a portrait neckline that exposed her from the shoulders up. Her belted waist was tiny. Written on the photo was *Sybilla and Hume. Christmas. 1950.*

"And she gave birth to Bertram the day before? Ha!" Sara leaned back in her chair. "That had to be Mary's child, but the Renlows claimed him. So what happened to Mary?"

"There was an expense for the burial of Mary Williams four months after she'd given birth."

"I wonder if Bertram ever knew that his mother was actually the maid? He —" She halted. "But Bertram thought he had a sister?"

"He was their only child."

"But what about Mary? She was a widow. Did she have any other children?"

"I don't know. I didn't see any mention of that. There were expenses for children, but I assumed they were the kids of people who worked at Oxley."

"Exactly," Sara said. "I'm trying to piece this together into a story. Mary Williams, a widow, gets a job as a maid at Oxley Manor, then she was quickly promoted to head housekeeper."

"So she was smart and good at her job."

"Or very, very pretty," Sara said. "Whatever, she was soon pregnant."

"By an unknown man."

"I don't think Lady Sybilla would have agreed to take the kid if his father was the local blacksmith," Sara said. "And I don't think that necklace was a coincidence of timing. Maybe ol' Hume gave her the diamonds as a peace offering.' "

Chris nodded. "Sounds plausible. Especially if she was barren. Then Mary died four months later. How convenient for the Renlow family."

"Byon's story said Bertram got drunk and talked about the sister he never wanted. He didn't like her. Said she was too bossy. Maybe the sister wanted a cut of the place. She wanted to share everything. And why not? They had the same mother."

"And Bertram's response to this proposition?"

"He told her to get the hell away from him." For a few moments, they looked at each other in silence.

"I bet she was really, really angry," Chris said.

"Like maybe she would do *anything* to get Oxley Manor. Maybe like crazy obsessed," Sara said.

Again, they were silent.

Chris moved his chair back. "I have to see to my horse, take him out for a run. When I get back, maybe we should . . ."

"Take a car and go see some of the sights of England? Leave Oxley Manor forever?"

"Perfect idea. Give me a couple of hours."

As Sara left the room, she texted a single word to Kate. Bella.

Twenty-Nine

Jack and Kate stopped for lunch at a pub in a pretty village. They sat in a little walled garden that was heavy with the scent of roses.

"Puck would like this," Jack said.

"She would. I wonder how she's getting along in London."

"I think that without her mother, she may blossom like one of these roses."

"I hope she stops hiding in trees." Kate was looking down at her plate. "Think Aunt Sara is okay without us?"

"I think she's probably doing exceptionally well."

She looked up at him. "It was like she couldn't wait for us to leave. Not like she wanted peace, but like she wanted to *do* something."

Jack frowned. "Something she doesn't want us to know about? Something dangerous that she wants to protect us from?"

"That's exactly what I mean," Kate said.

Jack lowered his voice. "The inspector said Mrs. Aiken was screaming that she had nothing to do with Mr. Howland's death. She said he was a nice man. He used to compliment her cooking and gave her a silk jacket from Japan. She said he didn't deserve to die."

"Unlike Sean, who did?"

"Welcome to the evil logic of Mrs. Aiken."

Kate didn't say anything for a moment. "What do you think Aunt Sara is investigating all by herself?" When Jack didn't answer, she looked at him. "Mr. Howland," she said softly.

"*Someone* was trying to get rid of us."

"You don't think Mrs. Aiken was the one who made Clive think a billionaire client wanted him back in London? And the party for Nadine?"

"Mrs. Aiken thinks Cambridge is a big city. I can't see her dealing with a bank in London or lord somebody." Jack looked at her. "Remember when we first met Mr. Howland?"

"Very well," Kate said.

"He mentioned a woman named Thelma Thompson."

"Who used to work at Oxley," Kate said.

"I was curious about her so I did a search

of the name. It's too common to come up with anything, but then Puck helped me. She knew where there was a tax list of employees — with their addresses."

"How very interesting," Kate said. "You wouldn't happen to know where she lives now, would you?"

"As a matter of fact, I believe she lives with her mother in a cottage about eight miles from here."

"What a coincidence. I wondered why you were so set on a scenic route."

Jack gave a bit of a smile. "It is remarkable, isn't it? You —" He broke off because Kate stood up.

"We are losing daylight. Let's *go.*" She signaled the waitress. "Could we have a dozen of these lovely scones to go? We're going to visit someone."

It was raining hard by the time they found the cottage. The building was what the English called "chocolate box" meaning it was cute enough to be on a box of candy. It had a stone path through a garden that was a mix of fruit trees and tall flowers that stood upright in the rain.

"I'm in love," Kate said as she looked through the windshield.

"It's too much to hope that's meant for

me," Jack said. "If it's for that thatched roof, it's too much maintenance."

"Spoilsport." She got her umbrella and the bag of scones. "Are we sure we want to do this? It was all a long time ago."

"Mr. Howland's death wasn't," Jack said as he opened the car door. "And yes, I want all the information I can get."

Jack took her umbrella, held it over both of them, and they hurried to the front door. They clanked the brass knocker but there was no answer.

They were about to leave when the door opened. An older woman stood there, her eyes dark and bright, her face wrinkled. She was too old to be the woman they were seeking.

"We're looking for Thelma Thompson, who used to work at Oxley Manor," Jack said loudly over the rain.

The woman smiled. "That's my daughter. She's just out to do the shopping." She pushed the door open wider. "Come in out of the rain."

Kate went into the house, and Jack followed her.

The ceilings were low, with giant, blackened beams across them.

"Come into the kitchen and I'll make a pot of tea. Or are you one of those Americans who only drink coffee?"

"We love tea and I brought scones." Kate held up the bag.

The kitchen was adorably quaint, and Kate thought Sara would love to photograph it. A narrow Aga in bright yellow was at one end. The warmth emanating from it filled the room. A side wall held a huge oak cabinet that was packed with dishes with many different patterns. "This is lovely," Kate said as Jack sat down at the table. "Truly beautiful."

"Just an old cottage," she said, but they could tell she was pleased.

"Can I help?" Kate asked.

"You can put the scones on a plate."

Kate enjoyed looking at the patterns on the dishes and chose one with a peacock on it, placed the scones on it, then sat down beside Jack.

"Your daughter used to work at Oxley Manor," he said. "We want to talk to her about that. When will she be back?"

"It will be quite a while," the woman said. "I'm Edna Thompson."

"Oh, sorry," Kate said and introduced them.

"Medlar?" Mrs. Thompson said. "That's the name . . ." She shook her head. "My memory's not what it used to be. Something to do with Bella."

"Yes," Kate said. "They're friends, and Sara Medlar is my aunt."

"Bella," Mrs. Thompson said. "That poor girl. She wasn't treated well. Her ladyship hated her. Then Bertram . . . Well, that wasn't fair at all."

"Sounds like you know a lot about what went on at Oxley Manor," Jack said.

"I should. I worked there for over forty years. Thelma was there for a while, but she wanted to work in an office. Don't blame her. There were things that went on in that house . . . Many times, I wanted to leave."

Jack and Kate were looking at her with wide eyes.

"My daughter says I talk too much. That's why it takes her hours to go shopping. She says train stations are quieter than living with me."

"We'd love to hear anything you can tell us about Bella Guilford and Oxley Manor."

"Guilford? Is that what she calls herself now? It was Williams when I knew her. But Bella always was ambitious. She said she'd own Oxley Manor someday. Said she'd find someone gullible and stupid enough to give her the money and the house and land would be hers."

At that remark, Jack looked angry. Under

the table, Kate put her hand over his and squeezed tight.

"Why did Bella want Oxley Manor so much?" Kate asked.

"She's Bertram's half sister. Same mother, different father. Only back then, that was a secret. Bertram! Now there was a nasty little boy."

"We didn't know Bella was Bertram's sister," Kate said. "Could you tell us everything, please? From the beginning?"

"Who was Bella's mother?" Jack asked.

Mrs. Thompson poured them cups of tea and sat down across from them. "That house! I don't know what about it made them love it so much. It was cold and creaky. I like this place better. It's always warm."

"The Renlows loved it," Jack said.

"They were a vain lot. They liked to say that the house and land were given to them by a king so they had to take care of it. That's why the old earl married Sybilla. She was a shrew."

"But a rich one?" Jack asked.

"Yes, very rich. But from trade, if you know what I mean. But she wanted something money couldn't buy. She wanted a son. And his lordship couldn't — not with her, anyway." Mrs. Thompson got a wicked gleam in her eye. "One day he told me, 'Edna, it just won't go up when I'm with her. It lays there like a dead fish.' "

"It sounds like you two were close," Kate exclaimed.

"Grew up together. Of course my pap was the gardener but that didn't stop us from playing together. He —"

"And Bella's mother?" Kate asked.

"That was Mary. Pretty girl she was, and we all liked her. Her husband had died in the war and she had a young girl to take care of."

"That was Bella," Kate said.

"Yes. She was an odd child. Rarely ever smiled. She wasn't pretty, but she had airs about her as if she had always lived in a Great House. When Mary had a swollen belly, we never said a word. We knew where it came from. But so did the shrew. We thought she'd throw Mary out, but she didn't. We should have known that she had something up her sleeve. She was always one for making plans."

Mrs. Thompson took a sip of her tea. "She took Mary's baby, and we were told to say that Lady Sybilla had given birth to the child."

"I guess no one protested," Jack said.

"Back then, things like that happened

often. Adopted children were never told they were adopted for fear that they'd feel left out. Mary had a hard labor and she never really recovered."

"So taking that baby looked like a kind and generous act," Kate said.

"It did. And Mary died just four months later."

"Of natural causes?" Jack asked.

Mrs. Thompson took her time answering. "There was talk among us. If Mary had recovered, Lady Sybilla might have had to give the baby back, but she doted on the child. Spoiled him horribly."

"What about Isabella?"

"She was sent away to boarding school and never allowed to come back. I'll never forget her screams the day she was taken away. Nearly broke my heart. She said she loved Oxley Manor and it was hers. *Hers!*"

Mrs. Thompson shook her head. "She came back only once from that fancy school she was in. Poor thing. It was like in that book . . . What was it?"

"Jane Eyre?"

"Yes, that's it." She paused. "They're all dead now so I can tell you. His lordship used to secretly take clothes down to Bella at school, and he sent her to university. He was very generous to Mary's daughter.

But . . .”

“But what?” Kate asked.

“His lordship died suddenly, just as she was about to finish university. He fell off his horse and broke his neck. It was hard to believe since he was a brilliant horseman. Then we found out that he’d lied to Bella over the years. She returned to Oxley Manor for the funeral, thinking she was part of the family and that she’d be staying there. His lordship had told her that he was leaving her the dower house in his will. But there was nothing in the will for Bella, and Lady Sybilla threw her out.”

“I can’t imagine her hurt,” Kate said.

“I heard later that her fancy fiancé dropped her. If he wasn’t going to get to live in a fine house, he wanted nothing to do with her.”

“Poor Isabella,” Kate said.

“Did you see her later?” Jack asked.

Mrs. Thompson frowned. “I saw her at Nicky’s funeral. Oh but that was sad. Bertram had no one to leave the place to. He was broke and didn’t know what to do. I think he and Bella had been fighting again. She had . . . well, she’d had too much to drink and she was very angry. She said, ‘The wrong one drove the car. It was supposed to be Bertram.’ I guess she meant fate had made a mistake. She said she could have managed Nicky, but not Bertram."

"Is that when she said she'd find some rich, gullible person to pay for it?" Jack's anger was showing.

"Yes, it was."

"What happened — ?" Kate began, but stopped when the front door opened.

"I'm home. They had a sale on salmon so I got us some. Oh! We have company."

"This is my daughter, Thelma."

She was older but still pretty — but she didn't look as friendly as her mother. "What's going on here?"

Kate stood and introduced herself and Jack. "Mr. Howland died a few days ago and —"

Thelma gasped.

"I'm sorry," Kate said. "He spoke very highly of you. Since you were on the way of our journey to Scotland, we thought we'd stop by and tell you in person."

Kate and Jack held their breaths to see what the woman would say.

Her face softened as she put a bag on the table. "Mr. Howland. What a lovely man. He used to tease me that we should get married. He kept saying he'd buy Oxley Manor for me. After I left, I should have let him know where I was, but I was too afraid of her to give out that information."

"Afraid of who?" Jack asked.

"Isabella, of course. She's why I left. Mr. Howland and I heard her tell Mr. Bertie that he *had* to let her live there, that Oxley Manor was hers as much as his since they had the same mother. He shouted back that her mother was the *maid* and had nothing to do with *him.* He told her to get out and never come back. Then she said she'd own Oxley Manor no matter what she had to do to get it.

"When she left, she saw us standing there. Mr. Howland was laughing. He thought it was all a joke, especially since *he* was planning to buy Oxley. He said to Bella, 'Maybe you can come clean for me. Like your mother did.' Oh, but he could be arrogant! Very proud of himself, he was."

"How did Bella react to that?" Kate asked.

Thelma's face seemed to lose color. "In all my life I've never seen anyone look like that. Pure hatred. Made my hair stand on end. The next day I gave in my notice. I knew she would find a way to make my life hell so I got out. I couldn't stand what went on there anyway."

Jack said, "And you broke the elephant."

Thelma didn't seem to know what he was talking about. "Oh yes. There was an ornament in a case. I was so agitated that I knocked it to the ground and it broke. I used it as my excuse for leaving. I didn't dare tell Mr. Howland the truth. I knew he'd laugh at me, and worse, he'd probably talk me into staying." Suddenly, the memories seemed too much for her. "Mother and I have work to do." It was a dismissal.

"Sure," Jack said, and minutes later, he and Kate were in their rental car.

"She said she'd own Oxley Manor no matter what she had to do."

"Think that includes killing her half brother? But Nicky got into the car instead?"

"At Nicky's funeral, Bertram said one of them had killed his son, but he was drunk so no one paid any attention to him. Bella was there so he was probably including her in his accusation."

"Whatever she had to do, she *did* buy it," Jack said.

"With the money given to her by a woman who likes to help people," Kate said. "Rich and gullible."

He glanced at Kate. "We may have left Sara alone with a murderer."

THIRTY

Sara didn't know why she was so afraid, but then, wasn't most fear irrational? She was in the bathroom dropping toiletries into her carry-on bag. There was no proof that Bella was . . . What? A criminal? A murderer? Just because all the pieces of the puzzle fit together meant nothing.

She looked at her watch again. How long would it take Chris to exercise his horse? It would be longer than a dog since a saddle was involved. But Chris was Australian. Maybe he rode bareback.

Trying to get a grip on herself, she stopped and took three deep, slow breaths. In the whole time they'd been searching for Sean's murderer, she'd never had any fear. Maybe that was because she'd always felt that his death had been a crime of passion. It had happened in the moment.

But Mr. Howland was killed because he *knew* something. There'd been no passion involved, just a cold-blooded need for survival. His life taken to keep somebody's secret.

Sara looked at the case she was packing. Why was she bothering with that? Inside her head a voice seemed to be crying, "Out. Out. Out." Over and over.

She left the bathroom, telling herself to grab her phone, her passport and her camera bag. The rest of it be damned.

The first thing she saw was that her phone wasn't on the foot of her bed. But that's where she was *sure* she'd left it.

She'd sent the text to Jack and Kate — her cutesy little one-word text that she now regretted — then she'd run upstairs to her room. She'd meant to write more to them, but instead, she'd started packing. At the time, getting her belongings out had seemed important.

She stood there staring at the empty bed. One of the worst things about getting older was the world's assumption that you became senile. This belief was so ingrained that the "accused" began to believe it. Every time you forgot something, misplaced an item, you felt panic. Was this forgetfulness or the beginning of Alzheimer's? Dementia?

All Sara could think was that she'd stupidly left her cell in the kitchen. She'd forgotten it, had walked off and left it.

She was going to have to leave the relative safety of her room to go get her phone.

Taking more deep breaths, she put her hand on the door. She was being ridiculous! Bella was in London. She'd known the woman for years. Just because some rotten things had happened in Bella's life didn't mean she was capable of murder.

Quietly, Sara unlocked the door and peeped out into the hall. It was empty — as was the entire hotel. It had that eerie feeling that old, abandoned buildings had. As though every deceased person who'd ever been there was waiting for the living to leave so they could come out.

"You write too damned much fiction," Sara said aloud, then straightened and started toward the stairs.

Her cell phone was on the second stair down. Smashed. Its little screen was cracked in a rather pretty starburst pattern.

She bent to pick it up.

An arm grabbed her, a cloth was put over her mouth and she felt a needle in her arm.

When she woke, she was sitting in the passenger seat of one of the Oxley Manor trucks. Vaguely, she wondered if it was the same one used to transport Sean's body.

No, of course not. That was too many years ago.

She tried to move but her body had the consistency of overcooked spaghetti. Besides, something tight was around her waist. She was tied in! She managed to turn her head a couple of inches. Her eyes were blurry, but she could make out who the driver was.

"You're awake," Bella said. "The trouble you have caused me!"

"Friend," Sara managed to say, although the word was slurred.

"You're saying I'm your *friend*?" Bella laughed. "Never! It took me years to find you. I needed someone alone and rich. Do you know how difficult that is to find? Money attracts people. Rich old men buy pretty young wives."

"Money," Sara said.

"Of course it's all about money, but even that wasn't enough. First, I had to get rid of Bertram. My *brother*!" She sneered the word. "A rotten piece of vermin, he was. But his drunken son drove the car that day. I could have managed that kid but Bertram was another matter."

"You *found* me," Sara whispered. She was trying to move her arms. Maybe she could get out of the truck. Then . . . Her mind was too fuzzy to think past that. She couldn't think how to untie herself.

"I researched," Bella said. "I used my job at the hotels. I questioned every guest who stayed in the presidential suite." She smiled. "I'd almost given up, then there you were. Writing those stupid, disgusting books, one after another, while money piled up in your accounts. I had contacts. I said I was doing background checks. In exchange for a free weekend I was told about your millions. Just sitting there. Your brother in prison, no husband, no children, no one at all. You were what I needed, what I *had to have.*"

When she stopped the truck, Sara saw they were at the Preserve. There was still yellow police tape around the site. The gate was standing open.

"That night when you thought we first met, in the restaurant in New York, I planned that. The rain was a godsend. How could you turn away someone as drenched as I was?"

She looked at Sara. "But then you were so alone that you welcomed anyone into your life. How hard that night was! I had to talk to someone like you about your despicable books and your petty problems. You've never known anything about true tragedy."

Bella got out of the truck, went around

the side and untied the rope around Sara's waist. "The problem with murder is that you're left with a body to dispose of. Howland was easy. I dropped pills in his drink, then covered his face. Everyone believed he'd killed himself."

"Not me," Sara whispered.

Bella pulled her from the truck. Sara barely managed to stand upright enough that she didn't hit the side of the vehicle. Her legs gave way, but Bella caught her.

"Do you know what hell you put me through this week? Had I known about that skeleton, I would have blown up that damned hole with that freak in it."

"Puck," Sara said.

Bella was half dragging Sara through the open gate. "Yes. Her! Always spying, always hiding. She was beginning to suspect me. She —"

"You called the bank," Sara said.

"Oh yes, that was me. I tried to warn you. Tried to save you from yourself but you and your little entourage wouldn't take the hint. You filled my beautiful home — the one I'd worked so hard to get — with that riffraff. Scum of the earth. Howland's death is *your* fault. *Yours!*"

They were standing at the edge of the pit. The rusty bars covering the opening and the vines were gone, cut away by the police in their investigation. It was just a big, open, deep hole in the ground.

"Who cared about some randy stable boy being shot? No one! But you had to stick your nose into it, didn't you?"

"I—"

Bella put her hands on Sara's shoulders, smiled into her face and gave her a push.

Sara fell backward into the hole. Her arms were too weak to flail. She just went down and down and down.

When Sara woke, she thought she was in heaven. A beautiful blond angel was leaning over her.

"You're awake?"

She closed her eyes again. Every muscle in her body hurt. She could feel bruises. She just wanted to lie very, very still.

"I think you should wake up. We've both been asleep and from the look of the light, it's been hours. We need to figure out how to get out of this place."

Reluctantly, Sara opened her eyes. Straight above her, she could see a round circle of light, but it seemed far away.

"I checked and I don't think any of your bones were broken. Didn't mean to be so forward but circumstances merited it."

"Chris." Her memory was coming back to her — and with it, panic. "She — !"

He put his hand on her arm. "You need to worry about your injuries. See what you can and cannot move."

With a nod, Sara obeyed. Starting at her toes, she worked upward. She could move all and nothing seemed to be broken. "Bella pushed me."

"Me too." Chris leaned against the wall of the pit. "She ran out in front of me. Poor horse bolted. Ran away. She said you'd fallen and she needed help getting you up. Of course I went with her."

Sara was doing her best to try to sit up. "Then she shoved you."

Chris nodded.

For the first time, Sara really looked at him. "How are *you*?"

"A bit smashed, I'm afraid. Cracked forearm, leg broken rather badly."

Sara's mind was beginning to function. What had cushioned her fall so that she wasn't broken into bits? "Did this happen before or after I landed on you?"

He gave a one-sided grin. "Leg before, arm during. I heard it crack."

"I'm sorry," she whispered, "but thank you."

"Least I could do." He looked up. "I don't

know how we're going to get out."

Sara swallowed. "I'm not sure, but I think Bella means to blow up this hole."

Chris blinked a few times, then recovered. "I can stand on one leg, and thank God, you're small."

She knew what he meant. "I can climb on your shoulders and get to the ledge. It's not far up from there. I think I can make it."

"With the vines gone, it won't be an easy climb."

Her eyes were clearing from whatever drug Bella had injected into her and from the trauma of the fall. "We can —"

There was a voice from the ground above.

Chris put his good arm in front of Sara, and they backed up against the wall and into the shadows. She felt his grunt of pain as he moved.

With pounding hearts, they looked up into the light.

When a woman's face appeared, Chris leaned in front of Sara, ready to protect her.

"They're not here," the woman said, then her face disappeared.

"It's Nadine," Sara whispered. "It's —" She broke off her words, took a breath, then let out a scream worthy of a horror movie.

Seconds later, Nadine's face reappeared, then Teddy's, then Puck's.

Sara stepped out from behind Chris and went to the center of the pit. "You have to be careful," she called upward. "Bella is here and she's —"

"We know. The inspector has her in handcuffs," Nadine said. "We figured it out. Like you taught us. We were in the car and we each revealed what we knew. She's Bertram's —"

"Half sister," Sara said. "Chris is hurt." She couldn't stand any longer and sat on the ground. "I broke his arm when I fell on him."

"An ambulance is on the way," Nadine said. "Willa and Clive went to get a ladder."

Sara looked up. "Jack and Kate?"

"They texted us that they're on their way here. They found out everything too. Mrs. Aiken told Puck about Bella, and she told us. Byon figured it out."

"Mrs. Aiken was trying to save her own neck," Teddy called down. "She suspected Isabella of killing Granddad so she told on her. Thought she could exchange one murder for another. She —" Teddy choked on tears and couldn't say more.

There were more voices, then Jack and Kate looked down into the hole.

At the sight of them, Sara lost all her bravado. She dissolved into tears. Minutes later, Jack and Kate had climbed down a rope. The three of them held each other. They were one solid being of tears and love combined.

ABOUT THE AUTHOR

Jude Deveraux is the author of forty-three *New York Times* bestsellers, including *For All Time, Moonlight in the Morning,* and *A Knight in Shining Armor.* She was honored with a *Romantic Times* Pioneer Award in 2013 for her distinguished career. To date, there are more than sixty million copies of her books in print worldwide.

The employees of Thorndike Press hope you have enjoyed this Large Print book. All our Thorndike, Wheeler, and Kennebec Large Print titles are designed for easy reading, and all our books are made to last. Other Thorndike Press Large Print books are available at your library, through selected bookstores, or directly from us.

For information about titles, please call:
(800) 223-1244

or visit our website at:
gale.com/thorndike

To share your comments, please write:
Publisher
Thorndike Press
10 Water St., Suite 310
Waterville, ME 04901